# THE
# ENCLAVE

Books by

# Karen Hancock

*The Enclave*

# THE ENCLAVE

## KAREN HANCOCK

Minneapolis, Minnesota

Published by Bethany House Publishers
11400 Hampshire Avenue South
Bloomington, Minnesota 55438

Bethany House Publishers is a division of
Baker Publishing Group, Grand Rapids, Michigan.

Printed in the United States of America

**Library of Congress Cataloging-in-Publication Data**

Hancock, Karen.
    The enclave / Karen Hancock.
      p.  cm.
    ISBN 978-0-7642-0328-2 (pbk.)
    1. Scientists—Fiction.  I. Title.
    PS3608.A698E53    2009
    813'.6—dc22

                                                     2008052074

To Pastor Robert R. McLaughlin

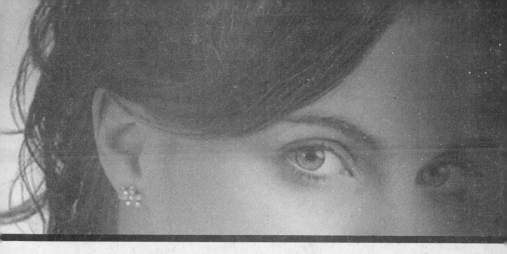

# PART ONE

# Chapter One

*Cameron Reinhardt is an idiot!*

Yes, he had a PhD from Stanford. Yes, he was widely acknowledged as a brilliant geneticist. Yes, Director Swain called him the field's brightest rising star, the Institute's greatest asset, and a fabulous hiring coup. But this wasn't the first time Lacey McHenry wondered how the man managed to get up in the morning and make it to his office fully clothed.

She stood in the frog room's open doorway, a large, rectangular steel tank hulking against the peach-colored wall across from her. One of its three hinged covers stood open, propped back against the wall. Live frogs and toads scattered the concrete floor beneath it, watching her with bulging golden eyes; more of them had trailed slime onto the gleaming floor of the corridor behind her in their break for freedom.

Apparently Dr. Reinhardt had come in sometime that afternoon and forgotten to close not only the lid but the door, as well. She pictured him collecting his subjects and hurrying off to his wet lab at the hall's end, heedless as a teenaged boy. Never mind that all the remaining amphibians could and did escape; never mind someone else would have to clean them up.

Surely he was living proof that a man could be a genius and a moron at the same time.

Conscience pricked her. It wasn't charitable to call anyone a moron, no matter how mindless and exasperating their behavior. And no matter how tired and irritated—and disappointed—she was.

*And that's really the problem here, isn't it?* With a sigh, she shut the door, rerolled the already drooping sleeves of her oversized white lab coat, and set about recapturing the slimy escapees.

Just last month she'd earned her master's degree in genetics, an accomplishment she was proud of and ready to make use of. Barely out of school, she'd been hired as a research assistant with the promise of eventually developing her own projects.

She'd arrived three weeks ago on the Institute's staff shuttle from Tucson, giddy with excitement. When the shuttle van had driven through the gateway in the massive berm that concealed the Institute's campus from the highway, and she'd seen the great glass-and-granite ziggurat stairstepping out of the desert into the sky, she'd been overwhelmed with wonder. To think they'd actually hired her, that she was to work at the Kendall-Jakes Longevity Institute, premiere research site on the genetics of aging in the country, and perhaps even the world. It had seemed the opportunity of a lifetime.

Now it seemed only an opportunity to develop humility and patience. Since she'd arrived, she'd done little more than tend the experimental animals in the bowels of that great ziggurat, run errands for everyone and his brother, and wash the unending river of glassware that poured from Dr. Reinhardt's fifth-floor research team. She didn't even have her own lab coat, but instead wore the oversized castoff of a former animal technician named *Carlos*, his name stitched in red on the coat's breast pocket.

Moreover her fellow staff members had made it *very* clear that she was junior staff—welcomed warmly, but hardly fit to kiss the feet of the exalted priests and priestesses of research who were the heart and soul of Kendall-Jakes, the brilliant men and women who would usher in a new age for mankind. Men like Cameron Reinhardt, who couldn't get his socks matched, rarely cleaned his glasses, forgot to shave more than half the time, and couldn't even remember to close the lid on the frog tank.

*And that,* her conscience informed her, *sounds very much like bitterness.*

She trapped the last frog in the far corner and dropped it into the tank with its fellows. As she closed the lid, movement in the corridor beyond the door's square window caught her eye. *Was that a face?*

Unease danced up her spine, eclipsed immediately by a wriggly embarrassment as she realized she hadn't yet captured the frogs in the corridor. Whoever was out there would surely think—

She stopped in the doorway. Except for the frogs, mostly congregated in front of the windowless door to Reinhardt's small lab at the corridor's end, the hall was empty. The door to Dr. Poe's salamander lab opposite the frog room, however, stood ajar.

She became suddenly aware of how alone she was, surrounded by thick, windowless walls, with almost no chance of anyone coming to her rescue. Most of her colleagues were attending the ice-cream social Dr. Viascola had arranged.

Lacey's heart throbbed against her breastbone. She made herself take in a long, calming breath and told herself she was being silly. The lights beyond the lab's open door were still off, so if someone had just entered, they were now blundering about in the dark. Not only that, she should have heard the echoing clack of the locking mechanism disengage, and she hadn't. The door had probably been open all along; she just hadn't noticed.

Rerolling her lab coat's too-long sleeves yet again, she crossed the corridor and peered through the crack into Dr. Poe's lab. Darkness steeped the room, gilt by the glow of starlight from a window on the far side. She backed out and closed the door to keep out straying frogs, then hurried past the frog room to the main hall. Gleaming floor stretched past the openings for two sister corridors on one side, and mostly closed doors on the other. Only the prep room was lit, its door wide open, as she'd left it.

She heard the squeak of Harvey the hamster running on his wheel from inside the prep room, then a rustle of bedding, probably from the mice caged beside him. In the silence she could hear the muffled drone of the refrigerator, but nothing else.

*I'm being silly.* Given the millions of dollars Director Swain had funneled into fences, cameras, sensors, alarms, lasers, and a cadre of brawny, black-uniformed guards, it was unlikely an intruder could penetrate even the grounds at large, let alone the zig itself. And even if he could, why come to the animal quarters? She'd probably seen the reflection of herself closing the tank lid. It wouldn't be the first time.

She went back to rounding up the frogs and had just dropped one into the tank and closed the lid when she heard a distinct click behind her. She caught her breath and her pulse once more accelerated. Someone was standing in the doorway at her back, blocking the exit, watching her, just as Erik used to do.

She fought down surging panic. *Erik is dead.* And the idea that anyone at the Institute would be watching her the way he had was absurd. If she'd just turn and face whoever was there, she'd see that.

Drawing a deep breath, she braced a hand against the tank and turned. A single frog sat on the raised threshold, sides fluttering, its golden pop-eyes gleaming in the fluorescent light.

She let out her breath and wiped sweaty palms down the front of her lab coat, feeling like an idiot. The frog hopped toward her. She stooped to grab it, then dropped it into the tank.

*It's the lack of sleep,* she told herself, returning to the hall in time to see two of her quarry disappear into the darkness of Dr. Poe's lab.

The fans in the physical plant below her dorm room had rumbled through her dreams every night for that first week. Even after Admin let her move, she still wasn't rested. Mandatory meetings and socials and nighttime lectures filled her evenings, after which she often had to spend several hours finishing up with the labware, before she could even start with the animals. Yet every morning breakfast was served at 7:30 a.m., regardless of how little anyone had slept.

And all that was in addition to the emotional drain of living in a new place and working among strangers she was desperate to impress. Every night she was asleep before her head hit the pillow. After almost a month of it, she knew her mounting fatigue was affecting not just her energy but her attitude.

She stopped with her hand on the knob of Poe's door, staring into the dark lab again, a square starry night sky visible through the window at the room's end. The light from the hall filtered in around her, limning shelved aquariums and Rubbermaid dishpans looming close on both sides. *Didn't I just close this door?*

Her nape crawled. She could almost feel someone in the darkness ahead, watching her, waiting for her. Down the hall in the prep room, Harvey's wheel stopped.

She nearly yanked the door shut and fled, but reason steadied the ridiculous panic. She drew a deep breath, pushed the door wide, and fumbled for the wall switch. The nearest bank of fluorescent lights flickered on, illuminating a narrow alcove choked with U-configured, shoulder-high wooden shelving units. The room's far end widened in the top stroke of a T, where a desk and a potted palm stood in the shadows. No one was there.

Squatting in the first U-shaped module, she nabbed one of her frogs between two of the dishpans and took it back to the main tank. Returning to move deeper into the room, she found another at the juncture of the third and fourth U's, almost to the wider part of the lab. It lay on the bare vinyl of the flooring and made no attempt to escape when she bent toward it. Only as she picked it up did she realize its hind legs were gone. She found one of them on the floor in the next U. Cool, damp, and still softly firm, its moist, ragged thicker end indicated it had been torn from the frog's body.

She stared at the limb uncomprehendingly. Even if the frog had gotten its legs caught between the pans and yanked it off in the struggle to get free, how had one of them gotten more than two feet away from the frog itself?

A cool waft of air, heavy with the scent of wet earth from the nightly watering of the grounds, washed around her. She looked up in surprise, realizing only then that the window was actually a door opened wide onto the shadow-shrouded courtyard beyond.

Even as the revelation dawned, a young man stepped from the shadows to face her. Maybe seventeen or eighteen years old, he was tall, lanky, and coarse-featured, with strong brow and jaw. He'd shaved the sides of his head close, leaving the top in a swath of peltlike hair that pointed to the big pimple in the middle of his forehead. His pale eyes glittered like bits of glass, and a nervous tic pulsed erratically at the edge of his right eye.

He smiled at her, revealing a chipped front tooth, then plucked the frog leg from her grasp and stuffed it into his mouth. She recoiled with a cry of revulsion as he grinned and chewed, cheeks bulging, saliva glistening on his lips. She heard the crunch of bones, and refused to give way further to the distress he clearly wished to cause her.

"Who are you?" she demanded, glad her voice came out firm and crisp. "You shouldn't be here."

He swallowed his morsel and drew the back of a dirty, long-nailed hand across his mouth, his palm marred with a bloody gash. He continued to grin at her, and a chill crawled up her spine. He stood at least a head taller than she and was unquestionably quicker and stronger. And there was something in those eyes that seemed older than his years. Something . . . hungry.

He stepped toward her and she flinched backward, bumping into the shelves of dishpans and glass aquariums behind her and pulling a laugh from him. *If you run, they always chase you,* she thought. *Better·not to run. Better to stand and face them.*

But the old fear was on her, just as it had been with Erik, though it had been four years since his death, and she knew she would take no stands, knew she was going to run.

Then out in the hallway the elevator pinged and its doors rumbled open, instantly reversing their positions. As the youth turned for the courtyard doorway, she grabbed his arm and screamed. He swung about, twisting free of her grip, then slammed her into the freestanding shelves behind her. She felt a blinding pain in her back and chest as she went down with the shelves in a crash of splintering wood and breaking glass. Water gushed around her, the room spun, and she gasped for breath.

Dimly she sensed the youth leave. Then there were others: Dr. Poe, Assistant Director Slattery, and several large security guards. The assistant director bent over her as she pointed toward the door and gasped out what had happened. She wasn't half finished before the guards had disappeared through the door after the youth.

As Slattery and Poe helped her to her feet, pain wrenched the room askew and she fought to draw more than a teaspoonful of air into her lungs. She felt them walking her forward, feet crunching on broken glass. A bright blue salamander thrashed amid the wreckage.

They were carrying on some sort of intense conversation that she had no context to grasp. Then Slattery drew his hand away from her and held it up, covered with bright red blood. "She's bleeding."

Poe hissed an epithet. "Is it bad?"

"I don't know. Her sleeve's soaked. Let's get her to the prep room."

They entered the corridor, Slattery pulling the door to Poe's lab shut behind them. Lacey's vision kept spangling with bright light, blotting the men out. Their voices grew dim and muffled. She wanted nothing so much as to lie down, to be able to breathe again.

The voices rose as someone joined them, and Slattery gave her over to the newcomer. After only a few steps, she was picked up and carried. Her arm didn't hurt, but she thought surely her back must be broken, or perhaps her shoulder blades. The last time she'd hurt this badly was when Erik had hit her with the baseball bat.

Her senses were clearing as they reached the prep room, and she realized with a mild shock that it was Dr. Reinhardt who carried her. He laid her on the floor in one corner, then shrugged out of his lab coat and wadded it up as a pillow for her. She heard the door shut and the lock click, even as Reinhardt leapt up and went to rattle the knob. The sounds receded around her, his pounding on the door growing distant, his demands that Poe unlock it, faint and irrelevant.

Panicked, she struggled to draw air into her lungs, sucking it in with a great painful gasp. The pressure on her chest vanished, her hearing returned, and as she breathed more easily, the pain ebbed to a manageable level. Reinhardt gave up on getting the door unlocked and returned to her.

In his mid-thirties, he had close-cropped auburn hair and gray eyes, which were almost hidden behind smeared wire-rim glasses. He had a pleasant face, open and almost boyish, despite its unshaven grizzle and a smudge—likely printer ink—across one cheekbone. His jeans bore similar smudges, though darker and wider, as did his tennis shoes—worn, run over, and gray with use and age. The rumpled red flannel shirt was both smudged and wet, the latter likely thanks to her.

He was blinking at her as if he had just awakened, as if recent events had transpired far too rapidly for him to follow. Likely they had. She supposed he'd come out of his lab all unawares and walked right into

Poe and Slattery helping her to the prep room. Having drafted him to assist, they'd left him locked in the room without a word of explanation, and he was obviously still trying to free himself of his nucleic acids and attend to reality.

"You're Miss McHenry, aren't you? The frog girl."

*Frog girl. Yes, that's all I am here, isn't it?* She nodded.

Concern creased his brow as he knelt beside her, plucking at the bloodied sleeve of her lab coat. "This doesn't look good. Can you sit up?"

"There was an intruder," she said. "He knocked me into Dr. Poe's shelving units."

"Yes, I gathered that. Here, let me help you." He lifted her to a sitting position, the action making her gasp at the pain it triggered. Gently he stripped off her wet lab coat, tossing it onto the wad of his own dry coat with no thought, apparently, of the consequences. His focus was on her wound now: a six-inch, straight-edged glass cut running along the inside of her left forearm, still bleeding profusely.

"It'll need stitches," he said, stepping to one of the cabinets. He pulled out a first-aid kit and set it on the floor beside her, then turned to the sink of soapy water Lacey had prepared earlier. "This intruder," he said as he plunged his hands into the bubbles, "what did he look like?"

She told him all she could recall, realizing as she did that the youth had seemed somehow familiar, though she couldn't imagine where she might have seen him before.

Hands washed and rinsed, Reinhardt was drying them off when two distant echoing booms halted the flow of her words. "What was that?" she whispered.

"Sounded like gunshots," Dr. Reinhardt said. He stood listening for a moment, then set about cleaning and butterfly-bandaging her wound, a service he performed with a swift and practiced competence that surprised her. As he worked he pressed her to continue her story, interrupting occasionally to question her more closely about the young man. Did he speak? Had she seen him before? Did she think he was truly unbalanced, or one of Director Swain's feared corporate spies putting on a show?

He was taping the last bandage to the slash in her arm when the door crashed open and Slattery burst in. A short, swarthy, vigorous man with a pocked complexion, he had straight black hair brushed back from a high forehead, bushy black brows, and piercing blue eyes. For a moment he paused as if surprised to find them as they were, then said to Reinhardt, "You've tended her, then."

"Only temporarily. She'll need stitches."

"Probably has a mild concussion, too." Slattery turned to the man who'd followed him into the room and gestured at Lacey. "Take her to the clinic."

A second man now angled a gurney through the door as Lacey tottered to her feet. "Oh, I won't need that, Dr. Slattery," she said. "I'm fine, really."

He scowled at her. "You could hardly walk a few minutes ago, miss."

"I just had the breath knocked out of me."

"And took a good knock to the head, too, from the look of that goose egg behind your ear. A concussion's nothing to take lightly. And there's the cut to stitch, as well. I won't risk any lawsuits. Now, hop aboard like a good girl."

Reluctantly she obeyed. "Did you find him? The man who attacked me?"

"Not yet," Slattery said, his scowl deepening. Irritably he motioned for the men to wheel her away, and immediately they complied.

As they lifted the gurney over the raised threshold of the prep room floor, the pain of her cut finally began to override the pain of the cramps in her back. Maybe a visit to the clinic wouldn't be so bad after all. She didn't have to walk, and they might have some Tylenol they could give her and maybe a compress for her back. In fact, she wouldn't even object if they wanted to take some X rays, just to make sure she'd not broken something.

## Chapter Two

As the gurney carried Ms. McHenry out of his sight, whatever had held
Cam Reinhardt together was loosed. A wave of trembling overtook
him and he found himself staring at the shockingly large puddle of
blood pooled on the floor at his feet. The deep red surface reflected the
fluorescent lights overhead and stirred up dangerous memories that
made his stomach flutter and light flicker at the edges of his vision.

A rumpled, bloodstained lab coat lay in a heap beside the puddle, so close it was almost touching. Fearful at any moment it would,
he stooped, picked it up, and slid it on, struggling a bit to work the
damp garment over his flannel shirt. It bound across the shoulders
as he stooped to pick up the other coat, which was also damp. And
bloodstained. He started to put that one on, too, then stopped himself,
bemused.

Out in the corridor, the elevator pinged, and its doors rumbled
open. He heard the rattling of the gurney as the attendants wheeled
Ms. McHenry aboard, then another rumbling as the doors closed.

Slattery stepped back into the room, his sharp blue eyes fastening
at once on the coat in Cam's hands. In three strides, he snatched it away
as if Cam were a child who had picked up a valuable antique.

"How is it you happen to be here, Doctor?" the assistant director
demanded.

"I was working in my lab, sir." The trembling had not yet left his

THE ENCLAVE — 19

fingers, and he kept getting flashes of other wounds he'd bandaged. Many wounds. Many times.

"Working in your lab," Slattery repeated, glance dropping to Cam's hands. "So you must have heard the shelving collapse. Why did you only emerge when we were helping Ms. McHenry to the prep room?"

"I . . ." Cam blinked at him. "I had my earphones on, Doctor. And I didn't think anything of it at the time."

"You didn't think anything of a crash and a woman screaming?"

"I didn't hear any screaming, sir. Only the crash, and then you and Dr. Poe talking in the hallway later. Even then I didn't pay much attention. I was focused on my work."

Slattery narrowed his eyes. "Why did you leave at all, then, if you'd heard nothing to concern you?"

"I was finished." Cam lifted the teal flash drive hanging on its lanyard about his neck and waved it at Slattery. "I was going up to my office to collate this data set with the others."

The assistant director regarded him suspiciously. What he thought Cam really might have been doing in the lab, or the real reason for his unseemly delay in coming to Ms. McHenry's aid, Cam couldn't begin to guess. But Slattery took his position as assistant director seriously, regarding everyone not part of the Inner Circle as likely spies or saboteurs.

"And Ms. McHenry?" Slattery asked finally. "Did she say anything to you of what happened?"

Cam let the flash drive slip through his fingers. It knocked against his chest as he shrugged. "She said she was attacked by an intruder who'd apparently broken in through the outside door in Poe's lab." Poe's was the only lab on this ground floor with such a door, which, given all the paranoia at Kendall-Jakes about corporate spying, seemed a gaping weak point in the Institute's otherwise prodigious security measures.

"Security searched the courtyard outside the door and the grounds beyond the courtyard walls," Slattery said. "They found nothing to corroborate her story."

"What about video surveillance?"

"I'll have to check the recordings, but I doubt there'll be anything."

*Recordings,* Cam thought, with another chill. *So the labs* are *under surveillance.* He didn't know why confirmation of what he'd already suspected should unsettle him so. Swain made no bones about the fact that he had every inch of this place under constant watch. Still, it set up the hairs on the back of his neck and made him feel strangely violated. *Do they have cameras in our apartments, too?* he wondered.

Slattery continued. "It was dark," he said, "and the girl was down here alone after a long day. She's a new hire, you know. Still getting used to things. They've already had to relocate her to new quarters on account of her complaints about the generator interrupting her sleep. I think she made an intruder out of a shadow and blundered into the shelves in her panic."

Cam did not know Ms. McHenry very well—these last weeks he'd been only vaguely aware of her as the new animal caretaker—but he did not think she had imagined the incident. For one thing, if there had been no intruder, not even one security man would have appeared at this hour, let alone five—plus doctors Poe and Slattery. If anyone was panicking, it was Slattery. The question was, why?

The assistant director continued to eye him. "You do realize that with the open house and the review coming up, it would be better not to get anything stirred up. After the business with Ms. Stopping last winter, the press would blow this all out of proportion. I trust you will practice the utmost discretion with regard to discussing this matter with the others."

"Of course, Doctor."

Slattery's swarthy scowl deepened. He held Cam's gaze a little longer than was comfortable, then nodded and stepped back. "You'll be going on up to your 501 office now, I presume?"

"Actually, I thought I'd give my lab a once-over before I leave, just in case there really *was* someone here tonight."

The frown returned to Slattery's brow. He could hardly forbid Cam to do precisely what their security procedures called for in such a situation, though, and the sudden vibration of the pager at the man's waist forestalled another lecture. "Let me know personally if you find anything amiss," he said as he pushed the response button.

Cam followed him into the hallway, then turned up the corridor toward his lab as Slattery proceeded toward the elevator.

The door to Dr. Poe's lab stood ajar, and Cam couldn't resist sticking his head in. What he saw shocked him. He'd expected a few dislodged and shattered aquariums, maybe a fallen shelf or two—not total devastation. Ranks of sturdy wooden shelving had fallen toward the doorway in which he stood, one upon the other in domino effect and on both sides of the central aisle. A chaos of broken glass, shattered aquariums, overturned Rubbermaid tubs, and thrashing salamanders covered the floor beneath them.

The room was lit by the harsh illumination of two freestanding electric lamps, set up in the clearer far end of the room, needed because the ceiling fixtures had been torn loose from their bolts, parts of them dangling toward the floor where lay the rest of them. It was as if a violent wind had slammed through the near half of the room. Even the small window in the lab door had been cracked by the event.

Poe was crouched at the juncture between the main room and the entry alcove, struggling to secure a thrashing red salamander. Beside him a man in janitorial gray swept shattered glass into a dustpan. The janitor—who was not the usual stoop-shouldered, white-ponytailed night man—stood to dump his dustpan into the gray plastic garbage can between them. As the clatter of broken glass tumbling into the near-empty container filled Cam's ears, Poe captured his salamander and flipped it into a blue storage tub nearby.

The dustpan emptied and the salamander contained, a relative silence ensued, and for the first time Cam heard the distinctive *wop-wop-wop* of a helicopter out in the night beyond the open door. It was a sound that always put the hair up on the back of his neck. Again the room flickered and swayed, as a sense of imminent danger jolted through him.

Poe stood up holding the tub and saw Cam in the hall doorway. He startled to a stop, his long, pale face furrowing into a scowl. "What are you doing here, Reinhardt?"

The question derailed Cam from his rising fear, though it took him a moment to collect his thoughts. "I thought you might like some help getting things back in order."

Poe nodded at the janitor. "Thank you, but as you can see, I have help."

Cam hesitated, scanning the wreckage. "Those shelves will be awkward to put upright with just the two of you."

"We're having new ones brought up." Poe hurried toward him, glass crunching under his sneakers. "You needn't concern yourself. We're fine."

Cam wasn't exactly pushed out of the lab, but the moment he had backed into the hall, Poe closed the door in his face and turned the lock.

He stood there in surprise, thinking wryly that Slattery must not have instructed Poe about being discreet. Or perhaps he had, and the eccentric scientist thought he was obeying the injunction, even as he all but screamed, *Don't look! Don't look! We've secrets to protect. . . .*

*Secrets to protect . . .* Again the sense of danger swept through him— so strong now he glanced over his shoulder at the empty corridor as he stepped to the door of his own lab. He swiped his ID card through the lock slot, the bolt retracted, and he pushed the door inward, stepping over the five-inch-high raised threshold as he snapped on the lights.

The square lab was a third the size of Poe's, with a row of narrow clerestory windows running high up along the opposite wall. Counters cluttered with lab equipment, working pans, and several ten-gallon aquariums ran along three walls atop Formica-faced cabinets. Those to his right butted up against a full-length wooden closet. Dead center, his desk and computer station stood as an island, piled with books, papers, disks, and various lab paraphernalia, looking almost as if someone *had* searched through it all. *When did I get to be such a slob?*

He stepped into the room, letting the door swing shut behind him, his neck crawling with the awareness that his every move was being recorded. Only when his jaw began to ache did he realize he was clenching his teeth. With a sigh, he relaxed his jaw and started around the small lab, sorting through beakers and flasks, opening cabinets and drawers, reading notes, making a show of inspecting his things, even as he wondered where exactly the camera was.

The heap of the frog bodies lying in the tray where he'd left them after removing their livers looked undisturbed. All still had their legs, so it didn't appear the intruder had breached his lab. They *were* beginning to stink, however. . . .

He continued around the counter, returning finally to the island computer station, where he slid out of his wet lab coat and tossed it carelessly over the back of the chair. Immediately it slid almost to the floor, and when he picked it up again and held it up to fold it properly over the chair back, his eyes caught upon the blood that stained its left sleeve and the red palm print on its shoulder. . . .

Suddenly the distant *wop-wop* of a helicopter's rotors grew loud and close. His chest constricted, and he clenched his teeth again—hard—as the bloody palm print flashed like a Vegas marquee. His hands shook and he gasped for breath as the image of another puddle of blood, much larger than what he'd seen on the prep room floor, overlaid the coat.

Suddenly he was on his knees in another ruined lab, this one on the other side of the world. Ranks of wooden cabinets had been splintered and wrenched from their moorings, huge examining tables lay on their sides, and jagged shards of glass glittered on the floor. Blood pooled around him and coated his arms to his elbows as he strove to hold closed the severed artery in the Afghan biologist's thigh until Rudy could get back with a med kit.

Automatic-weapon fire rattled in the cavernous chamber beyond the lab's shattered doorway, the sulfurous smoke of burned gunpowder acrid in his nose. He heard a chorus of screams; then all was drowned out by a lionlike roar. His trembling grew so violent he could hardly keep himself upright, his hand unable to hold the artery firmly, the Afghan's hot blood welling up against his palm. The roar sounded again, closer now, and panic seized him.

Abruptly he was back in his quiet southern Arizona lab, messy but not demolished. The floor was clean and clear, the walls solid, cabinets intact. Silence replaced the gunfire, though he could still hear the choppers, somewhere off in the distance—Institute security forces searching the desert for Slattery's nonexistent intruder.

Suddenly the coat in Cam's hands terrified him. He flung it away as if it were a flesh-and-blood attacker, surprised when it only crumpled to the floor about five feet away from him. He watched it warily, nonetheless, telling himself he was being utterly irrational as he breathed deeply and sought to regain control of himself.

Slowly it dawned on him that he'd had a flashback. His first in almost ten years.

He sagged back against the desk, horrified. That had been another time, another life, one he'd put firmly behind him. Why would he relapse now?

His gaze fixed on the bloody palm print just visible on a fold of the coat.

*Please . . . help us. . . .*

"No!"

He shoved himself away from the desk and went to the wooden cabinet, where he pulled out a clear plastic garbage bag. Weirdly unwilling to even touch the lab coat now, he picked it up with the bag, then shook the garment down into the bag's plastic folds. Knotting the ends, he dropped the whole thing into the hazmat bin at the end of the left counter, dumped the dead frogs on top of it, and followed that with a tray of used plastic test tubes. From there he went around the counters straightening and tidying, throwing away the trash that had accumulated—as if in doing so he might purge the memories that were even now trying to creep back into his present.

When the lab's door lock clacked, he nearly jumped out of his skin. As he turned toward it, the regular night janitor entered, a swarthy-faced, elderly Hispanic with snow-white hair. The old man stopped in surprise to see Cam staring at him. Then he dipped his head, apologizing in a raspy, heavily accented voice for "disturbing the doctor."

"That's all right," Cam said before the man could back out the door. "I was just leaving." And he did exactly that.

# Chapter Three

## New Eden

"Did you hear that the Enforcers took Andros away?" Terra's voice came from the other side of the goat, barely carrying above the rhythmic hiss of the milk as it streamed into the bucket between Zowan's knees. His hands, locked into the familiar cadence, squeezed and released in perfect alternation, one teat allowed to fill as the other was emptied. *Hiss. Hiss. Hiss.* He didn't miss the beat by even a hair, so if anyone was watching—always a possibility, particularly since it was Andros who'd been taken—they would not guess at the sudden sick lurch of his stomach, nor the wild acceleration of his heart.

The goat did, though, for she stamped restlessly and tossed her head as much as the stanchion allowed. Zowan kept the streams aimed into the ceramsteel bucket, alternating evenly, and clamped down on his panic. As Miss Malpi settled back, he leaned his forehead once more against her soft brown flank and spoke with careful casualness. "No." *Hiss. Hiss. Hiss.* "When?"

"This morning after service." Terra sat on her own stool, milking her own goat on the other side of Miss Malpi, the two of them alone in the small low-ceilinged milking room with the goats. Things had not gone well this morning. Three of their twenty-five milkers had developed early signs of bag fever, which necessitated isolating the sick trio and treating them, checking the others for potential illness, then sterilizing all the equipment and stalls. When the breakfast bell had rung, they still had fifteen goats to milk and all of them to feed. Zowan had sent his younger staff members to breakfast and morning Affirmation, staying on to finish up the morning's work alone. He'd been on the third to last milker when Terra had returned about fifteen minutes ago.·

"Gaias led them?" he asked, speaking of the Enforcers who'd taken his friend.

"Of course."

"What charges?"

"Blasphemy." She paused, her streams of milk shortening and faltering as she coaxed the last bit of liquid from her goat's udder. "He refused to say the Affirmation."

After what Andros had told him last night in the Star Garden, Zowan knew he shouldn't be surprised. But he was. Part of him rejoiced at Andros's courage and conviction; another part was horrified.

Terra's stool scraped as she stood. While she walked down to the cold room to pour her milk into the collection can, Zowan sought to express the appropriate words of shock and disgust for Andros's affront. He knew the hidden Watchers would frown upon him for saying nothing; nevertheless, he could not force the words past his throat, so instead, he busied himself with milking Miss Malpi dry. Then he stood and slid out of the narrow space between the stanchions to carry his own pail down to the cold room, which stood at the far corner of the narrow chamber in which they milked the goats. The roughhewn, cement-plastered ceiling hung but a foot above Zowan's head, and two rows of wooden stanchions stood end to end with a narrow walkway between them, six on one side, three on the other. A bundle of cables and pipes ran along the top of the wall just under the ceiling, bringing power and water to the cold room.

The cold room had a raised concrete platform for a floor, so when he stepped up through the doorway, he had to duck his head. Inside, the fifty-gallon cold can stood to his left, adjoined by a narrow counter and cabinets that ran around two and a half sides of the small, dim-lit room. The odor of disinfectant tickled his nose.

Terra stood at the double ceramsteel sink in the middle of the counter across from the doorway, washing her bucket in the soapy water of the left sink. She was a slim girl, her curves lost in the baggy green cotton tunic she wore over white cotton pants—the regulation uniform, with minor color variations, for all members of the Enclave. But even the baggy clothes could not diminish her beauty. Her red-brown hair fell in twin braids to her hips, and her heart-shaped face held a sweetness that belied her quick, strong mind.

He dumped his pail of milk into the fifty-gallon refrigerated ceram-steel collection can, careful to keep his distance from her—not easy in a chamber that barely accommodated one person. She helped by stepping to the right as she rinsed her bucket in the empty sink. Being only half an arm's length away from her, he felt her nearness with a keenness that made him realize belatedly that they probably shouldn't even be alone in the milking room together, much less this tiny cold room.

"I can't believe he would do such a thing," Terra said woodenly, shaking the last drops of water from her rinsed pail, then setting it upside down on the counter beside the others. "How could he be so ungrateful? So unthinking?" Her tone was so insincere, Zowan cringed. But she kept on, tension creeping into her tone. "Here, Father gives him life and he can't even offer simple thanks?"

Zowan said nothing. Better to keep silent. As she stepped away from the sink toward the door, he moved into the space she'd left and plunged his own pail into the sink of soapy water.

"He deserves the Cube, of course," she said from the doorway. "Which is surely what he'll get."

Zowan shuddered as he pushed the lever to turn on the water and rinsed his pail.

"Zowan?" She'd hesitated in the doorway, looking back at him, her tone one of question and of warning.

"Of course," he agreed. "Of course he does." But he sounded no more convincing than she had. He set his pail on the counter beside hers and turned to follow her through the narrow doorway back into the milking room. Like many of the outlying sections of the subterranean enclave in which they all lived, its walls were concrete-sealed, roughhewn stone. Two long tubes had been bored into the ceiling rock, equidistant from each other and topped with sky prisms at the upper ends, through which the sun's light was magnified and channeled. To his right, an opening led into the paddock chamber, where the goats were kept in one of two paddocks. To his left, beyond the rows of milking stanchions, another doorway led down to the Enclave's central complex of living and common areas.

Now he stood in the cold-room doorway as Terra unhooked her goat from the stanchion and led her to the near paddock. Once she was past, he stepped into the aisle himself and headed for Miss Malpi. Barely had he reached the goat's stanchion when a bald, dark-robed figure burst from the far doorway and strode toward him. Two others followed in his wake: Enforcers.

Zowan let his hands fall to his side and straightened to face them.

He'd done nothing wrong. Said nothing wrong. Had nothing to fear. All the same, his heart beat a tattoo against his breastbone, for he had recognized the leader at once.

The youngest of the three, Zowan's brother Gaias was also the shortest and slightest. Girls had once called him handsome, his deep blue eyes with their long lashes and level brows a cause for much sighing and giggling. Now only the lashes remained above his eyes, the brows fallen out along with his thick blond hair shortly after his third eye had begun to develop. It was bad enough to see his brother bald, but Zowan's stomach still roiled at the sight of the membrane-covered bulge gleaming in his forehead. The oculus itself was a dark indigo, its color softened by the milky translucence of its covering membrane.

He could not make himself look at it, could hardly make himself meet his brother's normal eyes. Not for the first time he wondered at the depth of his revulsion, for he'd lived with Enforcers most of his life. He'd attended his brother's induction ceremony, watching as he'd received the Breath of the Father that would ignite the yearlong development of the oculus and give him the second sight that all Enforcers had. He'd even joined in the congratulations and subsequent festivities. But it was still hard to see the reality of what had been done to him. For he and Gaias had grown up like two peas in a pod, close enough in personality and looks that people routinely confused them.

Now Zowan hardly knew him.

Gaias frowned. "What are you doing here, Zowan? Why have you missed the morning service and the Affirmation?"

"Oh!" Terra cried, a hand stealing to her lips. She gazed at Gaias wide-eyed. It must not have occurred to her until then that in sending the others while he himself did all the work, Zowan would not only have missed breakfast and the mandatory morning service, he'd not have said the Affirmation, either.

"I had to treat several of the goats for bag fever," Zowan explained calmly.

Gaias stared at him hard, and belatedly Zowan remembered the honorific, "Sir."

His brother's intense gaze eased. "You could not organize your time better?"

"I only discovered it this morning."

"And you did not feel you could wait to treat it until after?"

Zowan lifted his chin and refused to let that gleaming monstrous eye rattle him. "No, sir, I did not."

"Our workload was tripled this morning," Terra said. "He let the others go so they wouldn't miss and took the whole shift himself."

Zowan swallowed the words of admonition that rose to his lips, wishing she would stay out of it. Couldn't she see that Gaias was suspicious enough already? Couldn't she see the jealousy that had lately begun to flare in his eyes when she seemed to prefer Zowan over him and how much it goaded him that she had leaped to Zowan's defense? Didn't she realize how much power he had over her? As an Enforcer, Gaias could ask the Father for a union with her as soon as she came of age next month, and would most likely get her.

Gaias's hairless brow drew into a scowl. "I am an Enforcer of the Father's justice, girl. You will address me as 'Commander' or 'Sir.' "

And now Terra's own eyes flashed. It hadn't been so long ago they'd been playmates. Still she released a breath and submitted. "Of course. Sir."

His blue eyes narrowed. "He let the others go, but not you?"

"He sent me, too. I came back after service to help him finish."

"Came back when no one else is around, I note."

She blinked at him. Then a tide of red flooded her face and she averted her gaze.

Gaias looked down at her coldly. "How long have you been in the goat barn, Terra? Two cycles now?" He didn't wait for her to confirm the statement. "I think it is time you moved on. I hear the crèche has need of workers."

She almost protested, then swallowed the words and held her head high, straining not to look at Zowan as Gaias turned to him again.

"Your friend Andros required separation and reproof today. I suppose she told you."

"She did."

"He failed to say the Affirmation."

Zowan said nothing.

"When we called him on it, he fell into a pique, spilling all manner of blasphemy. It was despicable."

"I'm sure it was." Zowan focused on the cement-covered stone beyond Gaias's shoulder, trying not to see the eye, even as it filled his awareness. The oculus heightened an Enforcer's sensitivity to sound, vibration, emotion, tone, breathing rate, and other cues that enabled him to discern when someone was lying. And while Zowan wasn't lying, it had to be clear to Gaias that he did not share his outrage over Andros's "blasphemy."

"I find it difficult to believe you had no inkling of his sentiments," said Gaias. "Close as the two of you are." Again bitterness sharpened his tone. Gaias was jealous of Andros, too, for having replaced him in Zowan's affections when Gaias had become an Enforcer.

Zowan set his jaw. "I had an inkling."

"He spoke to you, then."

Zowan shrugged. "I thought it temporary madness. I cautioned him against pursuing such contemplation."

"Did you?" Gaias stared at him intently, third eye shimmering at the edge of Zowan's field of vision. No one spoke. Miss Malpi stomped her feet and bleated once, impatient to be off the stanchion and back with the other goats. Gaias drew a breath and released it as if reaching a decision. "You failed to say the Affirmation this morning, as well, brother."

THE ENCLAVE — 31

Zowan met his gaze with a slight smile. "How do you know, sir? Perhaps I said it to the goats."

Gaias's chin jerked up. "You are impertinent. You will come to the Sanctuary and say it now. I will watch to see that it is done properly."

Zowan's anger flared, pressing the bounds of his control, urging words of impropriety. He forced it down and finally glanced at Terra watching them wide-eyed from the paddock gateway. "See Miss Malpi back to the pen, all right?"

She nodded, and Zowan turned away from her, brushing Gaias as he strode past him toward the doorway and the corridor that led down to the Enclave's central complex. Gaias followed closely, his two Enforcer companions taking up the rear.

## Chapter Four

The harsh bleat of Lacey's alarm jarred her from a deep sleep. Groaning, she reached above her headboard to the dresser top, fumbled the alarm off, and brought it down to eye level. A green 7:30 glowed back at her.

It took a moment to register. Then, muttering a word Dr. Swain would find highly inappropriate—he was a fierce defender of civil conversation—she flung off the blankets and lurched up. Pain shot across her back, and stars dazzled her vision. She fell back onto the pillow, memory returning in a rush—her struggle with the stranger in Poe's lab and subsequent fall into the shelving, Assistant Director Slattery and Dr. Poe coming to her aid, and Cameron Reinhardt carrying her to the prep room, where he doctored the long, bloody glass cut she'd sustained with a row of butterfly bandages. Slattery had sent her off to the clinic for stitches and an examination—even made her ride there on a gurney.

Except . . .

She lifted her left arm, which had no bandage on it and no stitches, either. Just a fine white scar running across the delicate skin of her inner arm halfway from her elbow to her wrist. She stared at it, ran the fingers of her right hand along it, lightly at first, then with more pressure. It was slightly tender to the touch, pinkish along the edges, but obviously an old wound, not something she'd sustained mere hours ago.

She let both arms drop to her sides as a wave of disorientation swept through her. *Surely I didn't dream it all?*

She clearly remembered arriving at the clinic, but after that things got fuzzy. Had she stayed there longer than she thought? She picked up her clock from where she'd dropped it on the bed and pressed the Mode button for the date: *Friday, June 6.* A mere seven and a half hours since she'd been cut. And on her desk stood an orange plastic pill bottle of some prescription medication, indicating she *had* been to the clinic. . . .

*But how could this have healed so fast?* Her fingers trailed lightly along the scar again, and then it hit her: she worked in a place that was cutting edge when it came to research into tissue growth and gene therapy. Just last week she'd read the abstract of a paper describing a process of accelerated wound repair on rats. The rats' wounds had been burns, not cuts, and the acceleration had occurred over days rather than hours, but as Director Swain always said, the field was rife with competition. No doubt Kendall-Jakes had come up with a process of accelerated wound repair that applied to cuts and the clinic staff had used it on her arm. One of the perks of working at the Institute. "It's about time," she muttered.

She sat up more slowly this time, taking shallow breaths against the pain and dizziness. Eventually the small room stopped spinning. She sat in a stupor, watching as its pale undecorated walls grew increasingly bright from the fluorescent "sunlight" pouring through the mini blinds at the false window in the back wall—false because the room was underground, one level below the animal facility where she'd been working. Her roommate's twin bed stood along that wall under the "window," running perpendicular to Lacey's. It was tidily made, a stuffed dinosaur and pelican resting jauntily against the pillow. Slowly it dawned on her that Jade had already left for breakfast, which had started at 7:30. *Why didn't she wake me?*

The hurt and dismay of being ignored and excluded yet again swamped her for a moment. Sometimes her need for a true friend, for someone to see and appreciate her for herself, was so great she thought it would crush her. Yet there was always a barrier: age, social status, interests, personality, job. . . . She never had the right combination to fit in, to find approval . . . or even to be noticed.

She'd thought that coming to Kendall-Jakes, living and working among fellow scientists—the best and the brightest and the most dedicated in the world—would change that, but it hadn't. Already she was seeing the same old social-pecking-order politics, the gossip, the backstabbing, the sucking up, the ever-present competition. After three weeks, Jade was still no more than a casual acquaintance—one Lacey wasn't even sure she liked—and the others were even more distant. Nothing was turning out as she'd hoped, and she was beginning to think she was doomed by her own inadequacies to be alone and friendless for the rest of her life.

*But you know you can't leave now, so you might as well suck it up and stop sniveling. . . .*

When she finally felt stable enough to stand, she stepped to her desk to look at the label on the pill bottle. As she read the name of the prescription, a tingle of horror swept through her. "Valium?"

They'd given her mother Valium right before she'd gone to the hospital with her nervous breakdown, a tranquilizer to control her paranoid outbursts. *Why did they give me a tranquilizer?* Then she remembered that Valium was also prescribed as a muscle relaxant. And judging from the band of pain that tightened across her back just under her shoulder blades, she surely needed a muscle relaxant.

That would explain why she felt so stodgy and emotionally brittle, too, and why Jade hadn't wakened her, as well. For all Lacey knew, her roomie tried and failed—apparently her alarm had been going off every fifteen minutes since her usual wake time of 6:45.

Another glance at the clock reminded her she'd better hurry if she wanted breakfast—and if she wanted to hear firsthand the official report of last night's events, which would likely be delivered in the post-breakfast announcements.

Fifteen minutes later she walked stiffly into the staff dining hall, located on the south side of the ziggurat's main floor. The spacious room had a window wall facing eastward onto a rumpled landscape of oak-and-grass-covered ridges. The other three walls were adobe-colored and were decorated with large desert watercolor paintings interspersed with potted ficus trees. A small stage with a podium stood at the south end overlooking the forty-some round tables that accommodated the Institute's administrators and researchers. Director Swain's table stood front and center before the stage. With him sat assistant directors Frederick Slattery and Genevieve Viascola, Swain's gorgeous red-haired, sometime lover; Nelson Poe, head of Developmental Biology; Cameron Reinhardt, head of Applied Genetics; and the department heads of Molecular and Cell Biology, Chemical Engineering, and Senescence.

The waitstaff was beginning to disassemble the morning buffet when she arrived, but Lacey managed to load her plate from what was left. As she approached her usual table—where she was gratified to see her seat had remained empty—she noticed that diners at the tables she was passing were staring at her. Given the rumor mill around Kendall-Jakes, she wouldn't have been surprised if the whole room had already heard about her little escapade last night.

Indeed, at her own table, everyone was listening raptly to Aaron Stiles, resident "inside man," as he apparently shared yet another gossipy tidbit. As she walked into earshot, she heard " . . . complete breakdown. She had to be sedated. . . ." and glanced around to see if she could guess who'd been sedated. Instead she found the three junior lab assistants—Pecos, Lauren, and Tina—who sat across the table from her, staring at her wide-eyed.

"Well, you know," Melissa Magursky said to Aaron, "some people just aren't cut out for—"

Mel broke off as she and the remainder of those at the table grew aware of Lacey's presence, gaping at her just as the junior lab assistants had. Perplexed and blushing furiously, Lacey set her plate on the table beside Jade Kemmer and pulled out her chair.

"What are *you* doing here?" Jade demanded as Lacey sat down. Jade's blunt manner was not helped by her off-putting exterior. Thick black-framed eyeglasses perched on a narrow nose beneath heavy, unplucked brows, one of which had been pierced with a silver ring. Her ears were riddled with rings, as well, and her thick, wiry, two-toned hair had been cut in an asymmetrical style, chin-length black locks framing her face in contrast to the short-cropped blond hair in back. "The man who brought you back said you'd sleep all morning."

"My alarm woke me," Lacey said, noting that the conversations at the adjoining tables had started up again, glances flicking repeatedly her way.

"Oh," Jade said. "Sorry. I couldn't figure out how to turn it off, so I just kept hitting the Snooze button. I guess I should have put it in the closet or something."

"I'm glad you didn't," Lacey said. She cocked her head. "You said a man brought me back?"

"An orderly from the clinic. I think he meant not to wake me because he came right in. Scared the . . . er . . . stuffing out of me." Jade frowned. "You don't remember?"

Lacey shook her head.

"Well, you did seem out of it. He said you'd had a—" she hesitated, glancing uneasily at Aaron—"breakdown. Hysterics or something."

"A *breakdown*?" Lacey looked at Aaron. "*I'm* the one you were talking about just now?"

Aaron shifted uncomfortably in his chair. "Just passing on what I heard."

"Which is?"

"My friend Tom at the clinic—we play racquetball—said you started hallucinating in the animal rooms last night, had a panic attack and called security. I guess the security guys brought you in for . . . well, *he* said for sedation."

For a moment Lacey continued to stare, her drug-fuddled brain frozen into blankness.

"He said you'd bruised yourself up pretty badly," Aaron went on. "That you thought there was some sort of monster down there."

*Breakdown. Panic attack. Hallucination* . . . No wonder everyone was staring at her as if she were a freak.

She finally broke out of her stasis and snorted, shaking her head. "I can't believe the rumor mill in this place! I didn't have a breakdown, nor was I hallucinating. . . ." She paused, glancing around the table. "There was an intruder. The guards' arrival scared him off—*I* didn't call them. And I only went to the clinic because Assistant Director

Slattery insisted I go. To make sure I—" she hesitated, realizing she couldn't mention stitches when she had none to show—"didn't have a concussion or anything."

"No one's said anything about an intruder," Aaron said.

"Assistant Director *Slattery* was there?" asked Jade in astonishment.

"He came down with the security guys," Lacey said. "Dr. Poe was there, too. And Dr. Reinhardt."

The doubtful looks were deepening with her every word, and suddenly Lacey heard how it all sounded to the others: an AD and the heads of both the Genetics and Developmental Biology departments just happened to be down in the animal facility in the middle of the night rescuing her from an intruder no one had heard anything about?

She looked around the table in desperation. "Didn't any of you hear the helicopters last night? See their searchlights crisscrossing the grounds?"

An awkward silence ensued. The crease between Jade's dark brows deepened. At her shoulder, Aaron's angular face grew stoic while Pecos and Lauren exchanged sober glances.

"It's nothing to be ashamed of," Mel said presently. She sipped from her cup of coffee. "Hallucination is a common symptom of severe sleep deprivation—as is hysteria. We all know you got very little sleep your first week here, and I doubt you've had a chance to make it up. Plus, you've been working really hard."

"I didn't hallucinate," Lacey declared.

"If there really was an intruder in the AnFac last night," Aaron asked, "why doesn't anyone know about it? Why aren't we on orange alert like we were the last time they thought we had a break-in? When they hardly let us out of our rooms. Or our labs."

Lacey hadn't been at the Institute when the last security lockdown had happened, so that hadn't occurred to her. Now, as disparate pieces of the puzzle fell into place, a horrible suspicion bloomed. Was Slattery trying to cover up the break-in? Was that why they'd used a proprietary and possibly unapproved process to heal the wound on her arm so swiftly? So she'd have nothing to support her story should she try to tell others?

And on that line, what *was* she planning to tell them about her mysterious intruder? That he tore the legs off frogs and ate them for amusement? Even if she'd had a freshly stitched cut, they wouldn't believe her. A wave of frustration surged through her. "I only know what I saw," she said finally, mortified by her tremulous voice. Though her stomach had become a small hard knot, she stabbed her fork into a cube of cantaloupe and stuffed it into her mouth, desperate for something to do in the excruciating silence.

Snatches of conversation drifted from the adjoining tables:

" . . . let all the frogs loose . . ."

" . . . panic attack . . ."

" . . . overstressed . . ."

" . . . happens with new ones . . ."

Everyone thought she'd had a breakdown! She felt her face flame, and suddenly she wanted to fling down her fork and run away. But that would only make things worse. As would trying to explain further. All she could do was cling to what she knew was the truth. Maybe they'd caught the intruder last night and that was why security hadn't been tightened. After breakfast Swain would probably tell them all about it. Then Tom at the clinic and his busybody friend, Aaron, would be the ones with egg on their faces.

"You sure you're all right?" Jade asked.

"I'm fine."

" 'Cause, you know, it's really better to just admit it. Then you can get treatment for it."

"I appreciate your concern," Lacey replied tightly, wishing her voice wouldn't shake so. "But I'm fine. I didn't have a breakdown. I just needed a . . . a few X rays."

Jade frowned at her, and when Lacey added nothing more said, "Andrea Stopping wouldn't admit anything was wrong, either, and look what happened to her."

At Lacey's side, Mel gasped and the tension ratcheted up.

Andrea Stopping had been a postdoc from Johns Hopkins when she'd come to K-J last fall. Unable to handle the stress, she'd fallen into manic depression. One day in January she'd hiked into the mountains and vanished. Her body was never found, but everyone called it a suicide.

After a moment Jade said, "I'm sorry. I shouldn't have—"

"It's all right."

More awkward silence enfolded them. Finally Aaron asked with forced brightness if anyone had seen the heated exchange yesterday between Cameron Reinhardt and his new department assistant, Manny Espinosa, the Rhodes scholar from Argentina, a man who had demonstrated a marked preference for pursuing his own projects over Reinhardt's.

Given her experience with Reinhardt last night, Lacey should have been interested in Aaron's gossip, but she hardly heard him. Now that she was no longer the center of everyone's attention, her thoughts whirled in a tangle of disbelief and crushing disappointment that they would so dismiss her word . . . and the unsettling fear that things might not be as she'd recalled after all.

Not only was her story bizarre, but she could recall hardly anything of her time at the clinic last night. A bout of hysterics could certainly account for that. It would also explain the seemingly irrelevant questions she'd been asked by clinic personnel upon her arrival: *"Do you often work late? Have you been working overtime? How long have you been at K-J now? Been getting enough sleep? Would you say you have felt stressed lately?"*

She remembered being irritated. Remembered people standing over her, discussing her as if she weren't there, and thought maybe someone had given her a shot, which could have been Aaron's sedative.

*Had* she imagined it all? The frogs, the intruder, Reinhardt and Poe and Slattery? The question made her chest tighten so much she could hardly breathe.

Then she felt the new scar on the inside of her arm, rubbing against the side of her shirt as she ate. Still tender, and very real. No. She might not recall all that happened at the clinic, but everything before then was crystal clear, the memories too vivid for her to believe them figments of a panic attack. And as weird as the intruder was, as inexplicable as his motives were, there was logic and cohesion to all that had happened.

There were the helicopters, too, which she'd seen on the ride down to the clinic, their strobe lights lacerating the night sky.

"Esteemed colleagues…" Director Swain's voice blared over the loudspeaker, interrupting her thoughts. "May I have your attention?"

Still expecting an announcement that would put everything to rights, Lacey abandoned her ruminations and focused on K-J's director, standing now on the palm-flanked stage at the podium. Six-feet-four-inches tall, Parker Swain was still handsome and trim at sixty. His smooth skin, startling blue eyes, and thick, shoulder-length blond hair belied his years even more than his physique did, though the greatest marker of his youthfulness was the boundless energy that enabled him to work circles around men half his age. Institute rumor claimed he slept no more than four hours a night, and even a personal assistant and two secretaries on separate shifts strained to keep up with his demands. Which the particularly malicious rumors said involved frequent stints on the plush leather couch in his ninth-floor office.

His audience now waiting in expectant silence, he hesitated, regarding them all with that provocative wordlessness he so liked to use in his presentations. Then, just when it seemed someone had to move or speak, he raised his chin dramatically and said, "I have an honor to bestow this morning."

He paused to let his words sink in as Lacey's heart fell, her disappointment so great it nearly choked her.

Swain went on. "As most of you know, nearly a year ago we at Kendall-Jakes were pleased to welcome Dr. Cameron Reinhardt into our ranks. By now most of you have had the privilege of meeting him and some few the greater privilege of working with him. But I'll wager our modest doctor has not mentioned to any of you that he's just had his fourth paper published in the last three years. Nor that he has been selected by the ASHG to receive the Stern Award for that same series of papers at this year's fall meeting."

*Of course he'd make this announcement first,* Lacey told herself. *Just be patient. He'll get to the other at the end.*

"In light of these honors," Swain continued, "and the honor they bring to all of us, as well as his exemplary contributions to the field, K-J's board of directors has unanimously voted to grant him our coveted

Black Box Citation." Swain held up a large wooden plaque with a dark metallic glazing, the Institute's familiar ziggurat shape shining in hologram upon it. "Dr. Reinhardt, would you come up here, please?"

Polite applause echoed through the dining hall as Dr. Reinhardt rose from his spot at the table in front of Swain. Unfortunately, he took the edge of the tablecloth with him for a moment, giving all the place settings a good lurch—even as he tipped his chair backward out of control. It would have fallen to the floor had Dr. Viascola not caught it.

No one laughed nor spoke because it was so typically Reinhardt. *"The brilliant man in his bubble, wreaking havoc as he advances,"* as Aaron liked to say. Nothing like the man she'd seen last night who had carried her easily to the prep room and so swiftly and competently doctored the bleeding cut on her arm.

Reinhardt ascended the stage without further mishap and stopped at Swain's side, half a head shorter and dressed in jeans and a blue flannel shirt. Appearing bemused and embarrassed, he shook Swain's hand and accepted the plaque, mumbled an inarticulate response into the microphone, and looked as if he'd give anything to get off the stage. Instead of releasing him, however, Swain spoke again into the mike, going on about Reinhardt's educational past and his road to this moment.

Lacey hardly heard him as it became clear there would be no report about last night's intruder, and thus no exoneration for her from the nasty rumor someone had set into circulation. The realization brought tears to her eyes, and she spent a few moments blinking them back and fighting for emotional control.

After a moment, Swain's words registered again. "And now he's here with us." He turned to Reinhardt. "It's an honor, Doctor. You are an outstanding scientist and a brilliant mind, despite your archaic and irrational belief system."

Reinhardt smiled sheepishly, and a number of the audience tittered. Cameron Reinhardt, as Swain made sure everyone knew, was a Christian. A born-again, evangelical, Bible-believing Creationist. Aaron liked to mock that in him, too.

Swain's voice blared over the speakers: "We forgive you for it, though. Mere temporary insanity."

The director grinned good-naturedly, though Lacey did not think Reinhardt appreciated the jab nearly so much as Swain had enjoyed giving it. With that the director held out a hand toward Reinhardt. "Friends and colleagues, may I present our newest Black Box Fellow."

The audience supplied a round of dutiful applause, and Reinhardt was released with his plaque to return to his seat. Swain finished up his remarks with a few administrative details, a reminder of the coming review and open house for which they all needed to be ready, and nothing at all about the incident in the animal facility last night.

Though Lacey had accepted by then that he wasn't going to mention it, the reality of having her expectations fulfilled still hit her like a blow. As the others stood and headed over to congratulate Reinhardt, she sat unmoving, struggling once more to regain her composure and trying to ignore the glances of amusement, pity, and curiosity that came her way.

Later, as she passed through the congratulations line herself, it occurred to her that Dr. Reinhardt might be able to straighten all this out. If nothing else, he could explain to her what was going on. Thus, on her morning break she went to his office in Lab 500, only to learn he was down at the clinic gathering project data.

That took the wind out of her sails for a moment. Then she realized she could go down to the clinic herself and have a look at the records from her admittance last night. Nestled halfway across the bowl-shaped desert park planted at the center of the Institute's campus, it was only a five-minute walk from the zig.

At ten in the morning in June, it was already 103 degrees outside, and when she stepped out of the air-conditioned building, the sun's heat hit her like a cosmic pile driver. Heat waves shimmered off the asphalt path and wrapped her in an embrace that felt good after the chill of the Institute's excellent air-conditioning system. By the time she reached her destination, though, she was dripping with sweat.

Sliding glass doors bracketed an airlock that kept the clinic's cool air from escaping as people entered and exited. Inside, she crossed the spacious lobby and waited at the main desk while the two receptionists helped those who had preceded her.

The clinic was part of the Fountains of Eternal Life Health Resort, whose buildings occupied the western side of the Institute's campus. Though some said the resort and clinic paid a good portion of the Institute's expenses, many of the researchers considered it an embarrassment of commercialization that compromised their reputations as scientists. Even worse was the infamous Vault, also operated by the resort, which held the cryonically preserved remains of those who believed that one day the Institute's scientists would find a way to revive the dead and grant eternal life to the living. Membership numbered close to one thousand and was available to any willing to pay the two-hundred-dollar fee and sign over their life insurance to the clinic.

"Name, please?" The receptionist's voice brought Lacey back to the moment.

She gave her name, the woman typed it in, then said, "I'm sorry, but your appointment's not till 2:00 p.m. . . ."

"My appointment?"

"A follow-up on your admittance last night."

"Oh. Well, I'm not here for that. I was hoping I could see my records from that admittance, though."

"You want to look at your records?"

"Just from last night."

"That's a bit irregular. I'm not sure we can—"

"Lacey McHenry?" said the other receptionist. "I just gave that file to Dr. Reinhardt less than ten minutes ago." She looked at Lacey. "He stood over there by the door for a while and read it. You must've passed him on your way in."

Lacey was already turning away, for once appreciating the fact that Reinhardt was one of the few at Kendall-Jakes who did not rush around in a frenzy. She spotted him right off, some ways up the southernmost of the two paths leading to the Institute, walking slowly, reading as he went. It didn't take her long to catch him.

"Dr. Reinhardt!" she gasped as she came abreast of him, breathless from climbing the hill.

He looked up, the small photo-gray lenses of his glasses turned dark by the sunlight. "Ah, the frog girl."

"You *do* remember last night!" she cried.

When he said nothing, she added, "In the lab? You sutured my cut with butterfly bandages?" She showed him her arm, though of course there was only the mysterious scar. Behind her, a man called his name, but he seemed not to notice. She couldn't see his eyes because of the dark glasses but thought they might be fixed upon her arm and that any moment he might exclaim with surprise.

Instead he shifted backward and closed the folder. "That looks like a well-healed scar to me, miss."

She stared at him in astonishment. "It was bleeding all over the prep room floor. There was an intruder in Dr. Poe's lab." She paused. "Surely you remember, Doctor. Why else would you have asked for my records?"

Whoever was behind them called again, closer now. She began to feel hurried, even as Reinhardt grew stiff and tense.

He looked down at the folder in his hands. "I didn't ask. Gen asked me to bring back your file when I picked up the results of the blood tests we ran for the A-7 Project."

*Gen?* "You mean Dr. Viascola?" she guessed. "Why would she—"

"It says in here you have a history of mental illness in your family," he cut in, opening the file and thumbing through the pages.

"*What?*"

"Your mother, I think it said, had a . . ." He fumbled with the folder.

"Nervous breakdown," Lacey supplied. "Five years ago."

"You have a brother in prison for drug dealing and assault. And you yourself have been the victim of an abusive marriage that ended in your husband's death."

"Ex-husband. We divorced before he died. And what is all that doing in there?"

"K-J researches all prospective staff members thoroughly before they're hired. The security problem, you know."

She frowned, realizing he'd drawn her off the subject, and started anew. "Are you telling me, Dr. Reinhardt, that you remember nothing of the events from last night that I just described to you? The intruder, the bleeding glass cut on my arm, being locked in the prep room . . ." She heard the other man approaching behind them, huffing and puffing up the hill, his footsteps gritting on the path.

Suddenly Reinhardt grasped her forearm, rotated it palm upward, and rubbed the scar gently with his thumb. "This could hardly have healed overnight," he pointed out.

"Sure it could have," she countered. "If they used some sort of ATR process."

He looked up at her as if she'd startled him, then past her as the footsteps closed upon them. It was as if she had winked out of existence. Dropping her arm, he stepped around her to meet the man coming up the hill.

It was Frederick Slattery, carrying a folded, plastic-wrapped lab coat. "I've been looking all over for you, Doctor!" he said to Reinhardt as he seized the geneticist's elbow and hurried him up the path. They fell at once into a discussion of administrative nature, leaving her beside a mesquite tree, the sun beating down on her bare head.

# Chapter Five

Slattery dropped his talk of requisition protocols as soon as Lacey McHenry was out of sight and earshot and took Cam to task, first for talking to McHenry at all, and second, for having put on her lab coat last night instead of his own, then letting Slattery take Cam's in the belief it was Lacey's. Even worse, he'd thrown what Slattery had really wanted into the biohazard bin.

Of course, Cam had done none of it with conscious intent, having been completely rattled by the events themselves and the resultant flashback they had triggered. But he could hardly explain that to Slattery, since his stint in the army was officially designated as administrative and not the sort of work that might produce post-traumatic-stress flashbacks. Besides, he was trying very hard to forget the flashback entirely.

"Here is *your* coat," Slattery said, shoving the packaged garment into Cam's chest as they stopped together on the path. "Thanks to you we now have nothing with which to prove there was no intruder."

Cam looked at him in surprise. "I would think Ms. McHenry's alleged wee-hour hysteria and hallucination has removed all need for any such proof. Not to mention the near instantaneous healing of her cut," he added dryly.

Slattery's dark bushy brows drew together and he seemed momentarily at a loss for words. Then he harrumphed and leaned forward to pluck Lacey McHenry's file folder from Cam's grasp. "The director wants you in his office at your earliest convenience. I'll take this up to Gen for you." He continued on toward the ziggurat without further explanation, leaving Cam to stand with the packaged lab coat and a growing uneasiness in his gut.

Being head of the Department of Applied Genetics shielded him from the general stream of gossip and rumor, so he'd not heard of Ms. McHenry's late-night self-admission for hallucinatory paranoia until fifteen minutes ago, when the clinic receptionist had told him. That information had prompted him to open her file, which had shown him not only the false diagnosis but a notation in her physical evaluation that she had an existing hairline scar on her left inner forearm sustained during one of her berserk ex-husband's beatings. Barely had he read the fraudulent notation when McHenry had caught up with him and shown him the scar herself.

He'd recognized at once what they had done to her, for he'd worked on the ATR project a bit when he'd first arrived at K-J and had seen it in action. What he couldn't understand was why they'd done it.

The grit of her approaching footfalls on the graveled path behind him now intruded into his musings, and mindful of the AD's warning not to speak to her further, he hurried away before she could stop him.

Since "at your convenience" meant "immediately" in Swain-speak, Cam headed straight for the main elevators in the ziggurat's huge central atrium, stepping through a pair of sliding glass doors into the warm, moist, loam-scented air of the kidney-shaped atrium's artificial jungle. Seventy-foot-tall trees soared above him, encircled by nine stories of vine-cloaked balconies. More vines linked balcony to balcony, balcony to tree, and tree to tree in a riot of foliage that supported a collection of exotic birds, butterflies, reptiles, and small monkeys.

Where once he'd gawked in amazement, Cam now strode briskly along the artificial stream, past the thirty-foot-tall man-made waterfall to the bank of six glass-walled elevators that served the upper floors. One of them had just arrived, its passengers disembarking, and shortly he was ascending toward the ninth floor.

Watching the atrium's vine-cloaked balconies and tree trunks slide downward as the car glided up, he continued to chew on the rationale behind using what was certainly an unapproved medical procedure in their attempt to cover up the break-in. In light of Swain's past procedural indiscretions, it seemed a foolish action indeed.

Though it had been thirty years since the FDA had barred him from receiving federal research money, it had all come about because he'd dared to perform unauthorized experiments on human subjects, one of whom had died. Shame and exile had been Swain's reward, and he'd spent a decade working in various privately funded international research facilities. He'd returned to a mostly permanent residence in Arizona some nine years ago, living on-site to direct the last stages of the Institute's construction as he began recruiting staff and funding for its operation. It had only been five years, however, since he'd been fully exonerated by the FDA for his earlier crimes.

After all of that, why would he repeat his original sin now, when there was no need?

As the elevator stopped at the ninth floor, Cam turned from the view of the atrium, now plunging to dizzying depths below him, and stepped through the opening doors. He crossed the spacious common area and passed through another pair of glass doors into the foyer where the receptionist nodded him through. He strode past her and turned right into a busy, curving corridor.

Swain's office stood on the opposite side of the building. He had a private express elevator for his own use, but everyone else had to walk around from the main elevators, allowing visitors—and subordinates— the opportunity to appreciate the richly paneled walls, thick carpeting, sparkling chandeliers, and expensive paintings and replicas of the ancient artifacts that were Swain's passion—all of it a not-so-subtle reminder of the fabulous amounts of money and power it had taken to establish the Institute and to keep it running.

Inexplicably, as he neared the director's office, Cam's heartbeat began to accelerate. His hands went cold and damp, and the underarms of his flannel shirt grew clammy—and he had no idea why. He'd done nothing wrong and had nothing to fear. Besides, Swain liked him and he knew it. He'd all but begged Cam to join his team.

"Good morning, Dr. Reinhardt," said Deena Flynn, Director Swain's senior secretary, as Cam drew up to her desk. "And congratulations."

Curly black hair framed her pretty porcelain-pale face, wide blue eyes, and fetching dimples.

Cameron blinked at her. "Congratulations?"

"On the Black Box Citation." She regarded him with amusement. "Forgotten already?"

"Oh." He smiled sheepishly. "Thank you. And good morning to you, too."

She gestured toward the dark-paneled door in the dark-paneled wall behind her. "Go on in. He's waiting for you."

Cam rounded her desk and started toward the door. Suddenly a searing light exploded in his face and a thundering boom slammed him backward as it drove the breath from his chest. White heat flashed around him in the narrow, rough-walled tunnel and was gone. He stood reeling in the smoke that drifted before him, shifting ethereally in the beam of his head lamp. Sulfurous fumes stung his throat and nostrils, and he tried desperately not to breathe it in, but finally could not help himself.

As he gasped in the air his lungs demanded, the tunnel vanished and he was back in Swain's reception area, heart pounding. Sweat drenched him, and his knees trembled so violently he feared they might give way at any moment.

"Are you all right, Doctor?" asked Deena from behind him.

He swallowed hard, drew another breath, and felt the trembling subside. "Yes," he said as her chair squeaked and rolled back. He turned to give her a reassuring smile. "Must have been the elevator ride or something."

A slim brow arched. "Or perhaps you are working yourself too hard again?"

He ducked his head in a combination nod and shrug, then turned to close the gap still between himself and Swain's door. But as he grasped the pewter latch, he saw his hand still trembling and hesitated. Lifting his gaze to the dark, gleaming panels, he stood breathing softly, letting his pulse settle as he came to grips with the fact he'd just had another flashback. His second in less than twenty-four hours.

*What is going on?!* He'd suffered post-traumatic stress disorder during and after his deployment twelve years ago, and for a time it had ruined his life. But God had found him in the mess he'd made and pulled him out of it. *Oh, Father in heaven, please don't let me go back to that!*

He heard Deena's chair squeak behind him. She must have turned to look at him in renewed concern. Before she could speak, he drew himself together and pressed the latch.

Director Swain's huge corner office, with its sweeping, high-ceilinged expanse and odd dimensions, always gave him a sense of disorientation upon entry. Tinted floor-to-ceiling windows formed the two outer walls, providing a spectacular view of the Catalina Mountains looming to the south. Freestanding sculptures, replicas of ancient tomb decorations, and Canopic jars stood about the room, and the curving interior walls were lined with glass cases holding more artifacts than the state museum down in Tucson.

At first Cam thought Swain had stepped out, for the padded captain's chair at his massive mahogany desk in the midst of the archeological assemblage stood empty.

Then a voice called, "I'm over here," and Cam shifted position enough to see the director around the tomb panel that had obscured him. Swain stood at the south window peering through a telescope aimed at the grounds.

Wending his way through the artifacts and replicas, Cam felt his trembling increase and his chest grow tight. Thankfully he drew up beside the director without falling into another flashback, and his tension subsided. It helped to have the openness of the mountain view now spread before him.

Immediately below, the ziggurat's two lower sections stairstepped down and away from them, their flat rooftops glaring in the midmorning sun. Beyond them sprawled the Institute's desert campus, its inner mesquite park cradled between the long, curving berms formed of the earth that had been removed from what was now the ziggurat's multi-level basement. Paved and graveled paths wandered throughout the park, past several ramadas, a central bricked plaza, and a small lake as they linked the various outbuildings and maintenance buildings with each other and the zig.

To the right, about halfway down the bowl's slope, stood the white-walled clinic Cam had left some fifteen minutes ago. Beyond it, scattered across the northwestern berm and continuing up the surrounding hillsides beyond were the guest casitas, meeting rooms, and office buildings of the Fountains of Eternal Life Health Resort—adobe walls a warm contrast with the oak and cottonwood trees surrounding them. Between it and the ziggurat, the red-granite slabs of Swain's avant-garde Black Box Theater lifted from the side of the berm like a hatching pterodactyl.

The director, a wireless headset clipped to his right ear, had focused his telescope toward the southeastern boundary of the Institute's property, where a dissipating dust cloud rose off the distant draw that Cam knew lay just inside of the perimeter fence. He glimpsed a bit of the eight-foot-tall chain link, in fact, but only because he knew where to look.

Face still pressed to the eyepiece of his scope, Swain said, "Where is it exactly that you run on these morning jaunts of yours?"

Cam blinked. "Where do I run?"

Swain straightened from the scope to regard him blandly. "I was up early this morning—well, I'm up early every morning—and I saw you coming out of the desert down there by that ramada." He gestured toward the freestanding porchlike structure southeast of the park. "About half an hour after dawn. So where exactly do you go?"

Cam eyed the telescope, unnerved to think that Swain had been watching him at 5:30 in the morning. He turned his gaze to the wooded hillsides, taking comfort in the fact he'd done most of his run in the dark.

"I just go over the east berm, up the draw, and loop back on the trail there," he said, forcing himself to meet Swain's gaze. "Why?"

"Did you see anyone or anything unusual?"

"Just one of our vans. It was parked near one of those abandoned mine shafts. I assumed it had something to do with the search for last night's intruder." He paused. "I take it you haven't found him?"

"No." Swain returned to his scope. "Do you run every day, then?"

"Except Sunday." Cam was certain Swain knew the answers to these questions.

"Of course, not Sunday," Swain said, giving him a sidelong smirk.

"Well, I suppose given the level of dedication you devote to other areas of your life, that's hardly surprising. Still, I must warn you—it's dangerous out there, especially in the dark. You could stumble into a mine shaft or step on a snake. . . . How long does it take you?"

Shrugging, Cam turned his gaze toward the view. "About an hour." He traced his route with his eyes. "I have a head lamp. And I like to be outside. Like to see the sunrise and be alone to think." Though Swain's questions were superficially innocuous, Cam always had the sense that the man was playing with him, leading him to places he didn't realize he was going until it was too late. The director's personal magnetism was undeniable, and every time Cam was with him he felt its power— an assurance of affection, an invitation to relax and let down his guard with a kindred spirit, a benevolent authority. Yet the eyes, the mind, missed nothing.

"I thought you used the time to listen to those Bible lessons you download from the Internet every night," said Swain as he straightened and picked up the beige polishing cloth hanging from the telescope's tripod.

"Well. Yes. I do." *So he knows about those, does he?*

"I'll bet you use the time to pray, as well."

"Sometimes."

"My father used to pray at dawn," Swain said, carefully wiping down the telescope's eyepiece and knobs where he'd touched them.

*Okay. So* that's *where this is going. . . .*

Swain had declared months ago that his parents, both deceased, had been devout Christians, a failure for which he'd never forgiven them. Despite their increasingly desperate methods of evangelization, he'd refused to believe in Jesus. The whole idea of God demanding a blood sacrifice for the sins of the world, he said, was simply bizarre and barbaric. What kind of God would find red corpuscles and plasma a satisfactory payment for man's supposed transgressions? Swain's father, a pastor, had never been able to answer the question to his satisfaction. In fact, he'd apparently never tried, furious at his son's audacity for asking it at all.

"He was a fool," Swain said now, hanging the cloth on its hook. "Did not read—except the Bible, of course. Did not think! Heaven forbid he should ever seriously and thoughtfully entertain a concept that challenged his belief system! My mother was even worse. Anything they didn't understand—which was almost everything—they ascribed to the devil."

And the devil, in Swain's view, was nothing but an invention of religion, a nonexistent bogeyman used by one group of men to control another.

He sighed at Cam's side. "Faith is for fools, boy."

"So you've said." In the distance something flashed, and shortly a new dust cloud arose. There must have been another vehicle out there, hidden behind the foliage.

After a moment, Swain sighed again and chided, "Are you just going to let me say that, when we both know you disagree?"

"If we both know I disagree, why do I need to express it?"

"Because I want to hear your refutation. Give me a good reason to change my mind."

"There'll never be a good enough reason for you, sir. You don't want to change your mind."

"Are you saying I'm close-minded?"

"Your words, sir, not mine."

"Humor me, then. I want to hear your reasoning."

Cameron sighed. "Faith is for everyone, sir. You have faith yourself every time you get in your helicopter and take off—faith that it's been properly maintained and that the pilot is not going to make any mistakes."

"That's not faith, boy. That's certainty. I make it my business to know what the maintenance schedules are, and I see that they are followed. As for my pilot, he is a personal friend who has served me for years and proven his capability over and over."

"So it is with my God."

"A personal friend?" Swain turned to him with cocked brow, skepticism raising the pitch of his voice. "Proven His competence over and over, has He? Which is why you were all but fired from Stanford? Accused of doing something you did not do and never would?"

Cam met his employer's gaze with an arched brow of his own. "But that all led to my coming here, did it not? And in the end, my position was vastly improved."

Swain met his gaze silently, and Cam could sense his irritation warring with his pleasure at the compliment. Finally he smiled and stepped back with a nod. "Very well, I'll give you that one. For now."

He headed back to his desk. "It *is* dangerous out there, though," he said over his shoulder as Cam followed. "You never know what you're going to meet on the trail."

Swain sat in his captain's chair and gestured Cam into one of the two facing chairs across the sea of wood. On its flat surface, a five-inch cube of black glass balanced on end atop a stand of three curved silver prongs—the Institute's iconic Black Box. Beside it sat a silver tray bearing a matching pitcher, two empty glasses, and a folded cloth napkin.

As Cam settled into the thickly upholstered chair, the director touched a spot on the desk's flat, until now invisible control panel, and the window-wall behind him darkened. Then, folding his hands on the desk, Swain fixed his gaze on Cam and said, "Frederick is convinced you're a spy, you know."

"A *spy*?!"

Swain's eyes stayed upon him. "You didn't exchange your coat for McHenry's on purpose?"

"Why would I do that?"

"So someone else could pick it up?"

Cam regarded him dubiously. "Frederick thinks I'm in league with the night janitor, then? Who is *also* a spy?"

"He's not sure."

"He's paranoid, is what he is. And he's never liked me."

"True. He's jealous of you. But his concerns are valid. We're pretty sure the last hack job was done by someone inside. And our security has been picking up encrypted transmissions lately from somewhere on-site. . . ."

The director turned his attention to the Black Box on his desk, reaching out to stroke it gently, his fingertips leaving ripples of fading color in their wake. Watching him do so filled Cam with an inexplicable restless discomfort, and he worried another flashback might be about to seize him.

"Why *did* you throw the coat away?" Swain asked quietly.

An image of the bloodied handprint flashed before Cam's eyes as the light flickered at the edges of his world and dizziness swooped upon him. He swallowed and focused on the silhouette of the Egyptian frieze looming at Swain's right shoulder. "I . . . guess I thought it was unsalvageable." He explained about the handprint but did not mention the flashback, nor his sudden irrational fear of the coat.

When he finished, Swain looked genuinely puzzled. "But to leave a bloody handprint on her lab coat would mean his hand was bloody *before* he shoved her. And wasn't it the shove that was supposed to have caused Ms. McHenry's cut?"

Cam frowned at him. "Perhaps he had a preexisting injury."

"You're sure it was a handprint you saw, and not just random blood spatters?"

The question immediately recalled the bloody image to Cam's mind and, lurking behind it, others he was certain he did not want to recall. He was trembling again, his chest tightening, prickles of adrenaline washing over him. Swain's blue eyes bored into his own. He swallowed, tore them from the other man, and focused on the mountains outside the smoky windows. "It's what I thought at the time. . . ."

"And at the time you were somewhat rattled, I understand. Frederick said you were white as a sheet and unusually distracted, even for you. He thought you might pass out." Swain paused. "You're not one of those who faints at the sight of blood, are you?"

Cam slammed shut the incipient breach in the wall that kept him safe from unremembered horrors and drew himself together. The trembling and wooziness subsided. "I could hardly have cleaned and taped up Ms. McHenry's cut if I was, now could I? And my recollection of that, at least, is very clear, so don't think you're going to convince me it was all in her mind. Or mine."

Swain smiled at him, the expression odd for the sense it gave him that he'd just walked into the trap.

"Of course I know it wasn't in your mind. And I wouldn't dream of trying to convince you otherwise."

"Then, why are you trying to convince her? More than that, why would you risk using ATR on her when you've already set her up as a fragile, stressed-out nut case?"

"I would hardly call her a nut case." Using the folded napkin, Swain picked up the pitcher. "Lemonade?"

"No, thank you."

Cam watched as the director poured himself a glass, the gurgle of liquid and clink of the ice cubes stark in the silence. Swain replaced the pitcher carefully onto its tray, then sipped his lemonade. Presently he said, "If we acknowledge the break-in, our insurance and reviewers will wonder why we didn't call the police, as we should. If we call them, they'd have to investigate, and we'd have people poking into things that don't need poking into. There'd be interviews; there'd be technicians crawling about. There'd be *reporters* and their cockamamie stories, which are *never* an accurate rendition of the truth. It's the last thing we need with our open house next week." He sipped his lemonade.

Cam cut to the chase: "I'm not going to lie for you, sir."

"I'm not asking you to lie, just that you keep some information to yourself." Swain studied his glass, tipping it slightly this way and that. "I understand you did so routinely in one of your previous employments, with no angst of conscience."

*He knows about Afghanistan? No. Impossible. The mission was expunged from all records. . . .* "You mean when I was in the army? I was a bean counter."

"And some beans you let pass uncounted, I'm sure."

"Letting a few beans pass uncounted for the sake of mission safety is hardly the same as standing by while someone ruins the life of an innocent young woman. I—"

"This incident will in no way 'ruin' Ms. McHenry's life," Swain interrupted firmly. "She's a bright, adaptable young lady who will be a tremendous asset to our community. We used the ATR process primarily to persuade her to let go of the incident as quickly as possible without rousing undue suspicion with the others."

"You falsified her records."

"Only in regards to the actual incident that gave her the scar." He paused. "What did you say when she showed it to you down there on the path?"

Cam frowned at him. "I said it couldn't have healed in a night."

"And that's all?"

"If you saw her approach me, you must have seen Slattery intruding upon us. I hardly had time to say anything." A lame excuse. He could have said more. Could have shaken Slattery off. Could have phrased his first statement better. More truthfully.

"And did you point out her family history of mental instability?"

As Swain chuckled, Cam felt his face warm. "Do you have this entire facility bugged?" he demanded.

Swain's brows flew up in surprise. "I didn't *hear* you, Cameron. I simply *know* you. Those are just the sorts of things you'd blurt out, for I'm sure you were as shocked as she was."

"Maybe not quite as shocked. But definitely disappointed."

"See? There you go. Blurting your first thought again." He shook his head, smiling. "Cameron, you know ATR is safe. You know it's in process even now, and I'm told it'll likely get the go-ahead in the next week or so. We've jumped the gun by a measly two weeks, and for that you're willing to sacrifice eleven years of your life's work?"

He let the question hang and sipped his lemonade, ice cubes clinking in the glass.

And sacrifice it would be should Cam resign. Coming on the heels of that mess at Stanford, it wouldn't matter what excuse anyone gave. The community would view him as a rogue. A difficult loner no one would fund.

The same things Swain's contemporaries had once said of him.

Cam stared at his employer, chilled to the core, but the director avoided eye contact, letting the moment of distress draw itself out as he drank his lemonade. When he finished, he carefully wiped the outside of the glass with the napkin before placing it on the silver tray beside the condensation-fogged pitcher, and finally looked again at Cam.

"Consider carefully what you do here, son. You have incredible potential, and I am looking forward to the day when I can bring you safely into the fold. Stay with us on this, and you'll be rewarded beyond your wildest imaginings. Abandon us and . . ." He leaned back in his chair, shaking his head sadly. "Assets must be guarded. Much as it would tear me up to see it happen, if you leave us, your future in genetics is over."

Cam took his time responding. "I'll think about it," he said finally.

"And if she asks you point-blank what you know?"

Cam met his gaze unflinchingly. "I won't lie to her, sir."

Swain leaned back in his chair, tapping his fingers on its leather-covered arm, eyes narrowed. For several long moments he regarded Cam. Finally he stilled his hands and his face went bland and blank. "Then you'd better make sure she doesn't ask you."

# Chapter Six

## New Eden

At 1100 hours on the same day that Andros had refused to say the morning Affirmation, Zowan stood shoulder to shoulder with his fellows in the bowl-shaped Justorium located at the heart of the Enclave's central complex, awaiting the start of his friend's trial and punishment. As one who had only recently become old enough to participate, Zowan stood on the eleventh row of the small, steeply circular chamber where New Eden's trials were conducted and sentences pronounced and carried out.

Below him, ten rows descended in concentric circles of decreasing size to a central stage where stood the offender with two bald, black-robed Enforcers. Each row was partitioned off from the row below it by a continuous console that paralleled the row's curvature. On the consoles were numerous red levers, before which the audience parceled themselves out according to rank and seniority, one person to a lever.

If the judgment was reached that Andros was guilty—and there was little doubt that it would—he would be placed into the Justorium's Cube of Discipline, where the pain he endured would be directly controlled by how far down each member of the audience pulled his lever. Zowan had come with the determination not to pull it at all. How could he punish his friend for doing something he himself had not only contemplated but suggested?

Warm, stifling air, heavy with the odor of sweat, pressed upon him. An undercurrent of restlessness buzzed at the base of his skull, and his stomach churned with tension. Around him, the various colors of their tunics lost in the Justorium's red light, his friends and fellow Enclavers chattered nervously about the coming trial.

It had been over a year since the New Edenites had put someone in the Cube. Zowan's and Gaias's elder brother, Neos, had been the last, and it had killed him. Of course, he'd been a regular victim of the Cube's torment, a rebel to the end, and all those sessions he'd spent screaming between its electrified plates had weakened him. Or so said the Elders. Neos had refused to say the Affirmation, as well.

Andros had never been in the Cube. He was a shy, quiet kid, prone to contemplation and asking questions the Elders didn't like. Even now Zowan heard snatches of conversation around him as people marveled that Andros could have done such a thing. Zowan had always believed if anyone among the first generation followed in Neos's footsteps it would be himself. Not his quiet friend Andros.

Yet there he stood, his tall, thin form pinioned between a pair of black-robed Enforcers, awaiting the start of the trial as the last few attendees arrived. Finally a low tone sounded and a progression of Elders, robed and hooded, descended in parallel lines down the single rail-less stairway that led from the entrance on the top tier to all those below. They filed down in silence to fill up the lower two rows, each one taking his place, only the Father's central seat left vacant. Father was on the other side of the world visiting Babylon Enclave and could not possibly make it back in time.

From among them one arose and spoke the History, his amplified voice booming through the chamber as he droned through a narrative all present today knew by heart: the tale of how the enclaves came to be.

Over a quarter of a century ago, the Earth stood on the threshold of total destruction, all the result of man's ignorance, greed, and excess. Addressed far too late to stop it, the threat of global warming had disintegrated the ozone, melting the polar ice and triggering a catastrophic rise in sea level. Weather patterns were thrown into turmoil, and the ever-increasing heat evaporated the seas off into space, until all that remained were a few steaming, brackish lakes nestled amidst peaks that had once been covered by miles of seawater. Millions of people had died. Only those with the courage to understand and accept—what was happening had lived.

Father had been one such man, the brilliant scientist and visionary leader who had saved them all. With extraordinary insight he had foreseen the disaster and devised a plan for the enclaves, which he'd begun building long before the disasters had occurred, despite the mockery and ridicule of the world around him.

But rising waters silenced the laughter, and he and his followers, along with a carefully selected portion of Earth's plant and animal life, had entered the enclaves. Thus, life had survived and, by the Father's pronouncement, would rise again. The twelve enclaves scattered about the Earth were now the seedbeds of that vision. Initially protecting and stabilizing a remnant of the human population in the safety of their underground facilities, eventually they would resurface to spread the life they'd preserved across the Earth's barren, battered face.

Each Enclaver knew the debt he owed to the One who had saved him, and every morning in every Enclave each member affirmed that debt and gave thanks to the One he owed. To refuse was unthinkable.

As the first Elder came to the end of the History and fell silent, a second stood to read off the charges against Andros: "Rebellion, defiance, blasphemy. Refusal to say the Affirmation of the Father . . .

"Do you deny these charges?" the second Elder thundered.

"No." Andros's voice threaded, small and trembling, through the diminishing echoes of the Elder's.

"He created you, and this is your thanks?" the Elder sneered. "He has cared for you, protected you, nurtured you, and this is your gratitude?"

Andros trembled visibly in the hands of the Enforcers, his shoulders shuddering with terror. "I'm sorry!" he wailed, his voice a weak warble after the power of the Elder's baritone. "I'm sorry! Please, Father—" He gazed wildly about the Justorium, searching for the Father who was not there. "Forgive me. I don't know what I was thinking. Please, forgive me. Forgive me. Forgive me. . . ."

His voice shattered into desolate sobs, and he fell to his knees. As the Enforcers hauled him upright, Zowan gritted his teeth, wanting nothing so much as to flee this place, wishing he'd never come at all, despite the penalty for refusing.

"Will you say it now?" boomed a third Elder, standing now beside the others.

And to Zowan's chagrin, Andros did.

Silence followed his words. Then, "Father has heard you," intoned Elder Three. "He has forgiven you. Yet your crime demands a punishment."

Andros had known it would come to this. He'd said as much to Zowan last night. Claimed he was ready for it. But who was ever ready for this? Even Neos had wailed and pled and recanted.

"You must enter the Cube."

As Andros flinched and mewed with horror, Zowan clenched his teeth ever harder, hating this more than he had ever hated anything.

"May the Body have mercy in accordance with your crime."

The prisoner slumped between the two Enforcers, resigned now, but still trembling. They jerked him toward the opening at the side of the stage and disappeared into the bowels of the Justorium. The lights dimmed. The Elders burst into a song about the glories of the Father, and his unfailingly righteous judgments.

Zowan glanced across the small theater to where Terra stood with the other First Gen girls on his same level, her long red braids draped over the fronts of both shoulders. Seeming to feel his regard, her gaze shifted to meet his, and in it he saw all the helpless, furious sorrow that boiled in his own gut.

Why couldn't Andros have just said the stupid Affirmation in the first place? He'd been doing it all his life, most of that time unknowingly. What difference did it make whether he had come to the realization that he might not believe it all now? It was just a thing everyone did. Whether he meant it or not, who would know?

Now Andros would still have to say it, every day, morning after morning, but with who knew what handicaps. Memory loss, inability to concentrate, slurred speech, twitches, blackouts—those were only some of the recurring side effects of having gone through the punishment of the box. It had been a stupid, prideful, stubborn thing to do. But somehow Zowan couldn't hold it against him.

Terra's gaze flicked away from his and up to something behind and above him, then darted back to the stage below. It was Gaias she'd seen, Gaias who stood in the aisle at Zowan's back and who had promised him this morning as he'd brought him to the Sanctuary to say his own Affirmation that he would be watching him here. To be sure he did his duty. Even though the whole point of the Body doing this together was to allow each man to pull his lever as he deemed just.

The Elders reached the end of the first verse of their hymn, and the Body took up the chorus, voices filling the chamber. Beneath Zowan's feet, the cement trembled, the faint vibration escalating to a violent shuddering as the distant stage blossomed in petal-like sections and a gleaming black point emerged between them, spearing toward the red-lit ceiling. Part of the technology of the ancients, largely lost to humankind now, it rose slowly, gaining width, until it was revealed to be a massive cube of smoked glass floating above the dark petals.

The rumbling vibration stopped, the chorus's last note faded, and silence fell over the Justorium. Though Zowan's hands were ice, sweat dribbled down his sides beneath his tunic. He swallowed on a dry mouth, straining to see through the glass, knowing Andros was within, alone and sick with terror.

Tall, skinny, gawky Andros, with the pimply face and the dark, sad eyes. Andros, who never hurt anybody, who always seemed caught up in a mental flight of fancy, concocting some peculiar new invention, who hated talking as much as he hated exercise but loved anything to do with numbers. And who asked way too many questions.

*"What if all is not as the Elders have told us, Zowan?"*

Each Elder placed a hand on his lever. The Body followed suit in a susurrus of rustling fabric—Zowan, as well, his fingers so cold the lever burned beneath them. He felt Gaias's eyes on the back of his neck, imagined the oculus bulging in its bony socket.

"May the Body judge as the sin deserves," the Elder intoned.

A thread of light snaked across one face of the glass, and inside the cube Andros yelped. It was followed by another and another as the sides began to lighten, revealing the man within, already hopping and shuddering and yowling as he tried desperately not to touch any of the surfaces that enclosed him—a hopeless impossibility.

*"Do you ever wonder if they're really telling us the truth?"*

On Zowan's every side, levers were pulled downward along the console, slowly, for they were designed to resist a quick pull. Zowan stood his ground, fingers poised on the red lever but applying no pressure. He flinched at every one of his friend's cries, anger kindling within him, at both Andros and the system that punished him so unfairly.

More and more threads shivered across the glass. The young men at Zowan's sides had pulled their levers halfway down the track now and were still going. He held firm.

But in the back of his mind, a coward's voice said, *Gaias is watching you. If you don't do this, it will be you in there next time. It will be you. He'll make sure of it.*

Grimly he held to his conviction, reminding himself he had nothing to fear. The law said it was his right as a member of the Body to withhold punishment if he so chose.

As the flickering currents darted ever more thickly around the box, Andros became increasingly frantic. Revulsion rolled over Zowan in ever-intensifying waves, until he could hardly bear to stand there. He was on the verge of shoving his way past the youths and boys surrounding him in a bid for escape when the screams ceased.

Andros collapsed to the bottom of the Cube, and the glass walls darkened around him. As the floor trembled, the huge cube descended from whence it had come, the stage sections lowering smoothly into a flat surface once again.

It was done.

As the others returned their rods to the starting position, Zowan let go of his own, still in the full upright position. He was mildly surprised he'd actually carried through on his refusal and, at the same time, horrified by the inevitable ramifications.

As he exited the Justorium and headed down the wide corridor to the Enclave's central square and mall, Gaias stepped alongside him.

"You held back," he murmured in Zowan's ear. "There can be no holding back when it comes to supporting Father's honor."

"It will not be recorded."

"It already has been." Gaias tapped his temple. "Up here."

Zowan refused to show intimidation. "You can bring no charges. I have the right to show mercy, even in this."

"Yes, but everyone will want to know *why* you've chosen to exercise it now." He smiled, the grotesque oculus swiveling under its translucent membrane. "You walk the edge of a precipice, brother. It would be a simple thing to push you off."

With that, he stalked away, his black robes flapping batlike in his wake.

# Chapter Seven

After her less than satisfactory conversation with Cameron Reinhardt during her morning break, Lacey returned to her work in the fifth-floor prep and supply room. There she spent the rest of the morning hefting trays of glassware and steel instruments in and out of the two autoclaves and overseeing the receipt of a new shipment of lab supplies. Except for the inventorying, her tasks allowed her plenty of think-time, during which she chewed the encounter with Reinhardt to bits, deciding at the end of each cycle of rumination that he was either hiding something or was simply absentminded, weak in social skills, and talking to a woman prone to panic attacks made him nervous.

Technically he hadn't denied she'd been cut, or that any of the events she'd recounted had happened. He just hadn't confirmed that they had. Perhaps rightfully so. *He'd* not seen the intruder, after all—only the aftermath. For all he knew, she really had been hysterical and trashed the lab in her panic.

When the lunch hour came round, she bypassed the dining hall and went straight down to the animal facility, determined to find something to prove she hadn't imagined last night's intruder. As the elevator stopped at floor G, she half expected its doors to open onto barriers of yellow crime-scene tape, maybe even a guard and an investigative team searching for clues. But the floor was deserted. As she stepped into its quiet solitude, though, a sudden, irrational fear that last night's intruder might have returned stopped her in her tracks.

It took her several moments to convince herself to move on.

She found the prep room in a state of quiet order. Every cabinet door was closed. The water bottle nozzles had been washed and stood in ranks on paper towels beside the empty, shining sink. Harvey slept in a corner of his plastic cage, a furry ball nestled in wood shavings. The room's ivory vinyl flooring gleamed softly in the overhead fluorescent light, spotlessly clean. Even the first-aid kit stood in its place on the top shelf of the wall cabinet that ran perpendicular to the sink counter. And on the back of the prep room door on the hook where she always hung it was her oversized lab coat, *Carlos* red-stitched on the breast pocket. She stood before it, fingering its intact, unstained left sleeve as profound uneasiness churned in her middle.

*Carlos undoubtedly had more than one lab coat, though,* she told herself. *This could be another one, different from the one I wore last night. . . .*

Leaving the prep room, she went to peer through the small window in the locked door to Poe's lab. Beyond the cracked pane, all had been put to rights. The shelves were as they had always been, the rubber tubs standing between the aquarium tanks filled with their various inhabitants, as if nothing had ever happened.

She exhaled slowly, reminding herself that Swain would want things put to rights as quickly as possible, so this wasn't surprising, either. Still, she stared through the small window for some time, straining to find that one telling detail that would prove her rising fears wrong. In the end, she had to force herself to turn away.

Not surprisingly, a quick check of the frog room showed nothing unusual, either.

Increasingly unnerved, she descended a floor to B1, the technicians' dormitory where she slept. Stopping in the small gray-walled elevator lobby, she bought a package of cheese and crackers and a bottle of green tea from one of the vending machines, then went to her room to visit the bathroom and examine her clothing. She clearly recalled the blood that had saturated her U of A T-shirt—not a stain that would be easily removed.

Yet the shirt wasn't in the dirty-clothes hamper, nor even on the closet floor. Perhaps the clinic staff still had it or, more likely, had thrown it away as unusable. Despite that eminently logical rationale, she was dogged by the compulsion to check her T-shirt drawer and was horrified to find the garment neatly folded among her other shirts. Disbelieving, she pulled it out, unmindful of the two shirts that came with it. She held it up before her, aghast to find the white cotton knit behind the red-and-blue Wildcat emblem as clean and white as if it had never been worn.

*Perhaps it hasn't,* she told herself desperately. *Perhaps they replaced it like they did the lab coat, trying to cover the break-in. . . .*

Her eyes strayed to the orange bottle of Valium standing accusingly on the desk beside a curling pink appointment slip noting her 2:30 follow-up exam at the clinic.

Though she couldn't move her right arm without triggering a spasm beneath her shoulder blade, she refused to take the Valium. The possibility she might have been prescribed the drug for the same reason as her mother had, still made her sick and light-headed.

*"Schizophrenia tends to run in families,"* Ma's doctor had said that day in the conference room after they'd admitted her to the hospital five years ago. He'd regarded Lacey with cool, dispassionate eyes, as if he expected her to immediately confess some mental aberration of her own.

Drawing a deep breath, she cast Dr. Lane from her mind and stepped into the bathroom. Her reflection stared back at her from the broad mirror, dark eyes wide and haunted. Her face looked haggard, the wild, elfin look accentuated by her short dark hair. After a month's time she still hadn't gotten used to the new short cut, but today more than ever it was like staring into the face of a stranger.

"I did *not* imagine it all," she told the face in the mirror.

*"Prolonged, intense stress can trigger a psychotic episode,"* Dr. Lane's voice droned flatly in her head. *"We see patients suffering from delusions, hallucinations, and a severe divorcement from reality such as what your mother has suffered here. . . . And she has been under a great deal of stress."*

Thanks to Lacey. And Erik. The arguments, the threats, the rancorous divorce, the stalking, the restraining orders . . . Yes, it had been very stressful for Ma, but Ma had always been prone to worry herself into hysterics, and hadn't Lacey herself been under much more stress at that time? She'd not come unglued then—why would she now?

Because overwork and lack of sleep fed into existing stress levels—like the deep sense of unworthiness that dogged her, like her desperate need to succeed at Kendall Jakoo, and even the trauma that remained from the years under Erik's tyranny. . . .

What if she *had* imagined everything last night?

Nausea climbed up her throat as she braced both palms flat upon the counter. What if she *hadn't* fallen as far from the crazy tree as she liked to think?

Her ears began to roar. For a moment she could hardly breathe.

Then she recalled the scar and sucked in a great gasp of air. She pushed back from the vanity to examine anew the white seam curving up from her elbow and across the pale skin of her inner arm.

*I know I did not have this before last night.*

The tightness in her chest eased.

Somewhere out in the corridor a door closed, and hurried footfalls recalled her to the fact that her lunch hour was fast running out. Pushing the doubts from her mind as she brushed the tears from her eyes, she regained her equilibrium and went about her business.

When she emerged from the bathroom, she grabbed her cheese and crackers, bottled tea, and appointment slip and returned to the main floor, where she took refuge in a small garden along the zig's west wall, deserted now at midday because of the heat, despite its water-misting system.

There she called her mother, for once hoping Ma would actually pick up and sharply disappointed when she didn't. Lacey left a message asking if they had any photos of the scar on her left forearm. Then she called her family physician to ask if he had any records detailing the injury that had produced the scar on her arm. Of course she couldn't talk to him directly because he was seeing patients, but the receptionist promised he would return her call that night.

Flipping her phone shut, she tucked it into her lab coat pocket and sat down on a wooden bench to eat her crackers and drink her tea, feeling defeated and increasingly disturbed.

She wished she had someone to talk to, but even if Jade and the others had not been completely caught up in the problems of the day—a whole round of experimental data had been deemed corrupt and had to be redone—they'd already made it clear what they believed had happened to her. Her objection to her lab coat and T-shirt being in their usual places, her suggestion they were not in fact *her* garments but replacements put there to cover up what had really happened, would only persuade them further of her mental instability. Without more convincing physical evidence or someone willing to corroborate her story, she was stuck.

And the idea of trying to continue the conversation she'd begun with Dr. Reinhardt provoked such a deep sense of embarrassment in her—knowing he was privy to her most humiliating family secrets—she wasn't about to approach him again.

Worse were the unsettling questions that now began to nag her. How exactly *would* she explain the events she'd experienced if she hadn't imagined it all? Did she really believe K-J insiders would actually sneak a new shirt in her drawer, just to cover some Mohawk-haired adolescent's act of vandalism? Except for the damage created in his struggle with her, what had he done but eat the legs off a few frogs?

The only answer she could come up with was that even if she couldn't come up with an answer, that didn't disprove her hypothesis. There were undoubtedly a multitude of pursuits K-J administrators did not want leaked to the public, and as always the fewer who knew the better. Their paranoia about keeping company secrets was well-known. And while that reasoning might not satisfy anyone else, it was enough to encourage her to keep going.

Back in the fifth-floor prep and supply room, she resumed her work of shelving the contents of a carton of gel extraction kits and continued to ruminate, especially on her conversation with Reinhardt and her need for an ally. With the passage of time and multiple iterations, she began to wonder if that conversation was as negative as she'd taken it, or if Reinhardt was as absentminded as she'd assumed. Maybe he was as mystified and conflicted as she. If he *was* part of the cover-up, wouldn't he have denied flat-out that he remembered anything of what she was saying?

In the end she decided to swallow her embarrassment, and on

her way to the clinic for her afternoon appointment took a detour by way of Lab 500.

Like all the labs on the fifth floor, 500 was a maze of rooms, aisles, and work spaces that seemed to have no logical pattern. At the door into the main lab, she hesitated. About thirty people worked in the lab, seated or standing at various stations along the lines of lab benches that marched in ranks before her. The work surfaces were jumbled with test tube racks and boxes of pipettes, prepackaged solutions, and latex gloves. Bottles of reagents stood amidst various pieces of equipment—shakers, chromatographs, a spectrophotometer. Reinhardt's glass-enclosed office stood at the end of the long aisle down the back of the room, and she saw at once that he was in it.

Reluctance swelled in her again, but knowing how much she'd regret leaving without pressing for answers, she threw her timidity off and strode boldly forward. Tapping on the open glass door, she stepped into the office and asked, "May I speak with you privately, Doctor?"

He looked up in surprise, and his expression quickly turned to one of displeasure, though he nodded and motioned her in. She closed the glass door behind her and stepped toward him, noting peripherally the stacks of folders and binders and boxes and books that cluttered the tiny office. At his back, a white laminate bookshelf bulged with volumes whose titles reflected his line of work. He'd managed to prop his plaque for the Black Box Citation up against several on the second shelf.

"I don't mean to be impertinent, Doctor," she said, "but you never answered my question this morning when we met on the path outside. And . . . well, it's very important to me that you do."

His freckled face grew more guarded than ever. "Your question?"

"About what happened in the animal facility last night?"

He held her gaze for only a moment, then glanced across the room behind her as he settled back in his chair. Above the now-clear lenses of his glasses, his auburn brows drew slightly together. Finally he looked at her again. "Ms. McHenry, whatever you think happened last night, it really would be to your advantage to let it go."

She frowned at him. "I know what happened, Doctor. I know you know, too."

"Then why are you here asking me to confirm it?" Irritation crept into his voice.

She hesitated. "Because I think someone's trying to cover up what really happened." *And who cares if my reputation is destroyed as a result?*

"Someone? Like who?"

"Dr. Slattery, for one. You for another, apparently."

He cocked a brow. "And what exactly are we trying to cover up?"

"Whatever happened in the animal facility last night."

"I thought you knew what happened."

Her frown deepened. He was making her feel like a fool.

He sighed deeply. "Even if things happened as you say—there *was* an intruder and your arm *was* cut—why would anyone want to cover that up?"

And of course she had no more answer for him than she'd been able to come up with for herself. Her face started to burn.

His eyes dropped to his computer screen, and he tapped a couple of keys. "They're not going to fire you over this, Ms. McHenry. So you'd do better to let it go and concentrate on proving your competence with future actions." He looked up, snagging her gaze, suddenly sober. "If you can't, you should seek employment elsewhere. Or better yet, return to the U of A for your doctorate."

She frowned at him, grappling with his words, frustrated that he would so dismiss everything she'd said. But when he turned his attention back to his computer in clear indication the conversation was over, there was nothing for her to do but walk away. As she turned to do so, he said after her, "And, Ms. McHenry . . ."

She glanced over her shoulder.

"I'd appreciate it if you'd refrain from bothering me with this issue again," he said, his eyes still focused on the screen.

"Yes, sir." With that she turned and fled, sick to her stomach and so blind with mortification she nearly collided with the white-haired maintenance man coming up the aisle outside Reinhardt's office. Mumbling an apology, she skirted him and his cart of boxed fluorescent light tubes and hurried down the aisle in a daze of humiliation. She didn't come back to herself until she was riding downward in one of the zig's central elevator cars, the atrium's bright green foliage fluttering past her.

Why had she ever thought talking to Reinhardt would be a good idea? He said everything she'd thought he'd say, brought up every argument she'd brought up with herself. There'd been no sign of sympathy, no sign whatsoever that he remembered anything of what she said had happened.

"*They're not going to fire you over this,*" he'd said. Unless she made a stink about it.

It galled to think of giving up and letting the whole thing pass uncontested. But she had come to Kendall-Jakes with ambition burning in her heart, and that had not changed. After all the pain and heartache and failure she'd endured in her young life, she remained determined to make something good of herself, and believed her best chance was at the Institute.

It was the dream she'd had when she'd graduated high school, fifteen years ago. A dream that had seemed on the verge of being realized when she'd received a full-ride scholarship to the U of A, everything provided for her that her family never could have. If she'd just stayed the course, she probably would have earned her PhD by now. Instead, she'd squandered it all for love and religion.

Midway through the second semester of her freshman year, she'd believed in Jesus Christ and started attending church. She'd met Erik Ellison, five years her senior, in the church's college group, and married him after a three-week courtship, certain it was God's will.

At first their lives together had been idyllic. Then things began to change. Erik couldn't find an "acceptable" position after his graduation and became jealous of Lacey's mounting scholastic successes, resenting the time she gave to her studies instead of him. His increasing demands and unfair accusations had so distracted her she'd lost her scholarship, and dropped out of the program her junior year.

She'd stayed with him nine years before divorcing him. Even then he wouldn't let her go, stalking and threatening her until she'd obtained a restraining order. When he found out she'd changed her name back to McHenry, wanting nothing to do with him ever again, he'd broken into her house with a baseball bat and smashed everything in it. That had landed him in jail, and for a while she'd had a bit of peace.

Four years ago he'd hanged himself in his jail cell. She'd been both shocked and relieved, the latter filling her with a guilt that was only exacerbated by her insistence on trying to hold herself responsible. If she'd been a better wife, more forgiving, if she'd just held on longer, if she'd prayed more, gotten closer to God . . .

She continued to work at Barnes and Noble, and after a year pulled herself together enough to reenter the U of A at the age of thirty. Though, of course, there was no scholarship this time. She'd poured her life into the effort, sacrificing everything to attain her degrees— first the bachelor's, then the master's. She'd even considered a PhD, but her increasing debt combined with the arrival of the lucrative job offer from Kendall-Jakes had turned her down a new path. One she wasn't ready to abandon yet.

She blinked in the brightness of the midafternoon sun as she stepped out of the zig, following the same path down to the clinic she'd taken that morning. This time the receptionist had her fill out a form, then sent her to the waiting area until someone called for her.

The exam was a mere formality. The doctor, whom she'd never seen before, was a psychiatrist and clearly more intent on evaluating her mental state than anything else. He was disturbed to learn she'd gone immediately back to work and taken none of the Valium she'd been prescribed, but he didn't push hard, and she gave him no reason to. Finally he concluded his exam by writing her an official note of rec-ommendation to avoid the animal facility for a few days and get more rest. He also prescribed some sleeping pills, should she need them.

After he left, a girl in a burgundy smock escorted her to an office in the clinic's administrative wing and instructed her to sit in one of the two chairs on the visitor's side of a wide desk utterly free of clutter. "Dr. Viascola will be with you shortly," the girl told her, before taking her leave.

Lacey startled at the name. Dr. Genevieve Viascola? Head of K-J's Human Resources and CEO of Swain's Longevity Enterprises? *Why would she want to see me?*

Lacey didn't have long to wait. Less than five minutes later, Dr.

Viascola joined her. Though in her late forties, she had a youthful figure and an unlined face. Her luminous red hair was swept up into a fountain of curls at the back of her head, not a single strand of gray to be seen. She wore bright red lipstick and nail polish, and a tailored gray skirt and white blouse beneath a stylish white lab coat, her formality at odds with the laid-back blue jeans style most of her colleagues preferred. As was the big red straw bag hanging from her shoulder, large yellow flowers flopping off its front.

She greeted Lacey with a warm smile and firm handshake. "We are so pleased you elected to join our team," she said, a lingering accent betraying her high-class British upbringing. "We have such great hopes for you. Plans for you, truth be told."

"Plans?"

"Oh, all for your good, my dear. Please. Sit down." She went around the desk and settled into the big chair there, pulling a folder from her red bag before setting the latter on the floor beside her.

"I understand you've had a rough time of things the last day or so," she said as she opened the file and thumbed through the first few pages. " 'Stress-induced hysteria with hallucination.' " She grimaced delicately, then looked up at Lacey, her expression full of compassion. "I know it sounds dreadful, dear, but don't worry—it or something very like it happens to all of us sooner or later. You've only been with us, what? Three weeks?"

Lacey nodded.

"It's always a struggle for newcomers to adjust to the high-octane environment here. They neglect their sleep, work too hard, don't exercise or allow themselves any downtime. It's one of the reasons for our extensive recreation and social program." She smiled. "And the truth is, we *do* push our new people hard. Push them till they break, in fact."

Lacey shook her head in consternation. "Why would you—"

"Because we only want those who are willing to give their lives for this work, my dear. There is no such thing as burnout for those who really want something. . . ."

Lacey recognized her words as one of Swain's epigrams, or "Swain-speak" as they were affectionately termed.

"You think I don't want this enough?" she asked.

"Oh, not at all . . ." Viascola assured her. "Your break came a little sooner than we expected, but given your background and temperament, you've done very well. Studies show that creative, highly imaginative people have fewer filters in their brains against outside stimuli, and thus are less able to separate reality from imagination."

Neither the subject matter nor the phraseology could have been a coincidence. "So you see me as highly creative?"

Viascola laughed. "Of course we do. Because you are, my dear! We can't wait to set you free in a research environment and see what you come up with for us. And I promise you, that's coming soon. . . . We're searching for someone to take over the animal facility, and we've a couple of applicants who look promising. One from ASU up in Phoenix. We're trying to get him to come down tonight, in fact. So, you see, things could be changing dramatically for you very soon."

"*Tonight?!*" Lacey squeaked in astonishment.

Viascola lifted a cautionary finger. "Don't get your hopes up. We've been disappointed before, and we didn't give him much notice. Just know that it *will* happen." She leaned back in her chair, resting her forearms on its arms. "That is only part of why I've called you here, though." She paused. "I've been told you have a different version of the events of last night than I've read about, and I want to hear that version. I don't want to jump to conclusions here, and these are precisely the kinds of situations that breed wild stories."

Her warm, friendly manner combined with all the high praise and heady promises loosened Lacey's tongue as nothing else could have. Though she started tentatively, when Viascola continued to listen respectfully and with interest, she gradually warmed up, telling her the entire story in every detail.

When she finished, Viascola relaxed back into her chair, reflecting on all Lacey had told her, and for the first time Lacey felt she might finally have found her ally.

"So," Viascola said presently, "if I'm understanding you correctly, you believe there is a cover-up going on, and you suspect Doctors Poe, Slattery, and Reinhardt as ringleaders."

"More Slattery and Poe, I think—though Reinhardt *is* involved."

"Yet you have nothing to support these contentions. Reinhardt has not confirmed his role in your story?" Her brown eyes fixed upon Lacey, still kindly in aspect.

"No." Lacey sighed in disappointment. "But he's not denied it, either. Two times I've asked him, and he keeps evading me. I know I hardly have anything to prove what I'm saying is true. I'm almost convinced myself at times that I must have imagined it all. Except for this." She held up her arm. "I *know* I did not have this scar before last night."

"And you think the cut you got on the glass is now that scar?"

"It has to be."

Viascola frowned at the cut, then looked down at the open folder on her desk. She flipped a couple of pages and drew a red fingernail down the length of the third. Finally she looked up with a pained expression and said very gently, "Lacey, dear, I'm *sure* whatever you experienced last night seems very real to you, but . . . by your own admission you have nothing to support your account."

"Except this scar."

"Yes." Viascola paused. "But I think you know that stress has a way of altering perceived reality. Starvation, fatigue, sleep deprivation, anxiety—all can induce hallucinations, foster paranoia, even blot out previous memories. . . ."

Frowning, Lacey clasped her fingers in her lap. *Blot out previous memories?* For a moment she struggled to take a breath. Then she said, "You're saying I've had this scar all along, I just forgot I had it?"

Viascola grimaced at the distress in Lacey's voice. "Dear, I'm afraid I don't just think so—your preadmission records clearly note it."

*"What?"* Lacey lurched forward in surprise, straining to see what Viascola was reading.

Dr. Viascola reversed the folder where it lay open on the desk between them and pushed it toward her, pointing out the pertinent line of text. It was as Viascola said—notation of a fine scar on her left inner forearm, one in a list of the many other scars she had on her body.

Viascola looked pained but sympathetic. "Please do not feel that I will think less of you because of this incident. As I said, I *do* understand. And it's not unusual, as I'm sure you will soon find out. I want you to know that we consider ourselves one united organism here. A body, if you will. If one member hurts, we all hurt. So it is to our advantage to see that all members are well cared for—physically, mentally, and emotionally. Please know you can come to me with anything troubling you, and I will do my utmost to put it to right. Will you do that?"

After a moment of silence, Lacey nodded.

The smile returned. "Good. Now, you're no doubt aware that Director Swain will be presenting his vision for our operation in the Institute's Black Box Theater tomorrow night. I want you to attend. It will go a long way toward giving you the inspiration you need to survive here. It's ticket-only entrance, so I'll have one for you at this afternoon's unity meeting.

"I also strongly urge you attend one of our stress-management workshops. I believe one's coming up next Wednesday at lunch. We also have group meditation sessions in the Zen Garden every morning before breakfast. No need to sign up, and mats are available on-site. I think you will find both immensely helpful in your efforts to acclimate to the environment here.

"In fact, we'll be experimenting with some of the techniques at today's unity meeting, which will be focusing on stress management." She smiled at Lacey's surprise. "Yes, I changed it because of what happened to you last night, but only so you will know you are not alone in this. We have all struggled with the pressure here, and many continue to do so. We'd like to share with you some of the coping strategies we've discovered. Please, make sure you are present today."

Lacey felt a twinge. Already she'd lost so much time away from the autoclave with this appointment, she'd planned to skip the unity meeting to make up for it. . . . But if Viascola had changed the agenda just for her, she couldn't very well miss it.

"Of course, ma'am."

# Chapter Eight

Cam watched with chagrin as Lacey McHenry nearly ran over the maintenance man in her haste to escape. As she dodged around the elderly man and his cart and hurried away, Cam was already regretting the things he'd said to her and the inevitable reaction they'd caused. She'd taken him by surprise, barging into his office like that, and while he admired her chutzpah, he was also annoyed by it. And dismayed by how easily subterfuge and evasion had returned to him, despite his declaration in Swain's ninth-floor office/museum that he would be entirely truthful with her should they meet again.

His reflections were cut short by the sudden intrusion of the maintenance man's cart trundling through the open doorway of his cluttered office. As the man pulled his cart to a stop, Cam stood and came around his desk.

"Can I help you with something?" he asked.

"I'm here to fix the light, señor," the man said, a strong accent making his speech difficult to decipher. He pointed upward at the pair of rectangular ceiling fixtures whose steady white glow illuminated Cam's office.

Cam shook his head. "There must be some mistake. I didn't call for maintenance. And as you can see, my lights are fine." He thought the man looked an awful lot like the white-ponytailed night janitor who regularly cleaned his lab space in the animal facility but couldn't be sure. The name stitched in red on the left breast pocket of the man's uniform said *Juan*, but he'd never looked at the night janitor long enough or close enough to note his name.

"It's right here on my list." Juan pointed to his clipboard and read, " 'Fifth floor, Lab 500, room 501. Intermittent flickering.' "

"Well, none of my lights have been flickering."

"None of them?" The man looked up at the ceiling fixtures. After a moment, Cam followed suit. As if deliberately giving the lie to Cam's words, the tube closest to the door flickered.

Grimacing, Cam held up both hands. "I stand corrected. Go right ahead."

"Si, señor." Juan pulled a stepladder from the shelf on the bottom of his cart and set it up, almost knocking over a stack of binders in the process.

"You didn't happen to be cleaning floors last night in the animal facility, did you?" Cam asked as he watched.

Juan turned from the stepladder and grinned at him. "Si, señor doctor. They called me in at one. For half day. A lot of things went out last night, so they're needing many repairmen."

A lot of things went out last night? Now, that was interesting. "What kind of things?"

"Oh, door locks, video feeds, electrical circuits." He pulled open a drawer from the cart's middle portion and withdrew a screwdriver.

"They know what caused it?"

"Some kind of power surge." He climbed the stepladder and popped loose one end of the plastic cover on the ceiling fixture with the screwdriver, then shoved the latter into his back pants pocket.

*Power surge?* A shiver zinged up Cam's back as he recalled the gale-blown look of Poe's lab. "It must have done a number if they're having to pull in the janitors to do the electrical work."

"Oh, I've been an electrician for twenty years. That's what they hired me to do. I'm only in the animal facility because they can't get anyone else." He twisted the flickering tube, trying to work it free of the socket, and it went dark. "Because of the rumors."

"There are rumors about the animal facility?" Cam asked in genuine surprise.

"Some say it is haunted by the young woman who disappeared. Others fear Chupacabra. . . ."

"Chupacabra?"

"He comes in the night and sucks the blood of his victims. . . ."

"A sort of Spanish vampire."

"Not a vampire, señor."

"Does he eat frogs, too?"

"Frogs? No. Chupacabra feeds mostly on cows and goats. They've found drained bodies in the hills around here the last few months. One lady even saw him."

"Really?" Cam didn't have to feign his interest. "What did he look like?"

"Tall, thin, green skin, long sharp teeth, big eyes. A bony ridge on the top of his head."

"Sounds scary. But you're not afraid of him?"

"They pay me double not to be." Juan grinned at him, but something in the expression drove an inexplicable blade of shock into Cam's heart. For a moment he was certain he knew the man from somewhere else.

Juan turned back to the fixture, changing his position as he twisted the bulb and inadvertently brushing his shoulder and elbow against the dangling plastic cover. It swayed alarmingly back and forth for a moment, then twisted free and fell to the floor with a crash. Cam leapt back out of its way as the old man swiped forward with his arms trying to catch it. He only succeeded in toppling off his stepladder, which went flying in the opposite direction.

Juan fell into several three-foot stacks of manila folders stuffed with documents, sending them spilling across the floor under his cart and up against the bookshelf, which was surrounded by stacks of books and boxes.

Cam hurried to his side, concerned he had injured himself, but the man seemed more embarrassed than anything and brushed off Cam's inquiries gruffly. Then seeing the stacks of folders he'd disrupted, he apologized profusely and would have dropped to his knees to begin gathering them had Cam not stopped him.

"I'll take care of them."

"But, señor, it is my fault—"

"Or perhaps I distracted you from your work with my questions," Cam suggested with a smile. "In any case, they're my files, and Institute policy dictates I alone can handle them. You just take care of the light." He picked up several documents and inserted them into their correct folder, wondering if clumsiness rather than widespread fears of Chupacabra was the real reason Juan was mopping floors in the animal facility.

"Of course, señor."

The old man righted his ladder, then picked up the plastic light cover, now broken into three pieces. Tossing them into the plastic trash bag hanging from the end of his cart, he pulled out a dustpan and whisk broom and knelt to sweep up the smaller pieces. By the time he was done, Cam had collected all the folders. Rather than stay in the line of fire, he stacked the folders hit or miss and retreated to the relative safety of his desk, hoping the fellow could complete his task without further mishap and leave.

He did however keep an eye on him, as much out of a sense of self-preservation as from the nagging sense of familiarity the man provoked in him. Had he actually seen Juan somewhere besides in his adjunct lab, or did he simply remind Cam of someone else? A former co-worker or student? A long-forgotten friend? A movie star? Some political figure?

He groped after the memory, but it continued to elude him as Juan resumed his attempts to remove the faulty bulb. It came loose quickly this time, and he set it in his cart, then picked up a long, narrow cardboard box with a drawing of a fluorescent light tube on it. A sprig of fresh green cottonwood leaves sprouted from one end. How that had gotten stuck in the fluorescent tube box, Cam could only imagine, but it did not speak well for Juan's cart-manipulating skills.

Too distracted to concentrate on his work, Cam checked his e-mail. There were two from Gen. The first was a departmental reminder of today's 5:00 unity meeting to be held in the Desert Vista room on the third floor. It included the revised agenda, whose title, "Stress Management," made him grimace. Her second e-mail was a private missive requesting he make sure he was present at that meeting today—he'd missed the last three—and reminding him of the importance of bonding among team members.

The weekly unity meetings were one of the eccentricities of working at Kendall-Jakes. Devised by Director Swain to promote unity and cooperation, they were not explicitly mandatory, but nonattendance was frowned upon. They provided team members the opportunity to get to know one another outside the work environment, to play games, and have discussions both weighty and light. Once, they'd been called upon to cite five random things about themselves, four items of which had to be of a different category than anything anyone had said before you. Another time they'd shared the worst day of their lives, which for many of them was shortly after having arrived at Kendall-Jakes.

Cam had always felt they did more to undermine unity than promote it and, especially for those in upper management, were more a reminder of Swain's power than anything else.

He could hardly fault Gen for her frontal approach, but given his mental and emotional state today, the last thing he wanted to do was participate in one of their touchy-feely, reveal all and embarrass everyone, psychobabble meetings. He wished he'd never opened the e-mail, because now if he missed, it would be in direct violation of a superior's order.

"Señor?"

Cam looked up into Juan's swarthy, wrinkled face, framed with a halo of frizzy white hairs come loose of the ponytail. He stood before Cam's desk, his face clearly illuminated in the light of the overhead fluorescents, its familiar cast so compelling Cam could hardly stand it. *Where have I seen you before, Juan?*

He was on the verge of voicing the question when he realized Juan was speaking.

" . . . must have slid under my cart to the other side where you didn't see them." He waggled the manila folders in his calloused hands, then laid them on Cam's desk. "I just shoved everything together without looking, so maybe you'll want to go through and make sure everything's right."

Cam stared up at him, something in the voice finally triggering the door to his lost memory: *He looks like Rudy!*

Lieutenant Rudolpho Aguilar was the man who'd led a twenty-one-year-old new Army Ranger to Christ deep in the heart of Afghanistan. The two of them had worked together for almost six years, and Cam had come to trust him as he had no one else.

Until that final mission.

"Señor?"

"Oh. Yes," Cam replied belatedly to his question. "Yes, I'll go through them."

The maintenance man gave him a nod, then pushed his cart out of the office, heading left at the door and on toward the eastern exit.

Cam sat unmoving, transfixed by his realization. The man wasn't Rudy, of course. He couldn't be Rudy. Juan was easily in his sixties, whereas Rudy Aguilar would only be in his late forties now, his hair no doubt as raven black as ever. Besides, what would Rudy be doing at Kendall-Jakes working as a janitor-electrician?

A suggestion floated through his mind, but he rejected it soundly and, laughing off the resemblance as an oddity, counted the mystery solved.

But as the afternoon passed he found himself repeatedly contemplating the possibility that the janitor-electrician might actually *be* Rudy, despite the wrinkles, white ponytail, and mustache. Lieutenant Aguilar had, after all, been a specialist in covert operations. Colleagues even hinted his true employer was the CIA. If so, it was entirely possible he was in disguise.

Swain himself had mentioned the suspicion among some of the Inner Circle that one of their employees was a spy—the inside hack job on the Developmental Bio computers, the encrypted transmissions they'd intercepted . . .

And was it just coincidence that the man would have been serving as janitor in Cam's basement lab for weeks and, now, right after the events of last night, suddenly show up as an electrician changing light bulbs in Cam's fifth-floor office? Was it coincidence that a light that never flickered had suddenly flickered, almost on command, so that "Juan" would have reason to stay and do his work?

And what about all that clumsiness: knocking the light cover free, falling off the ladder into the files, even the man's chattiness? In retrospect it all began to seem staged, as if Juan had been trying to get his attention, especially there at the end, when he'd set the folders on Cam's desk. Why hadn't he simply called Cam's attention to them where they lay and let him take care of them? Especially after Cam had taken pains to explain Institute policy to him? Because he'd wanted a glimpse at them?

Cam began to search his desk for the folders, and finally found them, buried under other work he'd been trying to do since the man had left. Pushing the other papers aside, he pulled the stack of four folders toward him. The names on the tabs showed him immediately they were obsolete and probably needed shredding. If Juan had looked through them, he'd gained nothing of import, but if Juan was Rudy he'd have known they were useless and never bothered with them in the first place. A quick flip-through of each file's contents showed them pretty much in order, despite Juan's claim of just shoving them together.

Cam laid all four down flat before him and opened the folder on top again. This time instead of going right to the header at the top of the first page, his eye caught on the blue sticky note affixed in the lower right quadrant. The handwriting on the note was not Cam's. And the information it conveyed had nothing whatever to do with the rest of the file's contents:

*"Prelim DNA eval on lab coat blood anomalous."*

He stopped breathing, staring at the words that lurched across the two-by-two-inch square, understanding their meaning at once. A preliminary DNA evaluation on the blood in the lab coat he'd bagged and tossed into the hazmat bin last night had already come back: anomalous. Meaning it wasn't Lacey McHenry's blood, at the least. Meaning there had indeed been an intruder, one they hadn't yet identified.

He swallowed hard. Why not simply say *unidentified*, then? Why *anomalous*? Suddenly he jerked his hands off the folder as if it had burned him, the front flap falling back across that first page to cover the unnerving sticky note again.

*Anomalous . . .*

A roaring sounded in his ears as the room melted and oozed about him. Whereas a moment before he'd stopped breathing, now he was breathing too fast, the edges of his vision flashing as he hyperventilated.

Terror dropped upon him, hard and black. Narrow roughhewn rock walls closed in about him.

*No! Not another one!*

He clenched his eyes shut, willing the images away. They took him anyway.

Smoke filled his nose and burned his eyes and the ground shook as he raced after Rudy out of the narrow passageway and into a dark chamber, whose walls were barely visible at the end of their head lamp beams. The others of the team crowded around them, breathing hard, saying nothing, as from somewhere in the tomb complex a lion roared; only they all knew it was no lion.

"Which way?" Rudy asked in a low voice.

The pale green light of an electronic screen washed over Woofer's chest and face. "It's not coming up," he said after a moment.

Cam ejected the empty magazine from his pistol and slammed a replacement into the chamber, noting he only had five clips left.

"It's not coming up," said Woofer again.

"They must be jamming it," Rudy said. "We'll just have to—"

He was cut off by another roar, much closer, and they all looked around. The beams from their head lamps speared the smoky darkness, congregating on one of the chamber walls. A deep boom echoed around them and shook the ground, and in the light of their combined beams a crack opened in the rock wall.

"Hit the ground!" Rudy bellowed, a second before the crack exploded in a gout of rocks and smoke as they all dove for cover.

Cam came out of it to find himself crouching under his desk. Beside him, his stacked folders had sprawled across the floor at his feet. He could hardly breathe for the dust and smoke that filled his airways and thought he might vomit at any moment. He was shaking so badly his legs beat a faint staccato against the desk's wooden back, and of course his T-shirt was drenched with sweat.

"Dr. Reinhardt?" The voice of one of his lab techs sounded quietly from somewhere near the door, startling him so badly, he slammed his head into the underside of the desk. With a muttered oath, he tumbled out of his hiding place before the young man could grasp what was going on.

"I'm here, Pecos," Cam said as he arose from behind the desk and settled again on the padded chair. "Just looking through some of my files."

The young graduate student stared at him wide-eyed, his concern obvious, despite Cam's completely reasonable explanation for his actions.

"What's up?" Cam asked when Pecos seemed unable to find his tongue.

The young man shifted uncomfortably. "The unity meeting has begun, sir. Dr. Viascola sent me to get you."

"Ah." Cam glanced at the time on his computer screen and saw that it was indeed 5:10. . . . *How long was I out?* "Guess I got a little distracted," he said, with a sheepishness not altogether feigned.

As he set his computer to hibernation mode, he noted the lab outside his office was deserted and wondered if it was too much to hope no one had seen his little "episode." Then he recalled the lab's video surveillance cameras, and knew with dismay that it wouldn't matter. If Swain wanted everyone to know, they would.

It was as he came around the desk toward the office door that he saw the sprig of now curled-up cottonwood leaves, lying on the desk alongside the place where "Juan" had placed the folders he'd found.

Aware of Pecos's eyes on him, he looked away and continued walking, but as he followed the young man out of his office, he recalled how the sprig had been tucked into the end of the fluorescent tube box. That, too, had been no accident. Because every evening after dinner, Cam strolled down to the lake overlooked by the resort's restaurant at the other side of the campus. It offered solitude, tranquility, release, and a pleasant view of the setting sun across the water . . . and cottonwood trees. It was a habit with which Rudy was obviously familiar. The sprig testified to that, even as it served as a wordless request for a face-to-face meeting where they wouldn't be watched or overheard.

A request Cam wished heartily he could ignore, even knowing he would not be allowed to do so.

# Chapter Nine

## New Eden

After Andros's reproof in the Justorium's dreaded Cube, everyone went to lunch in the main cafeteria just off the mall in the Enclave's central commons. Like almost every other chamber in the Enclave, the cafeteria was a low-ceilinged, dimly lit space. Long folding aluminum tables with attached benches stood so close together there was hardly room to walk between them. They were serving sweet potato pie again today, with lentil soup and sliced cucumbers in a goat's-yogurt sauce.

Andros's trial and punishment was naturally the primary topic of conversation. With Terra already reassigned to crèche work and sitting at a different table with her charges, Zowan had to rely on his lifelong friends and sleepcell mates, Parthos and Erebos, for moral support. They sat to either side of him at Table 9—Parthos, tall, handsome, and dark-skinned; Erebos, shorter by a head with coarse black hair that stood up in an unruly brush from his head. Last night Andros had sat across from them.

Not in the mood to talk, they sat in silence, listening to the others prattle on about their shock and horror—not that Andros had been punished so severely, but that he'd needed it at all.

Gaias, who had taken a seat at the table not far from Zowan, commented loudly, "It just goes to show how you never know what might be going on in someone's head. Right, Zowan?"

He looked at Zowan as he said this, and by that drew everyone's attention to him, as well. Before Zowan could answer, Gaias asked what he knew of the affair. "Surely you would have reported it if Andros had spoken such blasphemies before."

Since Zowan and Gaias had already had this conversation, Zowan said nothing. But his brother would not be put off. "You're not answering me, Zowan."

"What difference does it make?" Zowan asked testily. "He's been punished, hasn't he?"

"It makes a difference because, in point of fact, you did not report his earlier blasphemies but dismissed them as foolish talk." The conversation at Table 9 all but ceased as nearby diners listened in.

"Is that why you didn't pull your lever today?" Gaias's words were met with the sudden combined hiss of indrawn breaths around them. At Zowan's side, Parthos turned to look at him in alarm, the whites of his eyes a stark contrast to his dark skin.

"Because your own failure led to his discipline?" Gaias let the question hang, eyes boring into Zowan. The cafeteria's soft lights reflected off his hairless skull, casting odd shadows beneath the lidded, quivering oculus, and obscuring his natural eyes in shadow. A smile twitched his lips. "Or was it your reluctance to punish someone whose blasphemies you agree with?"

Zowan glared at him. "Whatever I did, it is a private matter. It is our right to pull the lever as we deem just, and you are remiss for even bringing it up."

Gaias's hairless brows lifted. "How can there be any justice in the toleration of blasphemy?"

"How is not saying the Affirmation blasphemy?" Zowan demanded. "Don't you actually have to say something in order to blaspheme? And what meaning can any affirmation have if a person must be forced to say it?"

Powered by indignation, the words bubbled out of the deep doubts he'd long wrestled with, though he could hardly believe he was speaking them here in front of everyone. The other young men stared at him blank-faced. Except for his friends—who looked horrified.

Gaias glowed with triumph. "So you do sympathize with him!"

Zowan shot to his feet. "Andros is not a rebel. He did not deserve to be punished so severely simply because he had a few doubts."

His words were seized and swallowed by utter silence, as even the kitchen staff paused in their chores to listen.

"Father is wise and powerful," said Gaias sternly. "He knows things other men do not. Has he not saved us all? Does he not now keep us alive? If we lost him, where would we be? Why would anyone not want to affirm all that he is to us with humble gratitude? We owe everything to Father."

Around him others nodded and murmured agreement.

"The Affirmation is true and is a right thing to do," Gaias went on. "If a stubborn child, out of the promptings of his foolish heart, refuses to say it, we have every right to force him to do it. For his good and ours."

"Andros is not a child."

"But he was foolish."

Zowan refused to give in. "If we must be forced to say the Affirmation, we have no freedom to truly love Father at all. So what is the point?"

Gaias snorted. "We have life, Zowan, and for that we owe him love. Freedom to deny it will not change our debt of gratitude."

Zowan glanced down the long closely packed tables, the many faces turned toward him full of puzzlement. Did none here understand what he had said? No. There was Terra: he saw it in her soft brown eyes. He suspected Parthos did, too, from the way his clenched fist pressed against the edge of the table at Zowan's side.

Zowan returned his gaze to Gaias. "If we have no freedom," he said, "we can have no real love. And no life."

With that he turned and pressed his way between the opposing walls of diners' backs to the end of the tables, then strode out the cafeteria's main doors. A rumble of excited conversation spilled after him. He crossed the spacious central square with its four-faced statue of Father standing by the Sanctuary entrance ramp on one side, the mall with its long island of waterfall, running stream, and plantings of fan palms extending away on the other. Taking the corridor to the upper levels, he passed the library and the administrative and security offices, then  followed the long zigzagging corridor that traversed the Hydroponics sector, with its low chambers of lighted growing tanks. Finally he reached the shaft that accessed the animal and agriculture sectors and started up the long metal ladder inside it.

With Zowan's staff of youngsters all off at their afternoon lessons, the goat barn was deserted except for the goats in their paddocks. On the message board, beneath the chore rotation charts, a small computer screen informed him of the projection for when he might take the goats out for their biweekly dose of sunlight.

Having learned early on that the goats especially required sunlight to thrive, the Edenites had set up a protected area in a narrow ravine on the Earth's ruined surface. An invisible energy field helped shield them from the poisonous fumes' deadly rays. Even then, surface walking was dangerous, for the radiation and toxin numbers varied throughout the day. All trips were timed in accordance with projected and actual readings of the sensors both in and outside of the ravine. Right now the real-time readings were still too high, the safety window predicted to come in midafternoon.

While he waited, he busied himself with cleaning out the paddocks, hauling the collected droppings to the composters, and dousing the empty paddock with enzyme neutralizer. Then he transferred the goats that would go outside today into the holding chute before the passageway leading up to the surface.

By the time he finished, the external toxin and radiation readings had indeed diminished into the safe range, so he went to the change room and struggled into the stiff, bulky, brown-mottled protective suit. After securing its hook-and-loop fasteners, he pulled on one of the gloves, tucked the other into his belt beside the brown-lens goggles, and hooked the respirator around his neck. Then he went out to his charges, who waited along the holding chute fence calling for him.

As he slipped into the pen, they wheeled and trotted toward the enclosure's far side. When he opened the outer gate, they poured into the narrow, cement-walled corridor beyond, their hoofbeats and eager bleats echoing in the long, dark space. The corridor, barely high enough for Zowan to walk upright, led steadily upward, then leveled off in a series of U-turns before angling slightly downward. The air became noticeably drier and easier to breathe. Shortly after that, the cement-coated walls and floor gave way to damp, raw-faced rock and a muddy track pocked with old, water-filled hoofprints. The goats picked up speed, the kids jumping playfully as they hurried toward freedom, while Zowan labored after them, the mud sucking at his heavy boots.

The track ended at a solid metal gate, the goats bunching eagerly before it. Here Zowan finally put on his goggles and pulled up his respirator, then with his bare hand pressed the palm-sized activation pad beside the gate. As he pulled the other glove from his belt and slipped it on, the drone of purification fans sounded somewhere in the rock above him, followed by the loud grinding of the gate's motors. A familiar prickle rushed over him as the steel gate retracted into the ceiling and the goats trotted into the low-ceilinged chamber on the other side, down a short passageway, and out of sight.

Shortly Zowan emerged after them into a narrow, rock-walled canyon, the outflow of the Enclave's purification blowers rustling briefly around him as the gate in the cave at his back closed. The goats were already scattered about the ravine, browsing eagerly on its vegetation, so Zowan picked his way down a precarious footpath across ledges and boulders to the narrow pool—Enclave-fed and filtered—that nestled between the rocks at the heart of the drainage. A large madrona tree stood beside it, mottling the pool's glassy face with shadow. Tall long-leaved willows crowded the upper streambed until they were stopped by the forty-foot rise of sheer cliff that served as the grotto's upper boundary. Another cliff dropped away from the grotto's lower end, blocking travel downstream.

One old buck goat, Nimrod, stood at the lower precipice now, looking down longingly. Overhead, brown, blotchy clouds billowed across the gap between the ravine's steep sides, driven by the constant winds that scoured the planet's surface. Shreds of brown-stained fabric fluttered from anchor points at the top, all that remained of the Elders' initial attempts to shield the area.

Over the twenty years since, not only had the dust in the air increased, blocking out more radiation, but Enclave engineers had devised and perfected a new system of unseen energy shields. Extending from wall to wall, they had kept the churning dust and its contaminants at bay for over ten years.

Hampered by his spongy suit, Zowan settled awkwardly on the rock beside the pond. As he caught his breath—the respirator didn't filter the air fast enough for one to do much more than sit—he watched old Nimrod turn resignedly from the rocky edge and wander off to one of the shrubs.

And now, freed of his responsibilities, Zowan replayed the day's events, his anger having subsided to its usual dull burn, flavored by a twist of guilt. Gaias was right: it *was* Zowan's fault that Andros had been in the Cube today, but not for the reason he'd cited. Andros wasn't the only one to be frustrated by the Elders' refusal to answer questions. Zowan's own incessant questioning had four years ago led to his removal from the student guild and reassignment first to the furnace room, and more lately to the goats. Forbidden to enter the library or use the computer stations without supervision, he was allowed to read nothing but his red-bound New Eden Catechism. In it was a detailed account of the beginnings of the enclaves—and New Eden, in particular—as well as a listing and explanation of all the rules by which they lived. Rules for social interaction, for physical safety, for stability of the community, and for religious worship.

Once he had memorized the book and demonstrated his acceptance of its tenets in how he lived and spoke over a suitable period of probation, he might then be allowed to advance beyond the status of head goatherd. The position seemed deliberately chosen to give him time to read, and to think, while simultaneously protecting others from his bad influence. After four years he should have been well along in his rehabilitation. Instead he was farther away than ever.

For during his stint in the furnace room that first year, his most burning questions had centered around the origins not of the enclaves but of the Earth that held them. Did it really make itself as the teachers said? If so, why hadn't it fixed itself when man had come along and fouled it with his various emissions? Why was it here at all? Why people? Why the cataclysm? Was it all random? Was there any purpose to their existence beyond simple survival? Sometimes the sense of pointlessness grew so acute, he could hardly bear to go on.

Then one day in the furnace room as he shoveled refuse into the flames, the wind generated by their heat blew back a section of discarded book. Books arrived at the furnace room torn apart at the bindings and stripped of their covers by the refuse processors so they'd burn more efficiently, and this section landed right at his feet. On its front pages, barely readable for the scorch, were the words *Key Study*, which for some reason had caught his eye. He'd picked up the fragment, turned to the first page, titled "Genesis," and read, "*Chapter One. In the beginning God created the heavens and the earth. . . .*"

The words spoke so directly to the questions that had been plaguing him, he'd slipped the fragment into his trousers. It was forbidden to do such a thing—his Catechism made that very clear. It was also common practice among furnace workers.

Later he'd excised a block of pages from that same Catechism and glued the *Key Study* segment in their place. Since then he'd read its pages in their entirety—twelve partial chapters, as well as the fragmented commentary that accompanied them on what remained of the lower margins. Read them and reread them with the sort of concentration he should have been giving to the Catechism and never had.

Some of his intensity was born out of his frustration at not having the entire book. His fragment ended midsentence in chapter twelve, yet its words and stories had only sparked more questions. What kind of book was this? Why had it been designated for burning? Who was this LORD God who was said to have created the world and man and placed him in it? Was He real, or just a character in a story? The pages implied He was real. And deep in his heart Zowan thought they might be right.

Moreover, if this LORD God was real . . . He might still exist. In the stories He spoke personally with the men who served Him—Adam, Noah, and Abram. Might He still speak with those who served Him? He wondered, too, why no one in the Enclave had ever mentioned Him, or the *Key Study* story, seeing as how New Eden bore the same name as the garden God had made in the first chapter of Genesis. Surely whoever had given New Eden its name had known of the book. . . .

For three years Zowan's questions had simmered and stewed, breeding more and more doubts until his yearning for answers became one with his desire for purpose. For three years he'd kept them all to himself, fearful no one would understand, fearful of being censured even more than he had been.

Then came his fateful conversation with Andros—not the one they'd had last night, but the one they'd had six months ago, when Zowan dared to release his questions.

The brown prison of the ravine disappeared behind Zowan's remembered images of the darkened Star Garden in which he and Andros had spoken. The chamber's circular levels rose concentrically around a small fountain burbling on its bottom floor. Screens of fabric, wood, and vines divided the space and provided privacy for those who came to talk or meditate while soothing music played from hidden speakers, and carpeted floors dampened the sounds. Star patterns had spun slowly across the black domed ceiling overhead, re-creating what had once been the night sky as seen from the Earth's surface.

It was nearly curfew, and the two young men had sat alone on the highest balcony. Slouched side by side on a thinly padded concrete bench, their backs braced against the cold cement wall, they stared up at the false stars. They'd been sitting in silence for some time when Zowan finally voiced the question: "Do you ever wonder if all is not as the Elders have told us?"

Andros had regarded him uneasily. "You think they've lied to us?"

"I don't know. There are so many inconsistencies. Like my goats, for example. Why do I have to put on a protective suit and wear a respirator, yet they are fine?"

"Aren't they a hardier species than us? More able to withstand toxins and the deadly rays?"

"Even if they are, how can they munch on plants that grow in the poisoned air and soil and still make milk that we can drink? Milk is notorious for picking up contaminants."

"Isn't that what Dairy Resources is for with all their filtering and pasteurizing processes?"

"So they claim. Yet when we are exposed we have to go through days of quarantine, endless scrubbings, those awful purification meds. . . . If they went at purifying the milk like that, there'd be nothing of it worth drinking. And then there's our mission. We're supposed to be reforming the Earth's surface and repopulating it, yet most of us have never been outside the Enclave."

"The enclaves in South America and Australia have made more progress."

"How do you know? None of us have seen them."

Andros frowned at him. "Zowan, you've been outside the Enclave yourself—"

"Only in that narrow ravine. And I sure haven't seen any seeding going on."

Andros studied him with quiet concern. "Those are blasphemous thoughts, my friend."

"You're right. They are." Zowan braced his elbows on his legs. "And if the Enforcers heard us right now, we'd be taken away for readjustment. If I don't say the Affirmation tomorrow morning, I'll be put in the Cube. One would think there'd be no need for threats and schedules in getting a truly grateful person to express his gratitude. Yet every day we must listen to the Elders drone on, we must do precisely as we are told, no questions asked, and every day we have to say that cursed Affirmation."

"Zowan . . ." Andros said warningly.

"Well, it is a curse!"

"It is needed for unity." That was the justification they'd received since childhood. With so few people left they had to preserve their unity, and that meant rules not all liked.

"If we aren't thinking alike, can we really be united?" Zowan asked. "Why force people to be here if they don't want to be? If I refuse to say the Affirmation, why not just turn me out of the Enclave?"

"Because that would be a death sentence."

"Well, then, so be it."

Andros leaned forward now, too, studying his clasped hands, the long fingers pale and delicate. " 'If we don't live together, we won't live at all,' " he quoted.

"Yes." He sighed. "I'm just not sure I believe that anymore."

Andros had no response to that, and Zowan assumed it was because he didn't agree. They'd said no more of it until two nights ago when, back in the Star Garden again, Andros brought it up out of the blue.

Far from disagreeing, he'd taken Zowan's doubts and run with them, doing his own digging and asking his own questions, most of which had been met with the same evasion or outright condemnation that Zowan had encountered. Unlike Zowan, Andros had known when to stop pushing and had not ended up a pariah for his questions. But in the privacy of his soul, he'd continued to think and to question and to conclude until he reached the point where he no longer believed the Affirmation, and didn't know how much longer he could keep saying it.

Zowan had been stunned by his friend's revelations. "If you don't say the Affirmation they'll put you in the Cube," he'd pointed out, in an eerie reversal of roles.

"Maybe that's what New Eden needs," Andros had retorted grimly. "For more of us to refuse and be put in the Cube, so everyone can see how ridiculous and wrong it is."

Two days later, this very morning, Andros had done exactly that.

Now Zowan stared at the rock walls ascending raggedly around him, their upper edges lost in the churning dust. If he'd never expressed his doubts, Andros wouldn't have been in the Cube today. Yes, releasing them had been a relief, and how was he to know Andros would take them for his own and act where Zowan had lacked the courage to do so? He felt ashamed, in addition to guilty. Not for the first time he thought of removing his respirator, just to see what would happen.

The sudden rattle of gravel and the clatter of hooves down the hill behind him spun him around to see five of his goats charging wildly toward the precipice old Nimrod had earlier investigated. They veered around at the brink of disaster and stopped in a bunch, staring back up the slope toward whatever had spooked them. Zowan saw nothing but rocks and dust.

A little spooked himself, he stood and walked upstream to investigate. But though he made a circuit of the pocket, he found nothing suspicious and finally attributed the brief stampede to a combination of moving dust and herd mentality. He'd come to a stop at the brink of the lower cliff and stared idly at the scattered bones of the goat who had fallen off it last year. Over the months he'd watched the carcass disintegrate and wondered what exactly had eaten its flesh and moved the bones.

Gradually his neck began to prickle with the sense of someone watching him, and finally he glanced over his shoulder to see if someone was there. But the surrounding slopes stood quiet and empty, save for the goats. His gaze caught on the dark mouth of the Enclave's entrance in the hillside above. Was someone watching him from inside it?

A rush of pebbles on the uppermost slopes drew his eye up to where a man stood at the edges of the curtains of blowing dust. There for a moment and gone the next instant.

Incredulous, Zowan hurried up the slope after him. But he'd only climbed twenty feet before the slope's steepness and the limitations of his respirator brought him to a gasping halt, vision spangled with white sparks. "Hello?" he called, his voice muffled by the respirator. "Is anyone there?"

He heard only the rasp of his own breathing.

Suddenly six Enforcers burst out of the Enclave entrance, garbed in black protective gear. Fully alarmed, Zowan jumped, skidded, and fell down the steep slope, landing at the bottom unhurt. As he picked himself up and slogged toward his goats, who had bunched up by the pond, one of the Enforcers intercepted him. It was Gaias.

His gene brother frowned behind the mask and gestured toward the goats. "Toxicity levels are spiking," he barked. "Get them in now."

As Zowan stepped to obey, the toxin alarms went off, white strobe lights flashing across the ravine in time to the rhythmic blares of the Klaxon. The goats panicked and scattered, but he managed to snag one old doe and haul her bleating up the slope toward the cave opening. After a short time the others came running. But just as he and the doe neared the opening, the winds suddenly screamed so loudly overhead, he could hardly hear the Klaxons.

Thankfully this time the herd bolted into the cave instead of away, racing up the tunnel toward their home. Zowan followed at a wheezing trot, up the muddy floor and through the gateway, which was closing as he stepped under it. The moment its bottom edge hit the ground and he heard the whoosh of the air being exhausted from the chamber and replaced with fresh, he tore off the respirator and sagged against the metal barrier, sucking in air as if he'd been suffocating.

Once he'd caught his breath, he hurried after the goats, a deep fear curdling in his gut as he processed what Gaias had told him: toxicity spike. The rise so fast it had triggered the gate to shut before the six Enforcers could get back inside.

He was turning back to go try to open the gate when two medics from the clinic raced down the corridor toward him, both of them in hazmat suits. Ignoring his pleas for someone to go and get the gate open, they stripped off Zowan's suit and the tunic and britches he wore underneath, tossed neutralizing powder all over his naked body, then wrapped him in a protective shroud and escorted him hurriedly through deserted passageways to the Enclave's infirmary for emergency detoxification and treatment. One that all knew he might not survive.

# Chapter Ten

Unity meetings were held in various locations, depending on the department. Since the Department of Applied Genetics was almost entirely labs and supply closets, they met in the third floor's Desert Vista conference room. All meetings were mentored by members of K-J's revered Inner Circle, most of whom were the actual department heads, as well. Because Cam had been brought in to be head of AG, but had not yet been invited to join that Inner Circle, their meetings were mentored by Assistant Director and Head of Human Resources, Genevieve Viascola.

When Cam and Pecos arrived, they found everyone seated in a circle listening to Gen enumerate the causes of stress. As Pecos returned to his own seat, Cam took the only remaining one, which was immediately to Gen's right. She paused in her lecture to welcome him dryly and direct his attention to the handout that lay on his chair. With that dignified British accent she sounded perfectly poised, but he saw the anger in her eyes and knew there'd be reprisals.

He spotted Lacey McHenry right off, sitting across the circle and flanked by his technicians Jade and Mel. She seemed more relaxed than when she'd confronted him in his office earlier. Perhaps she'd grasped the meaning behind his words, and had taken his advice to heart to let the incident go. Certainly that's what this meeting was encouraging her to do.

Gen assured them that experiencing a crisis of mental stability was nothing to be ashamed of. She was willing to bet that everyone in the room had experienced one sort of breakdown or another—or at least had come very close to it. To illustrate, she talked of her own depression as a young woman years ago. Then, to Cam's horror, she encouraged everyone else to share their own experiences, in the interest of being "open."

Jade started off by admitting to her own bouts of paranoia and near breakdown when she'd arrived. Another girl confided she was on Valium for the first six months she was at the Institute. As each story was told, others grew more comfortable sharing their own events, speaking one after the other as they went around the circle.

Cam alone grew increasingly tense as the progression moved toward him. For the first time in years, he felt old shields going up, surrounding him like a tube of accumulating layers of Plexiglas. The others' voices grew increasingly garbled and faint, while his own heart beat a loud, rapid pounding in his chest.

Then they were all staring at him and he realized it was his turn. Sweat popped out on his brow and a prickle gripped the back of his neck, along with an old familiar sense of something stalking him. He wanted to jump up, cast the chair aside, and confront it, even though he had no weapon, even knowing there was nothing there.

Nothing there.

When the silence had stretched on too long to be comfortable, Gen nudged his arm, and for a moment sound and sense of the others returned as she prompted him: "I understand even *you* have struggled with a mental health issue, Cameron, religious faith and all." It was always on a first-name basis here in the unity meetings. And she always had to bring his faith into it.

He stared at her, struggling to keep his face and voice neutral. How could she know of his battles with post-traumatic stress disorder? His medical records had been expunged along with the rest of the mission details. "I think you've got me confused with someone else, Gen."

She cocked a skeptical brow. "You've never struggled with any mental health issues?"

"No," he said firmly. Nothing official, anyway. And certainly nothing he could talk about.

She held his gaze evenly, pushing at him with her silence and the pressure of twenty-eight pairs of wildly curious eyes upon him to spill his guts. He had a pretty good idea how they'd react if he told them he'd been irrationally compelled to turn on every light in his apartment last night, where he'd not even tried to sleep for fear of the nightmares he was certain he would have had. Where he'd popped a DVD into his player but had no idea what had been on it, for he was too busy jumping at every sound, checking all the rooms in his three-room suite, and shivering at the distant thumping of the choppers as they crisscrossed the desert with their searchlights. Which was how he'd known they'd flown all night and why he'd concluded they'd failed to find the intruder.

Of course, he couldn't tell them any of that, because that would lead to the flashbacks he'd suffered today, and then on to the PTSD, which he wasn't supposed to talk about, seeing as all the causal events were classified. Even if they hadn't been, he'd repressed so many of the memories, he couldn't remember them himself. And didn't want to.

When it became apparent he was not going to speak, Gen smiled, quite insincerely, and said, "Well, thank you for being so candid with us, Cameron." She turned to Espinosa on her left. "What about you, Manny? You've achieved a lot of things. You must have had your share of stress to cope with."

Manny—young, handsome, swarthy, and ultra-confident— shrugged. "Actually, Gen, I've never worried about that sort of thing. What others call stress, I consider a challenge. Maybe it's because I know I can always make things work out for me." He glanced past her to Cam and smiled.

As they continued around the circle, Cam began to relax, though with the withdrawal of fear came the inevitable embarrassment and self-condemnation. Thankfully, once the sharing got back to Lacey, the heart-baring session ended and Gen had them all get up and divide into teams of three. Each team she presented with two Nerf balls—one blue, one yellow—for a ball-passing exercise intended to relax them even as it "sharpened hand-eye coordination, stimulated areas of the prefrontal cortex, and provided an exercise in teamwork." Standing in a straight line, each trio would pass the balls from one to the other in a continuous loop all the while keeping time to the music.

When she was finished with her demonstration, Manny erupted in incredulity. "You really expect us to do that? Who thinks these things up?"

Genevieve's brightly painted lips tightened in displeasure. "Director Swain himself selects our weekly activities. But perhaps I should recommend your name to him as someone who would like to make the selections instead."

Manny said nothing to that, and Viascola got them started. It was harder than it looked but was still a waste of time in Cam's view, though better by far than the gut-spilling sessions. Thankfully, she only devoted fifteen minutes to the exercise.

Afterward, as she collected the balls into a mesh bag, she pointed out the moral: as long as everyone focused on his part, the balls were smoothly passed; let one mind drift to someone else's part, though, and the pass would be missed, breaking the chain of motion.

"What does this have to do with stress management? Just that, if we'd simply learn to focus on what we have to do now, not the past, not the future, but right now, we'd find ourselves a lot less stressed. The key is concentration. And here at K-J, we've found the practice of meditating to be an excellent way to develop that power and reduce stress."

She sent them all back to their seats, then slid a cardboard box from under her chair and pressed back the flaps to reveal it to be full of two-inch black plastic cubes. Plucking one out, she held it up for all to see. "Meditation is aided if you have a focal point, and we have one of these little cubes for each of you. The black box, as you all know, is the icon of our Institute, but do any of you know why?"

No one did, so she explained: "In science, a black box is something with known performance characteristics but unknown components and means of operation—we know what it does, but not why or how. Since our purpose at K-J is to discover those whys and hows, the black box is a perfect symbol. And the perfect item to use as a point of focus."

After a brief lecture on meditation, she devoted the last five minutes to a guided practice session and ended the meeting.

Cam leapt to his feet and started to slip between the chairs, but Gen caught his arm before he got more than two steps and asked him to stay behind. As soon as the room was emptied and the door had closed, she lit into him. "I asked you specifically to be here today, Cameron."

"I *was* here."

"Fifteen minutes late. And only because I sent Pecos to drag you out of your lab. Even here, you made your disinterest obvious, refusing to cooperate with our activities."

"I did your ball-pass thing without argument."

"And all the while made it obvious you thought it was idiotic."

"It *was* idiotic!"

"And now you continue to be disrespectful and insubordinate."

Cam drew a deep breath and said no more, enduring her subsequent tongue-lashing stoically. Since he'd been the victim of her antagonism—subtle and not so subtle—since the day he'd arrived at Kendall-Jakes nine months ago, that was getting easier. He thought at first it was his Christianity, for she never missed the opportunity to take a swipe at it. Lately, though, he'd begun to wonder if she was jealous; if maybe it wasn't just young, pretty women who threatened her, but anyone to whom Swain took a strong liking.

Born into an upper-crust British family, she'd been the wild, rebellious daughter, running off to France at nineteen to hook up with Parker Swain, American exile and bad-boy intellectual. Together they'd traveled the world searching out secrets in the medical and religious practices of both ancient and aboriginal cultures. Swain had tutored her in the sciences, and she'd become one of his top research assistants, eventually taking over as CEO of his research and development corporation.

Though they'd never married, she'd borne him two sons and was still so madly in love with him she alone seemed unaware that at forty-seven she'd become too old for his tastes. Though Swain still trusted her more than anyone, everyone knew she would never share his bed again.

In some ways Cam felt sorry for her.

"Are you even listening to me?"

He snapped back to the moment. "Come on, Gen. You hate these ridiculous games as much as I do. Why can't you just—"

"They are Parker's direct instruction and desire for us, his employees," she declared. "He believes they benefit all of us, help us to bond in shared endeavors and in baring our vulnerabilities."

He was tempted to roll his eyes but confined himself to shaking his head. "They're just more hoops for us to jump through so everyone will know he's calling the shots."

"He *is* calling the shots, Cameron. And he wants you at these meetings."

"He only suggests it."

"He's only being polite. It hurts him that you are so stubborn. Especially after all he's done for you. . . ."

Cam frowned at her. "I said I'd be there next time. On time."

She exhaled in exasperation. "I'll hold you to that, you know."

He nodded, shifting his weight to make his escape. She cut him off by addressing an entirely new subject. "I've reviewed your request of transfer for Manuel Espinosa, and the answer is no. We can't have him swabbing floors in the animal facility. It wouldn't be right—he's a graduate of MIT. Winner of multiple prestigious awards."

Cam folded his arms and frowned at her. "Well, apparently he's decided that's all he needs to accomplish in life, because he's been worthless to me. Too busy with his own project— his own *unapproved* project, I might add."

Her brown eyes narrowed. "You aren't doing this because he's Latino, are you?"

Cam barked a laugh of scorn. "That's ridiculous. I want him gone because he won't do a thing I ask him to."

She lifted the mostly empty cardboard box to the seat of her chair and laid the pile of unused handouts on top of the remaining black cubes. "Well, I'm sorry. You're just going to have to deal with him, because we have no one to replace him with."

"How about the girl taking care of the frogs?"

Gen stopped what she was doing to look up at him in surprise. Then her eyes narrowed again. "Why would you want *her*?"

"Because I saw her file this morning. She's got her Master's in Molecular and Cellular Biology. She's wasted down in Animal Resources."

"And Espinosa wouldn't be?" She laid the stack of manila folders on top of the handout sheets and looked up at him.

"Espinosa would benefit from a lesson in humility."

She lifted a finely plucked brow. "I hardly think *you* should be the one to give it to him, however. Besides, he'd more than likely walk out on us. And rightly so, if you ask me. The switch you're suggesting is preposterous." She returned her attention to layering the box flaps closed. "No. Ms. McHenry will stay with her frogs and you will have to find a way to make peace with Dr. Espinosa. Maybe if you treated him with a little more respect, you'd have an easier time getting him to work with you."

He huffed out a breath of exasperation. "Fine. Is that all?"

She tucked the last flap under the first, closing the box. "You will be here next Friday? On time?"

"I said I would."

"Very well. Don't forget to take your cube." She gestured at the plastic cube lying on his chair.

He picked it up with a sigh and headed for the door. But as his hand closed on its latch, she said, "You are such a wuss, Cameron Reinhardt. No wonder they drummed you out of the service. I don't know what Parker sees in you!"

He looked over his shoulder at her, shocked by the venom in her voice. She walked toward him. "You're just going to take whatever I dish out, aren't you?" she demanded, disgust souring her voice.

"You'd like me not to?"

"I'd like you to show some backbone." She stopped before him. "This passive-aggressive behavior is just . . . It's cowardly. And hypocritical. And I find it galling that you can stand there and ask me to transfer Manny for not being a team player when you yourself provide him such a sterling example of the same."

He frowned down at her, trying to make sense of what she was saying. First she'd told him he must do whatever Swain told him, then rebuked him for not standing up to her. Passive-aggressive? Show some backbone?

She grimaced and turned away from him. "Go. Your little girlfriend is no doubt waiting to speak to you in the hall. From the moment you walked through the door, she could hardly keep her eyes off you."

He stared at her in renewed befuddlement. What little girlfriend? He recalled no one who couldn't keep her eyes off him. . . .

"I said go," Gen repeated.

And he did. The moment he stepped into the hall, he realized she must've meant Lacey McHenry, though since the only looks McHenry had given him in the last hour had been fish eyes of astonishment and distaste, he had no idea why Gen would think she was his "little girlfriend." Nor why it would make her so angry.

The one thing he did know was that Lacey McHenry was not likely to be confronting him again about the events of last night.

## Chapter Eleven

At dinner every Friday, Saturday, and Sunday, it was the custom for department heads and senior managers to sit at the subordinates' tables, and according to the regular rotation, Cam was to sit at Table A5 tonight. Instead he arrived to find himself reassigned to B4, Manuel Espinosa's table. That was Gen's doing, for sure. Punishing them both for annoying her in the unity meeting, and a tacit reminder to Cam of her demand that he make more effort to be a team player.

Any other night he might have made such an effort, but the closer he got to the hour of his covert meeting with Rudy, the more preoccupied he became. It didn't help that someone had told Manny that Cam's mental health issues stemmed from an incident during his military service where his installation had been overrun by Taliban fighters. Cam refused to say whether it was so or not, and Manny refused to let him off the hook without giving an answer. It was not an enjoyable meal.

Finally it ended, and at 7:30, as had become his custom, he left the ziggurat to walk the paved paths that encircled the central park. He strode out around the loop, passing the Vault and the resort and the five-star Casa del Oro restaurant and finally circling back toward the ziggurat. It loomed ahead of him, a stairstep pyramid of glazed windows and polished granite walls reflecting the setting sun's warm light in a golden monument to the immensity and audacity of Swain's vision.

Cam rounded a bend, following the path down a gentle incline toward a line of cottonwood trees and the quiet pond beyond them.

Spiky stands of green cattails lined the water's edge, already steeped in shadow behind the stretch of protective railing that curved along the path.

He stopped at the bottom of the hill, leaned his forearms on the railing, and waited. A pair of ducks glided across the mirrorlike pond. Frogs croaked around him in shrill chorus as bats swooped and fluttered overhead. The scent of wet earth filled the still air, refreshingly cool here at the water's edge. Slowly darkness clotted among the cattails, as crickets added their songs to that of the frogs, and in the cottonwood leaves above him, a cicada started buzzing.

The minutes ticked by. He began to wonder if he'd overreacted. If Juan wasn't Rudy after all and this mission was nothing but the result of his awakening paranoia finding far too much meaning in a couple of coincidences.

After all, hadn't he told Swain this morning that it was *God* who'd brought him to Kendall-Jakes?

Caught in the midst of an intradepartmental squabble, Cam had been on the edge of no job at all when Swain's offer had come in. Though it had seemed like a career saver, he'd balked at the prospect of working at the Longevity Institute. He'd asked his Stanford department head, Sandy Ravenshead, flat-out if he should take the position. She'd said he should, convinced it was a phenomenal opportunity not only to advance the field of genetic investigation but his own career.

Despite her strong encouragement, he'd remained conflicted, praying repeatedly for guidance. Only after interviewing personally with Swain had he finally felt genuinely led to come to the Institute. All his Bible classes at the time had revolved around the importance of extending grace, of thinking the best, of focusing on the fact that Jesus had died for everyone, and willed that no man should perish. And on living in one's ambassadorship. If God wanted him to serve as witness . . . how could he say no?

Besides, there'd been no other door. Except Home Depot . . .

So he'd come, telling himself he really wasn't compromising his faith. But now . . .

Now he was up to his ears in compromise, with the grim specter of having been set up—tricked and betrayed in the worst possible way —hanging at the back of his thoughts.

Darkness had settled thickly around him when he sensed a presence in the shadows and was startled to realize he'd missed his friend's approach altogether. He stood near the rugged trunk of the cottonwood to Cam's left, barely an arm's length away, and almost invisible.

Cam felt the hairs on his nape lift as his stomach churned anew.

They stood for a long time in silence. Then, "That was fast thinking, you bagging her coat up like that and leaving it for me to find" came a low, familiar voice, utterly stripped of the Latino accent. "I wasn't sure you still had it in you."

Cam gripped the railing with trembling hands.

"Wasn't sure you'd recognized me yet, either."

Cam let out his breath in a low sigh, then murmured, "I hadn't."

"So why bag up the coat, then?"

"I couldn't stand the blood." Rudy was one of the few who would know exactly what he meant, and he telegraphed that understanding by a protracted period of silence. When next he spoke his tone was low and serious. "You're having flashbacks again?"

"Starting last night."

Another too-long interval elapsed. Then, "Did you see him? The intruder?"

"No. And what did you mean by 'anomalous,' anyway?"

"Exactly that. We suspect genetic modification."

Nausea swirled in Cameron's gut. There'd long been whispers that Swain's early work in those privately funded international research facilities had involved cutting-edge advances in human genetic manipulation. "So you're investigating Swain, then."

"Indeed we are. Kidnapping, murder, fraud, extortion, illegal experimentation. He's got a worldwide network of followers. Seven different international locations like K-J, but far less publicized, most of them where the local governments are happy to look the other way for the right price. There are rumors of reproductive human cloning, organ trafficking . . . slavery. Unfortunately, he's grown intensely paranoid after his last run-in with the law. Trusts no one but his Inner Circle— several of whom are also under investigation. His security systems are state of the art, with redundancy upon redundancy, and the vetting process is exhaustive. I'd originally wanted to go in as a biologist, but it was soon obvious that would never fly. As it was, it took me a year to get on as a janitor."

"I thought you hired on as an electrician."

"I did. And worked the last eighteen months waxing floors and emptying trash bins in various locations around campus."

Cam felt as if he'd been gut-punched. "So you brought me in."

Rudy said nothing.

Cam closed his fingers around the top rail, quietly furious. "So the debacle at Stanford was all a setup, then?"

Rudy let out a quiet breath. "More or less."

Cam's head swam. His heart pounded. "And Dr. Ravenshead? Was she in on it?"

"What difference does it make? It wasn't like she had a choice."

The coldness in the pit of Cam's stomach congealed into an icy, leaden lump. "I thought you were my friend."

"I am."

Cam choked on his expression of disbelief.

"I've been keeping tabs on you ever since you left the unit."

"I didn't leave the unit. I was drummed out of it."

"Only because they knew you intended to leave. And, anyway, you needed to. Back then. I've kept an eye on you, though. Prayed for you—"

"Don't tell me that!" He turned to look straight at the other man, a darker shadow in the shadow. "Don't you dare say that! You betrayed me. Not once but twice now. So don't tell me you're *praying* for me." He shook his head and swore softly. "I can't believe you did this to me."

"I had no choice, Cam. You are the only man for this job."

"This *job*?! I came here to contribute to the field, to uncover new information that might benefit the world. I came here to maybe give the gospel to some of these folks—not lie and scheme and betray them all. Whatever you want me to do, I won't. No matter how you pressure and position me. I won't. If Swain is dirty—"

"He most definitely is."

"Well, I'll not be the one to drive the knife in his back. I'll leave first. In fact, I've already drafted my resignation."

His words, soft but intense, died away into silence. The chorus of frogs and crickets filled his ears. Bats fluttered in brief silhouettes against the still-gleaming pond as over in the parking lot the street-lamps began to glow.

Finally Rudy loosed a long, low sigh. "He's not just dirty, Cam. He's playing with fire, something I suspect you've already figured out. We didn't select you just because of your expertise in genetics. Or even mainly because of it, though it helps tremendously. No, it's your experience in Afghanistan we need."

"Well, you're up a creek without a paddle," Cam said grimly, "because I can't remember anything from Afghanistan."

"You just said you were having flashbacks."

Cam said nothing to that. He'd begun to shake so badly, if not for the railing he'd have collapsed.

"There is literally no one else who fits the bill like you do, Cam," Rudy said. "In my opinion, God himself has prepared you for this."

"Rudy, you know I can't do this stuff anymore. You of all people *know*!"

Rudy shifted against the tree trunk, the fabric of his uniform rasping against its rough bark. "You did pretty well last night, my friend. Despite whatever demons you were fighting in your head." He paused, the silence between them filling again with frog and insect song. Then he whooshed out another breath and said more quietly than ever, "We think he might have some sarcophagi."

Cam's fear metastasized into terror. The air turned to thick, cold syrup as sweat popped out on his brow and chest. The tunnel of flashing fire flickered before him, but he fought it off, gripping the railing hard. "I can't!" he rasped. "Get someone else."

"There is no one else."

"Well, you'll have to find him, because it's not going to be me." His voice shook. "I've done my time. And it darn near killed me."

He pushed up from the bar. Rudy's next words stopped him from going farther.

"If you don't help us, he may kill us all."

Cam stood still, ears roaring.

"Start with their ATR program," Rudy said. A string of murmured numbers followed, then a coded password: "Golf-Zero, One-Delta, Three-Yankee-Three."

As old habits of mind kicked into action, already committing the sequence to memory, Cam shoved away from the railing, terrified he was going to lose everything he'd spent the last eleven years building.

Even as he knew deep down it was already lost.

# Chapter Twelve

Lacey returned with Jade to their dorm room on floor B1 around midnight. That was considerably later than she'd hoped to get to bed after her very long day, especially given her newly realized fragility. Nonetheless, she counted the time expenditure worth it.

After dinner Jade had invited Lacey to join her, Aaron, Mel, Pecos, and Lauren in the game room for a collaborative board game whose name she couldn't recall. Afterward they sat around talking, and for the first time since arriving, Lacey felt like she might actually belong.

It was as if she'd passed some trial by fire. She took comfort in knowing she wasn't the only one who'd come unglued from the stress. Yes, she'd fallen apart. But as Aaron had said just minutes ago, it was over now and she should move on.

Which was pretty much what Cameron Reinhardt had told her, though his words had carried a sense that she should simply ignore what she believed to be true and move on for the sake of her job. Which was probably more a manifestation of his personality than any reality of the situation.

"I'm glad you invited me to play, Jade," she said as they stopped before their door. "That was fun."

"*I'm* glad you said yes," Jade replied, swiping her card through the reader. "Lets me know you've taken some of our advice to heart." She opened the door as it unlocked and pushed into the room.

Lacey followed, shutting the door behind her. "Yeah, well, I really should have gone back to the prep room and run another couple loads of pans and tool packs. People will be howling for them tomorrow."

"Hey, it's Friday night. And you've taken next to no downtime since you got here. Besides, tomorrow's Saturday, so we can sleep in." She kicked off her clogs, then sat on the bed to pull off her red cotton socks.

"Which is why I said yes," Lacey said with a grin. "Since I knew I could go in early and get a head start on everything."

Jade looked up at her, eyes narrowed behind the dark-framed glasses. "Did you hear nothing that was said to you today? It's okay to rest."

"Yes, but having Dr. Yuen railing at me every hour because I still don't have his petri dishes ready, or his dissection packets, and then Dr. Ahmed-White comes in as soon as he's left and wants a hundred glass beakers *right now* . . . but I have to tell her to wait for Yuen's order . . . Well, that's stressful, too."

"Ignore them."

"They're shouting at me."

"That's what they do, Lace. Ignore 'em. They're only trying to intimidate you into giving them a leg up before the other one. Ahmed-White and Yuen have been competing since the day they got here."

"But the review board—"

"Won't be here till next week. Chill. In fact . . ." She stuffed her socks into her clogs, then pulled her laptop across the desk toward her and flipped it open. "How about we do one of those meditation sessions Viascola was talking about?"

"I need to get to bed!" Lacey protested.

"We'll do one of the ten-minute ones. You have your box?"

"She said not to do it if you're too tired. I'll probably fall asleep."

"Well, what's wrong with that?"

"Then let's get ready for bed first."

Fifteen minutes later Lacey sat on her bed dressed in her sleep tee, covers pulled over her folded bare legs as she watched Jade hang up her clothes. "By the way," she said, "thanks for sharing about your experience when you first got here. It really helped."

"Yeah, well . . . as you saw tonight, everyone has tales to tell. Even

Dr. Reinhardt. Despite his claims otherwise." Jade shook her head as she buttoned the collar of her shirt and hung it on the rod. "Though I'll admit I never would have pegged *him* as one having mental health disorders."

"What makes you think he does?" Lacey asked.

"You mean aside from how weird he was in the unity meeting today, not wanting to talk and all. Aaron said it was PTSD."

"Post-traumatic stress? What? From graduate school?"

"He was in the military before he went into genetics. Did a tour in Afghanistan." Jade shut the closet door. "And did you hear Pecos telling about how when he went up to get him for the meeting this afternoon, Reinhardt was on the floor under his desk? Said he was looking for a file folder."

"Well, given the piling system he's got going in his office, that could well be true," Lacey pointed out. Although the information that Reinhardt had been in the military in Afghanistan triggered the sudden recall of the practiced competence with which he'd cleaned and dressed her imaginary wound. How would she have known to imagine him competent in such a thing when she'd had no idea he had any experience at it?

"Pecos sure didn't think so. And for Reinhardt to refuse to talk about it—"

"I don't think I'd have told *my* story in there if everyone didn't already know about it."

"You're a newbie. You don't know anyone. It's harder for you."

"Maybe, but you're already hypothesizing he was having a . . . what? A flashback episode? Under his desk?"

"Hey, a car backfires or someone slams a door too hard and they dive for cover. Some of them never get normal. Some of them are *dangerous.*"

"You really believe Dr. Reinhardt is dangerous?"

"Well. No." Jade snorted a laugh. "The man's lucky if he remembers to zip his fly before he comes down to breakfast." She flung back the covers on her bed and plumped up the pillows—she had two—then plopped herself onto the exposed sheets and drew the covers over her folded legs like Lacey. Then she reached for the laptop on the desk, already booted up and ready to go.

She set it on the bed in front of her, moved her finger on the touch pad, then tapped it once and looked up. "Ready?"

Lacey held up the little black box Viascola had given them and sat forward from her own pillows propped against the headboard and dresser.

"Just put the box there on the bed in front of you," Jade said.

Lacey did so and Jade tapped the touch pad again to start the program.

A flat-toned feminine voice invited them to join her in a Buddhist meditation session, then suggested they should sit comfortably, relax, and be alert. A tone sounded.

"As a way of arriving in the present moment," the woman said, "allow your body to relax. Let your awareness roll across places of tension. . . ." She paused to let them do so. "Loosen the shoulders . . . the neck. . . ."

Her voice was quiet, deliberately unobtrusive. "The chest is open . . . the belly soft, enabling a full breath.

"Breathe . . ." Again, the voice paused, letting them focus on the action of breathing. "In . . . out . . . *Feel* a sense of embodied awareness."

*What in the world is embodied awareness?* Lacey wondered, thinking this was really quite ridiculous. She felt sillier now than she had in Dr. Viascola's demonstration earlier.

The voice continued. "You're aware of what your feet are touching, of where you're sitting. Of pressure. Temperature. Aware of all the body's sensations."

Again the voice fell silent as Lacey strove to become aware, staring at the box as Viascola had suggested. The woman instructed her to choose a place in her breathing to rest her attention—"the inflow and outflow of air through the nose, the rise and fall of chest or abdomen. A resting place to which you can return . . ."

"Note in . . . out . . . in . . . out . . ." the voice droned. "Or rising . . . falling . . . rising . . . falling . . .

"If some strong experience calls your attention, some difficult sensation or emotion, let go of the breath as the center of attention and include what's arising. Note it: 'Ah . . . tension, tightness, squeezing, heat.'

"Or, 'grief, sadness, fear . . . ' "

A faint light flickered in the box, seizing Lacey's attention and triggering a sudden gripping dizziness, as if the room had subtly shifted in alignment. Instead of merely noting it with a friendly aspect, as the meditation guide had suggested, she stiffened and leaned forward to study it more closely. It flickered again, and she sensed something. A presence. A heaviness . . .

Suddenly darkness enwrapped her, and she smelled the strong, sweet fragrance of jasmine mingled with the damp evening air. She sensed water nearby, though she saw only darkness. From somewhere ahead, more lights flickered and she heard voices talking in some other language, telling her to come, though she did not know how she knew that. She started toward them. Then, inexplicably, the voices silenced, and the sense of heaviness lifted. She felt the bed again, the rumpled coverlet beneath her calves and ankles, the tingling of a pinched nerve in her leg. Overhead came the faint rush of the air flowing through the air-conditioning ducts. After the fragrance of sweet jasmine, the room smelled like sweaty socks.

The meditation woman no longer spoke. Had the session ended?

She opened her eyes—and started violently at the sight of the black box floating before her eyes not six inches from her face. She flinched back sharply, swatting it to the bed as if it were some oversized insect. It tumbled across the folds of coverlet and came to a stop. She sat there breathing hard, blinking rapidly, and deeply alarmed. *Not again!*

After a moment reality reasserted itself, and she realized she hadn't been hallucinating, but dreaming. The clock on the desk read 12:55. They'd begun their ten-minute session at 12:25, so obviously she had twenty minutes to account for.

Nor was she the only one to have fallen asleep. Jade had collapsed back on her pillows and lay unmoving except for the rise and fall of her chest, her eyes closed, her mouth open. Lacey smiled at her roommate, wondering which of them had fallen asleep first.

She stood and set the box on her desk beside her cell phone, was about to turn back to the bed when she remembered the messages she'd left with her family physician and her mother. Though she hardly cared anymore, and assured herself those messages could wait until tomorrow, something prodded her to check. A latent hope that she really hadn't had a breakdown and they would actually exonerate her?

Whatever her reason, she picked up the phone and checked her voice mail. To her surprise there were three messages. The first was from Ma, who didn't remember any specific photos of the scar, nor even the scar itself, and wanted to know what difference it made, anyway.

The second was from her physician, who, not surprisingly, recalled no incidents involving lacerations, nor did he have any records of treatment elsewhere.

"But the urgent care centers don't always get the information to primary care, especially if the patient neglects to request it," he said. So. Nothing there, either. But then, she hadn't expected anything, and was okay with that. A tumble into paranoid hysterics in the middle of the night didn't seem so awful anymore.

The third call was from Gen Viascola, who'd tried to get Lacey on her pager but failed, so she was calling to let her know that the young man from ASU was not going to be coming down from Phoenix tonight, after all, due to lack of transportation.

"He should be here by Tuesday or Wednesday," Viascola said. "So you'll have to do the job for a few more days. Hopefully you'll get this message tonight, but if not, or even if you would prefer to wait until daylight, I'm sure everything can wait until morning. Sorry to spring this on you. Just give me a ping to let me know you got the message."

With a groan she dialed Viascola's number and left a voice mail, then flipped the phone shut and turned it off. Most times waiting until morning would have been fine. But as she'd told Jade earlier, tomorrow she needed to get right on the autoclaving. And she couldn't put the animal care off until tomorrow afternoon because she had a litter of newly weaned rats. If they didn't have enough food, they would start eating each other. She could, however, go down and make sure they had food and water to last the night.

With a groan, she stood, pulled her shorts and T-shirt from the clothes hamper and donned them, slipped on her flip-flops, and went up to the animal facility.

As she stepped out of the elevator into the dimly lit hall of the animal quarters, a chill of unease brought her to a halt. The elevator door rumbled shut behind her, and silence wrapped her like a shroud. A faint trickle of water drifted through the stillness. Only a couple of the fluorescent ceiling panels were lit, casting triangles of light and shadow across the walls. Ahead on the right, the ready room stood dark, door closed. What if the strange youth had returned and was waiting for her . . . ?

Her heartbeat accelerated and her mouth went dry as memory of last night's events returned with full and vivid force. It was only with great effort of will that she did not turn and slap wildly at the button to call the elevator back.

*He's not here,* she told herself firmly, drawing a deep breath and forcing the panic down. *He was never here. You imagined it, remember? Remember Poe's lab? My lab coat? My shirt? Reinhardt's denial? It didn't happen. There's nothing to worry about.*

She drew another breath and started forward, her rubber thongs flip-flopping loudly in the quiet.

She went to the ready room, snapped on the light, and frowned at the sight of one of the sink counter drawers open. It held pens, pencils, and broad-tipped black markers. One of the latter had been thrown back in uncapped. Its tip was mashed and drying out, so she cast it into the trash, wondering why whoever had used it hadn't done that in the first place.

With a sigh she retrieved her lab coat from the back of the door and put it on. By now fully awake, she decided to do all her chores and save herself the trouble tomorrow.

She tickled Harvey under the chin, then put him on her shoulder and dumped the wood chips from the bottom tray, replaced food and water, and moved on to the mice. Finally she put Harvey back into his home and went across the hall to the rat rooms, emptying the waste trays, refilling bottles and food bins, spraying down the floor to wash any stray droppings into the drain. There were five rooms and it took her forty-five minutes to finish them, all without incident.

Finally it was time to do the frogs, a task she normally did first but this time had unconsciously saved for last. She got a bucket from the ready room into which she would put the dead frogs—there were always a few to be picked from the tank—and headed with growing reluctance toward the corridor nearest the elevator.

She rounded the corner and stopped as suddenly as if she'd run into an invisible wall, her breath hissing against her teeth. The corridor was dark, but the frog room's light was on and its door stood open—inward, toward the room, exactly as it had been last night.

Tonight there were no frogs in the hall, though. Apparently Dr. Reinhardt had just been in and out, probably while she was in the rat rooms, and the frogs had not had time to escape. She could see a few on the floor, however, visible through the crack between door and jamb. At least she'd arrived in time to stop them from hopping all over the place. If only she could move.

Her pulse had once more careened into the hundred-twenty-plus range, her hands cold and shaking. She forced herself to move, but it was like walking neck-deep through a pool of water. Almost as if she knew what she would find there.

Except there was no way in the world she could have anticipated the sight that met her eyes.

# Chapter Thirteen

The steel tank lay on its side, frogs spilled across the painted floor, dead or dying, most of them legless. Bodies and legs floated separately on the water that had collected above the clogged drain. Here was the origin of the trickling sound she'd heard earlier.

She stared at the carnage in disbelief, more bewildered than afraid, and stepped into the room without thinking. Even standing in its midst, she couldn't believe it. No one person could turn that tank over with just the strength of his own arms. Especially not when it was full of water.

Yet there it lay, hinged lids gaping slightly open from the pull of gravity.

And the frogs. Dead. Mutilated. It was too bizarre and inexplicable to be real. *Oh, Lord! I must be hallucinating again.*

But . . . were hallucinations this vivid? The water cold on her toes where it reached over the thick soles of her flip-flops, the plastic bucket hard and cool against her bare leg, the dank stench of frog, the sucking sound of the water trickling through the clogged drain . . .

For the first time she lifted her eyes from frogs and tank and saw the words scrawled across the peach-colored side wall in fat black marker:

HIS EYES ARE OVER ALL HIS CREATION

She frowned, closed her eyes tight, opened them again. The tank, the frogs, the words were still there. And the words made no more sense than the rest of it.

She closed her eyes again, clenched the bucket hard, seeking to feel some sign that she wasn't really in the frog room but back in her bed dreaming. She took several deep, calming breaths, assuring herself of this, and trying to make herself wake up.

But the sick, surreal scene remained when she opened her eyes.

*Oh, Lord, what is wrong with me? Why do I keep doing this? Surely I'm not that stressed! I thought things were getting better. . . .*

"Do you like it?" The voice spoke low and raspy almost in her ear, catapulting her forward and around with a shriek. One foot landed on frog bodies and slid out from under her. Flailing for balance, she tumbled backward, landing with a splash on her bottom.

He stood in the open doorway, grinning at her, taller than she remembered him. There was the chipped tooth. The dirty blond hair with its short, bristled Mohawk, the heavy brow, the ice-chip eyes, the big boil on his forehead, larger than it was last night. He'd smeared mud across his grizzled cheeks—streaks of tan and reddish brown— which only added to the wild look.

"I did it for you," he said, stepping into the room.

She scrambled away from him in a backward crawl, hampered by the oversized, unbuttoned lab coat until her own movements pulled it down off her shoulders. Freed of it, she surged backward, only to hit the wall. He stopped a few feet inside the room, the hard blue eyes traveling downward from her face, over her wet T-shirt and skimpy shorts, her protective lab coat now a wet, rumpled mess beneath her. The muscles alongside his right eye twitched. His mouth opened slightly and the tip of his tongue darted out, running lightly across his lips. "I was afraid you weren't going to come."

A squall of revulsion sent her scrambling sideways and over the fallen tank, putting it between them. Using it to maintain her balance, she finally got her feet under her. Only to realize she was trapped. And if he had the strength to pull over that tank, what could she do to resist him?

"Oh, Lord, let me wake up! Let me wake up. Let me wake up."

"Wake up?" he asked, startling her. She hadn't realized she'd spoken the words aloud. "Yes. Let us wake up together."

He stepped back, his eyes never leaving her own, the tic in the right one working rapidly.

*Oh, Lord, please . . . please . . .*

He was reaching back to shut the frog-room door when the elevator pinged and both of them froze. The doors trundled open. Footfalls echoed in the silence.

Again, Lacey was first to react, screaming for help at the top of her lungs and leaping over the tank for the discarded bucket. As she grabbed it and flung it upward, her feet slid out from under her and she went down again. But not before glimpsing him dodging the bucket, his face full of undiluted fury.

But incredibly the stranger ran. She heard one of the heavy lab room doors slam, a rapid thumping of feet, and suddenly Dr. Reinhardt stood in his place.

"He was here!" she cried. "Just now. I think he ran out through Poe's lab again."

Reinhardt vanished, ignoring her cries to wait. She got carefully to her feet and finally had the presence of mind to kick off the treacherous flip-flops and put them into the bucket.

From the hall Reinhardt's voice echoed back to her: "You sure it was Poe's lab? 'Cause the door's locked."

"No. Not sure." She heard the *beep* and *click* of a security lock disengaging and reached the hall in time to see Reinhardt disappear through the doorway of his own lab at the hall's end. A warning rose to her lips and died there as the light flicked on and nothing happened. He'd left the door ajar, and she glimpsed him through the crack as he moved around the room beyond. A desperate disappointment flooded her as she realized the stranger had gotten away. Again.

She sagged weakly against the wall, shaking like an old woman, as much from reaction to the adrenaline recently surging through her veins as from cold. With her shorts and T-shirt drenched from all the falling and splashing, and her lab coat lying in the puddle of dead frogs and water, she had nothing to ward off the chill of the very well-conditioned air. Gooseflesh puckered her arms and legs, and her teeth were chattering.

Reinhardt emerged from his lab and pulled the door shut behind him, then stopped when he saw her standing there.

She pushed away from the wall, dreading what he would say next. "You didn't see him, did you."

He stood motionless for a moment, then gave a start and strode toward her, slipping off his lab coat as he came. "Here, you're all wet," he said. "No wonder you're shivering." He wrapped his too-large coat around her as if she were a child. She pulled its front edges together before her as her throat closed and tears blurred her vision. For a moment she wished he'd wrap his arms around her, too, for right then she wanted nothing so much as to cling to someone safe and let the storm of fear and heartache and frustration pour out.

But he touched her only enough to get the coat around her shoulders, then abandoned her to step into the vandalized frog room.

"I didn't imagine this," she called after him. "He was real! He was here!" She heard the rising pitch in her voice and cut herself off, knowing her words were more for herself than for him. She drew a deep breath, then stepped into the doorway. He was staring at the words on the wall.

"You see them, don't you?"

"I see them."

"And the frogs? The overturned tank?"

His head turned toward the tank and he nodded. She couldn't see his face.

"I'll admit I could have written those words on the wall," she said. "I didn't, but I could've. I could *not* have tipped over that tank, however."

"No. You couldn't have." He sounded almost dazed. Once more his gaze tracked over the various elements of vandalism in the small room, then he turned abruptly and met her at the door. "Nor do I believe you tore the legs off all those frogs. Come on. This place isn't safe."

Taking her arm, he steered her out of the doorway and down the hall toward the elevator. "For all we know, your friend is hiding out in Poe's lab, and I don't like it that security's not down here yet. That tank had to make quite a boom when it fell, so even if the surveillance cameras didn't— Well, no matter. You'll be safer elsewhere."

They stopped in front of the elevator, and he punched the single Up button. The doors opened immediately. But as he started to guide her into the car, she pulled free of him and stepped back, forcing him to turn and face her.

"If security's not down here yet, shouldn't we call them?" she demanded. "I mean, if their systems are down, and he *is* in Poe's lab, they might still catch him."

"We'll go straight up to security, if you like," he said. "But right now we need to get out of here. We have no idea where that nut case has gone, and someone who can do the things he has done is not to be trifled with."

With that he convinced her. She stepped into the elevator and he followed closely, slapping the One button for the security station as he entered. The elevator's doors rumbled closed and the car lurched upward, stopping moments later, one floor up.

But when the doors slid open onto the security center, Lacey stood motionless, staring past an empty waiting area to the receiving desk, where a young female officer sat reading a paperback book. Behind her stretched a roomful of desks and computer screens, most of them unmanned. From all appearances, it was a quiet, uneventful night.

Reinhardt had said there were surveillance cameras in the AnFac. Surely if they were down, someone would have noticed. And he was right about the boom of the tank falling. Even if they couldn't see it, even if audio transmitters were out, only one floor up they'd have heard it with their ears and felt it in the trembling of the floor. Shouldn't *someone* have come to investigate? *Especially* if their surveillance feeds were down?

*How could they not know what happened! Last night they were all over it!*

For the first time in hours she returned to her thoughts of a cover-up. In that vein, she could all too easily imagine how things would go should she approach the desk. How she'd tell the pretty blond officer that she'd seen the same intruder tonight as she'd hallucinated last night during her fit of hysterics.

This time there was the tank and the frogs, of course. But last time there'd been her wound and the destruction of Poe's lab. . . . Maybe they'd just been waiting for her and Reinhardt to leave and were even now down there cleaning everything up. . . .

If she told the girl her story, they'd no doubt hustle her down to the clinic again, claiming there was nothing on their surveillance cameras. Maybe they'd even blame her for the tank and the frogs. Hysteria sometimes gave people extraordinary strength—and given her record, who would be surprised if she were to jerk the legs off all the frogs?

By the time the desk officer looked up, Lacey had talked herself out of making any sort of report and, avoiding eye contact, reached to push the Two button, which would take them up to the main floor lobby.

"I thought you were living in the tech dorm on floor B1," Reinhardt said as the doors closed.

"I am," she said quietly. "But I can't go back there right now." Thinking about being trapped in that tiny underground, windowless room sent a wave of claustrophobic-tinged terror rattling through her. She realized now that it was a good thing she'd been sedated at the clinic last night, because she'd never have been able to sleep otherwise. As would certainly be the case tonight. . . . Unless she took a couple of those sleeping pills the clinic psychiatrist had given her. *Or maybe I'll just doze on a bench somewhere until dawn. Or head up to Prep and Supply to get a head start on the autoclaving.*

The south service elevator opened directly into the Madrona Lounge, which was located on the main floor, tucked away behind the great atrium and welcoming lobby. Intended for faculty, it was generally off-limits to the public.

She crossed the small elevator lobby and entered the lounge which, at two in the morning, was dark and deserted. Smallish round tables attended by plastic molded chairs filled the carpeted room, a few illumined by overhead security lights, most of them shrouded in shadow. Potted ficus and metal cactus sculptures stood at intervals around the space, which was bounded on the south by a wall of windows. Outside, more tables crowded a small balcony, beyond which a decorative balustrade held back the night, where only a few tiny grounds lights flickered in the darkness.

A coffee bar stretched along the room's east end, steeped in darkness save for the red lights of the automatic dispenser. The bar would open for business at 6:00 a.m.—and, yes, K-J employees had to pay—but for now it stood quiet and deserted, its curved glass cases empty except for a few bran muffins and crumbling pieces of leftover baklava.

To the west a wide hallway passed meeting and storage rooms on its way to intersect the main floor's central north-south corridor.

Reinhardt came up beside her. "What are we doing here, Ms. McHenry?"

"I don't know. I just . . ." She scanned the room, then turned to look up at him. He wore a blue plaid flannel shirt over T-shirt and jeans, his security keycard dangling on a blue lanyard from his neck. A faint red-gold grizzle gleamed on his cheeks, and behind his glasses, shadows cupped his eyes. In the dim light, he looked tired and more boyish than she remembered. Instead of the vaunted Dr. Reinhardt, or the absentminded geek, he seemed just a normal man.

"Did you see him at all?" she asked.

His eyes, which had been sweeping the room as if he expected an attack at any moment, came back to her. He didn't have to ask whom she meant. "No. But I heard someone running and the door slam. And when I came around the corner, you were still in the frog room with the door open. . . ."

She held his gaze soberly. "I didn't tip over that tank."

"I know." He drew a deep breath and let it out. "Why don't you tell me what did happen?"

So she did, though there wasn't much to tell he'd not already seen. "You'd back me up, then?" she asked when she was finished. "If I went down and reported this?"

"Of course. Though I don't think it would do much good."

She recalled their conversation earlier in the day, when she'd stopped by his office and he'd refused to acknowledge last night's events, and abruptly knew why she had come up here. "We need to talk."

He grimaced. "In that case, I'll need some coffee. Shall I get you some, too?"

"No, thanks."

She followed him to the machine and watched as he filled the paper cup, then added sugar but no creamer. She liked his hands—strong, well-formed, capable. He picked up the cup and led her to the table nearest the wall that framed the great window and sat down with his back to it, facing the room.

She settled beside him rather than across from him, and they sat in silence while he sipped his coffee and kept his eyes on the room.

Presently she said, "You lied to me, Doctor. You sat there in your office today and flat-out *lied* to me! You, the supposedly honorable, virtuous Christian!"

He grimaced but made no effort to defend himself. "I sin like everyone else, Ms. McHenry," he said, eyes dropping to the cup on the table before him, cupped by both hands. "I just happen to have the liberty of being able to confess it afterward." His eyes came back to hers. "And the situation is . . . more complicated than you know."

"Naturally," she said bitterly. "It's always complicated for everyone but the victim."

A crease formed between his pale brows. He looked more concerned than angry. "I'm not lying now, Ms. McHenry. I'm as much an unwitting—and *unwilling*—participant as you are. All they've really told me is that I'm not to talk to you about any of it."

She frowned, startled by his bluntness. "Why not?"

"Because I said I wouldn't lie to you. Because they hoped, with our cooperation it would all blow over. I'm sure they still do." He paused. "You must know how paranoid Director Swain is about drawing unwanted media attention. Especially now with the *Nature* article and the open house and review board coming up. It would be better for both of us if you'd let me escort you back to your room."

"You're going to hang me out to dry like everyone else? Just let them do this?"

"No one's hanging you out to dry. Director Swain assured me you have nothing to worry about. He has no intention of allowing this incident to derail the plans he has for you."

Dr. Viascola, she recalled, had also mentioned the existence of plans for her. She wasn't sure she liked that. "What sort of plans?"

"He didn't specify. I'm sure it has to do with promoting you." He paused. "You're a very attractive woman, Ms. McHenry. And bright, as well. If you play your cards right, you could easily go right to the top of this organization."

She stared at him blankly, trying to find the logic in his statement. Then it hit her. "You mean have sex with him? That's disgusting! I would *never* do that, and you insult me by even suggesting it. And Director Swain, as well."

He sipped his coffee as his eyes did another circuit of the room. "I don't know you, Ms. McHenry, so I wasn't trying to insult you, only to point out the reality of the situation. I *do* know Director Swain. I find it surprising you could have worked here three weeks already and not heard of his appetite for pretty young women, and his willingness to reward them for their . . ." He paused, searching for the right word. "Cooperation."

She stared at him, indignantly. "I can't believe you would spread that vile rumor."

"I'd say at least half the women working in this facility would not consider my words vile at all, but would be thrilled the director had taken note of them."

"Well, I am not one of them." She folded her arms and glared at him.

"Which is why I advised you to leave K-J and go back to the U of A." His lips twitched as if to smile, but he covered it by sipping from his cardboard cup.

After a time she unfolded her arms and rested them on the table. "I can't afford the U of A," she said quietly. "I have too much debt. And how could I ever get another job if I quit K-J because I 'couldn't handle the stress'?"

"Your grades and honors and the recommendations in your file are exemplary. I don't think it would be that hard."

"I mean a good job. A position that would enhance my career, not stymie it."

"Maybe not right away, but . . . in time you'll find something. You have too much to offer not to." He paused. "And Swain's checkered past is well-known. His enemies are many and his misdeeds legendary. There are any number of folks who would not begrudge you your decision to leave. . . ." He trailed off, lost in his own train of thought.

Suddenly some of the things he'd said earlier registered in a new way—the fact Swain had assured *him* no ill would come to her implied they'd discussed the situation. And apparently Cameron Reinhardt had been the one defending her. He hadn't lied to her outright, either, merely evaded her questions and turned her statements back upon themselves. And hadn't he just claimed to be as unwilling a participant as she was? A sudden, grim suspicion struck her,

"Did Director Swain threaten you, Doctor?"

Reinhardt released a weary sigh. "Let's just say he outlined the situation for me. He has assets to protect, after all."

"And you're not one of them?"

He shrugged. "Depends on whether or not I cooperate. Which"—he glanced around—"as it turns out, I haven't. Not very well, anyway."

"You're uncomfortable here."

"We're alone in the middle of the night. And we're being watched. Probably listened to, as well."

"But they already know what happened and what we know—"

"Do they?"

"I thought you said . . ." She frowned. "So they don't, then?"

"I don't know." He started to say more, then closed his mouth and glanced around again. Finally he pushed back from the table. "I really think you would be safer in your room. This big window . . . Your assailant is probably watching us out there in the darkness."

That spooked her. "I don't think I can bear it in my room, though. With no real windows, there's only one way out."

"No window means he can't get in that way. And I suspect they have a camera on the corridor outside your door at the very least. Probably in the stairwells, too. And the elevators and lobbies are standard. He may not yet know where your room is. So far he's apparently only broken into the animal facility. Your end of it. Where the door to the patio is. To access the residence floors, he'd need a security key. On the other hand, if he knows he's scared you, and he must, then he might think to head up a floor and see if you're there."

Huffing out her breath, she agreed he was right and allowed him to escort her back down to B1, where he followed her out of the elevator, insisting on seeing her to her door.

"You do have a roommate, don't you?" he asked as the elevator doors rattled shut behind them. "And she's there now?"

"I expect so," she replied uneasily. "She was asleep when I left."

She preceded him down the dim-lit, narrow corridor, the squeak of their shoes on the vinyl flooring echoing eerily around them. Suddenly the floor's familiar musty smell and cramped warrenlike corridors reminded her just how far down in station she was from her escort. Yes, he already saw her as the frog girl, but having him escort her to her basement dormitory quarters seemed to bring it all home. She was glad when they finally reached her door.

"Make sure you lock the dead bolt once you get in," he said as they stopped before it. The solemnity in his tone sent a shiver up her spine.

She stood looking up at him. "I'm sorry to keep you up so late, but thank you for staying with me."

"I'm just glad you're okay."

"Except for my reputation."

He shrugged. "At least you can take comfort in the likelihood that, after what happened tonight, you'll not be assigned to the AnFac anymore. Do you have your keycard?"

She pulled it out from under her lab coat where it hung on its lanyard and swiped it through the reader. The light blinked, the locking mechanism clicked, and she depressed the latch in silence, then turned to look up at him again. "If I leave this untrue accusation unchallenged, I'll have a black mark on my record for the rest of my life."

He grimaced. "Well, you certainly wouldn't be the first to have that problem."

"It's not fair."

"No." Some tiny sound drew his startled glance back down the hall; then he drew a deep breath and let it out, gray eyes coming back to meet her gaze. "I don't know what to tell you, Ms. McHenry," he said finally. "I don't like this any more than you do, but it's how things are. . . ." He leaned past her to push open the door, murmuring as he did so, "And all the walls here have ears. Don't forget that."

With that, he straightened, gave her a brusque "Good night," and walked back toward the elevators. She stared after him, chilled by his reminder. Her hand tugged the lab coat closer about her, and then she realized . . . "Doctor . . . I still have your coat."

He lifted a hand in dismissal and called back over his shoulder: "Leave it in the AnFac. I'll find it. And don't forget to lock your dead bolt."

She watched him until he stepped around the corner into the elevator's lobby and out of sight, then turned with a sigh and entered her darkened room. As the door snicked shut behind her, she wrapped her arms around herself and sagged back against the wood, where she was overcome with a fit of violent shaking.

Indignation tangled itself with dismay and frustration and a horrible sense of anxiety. The walls had ears? Surveillance cameras on the animal floors? And now in the corridor outside her room? What had she gotten involved in? How could what had seemed so golden an opportunity have turned so swiftly to such a convoluted disaster?

Maybe she should resign and give it up as Dr. Reinhardt advised.

But if she did . . . it would be the end. Her years of education lost. All that money spent, the loans she still had to pay back. Selling books would keep her in debt until she was an old, old woman.

"Oh, Lord . . ." she moaned, burying her face in her hands. "What am I to do?"

The only good she could see coming out of this would be if Reinhardt's prediction came true—that she never had to go to the animal floor again.

# Chapter Fourteen

The *rat-tat-tat* of automatic-weapon fire echoed sharply down the narrow crawl tube as Cam reached the hole in the ceiling at its end and pulled himself upward and over the lip. Gathering his feet beneath him, he looked up and froze. Parker Swain stood before him, wearing a white toga and a green camouflage military helmet. Behind him loomed one of the sarcophagi, a giant shadowy mound on a tiny cart that blinked with multifarious lights.

The sight startled him so badly it knocked him back into the hole— and out of the nightmare.

He sat blinking at the bars of too-bright light that lay across the green blanket covering his legs and struggled to figure out where he was. He took a deep gasping breath, then saw that the light was flooding in around the closed mini blinds on a window to his left. He was in his own bedroom in his suite at K-J, and he'd obviously overslept. Some three and half hours, a glance at the clock confirmed. It was just after 7:30. Which, seeing as he'd not gotten to bed until 3:30, was better than he'd planned. Better than Thursday night, as well.

As the terror birthed by his nightmare faded along with its images, grogginess flowed into its place and he collapsed back in the bed to stare at the ceiling. He didn't want to get up, but if he stayed here he'd miss breakfast.

*Do I care about breakfast?* His torpor had increased by now to the point of having almost physical force, as if a lead-filled blanket lay upon him. Everything felt wrong, and he dreaded what lay ahead of him this day.

It was all coming back to him now—Rudy, his claims about Swain and the sarcophagi, the anomalous blood report; Lacey McHenry's second encounter with the mysterious frog-eating intruder; Cam's own timely arrival in the animal facility to deliver her; the apparent obliviousness of Campus Security to the whole thing; his subsequent conversation with McHenry in the deserted Madrona Lounge, which he'd entered into in direct and deliberate disobedience to Swain's instructions. . . .

Now rising anger simmered it all into a stew of toxic thoughts and feelings. He felt as if he'd had the rug pulled out from under him— here, he'd made all the right decisions, sought God's counsel, believed he had been following God's will, all those years of being faithful in learning the Word and applying it, and this was how he was rewarded? He'd been manipulated and betrayed, prodded like a rodeo bull into a bucking chute so he could perform for someone else's pleasure a task at which he'd already failed miserably once.

And it was all wasted effort on their part, because he could not do what Rudy asked of him. Aside from the fact he was unwilling to deceive and betray the very people he'd come here hoping to give the gospel to, he was not physically, mentally, or emotionally capable of meeting the challenge this mission presented. His mind was already half unraveled as it was. Just the word *sarcophagi* turned his guts to water.

But if he couldn't do what Rudy asked of him, he also couldn't stay at Kendall-Jakes. Not knowing Swain was dirty. Not given the active cover-up Cam had already become entangled in. *"He's playing with fire,"* Rudy had said.

After their meeting by the lake last night, Cam had gone to the gym and run through multiple sets of his weight-training regimen as he'd planned his escape. His biweekly leave was coming up tomorrow—and he intended to make full use of it. He'd drive to Tucson, as usual, collect as much cash as he could from various ATMs before ditching his credit cards and Jeep, then board the first available bus out of town. It didn't matter where it went—Flagstaff, Vegas, Las Cruces, LA, even Mexico would work. In fact, the more random it was the better.

He had only to make it through this one last day without arousing anyone's suspicions of his intent, because he was fairly sure neither Swain nor Rudy would let him bolt.

At 8:20 he finally had enough energy to get out of bed, past time to make it to breakfast. Unhurried, he shaved, showered, pulled on jeans and a T-shirt, and went down to the animal facility. He wasn't surprised to find the frogs gone, the tank drained of water but returned to its upright position, and an orange pylon with a *Wet Paint* sign positioned in the doorway. All four walls boasted a fresh coat of peach paint, the frog eater's message completely obscured.

From the frog room, he went to his auxiliary lab at the hall's end, where the twenty frogs to which he'd administered a vaporized retro-virus yesterday still crouched undisturbed in their ten-gallon aquariums, all of them with legs intact. Looking at them gave him a pang of regret. He'd developed a genuine love for his chosen field these past ten years, and he'd miss it.

After half an hour's work, putting things to order and getting rid of things he preferred others not find, he headed up to Lab 500, reaching his glass-walled office just as Gen Viascola did.

"We missed you at breakfast," she said.

"I was up late last night."

"So I hear." Now her tone took a suggestive lilt. "Your little tryst with Lacey McHenry is the talk of the morning."

He frowned but said nothing. He'd known last night that it wouldn't matter what he and Ms. McHenry did; the fact they were there alone together would be sufficient to set the rumor mill in motion. All it would take was one security guard spotting them, and unless he was ordered to keep his mouth shut, the tales would fly.

"I'm surprised you got any sleep at all," Viascola said.

His frown became a scowl. "Why are you here, Gen?"

Now she pretended to pout. "I merely bring good news. We've transferred Manny. Here's his replacement. As per your request." She handed him Lacey McHenry's folder and strutted away on her six-inch heels.

Stunned to motionlessness, he stared after her until she disappeared around the corner. Then, as his lab techs began to trickle in, he turned and walked into his office. Kicking the door shut behind him, he opened the folder with genuine dismay.

He'd known they'd move McHenry off the animal floor after last night, but the last thing he expected was to have her assigned to him. And Swain himself had approved her reassignment—his signature was right there at the bottom of her promotion notice.

Well, this was going to be awkward. At least he had only a day of it to weather.

He came around his desk, laying McHenry's file atop the other folders and papers as he moved the mouse to awaken his computer. Then he settled into his chair and went back to paging through McHenry's file. He was peripherally aware of his desktop appearing on the screen, but it was a few moments before he noticed the little blue square blinking at the lower right-hand corner. Frowning, he reached again for the mouse and clicked on the unfamiliar icon.

At once a small window opened, asking for a password. He typed in the Golf-Zero number Rudy had given him. A new window appeared, an opening program he didn't know, which eventually resolved into a DNA profile, labeled *Anomalous Blood Sample*, complete with a summary text of the analysis.

He glanced away from the screen to the USB port at the side of the machine where a gray flash drive had been inserted, hidden by the piles of papers from the sight of anyone except the person sitting in Cam's chair.

Since he was leaving tomorrow, this information didn't concern him, but curiosity compelled him to read it anyway. According to the summary, the DNA did not match any they had on file. Furthermore, the blood chemistry registered a high white-blood-cell count, indicating a widespread systemic infection, probably viral. There was also the presence of unidentified proteins. The author speculated these might be contaminants from the collection process, but even so found the mysterious nature of these proteins to be "provocative."

Well, he understood now why it was labeled anomalous, and it was not at all what he'd thought. When Rudy had said they thought Swain might have sarcophagi . . .

His pulse fluttered and his mouth went dry. The memories were right there. All he need do was open the door in his mind and they'd come pouring out.

*No. Once was enough. Once was far too much. I can't do it again. . . .* He dropped his head in his hands and closed his eyes, breathing deeply and slowly through his mouth.

Scriptures rose to the surface of his mind. . . . *Greater is He who is in you, than he who is in the world . . . I can do all things through Christ . . . He will never leave you or forsake you . . . When I am weak, then I am strong, for His power is perfected in weakness. . . .*

He caught his breath and sat very still. Felt his heart slamming against his breastbone. Heard his pulse rushing in his ears. *Maybe this is not about what you can do, Cam. Maybe it's about Him. Maybe that's why He brought you here: to show you that.*

His mind backed away from those thoughts as if they were a virulent poison, a fiery furnace, a death sentence.

*And what's so bad about death, anyway? You'd be with Him. Or do you really not believe any of this stuff you've been studying all these years?*

The question hung in his mind, a grim indictment. He did believe. Sometimes. But at other times, like Paul, he was a miserable, wretched man. He who presumed to bring the gospel to these unbelievers . . .

*There is now no condemnation in Christ, Cameron.*

*What does that have to do with anything? Go away. I won't stay. I won't do this again.*

*If not you, who?*

Horror and denial welled up in him, and again the dark memories threatened to break free of their prison. *You know you can find someone else, Lord. You could take care of it yourself, for that matter.*

*But I am calling you to be my vessel.*

"Dr. Reinhardt?" The voice pierced his thoughts.

He dropped his hands and lifted his head. Lacey McHenry stood holding his office door slightly open, as if she feared to enter. He stared at her blankly, pulling his mind out of the darkness and into the now.

"You didn't appear to hear my knock," she added, giving him an odd look, "and they said I should report to you. . . ."

He shook off his distress and waved her in. "Yes, I just found out about your transfer myself. Come in."

He clicked the Alt and F4 keys, closing the window, wondering if he'd ever be able to access it again, or if the file would self-destruct upon closing. Probably the latter.

"Dr. Viascola said you asked for me specifically?"

He heard the notes of disbelief and uneasiness in her tone, and felt his face flush. Having gone to breakfast, she'd have suffered far more from the rumors regarding their actions in the Madrona Lounge than he had. "Yesterday after the unity meeting I suggested to her that you might make a suitable replacement for Dr. Espinosa. She turned me down, though. Apparently she changed her mind."

"Because of last night?" McHenry asked softly.

"She just said she'd reconsidered my request. Of course that's all she *could* say. Did the guy from ASU get here?"

"I don't think so. Everyone says they've sent Manny Espinosa down to the AnFac in my place."

Well, Cam had asked for that, too. And someone did have to take care of the animals. It was just that he suspected the frog eater would be back and would not be happy to find Espinosa in McHenry's place. But then, security had to suspect that, too. Surely they'd take care of things. . . .

Outside the glass walls of his office the lab techs and postdocs had arrayed themselves at their various cubicles and stations about the lab, nearly all of them gawking openly at the meeting going on in Cam's office. He frowned, and thought of going out to tell them all to get to work and mind their own business.

"So why *did* you ask for me," McHenry pressed, "if it wasn't . . . ?"

He looked around at her, and she trailed off, cheeks flushing, and he was struck anew by how appealing she was becoming. Every time he saw her, she seemed to grow prettier, and he couldn't deny the element of pleasure with which he contemplated having her stationed right outside his office. When she blushed and lowered her eyes like that, the dark wisps of hair curling along her soft cheeks and down the graceful neck, he could hardly pull his gaze away.

She shifted her weight and glanced up at him again. His flush of embarrassment heated as he leaned back in the chair and sought to make himself return to business.

"Why did I ask for you? I had your file yesterday, remember? I skimmed your master's thesis. Quite impressive. It was ridiculous they had you picking dead frogs out of a tank and autoclaving glassware when you could be doing real work. Especially when I've got a mound of studies that need examining."

And now he was saying way too much, way too defensively. Desperately he stopped himself and gestured toward the cubicle that stood just outside the office's glass door, all its flat surfaces piled with file folders. "It's all on Manuel's desk out there." He paused. "Well, your desk now, I guess." He smiled awkwardly, then tore his gaze away and turned his attention to the screen to open his *To Do* file for the day before he embarrassed himself further.

And still she didn't leave. Finally he glanced up at her. "Was there something else?"

"I was just wondering in what light, exactly, you want me to evaluate them?"

"Oh. Yes. Sorry. The overall project objective is to search for a genetic aging mechanism related to telomere reductions. But I suppose you should read the project proposal first. And the abstracts of all the research we're currently doing. It's on Manny's computer. You should be able to find it easily. Once you're familiar with what we're after, you can go through the folders of studies and note which ones have relevance to our objectives. Which ones we might want to replicate, or replicate with changes . . . With citations, of course." He frowned at her. "You *do* know what I'm talking about, right?"

"Of course. I'm compiling relevant studies from the literature. When did you want my report by?"

"When? When you're done, of course." He turned his gaze back to his computer screen and used the keyboard to call up a display of the gel readouts from Thursday.

She left him then and made her way to her new desk. He watched her surreptitiously over the top of his computer screen. The folders weren't merely piled upon the desk itself but ranged around the chair on the floor, for Manny had made little headway, considering such grunt work beneath him.

She spent a few moments looking around the station, opening drawers and paging through the folders. Then she turned to the computer and opened the document containing the proposal and abstracts, a fact that presented itself in a small box in the upper corner of his own screen.

As she settled in to work, he sought to do likewise—and found it an exercise in futility. He couldn't focus for longer than five minutes. If his mind wasn't drifting back to his plans for tomorrow, his eye was straying to his newest research assistant, and dredging up new waves of guilt with which to torment himself. Should he ask her to come with him into Tucson tomorrow? Alone, perhaps he could explain. . . .

But hadn't he already advised her to leave? And if she didn't, wasn't that her prerogative? And her choice to live with the consequences?

Except she had no idea what the consequences might be. Even he didn't know. . . .

At length, dragging eyes and mind away from her for the umpteenth time, he picked up one of the files on his desk and swiveled his chair around to face the bookcase behind him, then forced himself to start reading the file's contents. He'd gotten through two pages when the sound of his office door closing brought him back around; seeing who was there, he rocketed to his feet, papers from the file folder fluttering to the floor.

"Director Swain!" he exclaimed, alarm flooding him. "Good morning, sir."

"Good morning, Dr. Reinhardt," Swain said. "Just coming by to see how you're doing on that project of yours." He seemed completely at ease.

Cam regarded him warily. "Well, I'll have to order a new batch of frogs after last night," he said, bending to recover the dropped papers.

"Of course. Nelson tells me you're starting to see results, though. That you went through the first batch's livers yesterday."

Cam nodded, still on guard but playing along. "They all showed a remarkable vitality and almost complete freedom from disease or degeneration."

"So the f43 gene might have application?"

"It might, sir. . . ."

Swain nodded and turned to glance around the lab, his eye catching on Lacey McHenry outside the office. "Your new staff member has arrived."

"Yes, sir."

Swain chuckled. "I still can't believe you sent our Rhodes scholar to the AnFac."

"Your signature was on the transfer, sir," Cam pointed out.

"I was merely being accommodating." Swain's gaze came back to him. "Besides, it's safer for her this way."

"I'm not so sure, sir. Have you caught the guy who broke in yet?"

"Don't worry about him."

"A man who can turn a five-hundred-gallon steel tank full of water over with bare hands? Who can penetrate locked doors and leave them locked behind him?"

"It's not what it appears."

"Then what is it?"

Swain ignored the question. "What I find interesting is how *you* keep showing up at the same time he does."

Cameron said nothing, at a loss as to where his employer could be going with this but feeling like a mouse stalked by a serpent.

"Thanks to the intermittent function of the cameras," Swain went on, turning back toward the office door, "no one but Ms. McHenry there has seen him. Maybe he's you."

"You think *I* could turn over that tank?"

"Not with your own hands, no. But you're a clever man." His gaze held on Ms. McHenry for several moments while Cam wrestled with the insinuations in Swain's statement. Insinuations which made no sense, but which seemed to be threatening in a way he could not discern.

"So how is she working out for you?"

Cameron followed the direction of his gaze. Uneasiness slithered into his belly. "She only started this morning. It's a little too early to tell."

"Really?" Swain's voice dripped sarcasm, and for the first time Cam realized the tone of the meeting had gradually changed. The easy cheer had vanished, replaced by a subtle parry and riposte.

Outside the glass-walled office, McHenry had gotten up to move a pile of folders off the desk onto the floor, then move another off the floor and onto the desk. Now she stood stretching her arms and shoulder muscles, unaware of Swain's scrutiny.

"She's quite an attractive girl, isn't she?" the director said. "I can see why you'd want her here. Nice figure. Trim, athletic. I bet she jogs."

Cameron returned his attention to the folder on his desk, dismayed by the level of annoyance he felt that Swain would speak of her so. Annoyed with himself, as well, for his strong reaction to Swain's words.

Swain turned to him now. "Do you know?"

"Know what?"

"If she jogs?"

"I doubt it," Cam said.

Swain was looking at him with those snake's eyes again. "Because you'd have seen her if she did?"

"Most likely. Certainly *you* would have." He thought of Swain watching her through his ninth-floor telescope and scowled.

"Yes, I'm sure I would have." Swain smiled at him—a knowing, salacious sort of smile that only increased Cam's irritation. And was intended to.

"By the way," Swain said, "I want to thank you for seeking to convey to her last night my intentions regarding her career here." His voice was cool and calm, but it sent a shiver down Cam's spine.

When Cam did not reply or even look up at him, Swain added softly, "Did you hope to scare her off with your clumsy and disgusting allegations? If so, you clearly don't know her very well." He paused. "Or me."

When Cam held silent, he asked, "What? Not even an apology?"

"I told you I wouldn't lie to her, sir."

Swain snorted. "You did considerably more than 'not lie' to her, son. And I told *you* I'd guard my assets."

"That was before your mysterious intruder heaved over the frog tank with his bare hands. And tore all the legs off my frogs. It seemed ludicrous to pretend I couldn't see any of it. Besides, she's not going to make a report. You cut that avenue off firmly enough."

"I preferred to have her think she imagined it all."

"Why?"

"Because then she would stay out of it. We intended to transfer her all along. Things just didn't work out the way we'd hoped."

"Well, I'm not sure how much good the change will do now, seeing as that lunatic has conceived a warped infatuation with her. You must have heard her say he'd done all that for her."

Swain stiffened and looked at him sharply. "No. I didn't."

Cam frowned at him. "What happened down there last night, sir? I only saw what was done. Not how. Not who."

But the director claimed to know little more than Cam in that regard. With the cameras malfunctioning, Ms. McHenry was still the only one who'd actually seen the man. The security detail, having been earlier deployed across campus, had not arrived until nearly an hour after the tank was overturned.

"Your intruder set up a distraction to draw them off?"

"So it seems."

"And the tank?"

"We don't know how he did it," Swain said. But he watched closely, as if he thought maybe Cam did know. When Cam said nothing, Swain shrugged and went back to assuring him they were taking care of things.

When Cam only frowned at him, he turned his gaze again to Ms. McHenry, seated now at her desk, and smiled that slight, predacious smile of his. Then he faced Cam again, addressing him with a crisp, businesslike tone. "I'm holding a security meeting tomorrow afternoon in my office. Since you're so interested, perhaps you'd like to attend. In fact, I'd like your input. If you can make it, of course."

A security meeting. That was exactly the sort of invitation Rudy would want Cam to leap on. And one, given recent events, Cam would love to attend. But after nine months of shutting him out of such things, and not fifteen minutes after rebuking him for his "clumsy and disgusting allegations," why was Swain inviting him now, the very day before Cam planned to leave for good? *Is this bait to get me to stay?*

But how could Swain know his plans? Yes, he had written his resignation last night, but he'd done it in bed and used paper and ink, with only the dim illumination of the nightlight across the room. No camera could have picked up what he'd written.

Swain was staring at him intently, as if trying to read his thoughts.

"Is that an order?" Cam asked finally.

"Not at all. It's an invitation."

"You know I have the day off."

Swain tipped his head in acknowledgment. "And *you* know you can make it back early if it's important enough."

"Is Ms. McHenry going to be there?"

Swain snorted. "That would hardly be appropriate, given our goals."

"You just told me she's the only one who's seen this guy."

"We have surveillance records."

"I thought you said the cameras were out."

Swain's brow creased ever so slightly. "They were." The director shook his head. "You really should consider coming to our meditation sessions, Cameron. It would help you manage this paranoia that keeps interfering with your work."

"Paranoia, sir?" Cameron stared at him, derailed by the sudden change of subject.

"All this suspicion you harbor toward others, thinking they're lying or trying to hide something from you. You need to find some inner stability."

"Perhaps I do, sir. And thank you for the suggestion."

"But of course you'll decline." Swain grimaced. "So diplomatic. When the truth is, your Christian blood runs cold at the very thought of that evil meditation nonsense." He shook his head. "Whatever you Christians don't understand, you call evil."

"I never said it was evil."

"But you believe it is."

Cameron stared at him, hating the way the man persisted in his irritating game.

Swain chuckled and dropped it. "The security meeting starts at 4:00 p.m. tomorrow. My office." He paused. "You know my respect for you is such that I'll never willingly let you leave Kendall-Jakes. But it would be nice if, from time to time, you could at least *try* to seem as if you're beholden to me. Especially if you have any desire of advancing here."

He held Cam's gaze soberly a moment, then gave him a nod. "Now, if you'll excuse me, I think I'll conduct an impromptu departmental inspection. Rather like the review board committee will do." He stepped to the door, then turned back with an "Oh! Will I see you at my presentation tonight?"

"I've already attended one of your presentations, sir."

"Many of our associates enjoy attending subsequent sessions. I usually add some new twists, but even if I don't, they always pick out something they'd missed before. More importantly, they go away reinvigorated with the conviction that the goals we pursue here are profoundly important, not only to themselves but to all of humankind. Sometimes when things get difficult or confusing it's good to regain one's focus."

"I'm sure it is, sir. I don't have a ticket."

Swain arched his brows. "As a Black Box Fellow, you now have the privilege of attending anytime you wish. Just show your staff ID at the door." Swain gave him a big smile. "If you insist on skipping my meeting tomorrow, you'll go a long way toward assuaging my irritation by attending tonight."

With that he left the office and strolled along the back aisle, pausing to speak briefly to Jade Kemmer, where she worked at the end of one of the benches, then homing in on his target. Ms. McHenry looked up at him with that wide-eyed expression of surprise and wonder that was far too appealing for her own good. Though Cam could hear little of the conversation, their body language said it all.

Swain was charming, friendly, interested, careful not to come on too strong, but from Cam's point of view, obviously after her. McHenry was clearly overwhelmed, her elfin face so flushed with pleasure and embarrassment she glowed. And those eyes—huge and brown and innocent. When Cam had looked into them last night, tear-filled and pleading, he'd been smitten with the irrational desire to fold his arms around her and assure her everything would be all right—and then do all he could to make it so.

Now Swain leaned slightly over her desk as he spoke. She drew back in apparent surprise, seeming to stumble for words before finally saying yes. Smiling, he turned toward the mouth of the aisle where Jade worked, catching Cam watching him as he did. His smile widened ever so slightly and he wiggled his brows, then ambled down the first of the four lab bench aisles, where he stopped to talk to Lauren. Ms. McHenry stared after him in pleased disbelief. Another moment now and . . . yes, there was Ms. Kemmer, leaping up and hurrying to McHenry's cubicle.

Cam turned his eyes back to his monitor, intensely irritated. The strange vandal and ensuing cover-up were bad enough; now this blatant come-on by Swain? Of course he knew much of that performance had been for Cam, a mockery of the warning Cam himself had given the girl last night about Swain's "intentions regarding her career here." It might not mean anything at all.

He still didn't like it. He especially didn't like the way McHenry had gone all wide-eyed and breathless. And given what Rudy had told him last night, maybe it was only right he make at least one last attempt to persuade her of the danger here before he left.

Thus, just before lunch he called her into the office.

"I'm going into Tucson tomorrow," he informed her. "Would you like to come with me? I could drop you off at your church. Or your mother's house . . ."

She stared at him. "You know about my church?"

"It's in your file."

Distaste replaced her surprise. "Which you seem to have studied thoroughly. No, thank you, Doctor. I don't have leave."

He stared at her blankly, blindsided by the hostility of her rejection. Part of him knew he should nod and walk away. Instead he pressed her. "I could arrange leave for you." He couldn't, but it wouldn't matter once they were gone.

She fixed her gaze on the chair at his side, then took a deep breath and looked up with obvious reluctance. "Dr. Reinhardt, I'm grateful you requested me as a team member, but I want to be very clear that the only thing you're going to get from me in return is the very best work I can give on the project."

And now, finally, it dawned on him how his invitation had sounded. His face burned furiously and for a moment words failed him. Then, "Your very best work is all I'd ever ask of you, Ms. McHenry. I merely thought you might . . . want to get away for a bit."

"I have a morning tennis match," she said. "After that, I'd like some time to myself." She paused. "Frankly, given what happened last night and the way everyone is talking, I can't believe you even asked me this."

With that she turned and walked out, then kept going past her cubicle and on to the main hall. He stared after her—befuddled, embarrassed, frustrated, and wondering how he could have been so obtuse he'd not once considered how any invitation to spend private time with him this weekend was going to come across.

Worse was the belated realization that every technician and postdoc in the place had been watching them—and watched him still. Face flaming, he returned to the work on his desk and resigned himself to getting a sandwich from one of the vending machines in the lab lounge. Tomorrow couldn't come soon enough.

# Chapter Fifteen

## New Eden

Zowan lay on the hard mattress of his railed infirmary bed and stared at the canopy of translucent plastic sheeting overhead. Stretching from a central fastening point, it draped over the four poles at each corner of his bed, then down on every side to isolate him from his caregivers, lest the toxins that had penetrated his body during the wind surge contaminate them, as well. The clear plastic tubing of an IV set snaked away from the needle in his left wrist and out through a well sealed hole in the plastic, feeding fluids and nutrients into him as he lay there. Through the translucent sheeting, he saw the blurry shape of the fluid bag on its stanchion and the fuzzy lights of a monitor beside it. Those regular beeps must be timed to his heart—he felt the monitor's electrodes stuck to his chest.

The plastic sheeting let in enough light to reveal the shadowy forms of infirmary personnel occasionally moving around his bed. A small clear plastic window in the tenting to his left allowed them to look in on him if they chose to, but so far, no one had.

He'd been outside with the goats when a toxic wind had blown in, and he'd been taken to the infirmary for an immediate injection of anti-toxin medication, followed by an intensive decontamination regimen: they'd buzzed off his hair, washed his body with both chemicals and water, then blasted him with hot ionized air, and dressed him in a special neutralizing cotton tunic. By then his lungs and eyes had started to burn and his head was pounding.

They'd left him in the decontamination chamber, where Dr. Xavier and another man had questioned him through a window about his experiences in the ravine just before the wind had swooped in. Had he felt strange? Heard voices? Smelled or seen anything unusual? He'd told them of the man on the hill above him right before the wind surged, and they pressed him for details, though he had precious few to give.

By then he was alternating between sweating and shaking as the toxins took effect, despite the medication they'd given him. When the vomiting had begun, the questioning stopped. Not long after that, the diarrhea struck, and thereafter he'd grown increasingly weak and disoriented until all devolved into a miasma of watery blackness.

He'd awakened lying on this narrow bed in this dim-lit pocket of plastic-tented privacy, wondering if it wasn't the toxins but the anti-toxin medication that was making him sick. He'd felt fine before they'd given it to him, and it had burned fiercely going in. Within fifteen minutes he'd noticed the burning in his eyes, then the headache, and finally the pain and constriction in his lungs. He'd never actually seen anyone in the throes of untreated surface poisoning, the victims always administered anti-toxin medication and quarantine before the onset of symptoms.

He'd never even seen one of the goats struck down with it, yet every time he was exposed, by the time he got out of quarantine, the entire flock had been slaughtered. Why not give them the anti-toxin meds too? Weren't they supposed to be the hardier species?

Most disturbing of all was the fact that each of the three times he'd been exposed, he'd felt just fine until they'd given him that shot that was supposed to make him better. The more he considered it, the more reasonable his theory became. And what had Gaias and his five Enforcer buddies been doing out there, anyway? They'd done nothing to help him or the goats. So far as he could recall, they'd simply disappeared.

And why send six Enforcers to rescue Zowan and the goats, anyway? Usually they sent no one, the Klaxons alone enough to get everyone inside. Of course, usually the Klaxons sounded at the first indication

THE ENCLAVE — 151

from outlying sensors that a surge was on the way. This time, the wind had practically been upon them when the alarms had sounded. Why was that? Had the sensors malfunctioned?

The questions and attempted rationales tumbled through his mind until they snarled into oblivion and he closed his eyes, too weary to hold on to his train of thought. His head still hurt, though far less than it had, and his lungs ached dully. He wondered if this time the toxins might have finally done some long-term damage as the safety manuals warned—damage to his lungs, skin, or eyes; loss of his teeth; the development of a fatal—or merely grotesque—mutation. What if even now the beginnings of a third eye bulged from his forehead? The notion terrified him. When he finally forced himself to lift exploratory fingers to his brow and found nothing, he relaxed, realizing that was a crazy thought. Toxins didn't produce the eye. The Breath of the Father did.

Some time later the face of Dr. Xavier appeared in the clear plastic window. He had big rabbit teeth, sunken cheeks, bushy brows, and a thatch of strawlike blond hair sprouting from the top of his head. "Ah, you've awakened." His rubbery visage vanished as he checked the fluid bag on its stanchion, then reappeared. "How do you feel?"

"Worse by far than when I came in here."

Dr. Xavier snorted. "You're lucky to be alive, young man. The toxin levels outside were ten times the acceptable amount. External sensors registered the wind but not the toxins until it was right on us. You got a full blast. If you'd not been wearing your suit, you'd have died on the spot. If the Enforcers hadn't gotten you out as fast as they did, you'd be dead now."

But the Enforcers hadn't gotten him out. . . . "Where are those Enforcers, anyway?" Zowan asked. "Did they all make it back in?"

Xavier frowned. "Of course."

"You aren't treating them?"

Xavier didn't answer but stepped again out of Zowan's view. He felt a tug at the IV in his arm. "What are you doing?" he asked, vaguely alarmed.

"Just releasing your next dose of anti-toxin medication."

"No!" Zowan cried, recalling his suspicions about the medications. "I don't want any more."

Dr. Xavier's face reappeared in the plastic window, brows arched in surprise. "Zowan, your toxin levels spiked to one hundred percent over the normal limit. . . ."

"I don't want any more meds. They're making me sick."

Xavier's bushy brows drew down into a frown and his thick lips tightened. "The *toxin exposure* is making you sick."

"I wasn't sick until you gave me the meds!" The strength of his voice in accusation startled even Zowan.

Xavier's face cleared to blandness and his voice became soothing. "Why would you think such a thing, Zowan? I only want to help you. And you are not out of danger yet. Without these medications you will have no protection."

"They're making me sick—"

"It's the poison affecting your brain."

Zowan felt a burning run up his arm and into his shoulder. Fear electrified him, filling him with the certainty that they were going to kill him. He was the one who had spread the blasphemous thoughts to Andros, and they must have found out. Maybe they'd heard those conversations in the Star Garden. Now they would make him pay for his treacherous words and remove the cancer of doubt that was him from their midst.

With all his strength he sought to hurl himself upright. But he only got as far as his elbows, for his wrists were bound to the bed rails. So were his ankles.

He collapsed back on the mattress, aghast to realize tears were streaming from his eyes. He looked at Dr. Xavier. "Why are you doing this?"

Xavier regarded him sympathetically. "I'm sorry, Zowan. One of the side effects of your exposure is the paranoia. If you can't manage it, we'll have to sedate you."

"No!" The fear came rushing back, and he strained anew at his bonds, shouting imprecations at Dr. Xavier, who stood in the window watching him with sad eyes—and then dissolved into a column of smoke that somehow seeped in around the sealed edges of Zowan's IV tube, filling his small chamber with darkness. It pressed him into the bed, though he fought it with everything he had—gasping, choking under the weight of it, panicked at the notion it was trying to smother him. . . .

His thoughts scattered, remembering an afternoon in the Star Garden with Terra where he'd wanted so badly to take her hand, and hadn't, for fear of Gaias. The Star Garden was replaced by the grotto and the goats. Then a faint clicking. He turned to the rock wall and found the pale face of his bald brother staring at him through a little plastic window, the obscene third eye thankfully lidded.

"You're lucky you didn't kill yourself climbing up that cliff," Gaias said.

"What cliff?"

"The one I told you to come down from." Gaias frowned at him. "You don't recall?"

"It was just a steep slope. And I don't recall you telling me to come down."

"Why were you up there, anyway?"

"I saw someone. How did you get back into the Enclave?"

"Who did you see?"

Zowan turned his face away, annoyed. "I don't know."

"I don't think you saw anyone. I think you're lying. Trying to make trouble. Sow doubts. You're a rebel at heart, Zowan. And you know what happens to rebels. . . ."

Zowan stared at the plastic sheeting overhead.

"A pity about Andros dying."

The words wrenched Zowan's head around. *"What?!"*

"The Cube killed him. He couldn't handle the pressure. But he always was a weakling."

"You're lying! He's not dead!"

"He is. And it's all your fault."

The plastic window filled with the smoke again, and Gaias vanished.

Andros dead? Yes, he'd only been in the Cube once, but he was thin and weak and emotionally fragile. And the punishment had been near the highest intensity. It was possible. . . . Crushing grief surged through him, and he began to weep. *Oh, Andros, why did you have to refuse to say that Affirmation?* Guilt cut him alongside the grief. If only he'd kept his doubts to himself.

For some time he rode the heavy black-oil waves of mourning and self-recrimination. Then he began to wonder if Gaias had said those things just to make him hurt. He heard bells, men talking quietly, the Klaxon again . . . then a chime and the soft female voice alerting the New Edenites that the morning Affirmation would begin in half an hour. It must be Saturday morning. . . .

The sweet, haunting melody of the singing bowls and harps wrapped around him comfortingly. Then a choir burst into song: *"He is Father, He who saved us. Raise your voices loud and strong; Raise your voices thanking Him. Raise your voices to Him. . . ."* The God of the Genesis . . . who had made everything and saw that it was good. Who'd promised that the seed of the woman would crush the seed of the serpent. Who'd destroyed the whole world with a flood of water. *Raise your voices to Him. . . .*

Smoke rose around him again. Successive melodies wheedled through his consciousness. He heard snatches of the Affirmation as it was offered.

Suddenly Andros's voice intruded, pleading with him from a long way off, begging him to come and release him from the dark place they had put him in. *"It's your fault I'm in this place, Zowan. You owe it to me. You've got to come and let me out."*

Zowan puzzled over the words. Was Andros still in the Cube? How could Zowan let him out of that?

*Zowan.* Now a new voice spoke, different from the others. Quiet, even . . . but radiating authority and vast power.

Andros spoke again, frantically seeking to draw Zowan's notice back to him, but the new voice had captured his attention, galvanizing everything within him in a way nothing else ever had. "Who are you?" he asked the voice.

*I Am,* was the answer. *You must go from this enclave, Zowan, and from your people, and from your father's rule to a land which I will show you.* Zowan's heart leapt as he recognized the words. They were almost the same as the words God had spoken to the man Abram in the last numbered section in Zowan's portion of the *Key Study* pages he'd salvaged.

"You want me to leave the Enclave?" he asked the voice. "Go up to the surface?"

I Am did not answer, and Zowan feared that was all he would get, but he asked again anyway, "Who are you? Are you the LORD?"

*I Am.*

"I don't know the way."

*Come out of the darkness, Zowan, and you will find what you seek.*

The voice fell silent. Music drifted into its place, carrying Zowan along for a bit. He heard men talking in another room. . . .

Then a new voice spoke right beside him, shockingly familiar. "It's all lies, Zowan. There is no poison outside." A dark form stood outside the plastic, not on the window side, but on the other, so no features could be seen. He didn't need features. Zowan knew the voice as he knew his own. "Neos? You're alive?"

"The medications they're giving you are making you like this. They're hallucinogens so you'll discount it all, but it was me you saw outside. And me you're hearing now. Listen closely and remember. They'll discharge you Monday morning. Monday night I want you to go to the Star Garden half an hour before curfew, to the fifth level, beside the golden queen. I'll meet you there. . . ."

Zowan blinked. "Meet me? How? Why?"

"So I can set you free."

He made Zowan tell it back to him, admonished him to remember. Then he was gone. For a few moments Zowan considered all the meaning in his words, then lost them as he noticed the column of bright pink ants crawling down the pole of his canopy at the foot of his bed and across the sheet toward his face. He watched them in horror and alarm. Just as the first reached his chin, the lights flashed and a siren went off, and all fell into darkness. . . .

# Chapter Sixteen

Swain's bimonthly presentation of his Grand Vision for the Kendall-Jakes Longevity Institute was held in the newly completed and already infamous Black Box Theater, situated in the conference center across the campus from the ziggurat. An avant-garde structure, the theater's exterior was made of colossal red sandstone slabs that rose out of the concrete mass of the building to soar above it. Railed walkways led up from the parking lot to the entrance at the structure's highest end, where ranks of glass doors intermittently reflected the brilliant orange of an Arizona sunset as they were opened and closed by arriving attendees.

Admirers deemed it a bold, progressive design, its innovative flair an effective backdrop for the cutting-edge programs and performances presented there. Others called it an architectural disaster, a foolish waste of time and money, and nothing but another monument to Swain's overblown ego. The ziggurat itself was more than enough.

Those in K-J's employ laughingly called it the Phoenix, for from a distance it was said to resemble a great red bird rising from the desert. As Lacey observed it from the front seat of the employee shuttle van as it bore her and six others down from the zig, she supposed the granite slabs did sort of look like the bent leading edges of wings . . . and it did seem a bit excessive for what it was. On the other hand, it *was* a striking building, winner of several architectural awards. And Swain was an amazing man with amazing accomplishments in the face of great opposition. Why shouldn't he create something beautiful and innovative for his people?

Besides, she didn't believe his ego was overblown at all. She still marveled at the fact he had stopped to talk to her. Not only was Swain far more handsome up close than he'd appeared from the back of the room—his eyes were breathtakingly blue—but he was charming and personable, and amazingly down-to-earth. He'd actually introduced himself to her as if she might not know who he was! Had shaken her hand, talked to her like she was a regular person. In fact, he'd made her feel a lot more than regular; he'd made her feel greatly valued and specifically chosen for his team. He'd even claimed to have read her thesis, then commented on it so specifically and extensively, he couldn't have been lying. She was flabbergasted.

He'd apologized right off for keeping her down in the animal rooms so long. "Though serving in those menial areas *is* something of a rite of passage here, as you probably know," he'd added with a smile. "That's all behind you now, though."

He told her that after she'd done a brief stint as research assistant, he'd like to see her working on her own project. Thus, as she went through the abstracts and studies she was to do so with an eye to anything that might spawn her own inquiry. "If you see nothing that piques your interest, come to me and we'll talk." He'd paused. "Will you be attending the presentation tonight?"

When she said she was, he promised to keep his eye out for her, then said good day, assuring her they'd "talk again soon."

He'd left her so astonished she could hardly believe it had happened. But after he'd left and Jade came over to marvel with her, she'd gotten so excited she'd had to go off to the bathroom to be alone to grin and laugh and dance around squealing like a fool. Where last night everything had turned to darkness, gloom, and disaster, this new day had dawned with hope and luminous promise.

She thought of how Gen had assured her they had plans for her, how even Reinhardt had mentioned it—though his interpretation was disgusting and insulting; she could no longer believe Swain was any of what Reinhardt had implied. No, having met him face-to-face, having shaken his hand and looked into his eyes as he spoke to her, she knew he was genuine. And given the preparations that went into everything at the Institute, as well as Swain's reputation for being obsessively thorough in vetting his hires, she thought for the first time that they really did have plans. That they really had seen something in her that others had not, and had indeed chosen her to fill a very specific niche. A thought that filled her with a warm blush of confidence and self-assurance the likes of which she'd not felt in a long, long time. Now, at last, the hope for change in her life seemed on the verge of being fulfilled.

The van pulled up to an unloading zone, and the driver got out and came around to open her door and the side door behind her.

After showing her ticket at the door, she entered the theater's crowded, high-ceilinged lobby. Walls were layered with long white overlapping panels and cut out here and there in thin vertical windows, and a starburst chandelier of optical fibers hung dead center, aglow with multifarious points of light. The roar of conversation filled her ears as she shuffled forward, feeling suddenly self-conscious at the realization she was embarrassingly underdressed in a crowd decked out as if they were attending an opera. Diamonds, gold, and silver flashed amidst black evening dresses, dark suits, and well-coiffed hairdos, many of them the silver or auburn helmets of the older generation. Indeed, most were middle-aged or over, and the women far outnumbered the men.

She took consolation in knowing the fellow employees who'd ridden down in the van with her were equally underdressed—and that the crowd's close-quarters press would make it hard for very many to notice her too-casual apparel.

Windowed halls carpeted in deep blue ramped steeply down from either side of the lobby and were lined with a succession of open doors leading into the theater. She had to go three-quarters of the way down the ramp to find the door for her row and by then was glad she'd ridden the van, for her rarely worn dress shoes had already rubbed a hot spot on the back of each heel.

The theater held about a thousand people, its walls, ceiling, carpet, curtains—even the ranks of seats—all done in black. Irregularly shaped baffles extended from the walls and ceiling in serried ranks, and soft blue light shone down from fixtures hidden among them.

This Friday night presentation was a fundraiser, and Director Swain had told the employees at dinner that they expected the theater to be full this evening. From the number of people who already filled the rows, it appeared his expectations would be met. Lacey had to pick and semi-stumble her way along an aisle of knees wrapped in glittering fabrics while trying not to step on five-hundred-dollar pairs of evening shoes. As she worked her way to the middle right, she glimpsed Pecos and Lauren already seated two rows ahead of her, amidst others she recognized from the back tables of the dining hall, some of whom had shared her van. Farther down, she spied Cameron Reinhardt, standing at the far right corner of the front row, where it curved around the small orchestra pit. He faced the audience as he talked with Nelson Poe and a black man dressed in brightly colored African robes and headdress. Reinhardt wore a navy polo shirt and khaki trousers, and so was even more underdressed than she was. Not that *that* was any comfort.

Just then he glanced over the shoulders of the men to whom he was talking and looked right at her. Immediately she turned her attention to finding her seat. It was just right of middle stage, roughly eye level with the top of the podium on the stage's empty black floor. A heavyset man in full evening attire sat immediately to the right of it. He gave her a disdainful up-and-down glance and then turned away to resume his conversation with his much younger companion. With a grimace, Lacey pushed her folding seat down and sat beside him.

Immediately the older woman seated to her left touched her arm and leaned close to advise that she not let the old stiff disturb her. "Some people take themselves *entirely* too serious," she added with a wink.

Dressed in a red tapestry jacket and black billowing skirt-slacks, her silver hair cut in a sassy bob, Estelle Lederman had also come to the presentation unescorted. And though her face was wrinkled and her bejeweled hands pale and veined, she was as full of life as anyone Lacey had ever met. Estelle was an ardent supporter—both emotionally and monetarily—of Parker Swain and the Institute, her interest in K-J spawned by her CEO husband's death three years ago.

"You seem awfully young to be worried about death," Estelle observed when she'd concluded her introduction. "Though I suppose it's never too young to consider it."

"Actually, I'm a geneticist here," Lacey told her. "They encourage all the new hires to attend this presentation at least once."

"You're a geneticist here at the Institute?" Estelle exclaimed, her dark eyes widening with delight. "Oh my! What serendipity that I'd be seated next to you!"

"I suspect I am the beneficiary here," Lacey said, chagrined to realize she'd given Estelle the idea that she was much more than she really was. "I'm really just a research technician."

Estelle asked her a few questions about what she did and how she'd come to be at the Institute, but in the end, Lacey was right. In terms of information sharing, Estelle—who had attended the Grand Vision presentation many times—was a fountain of gossip and industry history. She told Lacey of Swain's early years roaming the globe with Viascola and Slattery, and how more recently he'd hooked up with American billionaires Ian Trout, John Kendall, and Maurice Jakes, and the Kendall-Jakes Institute was born. Of the three, Trout alone remained alive, Kendall and Jakes both having taken up residence in the tanks of liquid nitrogen down in the Vault.

She pointed out several venture capitalists in the audience, one of whom had, twenty years ago, allowed Swain to try his cutting-edge gene therapies on his cancer-stricken only daughter. Swain's procedures had resulted in a complete cure—the daughter remained alive to this day—and had bought the father's undying gratitude. And consistently generous support.

The brightly robed Africans seated in the front row were a delegation from the West African nation of Ivory Coast. Swain had worked there in his early, vagabond years, cultivating connections with men who were now in significant positions of power, including in the diamond trade. Many were backers of his research, and several were even signed up to go into the Vault, "when the time comes." Plus they had access to ancient African tribal lore that had potential application for Swain's research objectives.

"He's got quite a past, does Parker Swain," said Estelle. "Especially, so they say, with the ladies. Never married, but father of many. I think it's just jealous gossip. He's so charming. So handsome . . . when you meet him you just cannot believe he could be that cavalier. He really cares. You can sense that in a man, you know?"

Lacey nodded. She knew *exactly* what Estelle meant.

"He has such a presence, such high-energy integrity," the older woman went on. "He just seems to *collect* those of high intellect and spiritual attunement, as if they're drawn to him. Well, I believe they *are* drawn. . . ." She went off on a riff regarding the metaphysical properties of synchronicity that Lacey struggled to follow, and at the first lull Lacey asked about Cameron Reinhardt, her eyes seeking him out in the front row, sitting far right now, facing forward.

The older woman's glossed lips pursed and she gave a slight shake of her head, her shiny hair swinging like liquid silver. "Vastly overrated. I have no idea why Parker hired him."

Hardly the response Lacey had expected.

"Well, I guess I do," Estelle amended. "But, you know, he *was* on the verge of being fired at Stanford before Parker signed him."

"No," said Lacey. "I didn't know."

"I guess he's got something of a temper," Estelle went on. "Not to mention a full-blown persecution complex. And he's not at all a team player. Don't get me wrong, he *is* brilliant. And from what I understand, his ideas are innovative. But . . . he's so unstable, how do you trust someone like that?"

"But Swain hired him," Lacey pointed out, "so he must not be too concerned about him." Although after what Reinhardt had told her last night, she thought he should be. In fact, it made her angry to think that Swain would be so beneficent in hiring him only to have Reinhardt repay him so unjustly.

"Oh, it's not as if Reinhardt's troubles aren't justified," Estelle admitted. "He married very young, and went into the military barely a month after. Those two are hard enough to weather, but then his daughter was born with a genetic defect in the mitochondria. It's rare, but incurable. She only lived three years. They say it destroyed his marriage and lost him his position in the service. And was the reason he went into genetics in the first place. I— Oh! Here go the lights! I best shush up now."

And she did, along with everyone else. Which was just as well, for her revelations had startled Lacey enough that she would not have heard much more had it been said. Reinhardt had been married? Had a daughter who had died at three? Hardly the usual profile for the self-absorbed, ever-single, lecherous geek she'd assumed him to be. She had no time to think further, though, for by then, as both darkness and stillness lay upon them all, the chamber orchestra began to play a low, drawn-out note that enhanced the sense of something coming. It quickly gained volume and variation, glissading up the scale to a bright climax perfectly timed with the spotlight that exploded onstage, illuminating Parker Swain as if he had just been beamed down from heaven.

Striding toward the podium he made a tossing motion with both hands, loosing twin plumes of tiny butterflies that fluttered over the exclaiming audience, wings glowing neon blue and purple. Apparently drawn to shiny things, or white, they landed on women's necklaces, earrings, hair, or light blouses. Estelle was delighted when one of them came to rest on her big diamond pinky ring. She held it up so Lacey could marvel with her.

Then the lights darkened further, the orchestra quieted, and a low hum emitted from above, drawing the butterflies upward in a fluttering cloud until the darkness swallowed them and the audience burst into excited applause.

Onstage, Swain grinned, arms still outstretched from when he'd tossed the butterflies. He wore a white suit and tie, his blond hair styled in loose waves around his boyish, clean-shaven face, and he radiated youth, energy, and enthusiasm.

"Wonder," he said, his amplified voice echoing in the darkness. "It is the power of life. Our world is full of it, and much of it we are only beginning to discover."

Lacey was close enough she could see his eyes and face as he surveyed them paternally and grinned, flashing perfect white teeth.

At that moment his gaze caught upon her and the slight widening of his smile sent a zing up her spine. "I'm glad you came," he said, and she had the distinct impression his words were specifically for her. "Because tonight we shall explore the path to wonder, together."

# Chapter Seventeen

Warmth suffused Lacey's body, stoking the glow of optimism that had come upon her this morning until it burned as a joyous inner flame.

The podium, which had disappeared in the darkness, now came gliding back across the stage, Swain stepping to meet it. Blue light illumined the background as a huge smoky-glass cube descended behind him, turning slowly on invisible wires. From the podium Swain picked up a tiny replica, similar to the black cubes Dr. Viascola had given out at the unity meeting.

"It is a path," he continued, "that begins with a black box—the icon we use here to represent all the mysteries we have yet to unravel. In fact, once our entire world was a black box." A hologram of the Earth appeared in the center of the giant box behind him, turning slowly on its axis. "So were our own bodies"—the globe vanished as on each plane of the box, stunning video illustrated his words—"the plants and animals that share this planet with us, the weather, the stars, the rocks, the ocean . . .

"History is filled with marvels we have yet to explain." At his back, the flowers and ground squirrels were replaced by a giant boxcar of stone emerging from the ground. "In Baalbek, three perfectly dressed and fitted limestone blocks serve as part of the foundation for a later Roman-built temple, blocks weighing more than a thousand tons, quarried some three miles from the site. How were they quarried at all? And more, how did the ancients move what we would struggle with today using modern technology? We have no idea.

"Or consider the Nazca lines in Peru." The stone boxcar gave way to images of a barren plain into which a gargantuan, stylized monkey had been inscribed. "Inscribed a thousand years ago, and we still don't know why they were made, since one can only see the designs from the air, and the primitives we believe responsible could not fly. . . .

"The Judeo-Christian Bible, revered for millennia as the Word of God, lists generations of men whose lives spanned centuries rather than decades, and speaks of a race of giants spawned by gods. Nor is it alone. Greek, Roman, Egyptian, Sumerian, Persian, Nordic—each has their version of gods come down to unite with humans. But were they, indeed, gods? Or were they merely enlightened men?"

Swain stepped back from the podium, which glided stage right into the shadows.

"Clearly humanity once had knowledge it has lost. And if we found it once, we can find it again. In the last hundred years alone, we've put men on the moon, examined the very soil of Mars, and found a way to kill millions of people with a single explosion." In the box, appropriate video illustrated his words. "We've developed technology to the point we can watch what is happening on the other side of the world in real time—and travel there in less than a day."

Like a lion he prowled across the stage, tall, regal, fluid . . . mesmerizing. Periodically his blue eyes skewered hers, sending tingles down her legs.

"Yet nothing compares to the advances we've made in genetics. The single most radical event was when Watson and Crick figured out the structure of the DNA molecule." In the box behind him a double helix unwound, the two strands in turn winding into daughter strands as it replicated. "That, combined with the advance in computing systems, has led to the unraveling of the human genome and brought us to the beginning of a revolution in knowledge and abilities unmatched in all of history. A revolution that will lead to a radical change in life as we know it: the metamorphosis of man himself."

The orchestra's rendition of Strauss's *Also sprach Zarathustra* swelled through the auditorium as behind him a giant golden chrysalis floated in the darkness at the cube's center. Inside its transparent golden case, the pupa convulsed, forcing a split in the side of its prison. Before their eyes, the creature pushed itself through the breach, then spread its golden brown spotted wings, a worm no longer, but a newly born butterfly.

"As complete a change of form as any caterpillar," Swain intoned. "We stand on the brink of being able to rework the natural world and change our way of life, our own bodies and minds, even our mortality. Death, long the enemy of humankind, is about to be conquered."

Lacey felt a thrill of awe, tinged with undeniable uneasiness. Conquer death? Wasn't he overreaching? Didn't such things belong in the hands of God? Of course, Swain did not believe in God, so such a consideration would hardly be an issue for him.

But she *did* believe, though she had ignored her Christian faith for some years now. In truth she was angry with God for letting her marry Erik, for not answering any of her pleas to fix her marriage, to keep her in school, to work out all her problems. As He'd abandoned her, so she'd abandoned Him. Still, she wasn't prepared to push Him completely out of existence.

Unless it really was the hooey everyone she'd met at Kendall-Jakes claimed it to be.

Her thoughts broke off as she gazed in shock at the newest image on the screen, her attention returning to Swain's words. " . . . in the accelerated regeneration of skin tissue, allowing the near instantaneous healing of wounds. The one you see behind me took three hours from application to final scarring."

The image on the screen was her own forearm, cut in the same place hers was cut, encircled at the wrist with the same slender braided bracelet she had worn, and lost, that same night. Needles held by the hands of unseen workers made a series of brief injections into the tissue along the wound's edges, then withdrew as the laceration closed, scabbed, and formed into a scar before her eyes.

"Our process has already been patented, and we have just this afternoon received the approval of the FDA to begin our marketing campaign for it."

Swain's blue eyes found hers and her heart beat frantically.

Accelerated regeneration of skin tissue? Instantaneous healing of wounds? This was what they had done to her?

He held her gaze for an instant, then smiled and turned his attention to another, leaving her stunned and motionless in her chair. He'd just admitted everything: that there *had* been an intruder, she *had* been injured, and they *had* healed her wound instantaneously. And he'd asked her to come here. He wanted her to know that he knew, even as he couldn't admit it.

Her heart slammed frantically against her chest, and she felt angry, vindicated, and puzzled all at the same time. It made no sense. Why cover it all up, have everyone lie to her, make her think she was mentally unstable, leave a blot on her record, only to publicly admit her claims were true?

Because he was only admitting the part about the wound, not the intruder. As a courtesy to her. Perhaps as an assurance, as well. An assurance that he would indeed make all things right, if she would only trust him and be patient.

Swain, meanwhile, had moved on, outlining the kingpin of their research program, which was the aging process itself, and extolling the virtues of his scientists as well as the clinic and resort where their health secrets might be shared.

"I believe many of us in this room will be part of the generation that will never die."

The box withdrew into the ceiling as a forest of Plexiglas panels speared upward from the stage floor all around him. "Starvation, deformity, disease, death—for millions of years we have sought to free ourselves from them." As he walked among the panels, images formed on the transparent panes—a skeletal child, a young woman, face marred by the white sores of leprosy, a corpse draped in white linen.

"With immortality we can learn and grow as never before. We can unlock secrets closed to us for millennia, and we can at long last travel the distances that span the stars and be able to experience our destination when we arrive."

He strode from amidst the panels and faced them. "Tonight you can become a part of this vision. I see that for some of you it's already resonating." Again he caught her eye and again she sensed a question directed specifically at her. Was she one who knew this as the truth? She ventured a slight smile, which broadened his. The blue eyes flicked away, darted over the crowd.

"Consider what I offer you tonight—the opportunity to do away with poverty, disease, and even death. Will you ignore the call, sit back and leave it to others to answer? Or will you seize the chance to make your life matter in ways you can't even imagine? The choice is yours."

His gaze slid over them for a time. Then he drew his feet together, dipped a small bow, and said, "Thank you all for coming."

The spotlight and Plexiglas panels winked out, shrouding all in darkness. At first no one moved, and Lacey wondered if the others felt as disoriented as she did—as if she'd been riding a huge wave, careening past glorious sights, only to be dumped unceremoniously back into the regular world.

Something had happened during that speech. Somehow his words had reached into her soul and ignited a simmering excitement, filling her mind with a host of potential futures. She felt skeptical, yes, but energized. His vision, his challenge, had captured her, and she felt an undeniable yearning to be part of it. And then realized that she already *was*!

*"I'm a geneticist here,"* she'd told Estelle Lederman earlier. She'd felt embarrassed then, as if she were misrepresenting herself. Now, recalling that Swain himself had hired her, had specific plans just for her, plans that would take her far beyond her wildest dreams, she felt a burgeoning pride.

The blue ceiling fixtures brightened as people stood up around her. Director Swain had come down from the stage to shake hands with individuals who crushed forward to speak to him. She saw him for but a moment. Then her view was blocked as the people in the next row stood up. Lacey stood, but he was lost behind the ranks of shoulders and backs.

Beside her Estelle sighed with pleasure. "Wasn't that wonderful? Doesn't it just give you so much energy and hope? I could listen to it every week, I think." She took Lacey's arm and urged her along the row, which was rapidly emptying. "Come on, let's go down and see if we can shake his hand. I'd love to introduce you."

Lacey was tempted, but seeing the crowd already gathered around him, she knew it would be futile. "Thanks, but I need to get back to the shuttle before it leaves. With the blisters I'm putting on my heels, I don't want to walk any further than I have to."

"You should take off your shoes, dear," said Estelle.

They shuffled out of the theater into the outer corridor, which was only slightly less crowded than the inner aisles. Suddenly the crowd parted, and there was Director Swain, only a few steps away from her, shaking hands, laughing, but moving inexorably toward the side exit— which was also in her direction. As Estelle grabbed her arm again to draw her attention to him, he looked up and saw them.

In moments he stood before her. "Ah, Ms. McHenry," he said. "Did I make good on my claim?" He took her hand, and tingles crawled up her arm.

His regard was so intense, it set the blood rushing to her face again. She smiled and nodded. "I think you did, sir."

"Outstanding! I knew you would be a solid addition to our team." He patted her shoulder, then turned to shake the next person's hand and move on.

Estelle squeezed her arm. "He knows you by name! And you told me you were but a lowly research technician."

"Well, I am that."

"Not for long, if I'm any judge. Come on, I'll walk you to the shuttle."

"Hold on a minute, then," Lacey said. She bent to remove her shoes and they walked up the ramp together.

Lacey's moment in the sun might have ended, but that didn't diminish the optimism that soared in her soul. For the first time in years, all her self-doubts and uncertainty of purpose had vanished. For the first time she had the chance to do something with her life that really mattered, and she was determined to make the most of it.

# Chapter Eighteen

Unlike Lacey, who took the employee shuttle back to the zig, Cam walked the asphalt path alone through the darkness. He'd briefly entertained thoughts of trying to catch her en route to the shuttle and apologize, but one look at her—barefoot, her dark pumps dangling from her hands, old Estelle Lederman at her side—and he'd known it was not to be.

In truth, he was relieved, grateful for the solitude. His way was lit by the stars and the golden glow of the zig's exterior lighting. The bulk of the outer berm loomed to his left, while to the right lay the more organized campus park, occasional tall lamps illuminating paths winding through it.

He was still in turmoil, though its nature had shifted as the day had passed. Where before it had been pure outrage and an almost vindictive need to "show them," now second thoughts assailed him.

He'd not spoken to Lacey McHenry since the disastrous encounter before lunch, too embarrassed to attempt to explain himself. It didn't help that she'd refused to even look at him, nor that an interdepartmental meeting had taken up the bulk of his afternoon.

He kept telling himself it didn't matter, since he'd be gone tomorrow. But as the day wore on even that had been called into question. For if Rudy was right, how could Cam just leave her here and let it go? And not just her, but the other K-J employees and all the other people Swain was scamming.

Cam had gone to the presentation for two reasons: one, because he didn't want to rouse Swain's suspicions that he might be planning to leave; and two, because he was curious as to why Swain had specifically invited him. That was obvious now, but what he hadn't expected were all the things about the presentation he'd forgotten. All those desperate high rollers, nearing the end of their lives, trying to buy their way out of death.

Botox, exercise regimens, vitamins, hyperbaric chambers, and purification rituals might slow or hide or remove the evidence, but the fact remained their bodies were degenerating, and they all knew it. It was only a matter of time before they'd face their end. And it terrified them. So they sought to run from it, as desperately as he contemplated running from his own terror.

Nor was it just the elderly. Poe had introduced him to Hank Schroeder and his wife, a couple not much older than Cam, whose nine-year-old daughter had died as a result of injuries in a car accident ten years ago. As she'd lingered in intensive care, the couple had contracted with an organization called New Hope to have her cells harvested and frozen in preparation for cloning.

When Cam had pointed out the known failure rate of human cloning, and the problems of premature aging already cropping up in cloned animals, Schroeder brushed such concerns off as irrelevant. The cloning process, he informed Cam, had already been successful, the embryo implanted into the womb of a surrogate several months ago. "My wife has medical issues that preclude implantation," he added before Cam could ask. "The surrogate's already halfway to term."

"That's quite remarkable," Cam said. "And she's local, you say?"

"Oh no, she's in Europe," the man had told him. "Of course, you understand, I can't say exactly where. . . ."

"Of course."

Schroeder looked at Cam quizzically. "You're still skeptical."

"Actually, I consider the whole idea of trying to replace lost loved ones to be futile and misplaced. It might be the same body, but whatever soul God imputes to the child, should she be born, it would not be the same as your daughter's."

The man had looked at him as if he'd spoken gibberish. "God?"

he'd asked in a bemused tone. "I don't believe in God." He paused as if expecting Cam to argue. When he did not, the man dropped it. "Well, whoever she is, we will love her just the same. And I doubt she'll be that different. Identical twins, after all, are very much the same—in appearance, in medical history, *and* in personality."

Cam said no more. In all likelihood, there was no fetus and the man was simply being played. Thankfully, others joined them shortly thereafter and the conversation went off in other directions.

As for the new things Swain had hinted would be in the presentation itself, there'd been his announcement of FDA approval for K-J's patented accelerated tissue repair process and the video of the cut on Lacey McHenry's arm healing in three hours, the latter unquestionably inserted this evening as a peace offering to Cam and Ms. McHenry. Cam had no doubt that clip had already been removed from the program, and from any recordings made of it, with a new sequence inserted in its place.

There'd also been the shocking sight of Cam's own face up there on the planes of the massive box, touted as one of K-J's luminaries, a Black Box Fellow, winner of the Curt Stern Award. His face hadn't been part of the presentation he'd attended when he'd first arrived, though apparently it was not a new addition, from what Poe had said. He supposed Swain meant it as an honor, but seeing it tonight had smitten him like a blow. There was no way now that he could deny he was not intimately tied with Swain and all he stood for. Not with Christ . . . Not with truth. But with an institute that baldly stated its intentions of moving God out of the way and taking His place with their human knowledge and scientific expertise. All that nonsense about cheating death, changing the human race, conquering the universe—it was all straight out of Isaiah 14, the human equivalent of Lucifer's five "I will's."

Just like in the days of Noah, when the first attempt had been made at genetically manipulating humanity into a superior race . . .

Then came that final challenge . . . *"Will you ignore the call, sit back and leave it to others to answer? Or seize the chance to make your life matter in ways you can't even imagine? The choice is yours."*

Swain's words had echoed so closely those spoken by Cam's pastor over the last few weeks, they couldn't help snagging his attention. Even now, in recollection, he felt a zing at knowing the words had been for him, not from Swain, but from God himself. A call not to reengineer the world, but to stay at K-J and do what Rudy had asked him to do.

The presentation had doused his petty anger, reminding him of the bigger picture. Yes, he'd been tricked and manipulated, but not without God's knowledge. Not without His permission and perhaps even intent. . . . Just as Isaac had been tricked and manipulated into blessing Jacob instead of Esau.

Rudy might have meant it for evil—or at least for his own goals at the expense of Cam's—but God meant it for good. Cam *had* asked if he was supposed to come here, and believed God had said yes. To discover it was for a purpose not even remotely in Cam's sights didn't mean it was any less God's intent that he come.

The very fact it still terrified him could be part of that purpose. How many times had he been told that running from one's fears was futile because they always showed up again. The first time he'd fled this terror, he'd been new to the Christian life, his weakness and ignorance understandable. But after eleven years of near daily study, of consistently seeking to apply what he'd learned, of prayer and worship and fellowship . . . he had to conclude that if God had brought him back to face it all again, it could only be because He knew Cam was ready to face it.

*Except I don't feel ready, Lord. Gen's right—I am a wuss. As you know better than anyone.*

*My grace is sufficient for you. . . .*

Cam came to a complete stop, startled by the direct answer that had formed in his thoughts, the chill running down his back and shoulders again. He stared up at the ziggurat towering over him out of the darkness.

*My power is fulfilled in your weakness. . . .*

Protests and excuses flooded his mind—he couldn't even bear to let himself remember the things Rudy had called him here for, couldn't stop himself from the flashbacks, hadn't shot a gun in months, had no idea what was going on—

*My grace is sufficient. . . .*

Scowling, he strode on, continuing to list reasons why he couldn't stay.

When he reached the ziggurat, he found a crowd of people standing around in the lobby talking excitedly. From their fancy gowns and suits, he guessed a number of them were presentation attendees, having come over to view the atrium and the zig lobby. He spotted Lacey McHenry among them, in excited conversation with Estelle Lederman, who seemed to be egging her on. Judging from the look on McHenry's face, she'd been completely swept away by Swain's presence and persuasive words.

He skirted the gathering without stopping and went directly to his suite, where he changed clothes and did his Bible class. Not surprisingly the pastor touched briefly on Paul's own pleas for deliverance from his thorn in the flesh and God's answer . . .

*My grace is sufficient for you.*

Cam still liked the idea of running better. In fact, every time he let himself contemplate what might lie ahead of him if he stayed, he was overwhelmed with the compulsion to flee. Besides, he was going to Tucson tomorrow regardless, so he could always decide later. For now he needed to go down and check his frogs and gels since he wouldn't be doing it in the morning.

Five minutes later, he stepped out of the service elevator into the tomb-quiet animal facility. The floor lights were off, but a swath of illumination poured through the open prep-room door to the right of the elevator, falling in a distorted rectangle across the gleaming vinyl floor.

Seeing it he stopped in dismay, realizing it had to be Manny. Cam had no desire to encounter his undoubtedly disgruntled former postdoc, especially not here in the middle of the night. And, really, he needn't. His lab was at the end of the first corridor opening left off the main hall, well out of view of anyone in the prep room unless they came to the door, so no reason he couldn't go about his business without drawing the other man's attention.

He started down the hall and had just reached the turn when a shadow occluded the rectangle of light and a man stepped out of the prep room.

Though Cam intended to pass by as if he hadn't noticed, a congruence of unnerving observations reversed that decision: the light on in the now-unused frog room, the fact he'd be blocked from any escape route should he continue to the hall's end, and the overwhelming oddness of the man who had emerged from the lighted prep room.

A man who was obviously not Manny. This person was lean and tall, dressed in dirty jeans and a dark short-sleeve T-shirt. His fair hair had been shaved into a bristly Mohawk, the crest rippling like a bear's pelt above a heavy brow marred by a huge red pimple, and half obscured by smears of dried mud.

It was Lacey McHenry's intruder.

He was bigger than she'd described him. As tall as Cam himself— maybe taller—and broad across the shoulders with a solid, muscular build. His face was flushed and he was sweating profusely. And the look in his pale eyes was not at all friendly.

With Lacey the youth had always fled, so Cam was surprised when this time he attacked. Reacting with reflexes he'd not used in years, Cam stepped aside and used the other man's momentum to send him sprawling face forward. Cam didn't stick around to continue the struggle but fled up the main corridor toward the stairwell door. The elevator—if the car was even still there—would never get him away fast enough.

As it turned out neither did his own legs. He closed his hand on the door latch, only to be grabbed from behind and flung away. He hit the opposite wall some twenty feet down the hall and slid to the floor. Gasping back his lost breath, he scuttled backward as his assailant approached.

The stranger was angry—red-faced, eyes flashing, the boil on his forehead glistening as if it had popped from the pressure of his rage. For a moment the corridor flickered and Cam smelled sulfur, saw a warrior's bronzed face, eyes gleaming like gold orbs—

Desperately he shook it off, readying himself for the imminent attack as he saw the other's muscles tighten and heard the labored wheeze of his breathing. The sudden rattle of the elevator's cables disturbed the silence and drew his assailant's gaze. At the *ping* of the car's arrival, the intruder whirled, bolting for the stairwell door Cam had just sought for his own escape. Yanking it open, he disappeared into the stairwell.

Their roles reversed and Cam now raced after him, barely catching the closing door before it latched. As he heaved it open, he heard the security guards exiting the elevator. Confident they'd see the closing door and follow, he didn't wait for them.

Flying down the concrete steps after a rapid thudding of footfalls, Cam had barely reached the first landing when he heard the buzz of an electronic door lock somewhere below. Desperately he accelerated, taking the flights one leap at a time as he descended. Even so he heard the *clatter* and *click* of the door closing as he came around the last flight, arriving seconds after the final *clack* of the door's steel-hardened lock latching.

He jammed his thumb into the hooded print reader beside the door, but that only lit up the red Access Restricted sign over the pad. Sweeping his security clearance card through the accompanying card slot produced the same results. Vainly he tugged at the door's handle. How could the intruder have hacked the Institute's security so deeply he had access to areas Cameron himself was denied?

Before he could begin to contemplate the answer, he was grabbed firmly from behind and shoved into the door, right arm twisted painfully up his back. Being seized like a criminal shocked him. The cold bite of a metal cuff as it was snapped around his wrist shocked him further. "What are you . . . ? Wait!"

His right hand was dragged down and a second cuff snapped onto his left wrist. "We got 'im, Captain!" his captor called out, apparently to a superior who was waiting in the AnFac doorway above.

"No!" Cam protested. "The man you want is getting away!"

"Tell it to the captain," the guard commanded, spinning him around. Cam recognized neither of the men standing before him.

They were both well over six feet tall, broad as Goliaths across their chests, and all muscle. They wore black uniforms and each had a small crescent-shaped communications piece in his ear. The guard who'd cuffed him had coarse, broad features and dark hair bound in a six-inch braid at his nape. The other had a narrow face, with pale blue eyes under a heavy brow and fine blond hair cut closely to his scalp.

They were stern-faced men, probably former Special Forces or SEALs. He knew Swain had recruited from one of the premier security agencies in the country—most of whose agents were former military— for his Institute guards.

Realizing they couldn't have seen the intruder—only Cam in flight—he saved his protests and let them escort him back up the stairs. Only then did he realize how far down he had come in pursuit of Ms. McHenry's frog eater: at least three levels lower than the animal facility and possibly four. It was hard to tell because, although there were the correct number of doors—one for the auxiliary housing level and one for the physical resource plant—there were too many steps.

As they ascended the last flight of steps, the captain awaiting them at the door got his first look at their captive. "Dr. Reinhardt?! We knew our intruder had to be someone on the inside. But you?"

The fact he knew who Cam was, when Cam was pretty sure he'd never seen the man before, unnerved him.

"Definitely someone on the inside, Captain"—Cam glanced at the man's name tag—"Jablonsky, but not me. I came down to check my gels and surprised him."

"At one in the morning?" Jablonsky stepped back as they entered the corridor and let the stairwell door shut with a clank. He was a tall, lean, well-muscled man with deep blue eyes, a weathered face, and short brown hair graying at the temples.

"If you know me, Captain," Cam said, "as you apparently do, you must know that's not unusual for me."

Jablonsky frowned at him. "Then why did you run from us?"

"I was chasing him."

Jablonsky glanced at the other two guards, then turned away as he touched a finger to his earpiece and said, "Yes, we've got him." He paused, listening, then, "Yes, it's Dr. Reinhardt. You can see us now? The video's back online, then?"

He paused, listening again, then nodded. "We'll check it out, sir." He looked up at the blond guard—Armstrong, according to his name tag. "Visual's still out in the frog room. Go see what's wrong."

As Armstrong moved down the corridor, Jablonsky looked at Cam and asked, "What'd he look like?"

"Exactly as Ms. McHenry described him—tall, lean, pale blue eyes, his hair in a Mohawk, big pimple on his forehead, face covered with streaks of mud."

"Mud?" Jablonsky cocked a graying brow.

"Sir!" Armstrong's voice echoed from down the hall, sharp with sudden urgency. "I think you'd better see this."

All three of them hurried down the corridor and around the corner to the frog room, where they stopped in the doorway, Jablonsky in the lead, Cam just behind him, the dark-haired guard bringing up the rear.

The frog tank still stood in the empty room, two of its hinged lids shut. The third, farthest from the door, was open and propped back against the wall. Seated in the opening was Manuel Espinosa, face pale, dark eyes wide and staring, head cocked at an unnatural angle. Above his head, black jagged letters slashed across the freshly painted peach-colored wall at his back:

SEND THE GIRL BACK. I WANT THE GIRL!!!

## Chapter Nineteen

Cam stood in astonished rigidity. He didn't need to check the young scientist's pulse. The cocked head and unblinking eyes told it all. Nevertheless, Jablonsky stepped over the lip of the doorway and checked it anyway. He stepped back with a grim face, then pressed his earpiece and reported what they'd found. Cam heard his words without registering them, staring at the jagged, angry letters lurching behind Manny, their ramifications lifting the hairs on the back of his neck.

*I WANT THE <u>GIRL</u>!!!*

"The camera lens is fine," Armstrong announced, glancing over his shoulder at Jablonsky from where he stood under the mount in the corner. "He must've jammed its transmission with a remote."

Both of them turned to Cam, expressions grim. Jablonsky nodded to the dark-haired guard, Herke, who gave Cam yet another patting down. He found no remote. "Must've dropped it in the stairwell before we caught him."

Jablonsky sent Armstrong to find it.

"You think *I* did this?" Cam exclaimed, nodding at Manny. "I didn't even know he was down here!"

"You had him transferred here," Jablonsky pointed out.

"With Dr. Viascola's and Director Swain's approval."

"Still, you asked for his reassignment last night and now he's dead. And your relationship wasn't the best. For all I know he jumped you and it was self-defense."

"I had nothing to do with him. I never saw him, only the guy with the Mohawk." Who had, he realized now, seemed vaguely familiar.

"You can give us your full testimony in the briefing room." Jablonsky turned away and informed whoever was on the other end of his earpiece that he and Herke were bringing the suspect down, and would they send up a team to deal with the body? He said nothing about searching for the man Cam had chased.

In the elevator, Jablonsky slid a keycard through the slot above the floor number buttons, and a small panel slid aside to reveal a thumbprint pad, which activated a grid of lighted keys beside it. Cam couldn't see which keys Jablonsky pressed, but suddenly the elevator floor dropped beneath their feet.

Alarm was thick in Cam's throat by then. He'd assumed they'd take him to the security center on the first floor, not some area of restricted access deep beneath the Institute. And he couldn't believe they really thought he'd murdered Manny. Had they seen his meeting with Rudy and guessed the worst? And if they had, could he possibly convince them that he'd come to K-J innocently, with the best of intentions, and had no intention of doing what Rudy had asked of him?

The car slowed to a stop, and they stepped into a bare-walled lobby, then turned left through a set of glass doors. Beyond lay a shadowed, sunken room filled with glowing computer monitors. They ringed the walls and sat on long banks of consoles, attended by at least fifty people. Though some of the screens displayed data in graph and table form, most showed visual images of empty corridors, doors, lobbies, and deserted semi-darkened labs. All of them changed on a regular basis, flipping from camera to camera so that one screen might show the views relayed by twelve different cameras. Each attendant appeared to have at least two such screens to monitor and sometimes double that.

Cam was steered leftward along the upper level, away from the well of monitors to a second set of glass doors. These led into a baffle-walled corridor lined with knobless panels, one of which Jablonsky opened to reveal a small briefing room with a table, two chairs, and a long window of darkened glass on the inner wall.

Herke pushed Cam down into the chair on the table's far side. Shortly they were joined by Assistant Director Slattery and Colonel

Paul Nevins, head of security. Slattery set his laptop on the table across from Cam, and sat down before him. As he opened it and set up a small microphone, Colonel Nevins dismissed Jablonsky and Herke. When the door had shut and locked itself in their wake, Slattery asked Cam to state his full name and security clearance code for the record, then tell them what had happened.

Cam did so as simply, clearly, and unemotionally as he could. From time to time Slattery interrupted him, pressing for more detail than the guards had, particularly with regard to the intruder's appearance. When he was finished the AD leaned back in his chair and scowled. "So tell me, why in the world were you down there at one in the morning?"

"I often go down late. And you know I was at the presentation."

"The presentation ended at ten."

Cam told him how he'd listened to a sermon in his room, and then gone down to the AnFac to check on his projects, seeing as he wouldn't be doing it in the morning.

If anything, Slattery's scowl deepened. "Or perhaps you were just waiting for a good time to confront Espinosa."

"Actually, I hoped not to see him at all."

"So that you might eliminate him and try to blame it on our intruder. If there is one at all."

Cam frowned at him. "Why would I want to eliminate Manuel Espinosa? And with your security cameras and microphones, you must know I didn't."

"Our cameras have been going in and out all night, not just on the animal floor but everywhere. We have the audio of what we believe to be Espinosa's death, but no visual. Here. Have a look."

He spun the laptop around so Cam could see the screen where Manny stepped out of the elevator into the animal facility's main corridor and headed for the prep room. As he entered, the screen shifted to view him heading across the room to where Harvey the Hamster ran madly on his squeaky hamster wheel in his Lucite cage. At that point the screen went solid blue, but as Slattery had said, the audio continued. They listened to the sounds of water running and splashing, the squeak of the handle as it was cranked off, a rustling of paper toweling, more squeaks of doors and drawers, implements rattling, glass clinking. Then a deep, harsh voice, surprised and a bit imperious: "Who are you? What are you doing here?"

The words were followed by a bang, a curse, and an extended rustling attended by thumps and grunts. There was a loud cartilage-cracking sound, then a few moments of labored wheezing. A drawer rolled open, then closed again, and all went quiet. Presently the faint *thump-slap* of footfalls sounded, faded to silence, then returned in sudden loudness as new microphones picked them up. Cam heard the familiar squeal of the frog tank's metal lid being lifted and finally a great gonging thud as the intruder apparently dropped Manny's body into the empty tank.

More silence, then a faint erratic squeaking that Cam finally identified as a marker being used to write on the wall. Again the footfalls faded and sharply increased as the spinning hamster wheel became loud again—the intruder had returned to the prep room. Various unidentifiable sounds ensued, then the *ping* of the elevator and the shouts of the guards. At the same moment the screen flickered from blue back to imagery, showing Cam racing for the stairwell doorway as the guards shouted behind him. He vanished through the door, and moments later the guards followed—except Jablonsky, who stood at the doorway. At that point the image froze.

"Now what do you have to say?" Slattery asked smugly, turning the laptop back to face himself.

"I'd say you have a big problem on your hands," Cam replied. "Because it wasn't me, and the man you're after is not only still out there but has somehow acquired clearance to enter places even I can't."

Slattery's dark brows drew together. "You were right there, obviously running from the guards. There was only one ping of the elevator—that which sounded when Captain Jablonsky and his men arrived."

Cam stared at him. "No doubt because the microphones were focused on the action in the prep room." Or perhaps because some audio technician had taken it out?

"I was still on the fifth floor when this happened," he added. "You must have surveillance footage from the corridor and elevator lobby showing me there. Compare the time on those to that on the audio and you'll see I wasn't there." He paused. "Besides, why would I ask Manny who he was, if it was me coming through the door?"

Slattery and Nevins exchanged a glance.

Cam frowned at them. "You both know it wasn't me. I could never have turned that tank over the other night, and don't pretend you know nothing of that. He was very strong, very fast, and he had a wild look in his eyes. Not quite sane, I'd say. Which his actions confirm."

"And yet," Slattery said, "you survived. Why did your mysterious intruder kill Espinosa for no apparent reason other than a chance encounter with him, and not you?"

"He killed Espinosa because Espinosa was there instead of Lacey McHenry. Which is obvious from the words on the wall."

"Well, you were there, too, instead of Ms. McHenry." Slattery poked at the keys on his laptop. "And you said that he did, in fact, attack you. A man as strong and fast as you say he is—"

"He wasn't that adept at fighting," Cam cut in.

"And you are?" Slattery asked sarcastically.

Cam said nothing.

Slattery frowned at his computer, typed something briefly into it, and pushed Enter. "It seems to me that if he's as strong and fast as you say, your intruder should have easily overpowered you regardless of the level of his fighting skills." He looked up from the screen. "I don't think there was any intruder. I think you are the one who's been staging all of this. I think you are the one who has disrupted our surveillance network, and that you are responsible for Manuel Espinosa's death. Out of jealousy and fear that he would supplant you, given his superior credentials."

Cam stared at him, struggling to believe he was serious.

Slattery stood up, Nevins punched in the code to open the door, and the two men departed, leaving Cam alone with whomever was on the other side of the glass.

He sat rigidly, fighting down the incipient panic with long, slow breaths. Of course, that was Slattery's intent. They didn't have a case. Their surveillance records were admittedly compromised, unreliable. If the intruder had been able to disrupt transmission, who knows what else he was able to do? Slattery might pretend to believe Cam was guilty of murdering Manny, but Cam was nearly certain he knew the truth. Probably knew exactly who the intruder was and was covering, as he had been covering from the beginning.

The question was, what was he covering? And why?

Presently Captain Jablonsky returned to escort Cam through a maze of corridors to a small elevator lobby. Jablonsky swiped his card through the adjacent slot, opening the elevator's doors. Cam entered the wood-paneled car alone. The doors closed and the car lifted, gathering speed quickly. Cam barely had time to realize that there were no observable internal controls, when the elevator slowed and came to a gentle stop.

As he stepped out into another small, shadowed lobby, he realized he'd just ridden the director's private express elevator.

An unlit paneled corridor led him past several closed doors to one that stood open, light gleaming off its polished wooden surfaces, inviting him into a modest-sized meeting room with a long window along its outer wall. It was furnished with several overstuffed chairs ranged in a U-shape around a low rectangular table. A huge abstract painting of a stern-faced Native American warrior swathed in a robe of watery colors hung on the wall at the end of the table, lit by a recessed ceiling lamp.

Other Native American art forms graced the adjacent walls—flat baskets, black pottery plates, war hammers. A tall cabinet of rough-hewn mesquite hulked on the wall opposite the painting. Swain himself, as before, stood at the window, awaiting the arrival of his guest. As Cameron drew up beside him, he did not speak nor glance aside, but continued staring at the quiet campus and the bright stars overhead. The low light of the various table lamps scattered about the room cast enough illumination that Cam could clearly see the director's face, which was calm and placid.

Below them the Institute's inner park lay in a well of darkness scattered with pools of warm light from the security lamps. Above, the dark bulk of the Santa Catalinas loomed beneath a vast star-spangled sky in which Cam easily picked out the three-star belt of Orion hanging directly over the mountains.

"They tell me you claim not to be the murderer," Swain said, "but to have chased him down a stairway."

Cam eyed him, certain Swain had seen the interview himself, if not from the other side of the one-way glass, then from monitors in the room.

"I chased him right up to a door he went through easily, but to which I was denied access."

"So of course you couldn't capture him. A convenient excuse." He paused. "Do you think you could have held him had you caught up with him?"

"I knew the guards were behind me."

Swain turned to look at him, eyes piercing, expression inscrutable. Then he stepped from the window and gestured toward the chairs and table. "Please, sit down. I've something to show you."

As Cam went to the chairs, Swain strode to the mesquite cabinet and opened its doors to reveal shelves of liquor in exotic bottles. He pulled a squat-bellied red one from his collection and set it on a tray, added two small glasses, a silver bowl of some sort of crackers, and what appeared to be a remote. Closing the doors with a faint snick, he brought the tray to the table, then sat in the chair at the table's end, kitty-corner to the seat Cam had chosen. "I suppose your theory is that he found his way in through one of the service access ports," he said, using a napkin to pull the glass stopper out of the liquor bottle.

"Why would he need to do that when he has security clearance beyond mine?"

"Oh, I wouldn't say he has that." He poured deep amber liquid into one of the glasses, then glanced up. "Brandy?"

"No, thank you," Cameron told him.

He smiled. "I knew you'd say that." He set the carafe back on the tray, replaced the stopper, then picked up his drink and settled back in the chair. "The door you reference leads only to one of the physical plant floors—electrical tunnels, drains, fans, vents, that sort of thing. Your card isn't coded for that floor because you're not one of our maintenance personnel. Coding is always on a need-to-access basis."

"So this man has a keycard that admits him to the animal facility and to the physical plant."

Swain shrugged. "It's your story, Cameron."

"It is *not* a story. It's the truth. There was a thumb-pad device by the door. Why would that be on a stairwell entrance to the physical plant?"

"A thumb-pad device?"

"I jammed my thumb into it."

"Most likely some sort of electrical housing. You're lucky you didn't get electrocuted. . . ." He smiled and sipped his drink, watching Cameron sharply.

After a moment he said, "Actually, I do believe you."

"You know who he is, then."

"Not specifically, no. None of our cameras has yet been able to capture his image. What we're trying to understand here is why he's suddenly resorted to murder. As you must have guessed, professional technology thieves do not develop sudden, irrational crushes on random lab technicians they happen to run into."

"You think the messages on the walls are meaningless, then?"

"Diversions, yes."

"That still doesn't explain why he'd resort to murder."

"Manny must have seen him doing something compromising."

"The audio tape certainly doesn't indicate that."

Swain cocked a brow at him. "So then, what? You think he's a lovesick vandal?"

"I do think he's sick. He certainly didn't look well."

Swain went suddenly still and alert. "You mean, ill? Like sweating, chills . . ."

"Flushed, dripping sweat, rank odor, wheezing . . ." He fell silent as it occurred to him that one of the symptoms of genetic therapy gone awry was the sudden onset of flulike symptoms. Fever, body aches, vomiting, diarrhea. . . . He looked at Swain in horror. *By all that's holy, Director, what have you done?*

Swain shook free of his paralysis. "Well, I guess we can find that out once we capture him."

"Capture him? Don't you think you should wait until the police get here? I mean, you're going to mess up evidence, and they may have this guy's profile in their database."

Swain regarded him steadily. "You know what I think about calling the police, son. We've already had this discussion."

"That was when the subject was a relatively harmless vandalism. This is murder."

"The police aren't going to do anything we can't. And they'd bring those jackal reporters. Then we'd have another Andrea Stopping mess on our hands, and—"

"But it's murder."

"Indeed it is. Which means you, of all people, do not want the police here."

"What?"

"Think it through, son. . . . Who will be their most likely suspect?"

A chill crawled up Cam's spine as he stared at the other man. "I didn't do it, sir. And you just said you believed me."

"I do, but given the available evidence, it appears as if you are guilty. You had motive and opportunity. We have all the records of your many arguments with Manuel Espinosa, which they would request and we would have to supply them with." He paused. "I'm sure you can imagine what the reporters would do with that: the white German star scientist versus the poor minority student."

"Manny was as much a star as I am, and you well know he wasn't remotely poverty-stricken." His parents owned a vast ranch in Argentina. "Furthermore, I'm not German—I'm American!"

"Your name is all they'd need." Swain hesitated. "Then, of course, they'd uncover your military background—your knowledge of how to penetrate a facility like this, short-circuit cameras, even provide false visuals. Not to mention your mental health issues."

Cam stared at him, cold to the core. *How can he know I have that knowledge? That information is classified.* But then, so was the matter of his "mental health issues" which both Swain and Gen apparently knew about. Which meant Swain somehow had access to government files, even those the government had supposedly destroyed. And he wanted Cam to know it. . . .

His coming up here alone, the lack of guards, the relaxed meeting with Swain had eased somewhat the sense of being regarded as a criminal that he'd experienced when escorted handcuffed into the lower security level. Stepping into the familiar meeting room, eerie as it was in the semidarkness, had implied that he was an equal—valued, free, and innocent. And that was exactly what Swain had intended, he realized now. To relax him, then drive in this knifepoint of potential disaster.

Swain smiled. "Still think we should call the police?"

"But you have his body. You can't just dump it somewhere in the desert and hope no one will find it."

Swain sipped his brandy. "We do have on-site facilities for taking care of the dead, you know."

The Vault. He meant to put him in the Vault. There were over two hundred bodies frozen in their cryogenic canisters, four to each canister. To demand an inspection would be like opening a score of graves at the local cemetery.

"You can't just make him disappear."

Swain shrugged. "He was distraught. He took a hike into the mountains. The terrain is treacherous there. People get lost all the time. Most are never found."

Cameron shivered. This was the story of Andrea Stopping.

"On the other hand, many here will testify that Manuel was an irresponsible person, egotistical and easily angered. No one would be surprised if, in a fit of pique over his unjustified—in his eyes—demotion he might decide to simply walk away. It would be an easy matter to hitch a ride back to Tucson."

Cam swallowed the nausea crawling up the back of his throat.

"We've deliberately restricted knowledge of this incident to a handful of people," Swain went on. "You, myself, Frederick, Paul Nevins, and the three men who arrested you are the only ones who know. The guards know only what you claimed and they saw, which unfortunately is significant enough to create a security risk for us, so we'll be sending them off to our South American facility before week's end."

Swain finished off the rest of his brandy, set the glass on the tray, then raised his eyes to meet Cam's. "Thus we can leave things . . . for as long as you like."

Cam could hardly breathe, Swain's cobralike gaze holding him spellbound—horrified, helpless, waiting for the fatal strike. At length, when it did not come, Cam swallowed and pulled his eyes away, staring out at the three stars of Orion's belt lowering now behind the mountains. Other stars, brighter than those in the dark sky swam across his vision.

"There is another bit from our surveillance videos you should see," Swain said, picking up the remote off the tray. He pressed a button and the painting of the Indian warrior rotated clockwise to horizontal aspect and became a flat-screen monitor.

He pressed the remote again, and the screen lit with a frozen, fuzzy night shot of a loading dock dimly lit by a light source offscreen to the right. As they watched, one of the campus's service carts appeared out of the shadows and backed up to the dock. The driver had Cam's build and wore a baseball cap, sweatshirt, and jeans very much like ones Cam owned. His face obscured by shadows, the man leapt onto the dock and disappeared through the door. Shortly he returned with a gurney, which he collapsed at the dock's edge. Then he stepped into the back of his cart and wrestled what appeared to be a corpse wrapped in black plastic onto the gurney's bed, then extended the stretcher's legs and wheeled it into the Vault.

"Records, of course, will indicate which canister went online tonight," Swain said.

Cam sagged back into the chair, swallowed hard, and finally said, "What do you want from me?"

"I want your mind, son. I want your heart and soul and strength." He smiled at Cam's shocked expression and shook his head. "I just want your loyalty, Cameron. I want you to believe me when I say I have your very best interests at heart and trust that I know what I'm doing. And I want you to share my vision."

Cam could only stare at him, drowning in the depths of sudden disaster.

Finally, Swain sighed wearily and said, "Never mind. For now just go on with your plans. Head in to Tucson tomorrow. Have your day off. If you can make the security meeting, do so." He paused. "Just make sure you *do* come back."

He led Cam back to the elevator then and, as the doors opened, clapped his shoulder with a warmth that seemed utterly inappropriate.

THE ENCLAVE — 189

"We're in this mess together, Cameron, but your part is by far the most precarious. I know you didn't kill him, but my loyalty and heart-felt endorsement of your character will not go far in a court of law. Especially when they bring out the circumstances of your military discharge. . . ."

He gave Cam a quick smile, then pressed him into the car. "It's late. You should get some sleep. It'll all seem better in the morning, I promise."

Cam stood in the car, facing his superior as the doors closed between them. He put a hand to the railing as once more the floor dropped sickeningly beneath his feet, almost like his life was doing right now. And he was certain that not much of anything would be better in the morning.

# Chapter Twenty

At 5:00 a.m. on Sunday, Cam checked out at the reception desk in the ziggurat's high-ceilinged main lobby, then headed down to the underground parking garage northeast of the building. It was earlier than he usually left, but despite a second night of getting to bed around 3:00, he'd found himself unable to sleep.

There was something deeply disturbing in knowing he was being framed for murder. It was the sort of thing that happened to other people—most of them on TV crime dramas—not to him. Especially not the "him" of today, the mild-mannered, absentminded but respected geneticist with several important papers published in the better journals and winner of more than one research award. Memory of his interview with Swain in that cozy theater room beneath the gaze of the stern-faced Indian seemed as much a part of some bad dream as his race through the Afghan tunnels. And yet, like the tunnels, the theater room was real, and both the race and the interview had happened.

This early on a Sunday morning, the garage was tomb-silent. His footsteps echoed eerily around him as he strode down the concrete ramp past shadowed rows of parked cars. The back of his neck prickled with the sense of being watched. And not just by security cameras, but by actual human eyes.

Despite his efforts to appear relaxed, he found his pace quickening, especially when he spied his red Jeep Cherokee in the line of cars on his right. He reached it without incident, opened the door, tossed his duffle and laptop onto the passenger seat, and got in. And immediately hit the door-lock switch.

Then he sat there, staring at the concrete wall beyond the Jeep's hood, breathing deeply as his stomach churned and his hands trembled and lights flared across his vision with such brightness he thought he might pass out. Or fall into another flashback.

But he did neither, and the anxiety passed. When he was himself again, he unzipped the external pocket on his duffle, pulled out his iPod, hooked it to his belt, and put on the earphones. Then he switched on the ignition, fastened his seat belt, and put the Jeep in reverse. As he backed out of his parking space and headed up the ramp toward the ground-level exit, still several turns above him, his rearview mirror showed a figure standing in the lane behind him, watching him go.

So apparently his paranoia wasn't as baseless as he'd thought. Swain had implied Cam would be watched today, and Cam did not doubt for a moment that the RFID adhered to his windshield not only lifted the parking garage gates from his path but transmitted the exact location of his vehicle to that high-tech security center hidden in the ziggurat's bowels. But with all of that, the fact they'd set an eyes-on tail after him, too, gave it all a greater reality. And confirmed his fears that Swain did indeed suspect he might bolt.

Thus, as he drove out the garage's exit and onto the divided two-lane road that led out to Highway 92, he was not surprised to see a blue sedan slowly emerge from the parking garage in his wake.

He kept his speed moderate, noting the sedan pull out onto the blacktop behind him. It was a Honda Accord, and it matched his speed, keeping the distance between them constant. The curving blacktop rolled up and down over the hilly terrain, beneath a cloudless sky washed with the rose of the coming dawn.

It took Cam about five minutes to reach the curving stonework walls of the Institute's main gate. He waited a bit at the stop sign, hoping his tail might pull up behind him so he could get a look at the driver, but when the car didn't appear, he gave up and turned onto the highway, heading west. Only as he crested the first hill did one last glance in the rearview mirror show the Honda pulling up to the same stop sign. Cam was over the hill and out of sight before he saw which way it turned, but it didn't matter. If the car was following him, he'd see it soon enough.

And so he did, not five minutes later, the Accord hanging back enough to be frequently obscured by the road's dips and turns. Just for fun, one time when he had the tailing car in sight, he suddenly sped up as he went over a hill, hoping to trick the driver into thinking he was making a break for it. Instead he slowed on the downslope, so that he was going about half his original pace when he started up the next hill, a long, straight ascent that would keep the two of them in sight of each other for some time.

Sure enough there came the Honda, popping over the top of the hill at a fair clip, then braking sharply when the driver saw him much closer than expected. Cam chuckled his amusement and wondered if he should try it again. Eyes on the rearview mirror, he was readying himself to gun the engine when a gold Chevy Corvette came flying over the hillcrest, blasted around the slow-moving Accord, and raced up the incline toward Cam. The coupe blew around him on a double yellow line and thundered up the highway way too fast for the road.

It was still in the other lane as it approached the hilltop when a white cargo van appeared in its path. The Corvette swerved hard right, then left to avoid the shoulder, fishtailing over the crest and out of sight. Cam came over the hill in time to see the car swing wide along the leftward curve, hit the dirt shoulder and go airborne, tumbling off the roadway in a cloud of dust.

By the time Cam caught up, it had come to rest upside down on the grassy slope of a shallow drainage area, front fender smashed into a small yucca. Its roof was crunched, its windows shattered, its wheels still spinning.

Pulling off the road, Cam parked and ran down the hillside, through the ruptured barbed-wire fence, and on to the car. When he arrived, the driver was already wriggling out through the empty windshield frame.

Cam pulled him the last bit out and helped him to his feet. He was a heavyset, balding, middle-aged man, covered with dust. A cut on his forehead bled profusely, but otherwise he seemed unharmed. "You all right?" Cam asked.

"Yeah . . . just shaken up a bit." The man looked at his car and swore softly.

"Let's get you up to the road," Cam said, "and I'll call an ambulance."

"I don't need an ambulance. A tow truck, though, *that* I'll need."

As they climbed back up to the road, the white cargo van pulled off the road in front of Cam's Jeep. It eased forward to the middle of the curve where the Corvette had gone off and stopped, keeping the engine running. The passenger window lowered, and from his seat inside, the driver asked if the man was all right.

Cam said he was, and after helping the bleeding stranger settle at the roadside, he stepped to the van's window. "He says he's okay. Just cut his brow."

"Could be in shock," the van driver said. "Could have a concussion, too. I better call." He picked up his cell phone as Cam glanced back at the Corvette driver, still sitting where Cam had left him, mopping the blood from his face with a handkerchief. At Cam's back, the van's side door slid open. Suddenly a bag dropped over his head and he was yanked into the vehicle. The side door slammed, the engine revved, and the van made a hard, screeching left turn, heading east as it had been when it first met the Corvette.

Everything happened so fast, by the time Cam realized he was being kidnapped, it was too late: the strong sweet smell of a soporific was filling his head with black cotton.

The next thing he knew, the hood was gone and he was reclining in a raised-back hospital bed. Rudy Aguilar sat in a chair beside him. The janitor disguise was only partially gone. His white hair fell in thick locks over his shoulders, but he was clean-shaven and minus the wrinkles, his dark eyes a sharp contrast to the pale hair and brows.

"I kinda thought I might see you today," Cam murmured.

Rudy held up a white plastic cup. "Water?"

Cam took it, drank, then pushed himself up in the bed and glanced around at the tiny featureless room. "Where are we?"

"Command HQ," Rudy said with a wry smile. "Such as it is."

Which wasn't exactly what Cam had meant, but obviously Rudy was going to play things close to the vest for a while.

"Swain had a tail on me."

Rudy nodded. "Blue Honda Accord. Pulled over to watch when the Corvette crashed. So far he's still on your tail. Or at least he thinks he is." Rudy explained that as his men were yanking Cam into the white cargo van, a double had stepped out of it to take his place. The double would stay with the injured Corvette driver—also one of Rudy's team—until a tow truck arrived. Relieved of his charge, the double would continue on to Tucson, where he'd do Cam's laundry, visit the U of A, then lead the Accord on a roundabout journey through town, withdrawing cash from various ATMs. Around midafternoon he'd head south toward Nogales at the Mexican border, only to change his mind when he got there and turn back for the Institute, stopping at Catalina State Park, just north of Tucson, to eat and watch the sunset.

"There you and he will change places again," Rudy said, "and you can return to the Institute, hopefully no one the wiser." He paused, then added quietly, "Or simply disappear, if that's what you want."

Cam cocked a brow at him. "Really?" Skepticism soured his voice.

"I can't force you to help us," Rudy said. "But neither can I leave you in now that you know we're involved. Not without a firm commitment that you're with us."

He fell silent, waiting. Seconds ticked by. Cam listened to the sounds coming from beyond the partitions—the whir of some machine, maybe a centrifuge, an intermittent bump, the sudden thumping of footsteps, low voices in muffled, erratic conversation. The faint aroma of acetone revealed the presence of a lab . . . most likely one with DNA, fingerprinting, and other forensic capacities.

Cam brought his attention back to Rudy, his anger only a slow burn now. "Give me one good reason why I should trust you."

"I can't." Rudy braced his hands on both knees and dropped his gaze to the side of Cam's bed. "I'm hoping maybe God already has."

"You stabbed me in the back in Afghanistan."

Rudy grimaced and looked up, seeming genuinely pained. "You *know* we had to shut down that installation. The chance was too great those things would get out."

"I'm talking about afterward. At the medical hearing."

The furrow in his friend's brow deepened. He sat in silence a moment, then sighed. "You were a man raving about monsters and voices in your head."

"You heard those voices, too. And you saw those . . . *monsters* with your own eyes. At least the one. You know they were real."

"Yes, but by that time, they were all dead, the mission abandoned, expunged, nonexistent. Just the little bit Ruyker saw of what happened— before the EM pulse blew out all our surveillance and communications—terrified him. None of us had any idea what we were up against, only that it was far more than we could handle." He leaned back in his chair. "Ruyker did the only thing he could think to do: he sent in the birds with the bombs, praying it would be enough, praying those monsters would not somehow survive and dig out, wondering how many more of them were down there and if some of them might have survived.

"I still have nightmares about that chamber Khalili showed us full of unopened sarcs. . . ." He paused, rubbed a hand up his forehead and through his hair. "We searched the surface for days—with probes, sonar, everything you can imagine. No sign of life. Little by little we began to hope it was over.

"Then you walked into that warlord's camp a week later, the lone survivor, terrified out of your mind, raving about things that couldn't be real. *Couldn't* be, Cam, because if they were, that would be the end of us, not just as a civilization but as a species. We had no other way of stopping them. They'd have wiped us off the face of the Earth."

Cam sat there, staring at Rudy's crossed arms, knowing what his old friend said was true—they *could* have wiped humankind off the Earth—without knowing how he knew it. He shivered.

The movement drew Rudy's gaze back to his. "Have you remembered anything more about it?"

"No." Cam looked away from his probing gaze. He'd begun to tremble and sweat again, the restless darkness struggling against its bonds.

"Can you try?"

"*No!*"

Rudy said nothing. Somewhere beyond the tiny briefing room's walls a buzzer sounded. Footfalls thumped on the raised floor, followed by the sharp hiss of some releasing gas.

"I remember bits and pieces," Cam said suddenly, hitching himself higher in the bed. "Running through dark, large chambers. Explosions." *A ruined lab, floor puddled with blood, littered with glass and bodies . . .* "Nothing coherent. Some things I think might have happened. Others I'm not so sure." He caught Rudy's gaze. "Mostly what I remember is you not coming back. The other guys dead. The rumble of the explosives detonating, the collapsing tunnel, and me trapped there. With them." His voice had acquired an embarrassing tremor and he fell silent.

"But you did get out. . . ." Rudy said softly.

When Cam did not speak further, he prodded, "You were in there for a week, Cam. You must have killed them all. How can you not remember?"

"Probably because I *wasn't* entirely sane." He toyed with the plastic cup in his hands. "Or maybe I've subconsciously done what Commander Ruyker did: declared the mission unacceptable and expunged it from my memory." He paused. "Except it hasn't really been expunged from anything, has it? Because here you are dredging it up again."

Finally he met his friend's worried gaze. "Why do you think Swain has sarcophagi?"

Rudy leaned back in the chair, brows raised, eyes wide. "Does this mean you're on board, then?"

"Maybe."

"Maybe?"

"Rudy, be reasonable. It's been eleven years since I've done anything like this. I'm out of practice, out of shape, far from the cutting edge of whatever's going on in the spy world these days, and let's face it, mentally and emotionally unstable. I'm not sure I could be all that much help to you."

"I'm not asking you to get in on the action, just be our eyes and ears. There may be a few things we'll want you to do, maybe collect some DNA—we have nothing whatever on Swain, for example. Not even prints."

"You've been in the place for a year and a half and you don't have prints?"

"He rarely comes to the places I'm assigned, and when he does, he touches nothing. Usually he has others to do it for him. I couldn't get into his penthouse, or even his fancy office. Even our guy in security hasn't been able to. But you—"

"I eat with him three times a day. It shouldn't be too hard to grab a used fork."

Rudy eyed him in surprise. Then he grinned. "Well, there you go. Mostly, though, we need information, and right now you're perfectly positioned to look in the places we think it will be found. More than that, I believe you are singularly qualified to see clues the rest of us would overlook entirely."

"Information only?"

Rudy nodded.

"Because, you know, I'm not an Army Ranger anymore. I'm a geneticist."

Rudy's expression turned wry. "Don't worry. We've got a whole passel of young hotshots to do the Ranger stuff. Though I have to admit, in your day you were better than all of them. . . ."

"Flattery will get you nowhere, friend. I get enough of it from Swain. I never believe a word of it, and I always know he's after something."

Rudy's amusement faded. He made a face, turned his attention to his knees, and after a long moment breathed a weary sigh. "All right, I'll cut to the chase, then. Good as you were, it wasn't enough to escape Tirich Pazu. God's the one who got you out of there. For a reason. I'm convinced part of that reason has to do with what's happening here."

Cam sat very still, holding his mind carefully blank.

"We may have set up the thing at Stanford," Rudy went on, "but we didn't cause you to go into genetics. Nor were we responsible for your successes in that field, which, as I understand it, are pretty phenomenal. We only set you up *after* we realized Swain was pursuing you. And I have to say, the day I learned he had you in his sights, given what we suspected he was up to even then, the hairs on the back of my neck stood up. The connections are just too strong and too timely to dismiss."

His tale made the hairs on the back of Cam's neck stand up, too. *Oh, Lord, do you* really *want me to do this?*

"So why do you think he has sarcophagi?" Cam asked again.

Rudy's pale brow arched in question.

Cam made a face. "All right, yes," he said, crumpling the water cup and tossing it into the nearby trash can. "I'm with you."

Rudy smiled his crooked grin and bent to pick up a laptop that had been sitting on the floor beside his chair. "I figured your first question would be about the sarcs." He adjusted the screen and set the device on Cam's lap. "These were taken over the last decade, the most recent being five years ago."

The first photo was of a large helicopter lifting what looked like a boxcar off the side of a mountain. It was taken in the Andes, Rudy told him. The next showed the plume of fuel jettisoned by the chopper so it could get airborne in the thin air while lifting such great weight. Several more showed the helicopter moving away from the lift site.

Then a new series began of three covered military transport trucks backing in turn up to an opening in a hillside near Baalbek, loading something dark and large into their beds, and driving away. The final shot showed all three moving along a dirt track through the desert, a cloud of pale dust churning in their wake. A fourth series, taken at night, showed a large covered mound being transported on a flatbed truck through the sandy deserts of Iraq near one of the ancient ziggurats along the Euphrates River.

None showed a clear shot of anything that looked like one of the sarcophagi, but the locations coupled with the size and shape of the transported containers added convincing support for Rudy's story.

So did the record Cam was shown next of all the funding that Kendall-Jakes had discreetly been directing toward various archaeological projects. Clearly Swain's interest in archaeology went beyond the hobby level. The sites included a small dig in the Bekaa Valley near Baalbek in Lebanon, a project in the Peruvian Andes, an effort in Norway, another two in Iraq, and three in Afghanistan, two of them ongoing, the third closed, its name raising the hairs on the back of Cam's neck: *Tirich Pazu.*

"Swain was connected with Tirich Pazu?"

Rudy nodded. "We don't know if he actually got one from those tombs, but we do know he paid the project an awful lot of money. He did it through several fronts. It's a complicated path, but if you want to study it . . ."

"No. I know how he works. How much does he know about Operation Nimrod?"

"That I don't know."

Cam sat silently for a moment, gripping the rail beside the bed, forcing himself to breathe deeply, calmly. Dark memories stirred and shifted, and he knew he could touch them if he wanted to. But he didn't. All Rudy had asked of him was to be their eyes and ears, and for that he knew all he needed to know.

And fear was a sin. An insult to God. If he ran from this now, it would only follow him, so he might as well give in and face it, test God on that promise of His grace always being enough, His power perfected in man's weakness. Cam drew a deep, shuddering breath and let it out. "Okay, then," he said. "Where do we start?"

Rudy, who'd been watching him closely, relaxed in obvious relief and got down to business. "How about you tell me what's been going on from your end?" he suggested. "Then I'll add in what we know or suspect."

Thus Cam had his first debriefing since the days following his emergence from the tombs of Tirich Pazu deep in the mountains of Afghanistan.

That was followed by Rudy's lengthy verbal download of the intelligence they had gathered so far, and then a tour of the facility, which was comprised of two semitrailer trucks that had been converted into a state-of-the-art forensics lab and surveillance-command post. Ostensibly there as a base for a team of ecologists doing a habitat survey for the Arizona Game and Fish Department, it also sported a small but excellent armory—the narrow, low-ceilinged underground passage that connected the two trailers doubled as a firing range—fax, phone, and wireless facility, a satellite uplink, and other monitoring systems.

From the facility, Rudy or his second-in-command, a woman named Brianna, coordinated their fourteen-person team, five of whom were at the command site now. The other nine stayed mostly in the field. Seven of those nine were employed on a full- or part-time basis at the Institute or resort—one in security, though Rudy said no one had heard from him in a couple of days.

The other two served as couriers of materiel and information. Wireless communication was tricky because of the constant danger of interception by the high-power antennae and receiving discs that sat atop the ziggurat—as well as at other locations around the property.

They stopped in the tunnel firing range so Cam could practice shooting. This was the one aspect of his former profession he'd kept sharp, driven by his residual fears to stay ready to defend himself. Until he'd come to K-J—where personal firearms were prohibited—he'd been a regular on the practice ranges for both handgun and rifle. Thus he acquitted himself favorably with the pistol.

After lunch, Brianna familiarized Cam with the array of equipment and devices he'd be bringing back with him to K-J: a special BlackBerry Smartphone to replace his old one, a master lock release device disguised as a ballpoint pen, an upgraded pair of binoculars and a replacement iPod, both with special surveillance and transmission capabilities, as well as a Taser and a handgun plus ammunition concealed in two booklike CD cases, all of it distributed throughout his duffle bag and his laptop case—which had been passed by his double to the Corvette driver and brought to HQ shortly before noon.

His laptop would also be replaced by one with larger capacity and greater protection against surveillance. In shadow mode, it would be impervious to Institute monitoring devices designed to pick up and replicate whatever was on his screen. They were still in the process of uploading its contents onto his new machine, so he went down for additional shooting practice. Which Cam had to wonder about—was it really necessary given the fact he was supposedly only doing information gathering. He didn't ask, though, for it felt good to have the gun in his hands again, and he did considerably better during his second session.

By early afternoon, the new laptop was ready, and Rudy went through the Top Secret encrypted files they'd loaded onto it. These included a comprehensive personality and background profile of Parker Swain and ten of his closest followers; a file on the eight young women who had disappeared from K-J over the last six years; an extensive array of area topographical maps, displayable as flat images or in three-dimension, including GPS coordinates. Finally, there were several pages of blueprints obtained from the contractor who had built the ziggurat, which Cam noted at once showed nothing past the door at the base of the east-wall stairwell.

Rudy listened to his suspicions with keen interest and said he'd have someone look into the possibility of some sort of deeper complex beneath the zig. But it wasn't something he wanted Cam to waste his time on. "We can get geographical soundings done, compare the lay of the land now to what it was before construction, and do the earth displacement calculations. We don't have a chance of getting into Swain's Inner Circle.

"*We* can't enlist Lacey McHenry to our cause, either. It's all up to you. In fact, courting her should be second only to your priority of getting into Swain's private club. As for your concerns about putting her at risk . . ." He sighed. "You know full well she was at risk the day she arrived. Swain drew her to the Institute for a purpose, just like he's drawn you. And it has nothing to do with her researching abilities. She's just like Andrea Stopping and the other girls: strong, pretty, healthy, and intelligent. If we get her on our side, she might be able to lead us to the others. Or else let us know what's become of them."

To that end, Rudy had provided a disk with the same articles and reports on the lost girls as Cam had on his new laptop. He slipped it between stacks of gel readouts and research abstracts and put it all into a manila envelope for Cam to either hand her directly or slip unobtrusively onto her desk.

Finally, all had been covered: the equipment provided, exigencies discussed, goals outlined, lines of communication set up, code words, drop and pickup locations memorized. It was time to go back. They would leave Cam on a forest-service road near the state park, and he'd hike several miles across country to the meeting site, which he'd find by GPS coordinates on his watch. There he'd wait for his double to show up at dusk. Someone else would see to exchanging the equipment in the Jeep.

He left the station wearing the hood again, never having had a look at anything outside. Rudy led him by the elbow into the back of the cargo van, and once the doors were shut and the van in motion, they spoke no more.

Cam's respite was over. Only God knew what he'd find at the end of this path he'd chosen. One that seemed more and more like a rendezvous with a past he'd never in a million years have thought he'd have the guts to revisit.

# Chapter Twenty-One

That same Sunday afternoon, while Cam was being dropped off on the forest-service road, Lacey McHenry sat in the Institute's first-floor laundry facility, waiting for her clothes to cycle through two of the ten washing machines and trying to come up with a project to propose to Director Swain. Around her, other machines were sloshing away, as well, while various residents' clothes tumbled in all fifteen dryers. The warm, slightly humid air was heavy with the fragrance of soap and fabric softener, and except for the clothing and machines, she had the place to herself. Wrapped in a well of rhythmic mechanical noise, she had little excuse not to concentrate.

Yet she'd been working since breakfast to come up with something and still couldn't seem to make herself attend to the task. Right now, in fact, her laptop screen showed a page from the Kendall-Jakes Web site on which she'd just finished reading a description of its newly patented accelerated tissue repair process, which was indeed a form of transitory gene therapy. The modified gene was placed into a specialized virus, which was then allowed to replicate in solution before being injected along a wound's open edges to accelerate the repair function and growth of skin cells. In the case of a wound like hers, the injury would be taped shut and full healing completed within three hours. Hence the need for her stay in the clinic and the sedatives. K-J's process had already gone through clinical trials to the third stage and had been awaiting

FDA approval for the last six months. Everything Swain had said in last night's presentation had checked out.

All of which at best only peripherally concerned her goal of conceiving a whiz-bang research topic she hoped would wow Director Swain. The problem was that her preparatory reading of research abstracts had left her painfully aware of how far out of her league Kendall-Jakes really was. Not only did she lack her doctorate—with no real hope of ever getting it—but she'd discovered just how much she *didn't* know about what was going on in the field of Applied Genetics. And even K-J itself: Estelle Lederman's summary last night was the most detailed and substantial recounting she'd heard, and not until Lacey had taken time to seriously peruse the Web site today had she seen what an awe-inspiring organization it was.

Where last night's presentation had inspired her, this afternoon's exposure to the hard facts had filled her with self-doubt. Now all the potential project ideas she'd dreamed over the years of developing had turned dull and elementary, the sorts of ideas a third grader might come up with for a science fair. Frustrated and discouraged, her mind hopped from subject to subject like a flea. One minute she was reading through an abstract on cloning frozen mice, and the next she was at some archaeological site looking at the mammoth monoliths Swain had mentioned in his talk last night. She'd start sorting through the complexities of a project on the reduction of roundworm telomeres, only to find herself reading about K-J's Accelerated Tissue Regeneration, or ATR, process.

Grimacing, she clicked back into Word and reread her encapsulation of Swain's vision—a statement she'd taken from the presentation and modified for her own use, determined to get herself back on track. She thought of the butterfly, and asked herself which of her potential avenues of investigation would most echo the concepts of *"We're going to change the world"* and *"make everything new."*

But thinking of the presentation made her think about Swain, his incredible presence on the stage, his mesmerizing voice and words, the excitement they'd generated in her, the desire she'd felt to be worthy of him . . . to join him in his quest. . . . For a moment she reveled in the revival of her feelings of optimism and hope. Then, one thought led to another until somehow she ended up reading through an online version of the book of Genesis in search of the passage about the giants he had mentioned. She found it in chapter six and was surprised that it really did seem to say that some sort of greater beings had come to Earth and gotten together with human women.

"Is that the *Bible* you're reading?!" Jade spoke from right behind her, and she jumped in surprise. In the rumble and whine of the machines around her, Lacey had not heard her roommate's approach.

"Just checking something Director Swain said last night in the presentation. . . ." Lacey said, her face flaming. "Your game over?" Jade had gone to the recreation center after lunch to play volleyball.

"Yeah. You shoulda come. We coulda used you." She went to one of the stopped dryers, pulled open the door, and felt through the clothes. With a grimace, she shut the door again and pushed the button for more time. "I'm surprised to hear Parker Swain was quoting the Bible."

"I thought you went to one of those presentations."

"I did. Ten months ago. I don't remember anything about the Bible."

"He just mentioned it briefly when he was speculating about the different myths about gods coming down to human women and making giants—that maybe they weren't gods but enlightened men."

"Oh yeah . . . That's in the Bible, you say?"

"Sort of." Lacey read the passage: " 'And it came to pass, when men began to multiply on the face of the earth, and daughters were born unto them, That the sons of God saw the daughters of men that they were fair; and they took them wives of all which they chose.

" 'And the LORD said, "My spirit shall not always strive with man, for that he also is flesh: yet his days shall be an hundred and twenty years."

" 'There were giants in the earth in those days; and also after that, when the sons of God came in unto the daughters of men, and they bare children to them, the same became mighty men which were of old, men of renown . . .' "

"Giants? It says that?" Jade dropped into the chair at Lacey's side and read the passage herself. "Huh," she said after a moment. "That's even weirder than I thought."

She leaned away from the laptop and forward to pull a green lollipop out of the back pocket of her jeans. "It blows me away to think there are actually people out there who believe that stuff," she said, peeling off the clear cellophane wrapper.

Lacey knew she should say something like, "I *believe that stuff*," but she didn't. For one thing, she had no desire to be the recipient of Jade's scorn just when they were getting to be friends; for another, she wasn't even sure she *did* believe it anymore.

"Some people even take it *literally*," Jade went on, thankfully oblivious to Lacey's discomfort. "You'd think after all the advances we've made in understanding our world and how we fit into it, it'd be a dead book." She lounged back in the chair, legs stretched out before her, holding the sucker up to inspect it. "Or at the very least only ignorant, redneck yokel types would be the ones who clung to it. Then you meet someone like Cameron Reinhardt and you have to scratch your head."

She licked the sucker's bright green face, then looked at Lacey. "Did you know he's a creationist? Doesn't even mess with that Intelligent Design hooey. Just says flat-out that God did it all. It boggles the mind, I know. Viascola's going to confront him next unity meeting. Ask him outright before all of us how he reconciles his position with the facts of evolution." She licked the lollipop again. "Assuming he ever *comes* back. Have you heard the latest on Manny?" She stuck the sucker into her mouth.

"I don't know. What's the latest?" Lacey surreptitiously closed her Word files. She'd said nothing to Jade about her work on a subject for a possible research project, as much because she suspected it would make the other girl jealous as because she feared nothing would ever come of it anyway, and she'd just make herself look stupid.

"He's gone missing," Jade said around the sucker. "He doesn't have leave this weekend, but he didn't show up today for breakfast or lunch and no one's seen him since the presentation last night."

"Well, he was just demoted to rat-man, so he's probably sulking in his room."

"If so, he's not answering his door. There's also a rumor he and Dr. Reinhardt had a huge fight in the AnFac last night. And that Reinhardt checked out this morning at 5:00 a.m. with duffle bag and laptop."

"So big deal," Lacey said, mildly annoyed. "Reinhardt *did* have leave." She closed her browser and powered off the laptop. "I know, because he asked me yesterday if I'd like to go into Tucson with him."

"Get out!" Jade pulled the sucker from her mouth and stared at Lacey. "After what happened the other night? I think he really *is* interested in you. Why didn't you go?"

Lacey frowned at her. "I told you: he's not for me." She had already explained to Jade that her so-called tryst with Cameron Reinhardt in the Madrona Lounge had been nothing of the sort. She'd only "gotten disturbed" going back to the AnFac that night, and he'd helped her regain her composure. Which was the truth. As far as it went. "Besides, I didn't have leave."

"Well, it's probably good you didn't, because some people think he murdered Manny and stuffed his body in the Vault."

"*What?!* Who's saying that? Aaron and his gossipy friend Ted?"

"It's Tom, and why act so surprised? Manny's disappeared, Reinhardt's gone—"

"You need a *body* to accuse someone of murder, for one. And I don't think it's even possible to just stuff it into one of the Vault canisters. Especially not single-handedly. And what would his motive be? He'd already demoted the guy. Why kill him?"

"Maybe it was self-defense."

Lacey rolled her eyes. "Why don't people here just take the most rational explanation when things like this come up? Which is that Manny's in a snit over the reversal of his fortunes." But even as she said the words she thought of her own situation, where people *had* taken the easiest, most rational explanation—that she'd had a panic attack and hallucinated an intruder, and been wrong. "Besides, I don't believe Reinhardt could do something like that."

"I don't know. He was pretty weird in that unity meeting yesterday," said Jade. "With the PTSD and all. And I've heard you can't always tell with psychopaths. How many times on the news have you heard how they seem like fine, upstanding people—the parents, the wife, the friends, the neighbors, all say, 'I can't believe he did that!' "

Which had certainly been true enough in Lacey's case when it had come to Erik Ellison. She'd misjudged him completely.

208 — KAREN HANCOCK

"If there was a fight, surely security would have seen it," Lacey pointed out. "And if Reinhardt *had* killed Manny, they'd have to know. In which case they'd have him in custody already, and it wouldn't be rumors, it'd be official."

Jade was looking at her oddly. "I can't believe you're *defending* him."

"I'm not defending *him*," Lacey protested, her face suddenly hot with embarrassment. "I'm defending truth and level-headedness."

"Level-headedness?" Jade grinned at her. "For someone who claims no interest in this guy, you seem awfully unlevel about it all. In fact, I'd say you're annoyed."

"I'm not *annoyed*!" Lacey frowned at her, then shrugged. "Okay, maybe I am. But not because of him. I just hate all this rumor-mongering."

Jade shook her head, still grinning. "Lighten up, girl! I'm just yanking your chain."

A strident buzz interrupted the conversation and Jade glanced around. "Ah. There's my dryer." She grabbed one of the rolling baskets and wheeled it up to the dryer as the clothes within tumbled slowly to a stop. After that several others came in, everyone talking of Manny Espinosa and Cameron Reinhardt and what each person had heard or thought. Lacey slid her laptop into the messenger bag she'd brought and got up to transfer her clothes from the washers to the dryer Jade had just emptied.

By dinnertime both Espinosa and Reinhardt were still missing, and the story of their alleged fight had achieved epic proportions. Some people were actually taking bets on whether Espinosa was dead or had simply left for good. Others murmured about Andrea Stopping and how Espinosa's mysterious disappearance certainly wasn't the first. Maybe he'd gone out hiking, too, they'd suggested ominously.

That was the first time Lacey heard there'd been other girls besides Andrea who'd disappeared. At least two, and she couldn't help thinking of her mysterious intruder. Wondering if perhaps he was behind all the disappearances. If Swain was executing yet another cover-up. After all, Manny had replaced her in the AnFac. What if Frogeater had come back and found him instead of Lacey and been angry?

The thought chilled her.

Swain cleared his throat into the microphone up on the front dais. "I have an announcement, if you please." The room quieted at once, and he continued. "I am sorry to report that Dr. Manuel Espinosa, our recent postdoctoral hire, has apparently left the Institute without checking out or giving notice of his resignation. We've confirmed that he was quite angry over his demotion to support technician yesterday, and we believe he has left us for this reason. The fact that all of his belongings have been cleared from his quarters corroborates this conclusion.

"As for the rumors regarding a fight between him and Dr. Reinhardt last night, those are *entirely* unsubstantiated. We have no eyewitnesses of this supposed occurrence, and surveillance records show nothing. For those of you stimulated to flights of speculation by the fact that Reinhardt is also absent this evening, please recall that today was his regularly scheduled leave rotation and also that it is his custom to eat dinner in Tucson and return late in the evening.

"With absolutely no evidence of foul play, we must conclude that Dr. Espinosa has left of his own accord, and that we will receive notice of his resignation soon. If not, we'll have to file a missing person report, which means the police will be out here—along with the press. Thus, in the interests of guarding the Institute's reputation and integrity, as well as that of doctors Espinosa and Reinhardt, I would appreciate it if you would all curtail your conversations regarding this matter until you have something factual and verifiable to discuss." He paused. "Thank you."

"So much for your ridiculous Vault theory," Jade muttered at Aaron.

"Hey, it could happen."

"Those canisters are like twenty feet tall or something. How's he supposed to get the body into one by himself?"

"And not trigger off-line or leakage alarms," Lacey added.

"Maybe he had help."

Groans and hisses of disgust greeted his suggestion.

As she turned from the conversation, Lacey's eye caught on Director Swain heading in their direction. He stopped to chat with Dr. Yuen at the table next to them, and then suddenly there he was, taking the empty faculty member seat between Pecos and Tina. For a moment everyone at the table was so shocked, no one said a word.

Swain smiled and said, "Please, don't let my position intimidate you. I'd rather you see me as your loving father than the distant director of the Institute. It's important that we get to know each other. You, so you'll know where I'm coming from and trust me; me, so I can know how best to serve you.

"Now, let's go around the table and each of you tell me how you got here, why it was you chose genetics in particular as your field of study, and what your long-term goals are. Where do you see yourself five years from now?" He turned to Pecos, who sat directly to his left. "You may start, young man."

Pecos hastily introduced himself.

They proceeded from Tina clockwise around the table to Aaron, Jade, and all too soon, Lacey. "Ms. McHenry," Swain said, making a point of showing her and everyone else there that he knew her name already, "what is it that *you* would most desire to research?"

Since she'd not come up with a single clear thing all day long, she'd been striving to come up with something intriguing before he got to her. Now that his attention was upon her, her mind went absolutely blank. Moments stretched by, and then, right out of the blue, words: "I think right now I'm mostly interested in the factors that direct growth. Particularly accelerated growth."

She heard her own voice with a measure of horror. What in the world was she saying? Was she deliberately trying to provoke him?

She was relieved when he simply lifted a brow, seeming more amused than annoyed, and said, "Well, now. That just happens to be an area that K-J is actively pursuing, as, of course, you know."

*Touché*, she thought.

Swain held her gaze. "And where do *you* see yourself five years hence?" he asked.

"Why, right here, I hope."

"No thoughts of running off to get your doctorate?"

"Well, if an offer came, of course, that would be great. . . ." But there was no chance of that. She suspected he knew it.

Finally he smiled, as if she had passed some sort of test, and said,

"I'm delighted you feel that way, Ms. McHenry. You wouldn't happen to have come up with any specific project ideas in line with your interest in accelerated growth, would you?"

"Project ideas? I . . . no, sir. Nothing specific."

"No? Well, why don't you see me after dinner and we'll discuss it further."

His attention moved on to Mel, sitting to Lacey's left. But the poor girl was so disarmed by what he'd just said to Lacey that she stumbled and stuttered her way through whatever it was she said. Lacey herself was so stunned she hardly heard her.

*Did Director Swain really just ask me to see him after dinner to discuss a potential project?* she wondered. When it finally penetrated that, yes, indeed, that was what he had done, she wanted to leap up and shriek, except . . .

Except she wasn't entirely sure it was for real. Perhaps he'd been annoyed by her comments about the ATR and was simply baiting her. He probably suspected she'd not been serious, given the thoroughness of the profiles he compiled on his employees. When she admitted as much, he'd send her back to Reinhardt and that would be the end of it.

Nevertheless, she could not extinguish the hope he'd birthed in her.

They continued around the table and, once the introductions were completed, had embarked on a lively conversation. Swain was engaging, generous, and funny, and by the end of dinner, she was utterly enthralled with him. That he'd take the time to sit with them, talk to them in such a respectful way, not as peons but as equals, blew her away. Every time she had any personal dealings with the man, it seemed, she just got more and more impressed.

The only weird part of it was that during the conversation he did not speak directly to her again, or even acknowledge her presence. His eyes would fix upon each of her tablemates, but would jump from Jade on Lacey's right straight over to Mel on her left, never again making eye contact with Lacey herself. It left her feeling quite confused, unable to celebrate, unable to lament, unable to do anything.

Even at dinner's end, as he'd left them and her cohorts gathered around to congratulate her in surprise and apparent joy, she couldn't shake her ambivalence. All he'd promised was a discussion. Congratulations seemed entirely premature.

Indeed, he'd left the table so rapidly, she wasn't sure he even remembered he'd asked her to talk to him afterward. At first she thought he'd left the room entirely, but then she saw him, locked in conversation with the head of Chemical Engineering. Not knowing what to do, she drifted in his direction, and as the others left to attend the evening forum, she waited in his periphery, slowly talking herself over to the view that he had forgotten what he'd asked of her, or she'd misunderstood, and even if he did mean to discuss a project with her he'd not meant that evening.

"Ah, Ms. McHenry." His smooth and pleasant voice broke into her dismayed rationalizations. "I've been making a few inquiries over the weekend, and it looks as if we may be able to get you into the U of A graduate program."

She gaped at him. He held up a cautionary finger. "Before you protest, hear me out. I spoke to Dr. Essex yesterday, and today he has agreed to approve on a trial basis your admission into the university's doctorate program. I will serve as your adjunct doctoral advisor, though officially it will be Dr. Essex who mentors you."

Her ears were roaring, and she wondered if she really was hallucinating this time. "I hardly know what to say, sir."

"How about, 'Thank you. I accept'?"

"I would love to. . . . I would say yes in a moment, except I—"

"Your funding problem," he guessed, cutting her off. "No worries. I have secured you a full sponsorship from among our many donors, one who has asked to remain anonymous."

"Estelle? Is it Estelle?"

"Now, now, Ms. McHenry." He smiled. "You can't ask me to betray a confidence. You have only to say yes."

"Well, then . . . yes! Of course I accept. I—" Words failed her as her throat closed up and tears blurred her vision.

"I'm transferring you out of Applied Genetics and into Human Resources for the time being. That's where we've located our other independent researchers. You'll be directly answering to Dr.

Viascola—though, as I said, I will be your advisor. Anything you need, anytime you wish to talk, just let me know. For now, report to Dr. Viascola tomorrow at nine, and she'll get you settled into your new office."

"Office?"

He smiled. "I told Essex you could have a rudimentary proposal ready by the end of the week, so why don't we set up an appointment for ten-thirty Thursday morning. You can bring in what you've got and we'll go over it. Then I'll fax the final version on Friday." He paused and smiled again. "I consider it a matter of honor to see that my loyal employees are very well treated, Ms. McHenry. Anything you need, just let me know."

"Yes, sir."

He said good night and left her there, too dazed to move, reliving the encounter in her mind, certain she must have misunderstood. To have her chance at a doctorate after all? Practically handed to her, money and all?

Eventually she ended up back at her room, which she had to herself, since Jade had gone to the forum. She shut the door and began to squeal and jump around with glee, reveling in the astonishing change in her fortunes. Soon enough, however, her ambition superseded her rejoicing, reminding her that if she had nothing to present on Thursday, the offer could well be retracted. She'd best get to work. Today's effort had been playtime. Now she needed to get serious.

As she sat down and powered up her laptop, Swain's parting words returned to her: "*I consider it a matter of honor to see that my loyal employees are very well treated.*" This time they struck her with a significance that her high-running emotions had blinded her to earlier, and she wondered suddenly if Swain's offer was not as much happenstance as it had appeared. Maybe his offer was not made because he'd noted potential in one of his young employees and wished to develop it, but because he was rewarding her for her silence regarding the events surrounding Frogeater. His way of making up for that small black spot she would always carry on her record.

It rankled a little, for she'd rather be promoted solely on the basis of her own work. And yet . . . after all the trouble she'd had, all the grunt work she'd put in, all the embarrassment and mental trauma she'd suffered, perhaps it was only fair she be recompensed in some way. Besides, it was only the opportunity that was being offered, not full-fledged success. That she *would* have to earn by her own merits. So why not take advantage of this opportunity to show him what she could do?

Her eyes drifted to the black box sitting on her desk. Strangely unreflective in the overhead lights, it looked more like a cube of shadow than obsidian or plastic—or whatever it was made of.

She picked it up and sat on her bedside. "I don't suppose *you* have the answers, do you?" she asked it jokingly, as if it were a Magic 8 Ball. Maybe if she turned it round she'd find the solution in a little answer box: *Signs point to yes. Reply hazy, try again. Without a doubt. My sources say no. . . .*

She did turn it round, but no answers appeared. Then a wave of dizziness swept over her and she plummeted through blackness. The sensation was so startling she dropped the box with a gasp. But as she stared at the cube on the floor, fear beating irrationally in her throat, nothing further happened. After a moment, fear turned to amusement—sleep deprivation and stress were no doubt rearing their ugly heads again.

With a grimace she replaced the cube on her desk, then pulled out her chair and reached for her laptop, because she'd just gotten the perfect idea for a project.

# Chapter Twenty-Two

## New Eden

Neos was right in his prediction that Zowan would be discharged from the infirmary on Monday afternoon, seventy-two hours after his exposure to the toxic wind surge. Though he felt fine—one hundred percent normal again, except for his buzzed-off hair—he was forbidden to go outside again for a year, due to his now-increased sensitivity to the toxins. Thus he was to be reassigned from the goat barn once he'd trained his senior assistant to take over his job, a task he had begun that afternoon.

And that same Monday, in the evening, as Neos had instructed him, he headed for the Star Garden shortly after dinner. He went alone. There was to be a performance of a string quartet that night, and he wanted to get to the fifth level before the place got too crowded. Plus, he didn't want to talk to his friends just now. Not only had his ordeal with the toxins left him shaken and emotionally brittle, but he'd learned that day—for real—that Andros had indeed died while Zowan was in recovery, the result of his inability to withstand his punishment in the Cube. His body had been cremated while Zowan was still in quarantine. Because he'd died as a result of his punishment, there would be no memorial service.

The news hit Zowan hard, all the grief and guilt he'd suffered during his time in quarantine returning tenfold, his pain no longer blunted by a drug-induced haze or confusing hallucinations of Andros's voice begging him to find him and free him. One moment he was on the verge of tears, the next boiling with anger over something petty and insignificant. He'd been snappish and impatient and downright mean to his poor senior assistant in the goat barn, and just trying to be civil and normal at dinner had been a challenge. It was hard to function properly when he felt as if his life had been turned upside down and shaken into a disorganized muddle. Reality had blended with fantasy, and he struggled now to pull them apart.

He'd told no one of the things he'd experienced during his recovery—not the pink ants, not his exchange with Gaias, not the strange visitation from the one who called himself *I Am*, and especially not his encounter with Neos. Dr. Xavier had cautioned him upon his release against giving credence to anything he might recall of his time there because the toxins had caused him to hallucinate various visitors with whom he'd spoken. But the truth was he'd had no visitors.

Perhaps. All Zowan knew was that he'd first learned of Andros's death through Gaias. And so far, everything Neos had said would happen had happened. Moreover he'd not been able to get the memory of the one who'd called himself *I Am* out of his mind, nor his command to leave the Enclave. Nor had he forgotten Neos's promise that if he came to the Star Garden tonight, Neos would set him free. Maybe it really was all hallucination, manufactured by his deepest dreams and desires, but in case it wasn't, he'd be here. If nothing happened, then he'd know for sure. . . .

The Star Garden's lights were always kept low to highlight the artificial stars in the night-sky dome overhead. As Zowan arrived, the musicians were unfolding their music stands and setting them before the four chairs clustered to one side of the garden's central fountain. Chairs and benches had been set out on all the levels for the people to sit on, the first level already completely filled.

Zowan made his way to the top level and around to the side opposite the stairs, where two empty padded benches flanked the golden portrait panel of the ancient Sumerian queen Summat-rama. The same place he'd sat with Andros the two times they'd engaged in heretical conversation. Had Neos known that somehow?

As he approached he eyed the panel, in case his brother had left a clue or sign to reassure him, but saw nothing. Turning his back on the benches and panel, he braced his forearms on the railing and watched the crowd grow beneath him.

Of course, Neos's instruction had made more sense when Zowan hadn't known there'd be a special function going on in the garden at the same time. Tonight would be a difficult time to make contact, with so many people, including Enforcers, packed into the place. And meeting at the highest level, with five flights of spiraling stairs to descend to the exit, didn't make very much sense, either.

His gaze caught on the tall, lanky form and dark face of his friend and sleepcell mate Parthos, climbing the spiral stair between the second and third levels. He was one of a continuous moving line heading ever upward through all four levels. Erebos, their third cellmate, followed Parthos, and after him came Terra, dressed in a white linen tunic and dark ankle-length skirt, her two red braids tied together at the middle of her back. Two young men followed her, and then, sure enough, little black-haired Helios appeared around the curve.

Zowan watched Parthos reach the third level and step immediately onto the next spiral to the fourth. When the others came right after him without hesitation, Zowan knew they were coming up to join him—despite the fact he'd been a cranky pain in the neck today, and that he'd told Parthos he didn't intend to come at all.

But they were his friends, and they had been Andros's friends, too, and they were grieving as badly as he was, so how could he drive them away? Parthos reached the fifth level and for the first time made eye contact with him, then led the others around the railing to where Zowan stood. Without a word they took up flanking positions, Terra to his right, Parthos to his left, the other three at the ends of the row. Not one of them said a word.

Well, this would certainly put a new wrinkle in whatever plans Neos had for contacting him. He wanted to tell them all to go away, that he didn't feel like having company right now. But he couldn't make himself utter the words. Maybe they would all lose interest and go off to bed before time for his meeting. Maybe his meeting would never happen, and he'd have driven off his friends for nothing. And the truth was, he welcomed their presence, even if he didn't want to talk.

Finally the Star Garden was filled with listeners, and the string players who had spent about ten minutes tuning up their instruments stopped and waited. Two Elders pressed their way through the crowd below, followed by several Enforcers. The Elders took their reserved seats immediately across the fountain from the quartet. Some of the Enforcers took up positions nearby, while four headed for the spiraling stairway in the corner. Seeing them approach, those on the stairway increased their pace to get out of their way.

"Yup, that's Gaias, all right," Terra remarked, her arm pressing against Zowan's as she leaned toward him. One of the four Enforcers heading for the stairway had stopped to look around. Despite the milling people, he stood in a well of space, the others unwilling to come too close to him.

"You know, they talk about Andros malfunctioning," Terra said quietly. "I think they should take a look at Gaias. He's become obsessed with you. Every time I went to the infirmary this weekend to see if they'd let me visit you, he was there. Asked me what I knew about Andros, you, your times in the ravine—all kinds of weird questions."

Having scanned the main floor, Gaias now lifted his gaze to each successive level, eyes carefully cataloguing each person standing in his view at the rail. Zowan gave thought to stepping back for a moment and taking a seat on one of the benches behind him, just to make things more difficult for his brother—if Gaias didn't see him, he'd inspect each floor on foot—but he did not act on it.

"He even asked if you'd ever talked about seeing or talking with Neos. *After* his death, that is. I thought he was trying to make a case for you malfunctioning, too."

He listened to her with half an ear, eyes upon his brother, who was just about finished with his scan of the fourth level. Now his eyes lifted and . . . sure enough, they fixed almost immediately on Zowan, the third eye gleaming phosphorescently in the low light. With a small smile, Gaias turned abruptly and headed for the spiral stairway. He cut across the open area where the musicians were playing, forcing at least one of them to miss a few notes when he passed a bit too close.

Beyond the clear space, he pushed easily through the spectators, who parted before him like water under a boat's bow.

Terra was leaning even more closely against him now as she murmured, "But then yesterday I heard a rumor that you'd actually seen a *man* out there when you were in the ravine with the goats. Right before the winds came."

Zowan turned to look at her in surprise. "Who told you that?"

"One of the girls I'm working with."

"How would she know?"

"*Did* you see someone?"

He shrugged and told her how they'd said he was already being affected by the toxin spike at that point and must have hallucinated. She snorted her disbelief.

Gaias had reached the fifth level and now emerged from the stairway's shadows on the opposite side, gaze fixed on Zowan. As he started around the level, Zowan dipped his head toward the Enforcer and said to Terra, "Maybe you should ask Gaias, since he was out there, too."

Stuck out there, in fact, and apparently no worse for it. But then, Xavier said Zowan had hallucinated the Enforcers coming out to warn him, as well.

Zowan turned his gaze back to the performance below as Gaias came round and found a spot against the railing not far from Helios. When Zowan realized he meant to stay there for the duration, he was filled with a powerful dismay. How could Neos ever meet him with Gaias standing right there? He had to make him go away!

But even as he thought it, Zowan knew it would be impossible. Even if there hadn't been a concert, it wouldn't have worked, for how would Neos walk through the commons and mall and into the Star Garden without being caught? It made no sense. It had never made any sense. He'd simply desired so strongly to believe it, sense didn't enter into the matter.

Neos was undoubtedly dead. Zowan probably overheard someone say that Andros was dead when he was in one of his hallucinatory states in the infirmary, and from that had conjured not only Gaias's visit, but Andros's pleading voice. And the voice of I Am, as well. Who most likely hadn't spoken in parallel to words from the *Key Study* because

He was real, but because Zowan had assigned those remembered words to Him in the hallucination. Besides, what kind of name was "I Am," anyway? He must've made it up.

There would be no meeting with Neos, there was no Light, and there would be no freedom for Zowan. He'd best just accept it and get on with his life in the Enclave before he made so many mistakes they would put him into the Cube.

Though this was the reasonable conclusion, for a moment his disappointment was so bitter he wanted to weep. Then, in the next moment, he wanted to stride around to his brother and smash a fist into his face, maybe grab him by the throat and strangle him right there in front of everyone.

*Why can't they just leave me alone? Let me leave if I want? Let me wander off across the poison-filled surface of the Earth and die?*

The urge to weep was back, and he swallowed hard against the lump in his throat—mortified, blinking, lest the tears welling in his eyes break free and trail down his cheeks. He would have left right then could he have done so without drawing an inordinate amount of attention.

The quartet had just finished their third selection when the lights went out—stars and wall lamps together—steeping all in sudden and absolute blackness. Since power disruptions occurred frequently in the Enclave's electrical circuits, blackouts were a common occurrence, and all Edenites were trained from early childhood to freeze wherever they were and wait for the lights to return or instructions to be given. Block leaders all carried portable hand lamps in case the power outage lasted longer than a few minutes.

Thus, when this one occurred, everyone obediently stood or sat where they were and waited patiently for the lights to come back on and the concert to resume.

Instead, the alarm Klaxons went off, and a rough male voice bellowed, "Breach!"

At which point, pandemonium erupted. Zowan immediately reached for Terra, pulling her snug against him as he stepped back from the railing toward the wall and the two benches, lest in the chaos they might be pushed over and fall five levels. His grasp on Terra was broken as they tumbled onto one of the benches. Screams and shouts and a thunder of running footfalls filled the air, and the wood floor trembled underfoot. Where were the hand lamps? Where were the leaders? Why didn't they act?

If the sealed integrity of the Enclave had truly been breached, precious oxygen and water were not only leaving New Eden, but deadly poisons were entering. Shouldn't the garden be locking itself down, guarding the precious air it had? Everyone knew the Enclave was equipped with a system of self-closing emergency steel doors that would be automatically activated should the Enclave's outer walls be breached. Could they still function if there was no power?

A sudden gust of air washed around him, heavy with the odor of unwashed flesh. Probably someone had just raced along the walkway searching for the stairwell. The thought had no sooner flashed through his mind than it was proved wrong as he was seized from behind and pulled off his feet. Another whoosh of air, like a heavy door closing on him, preceded a sudden close thump, and immediately the noise in the Star Garden was reduced to muffled cries and indistinct thumping.

After the absolute darkness of the garden, his pupils had dilated enough to detect the faint light that illumined what was a narrow passage paralleling the curved wall of the Star Garden. He heard someone breathing behind him. *Neos?* He turned, excited. But his hope gave way to panic when he saw a man robed in Enforcer's black filling the space there. Gaias! But why would Gaias snatch him like this? And why was he suddenly wearing his cowl over his head like that?

Then the stench of old sweat and stale clothing, made worse by a tang of vomit, became so overpowering Zowan could hardly breathe, and he knew it couldn't be Gaias. No one would be allowed to live in the Enclave with that kind of body odor.

Motioning for Zowan to follow, the other man sidled away through the narrow passage. Zowan gave him a couple of steps headstart to clear the air, then followed, thinking he was nuts to follow a stranger in Enforcer black, especially one who smelled so bad. But hope and curiosity had overruled his common sense, for it seemed Neos's words were coming true, impossible as it was. Or maybe it was all hallucination again. Dr. Xavier had said he might suffer isolated episodes of delusion for another few weeks.

They crept past the wooden frames and studs that supported the backside of the Star Garden's finished interior walls, the passage lit by oblong stones aglow with blue-green phosphorescence, sparsely placed along the stone wall near the floor. Though Zowan had never seen the likes of them before, he guessed now was not the time to remark on them, even if pandemonium still raged on the other side of the wall.

As they rounded the curve, Zowan noted several places where makeshift stepladders sat beneath what appeared to be peepholes bored through the facing material. Seeing as the Star Garden was a place where Edenites came for solitude and privacy, Zowan found this both understandable and outrageous. Had someone spied on him and Andros here last week? Heard their heretical conversation? Or worse, the one that had preceded it six months ago?

But his whispered "What is this place?" only provoked a hissed order for quiet from his guide.

Before long they came to a closetlike opening in the rock wall to their left. As Zowan's guide turned his back to the opening, then reached up and pulled himself out of sight, Zowan realized the "closet" lacked both floor and ceiling and was actually a vertical ventilation shaft cut through the stone.

Cautiously, Zowan backed into the place the other man had just vacated and reached up as he had done. His fingers closed about the metal rung of a ladder ascending the side of the shaft. Bracing his feet on the sides of the opening until he'd ascended far enough to get them on the ladder's bottom rung, he remained unnervingly aware of the space at his back and the indeterminate drop below him.

After what seemed like forever, his hands reached the end of the ladder. Groping about, he found a flat landing, and was considering how to execute the transition from ladder to floor without anything to hold on to when a hand seized his arm and pulled him off the ladder onto the flat as if he were a child.

The hand was hot as fire as it drew him away from the shaft and through a doorway—though only the snick of a door shutting behind them told him so. He was released then, and a palm-sized lamp was pressed into his right hand as a rough but familiar voice grated, "Turn it on. Keep your voice down."

"Neos?!" Zowan flicked on the hand lamp, its weak light illuminating his dark-robed guide once more. It was Neos, all right, but his brother had changed considerably since Zowan had last seen him six months ago. His face had grown more angular, his brow heavier, his cheeks gaunter. It was just now sweat-sheened and streaked with some sort of dark pigment, and the angry red boil in the midst of his forehead looked ready to burst.

Zowan had no more than a glimpse of it, though, for the moment the light hit him, Neos gasped and turned away, shielding his eyes with a huge, knobby, long-nailed hand, also streaked with pigment, dirt . . . and blood.

"What is that on your forehead?" Zowan angled the lamp away from the other man, all his excitement now turned to horror. It couldn't be an oculus. Why would they do that? Neos was never selected to be an Enforcer. Enforcers were supposed to have affinity for the position, to be reliable and obedient and stable. . . .

"I don't know," Neos said, so softly Zowan had to lean toward him, trying not to gag on his pungent body odor. "I don't want to know." He said it so vehemently, Zowan veered off from questioning him further. He was obviously unwashed. Perhaps it was just a big pimple.

"Is there really a breach?" Zowan whispered, trolling about for something else to say, and realizing now that it must have been Neos who'd yelled that panic-igniting word in the blacked-out Star Garden.

Neos made a huffing sound that might have been a snort. "There's *always* a breach. New Eden's air comes unfiltered from the surface and always has." He shook his head. "There are no air scrubbers, no seals, no poisons. The surface is fine. Everything they've told us is a lie. Everything."

"Are you all right?" Zowan leaned closer, lifting the lamp a bit, to see that Neos really was shivering under the heavy cloak. "You seem ill."

"I *am* ill. They've infected me with something. I don't know what. I don't even know if I'll survive it. Probably not."

"We should get you to the infirmary," said Zowan. But the moment he uttered the words he knew it was a ridiculous suggestion.

Which Neos confirmed with another snort. "Why? So they can finish the job?" He fell into a coughing fit—deep, wracking, mucus-filled coughs that made Zowan draw back in alarm. His thoughts went back to the heat of his grip, the boil on his forehead, and the clumps of fair hair on his red tunic. All symptoms of the development of an oculus . . .

Suddenly his brother's hand shot up from the dark folds of his cloak to grip Zowan's forearm again, the burning on his bare skin now carrying profound significance. "The world is not what they said it was. You have to go and see it. They're holding us here like prisoners. Doing things to us that shouldn't be done to—"

He broke into another bout of vicious coughing. When he had recovered, they sat silently for a moment, and then he said again, "You have to go and see it."

"How?" He waited and, when Neos said nothing, added, "*Is* there a way out of the goat ravine?"

Neos grunted. "It would never be that obvious." He heaved a shuddering sigh and shoved to his feet. "Come. I'll show you."

Between the continued darkness, and the exit from the Star Garden through various ducts and shafts, Zowan had lost all sense of direction. He followed Neos through a maze of passages—some wide and high and recognizable as corridors in the Enclave proper, others dusty, cramped, and unfinished. Once they walked around the edge of a huge shaft, toes balanced on a narrow walkway as they held on to the pipes and cables that snaked down the stone wall.

Zowan had no idea how long they walked, or where they were, and sometimes he wondered again if he was just hallucinating all of it.

Finally they entered a low-ceilinged chamber full of the whir of machinery and the odor of damp earth, metal, and concrete. Zowan's hand lamp reflected off huge pipes sprouting out of the floor, running parallel to it and then turning away, or dipping down again. Some were marked with red painted lines, others with blue. They followed one such pipe, marked with red, all the way to the back of the chamber, where it dove into the floor so close to the back wall they practically touched. About five feet away from it, Neos rolled aside the large metal drum

THE ENCLAVE — 225

that was holding a four-foot square of steel plating in place against the wall. Pulling the plating aside, he revealed a small tube that had been drilled through the stone, slightly over two feet in diameter.

"It's through there," he said, gesturing for Zowan to enter. "Crawl on to the other side and wait for me there."

"Wait for you?" Zowan looked at him aghast.

"There are some things I need to do."

"Like what?"

"Set up some diversions. I can feel Gaias getting closer. And they'll probably have some of the power lines up soon."

"What difference does that make? Can't we just leave?"

"If they know where we've left the Enclave, they'll know where to look for us on the surface. Besides, I want to keep things confused enough they won't know for sure you're even gone yet. It'll give you a bit of a head start. And believe me, you'll need it. If they think you've gotten out, they'll hunt you down. And when they catch you, they'll add you to their collection of experimental subjects."

"But how will I know which way to go?"

"You won't have any options. Just crawl to the end of the tube and wait for me there. Now hurry up. I want to close this back up before I leave."

And so Zowan shoved hard into the narrow tube, which was barely wide enough for his shoulders. Wriggling forward on his elbows and hips, the beam of the hand lamp spearing about erratically, he tried not to think of where he was or where he might be going. But when he heard the sound of the metal drum being rolled back into place against the steel plate, intense anxiety accelerated his pace until he was crawling as fast as he could, desperate to get to the end of the tube and wondering how he was going to be able to stand waiting in a space not much bigger than his sleepcell bunk for who knew how long.

Especially since he was growing more and more convinced this was all a trick and Neos had only brought him here to bury him alive in this bizarre way. His breathing rasped loudly around him as blisters formed at the pressure points where he sought to push himself forward.

Then abruptly his outstretched elbows came down on nothing and he pitched headfirst out of the tube.

Zowan fell only about two feet to a dirt floor below the crawl tube's ending. At first he lay panting, disoriented in the total darkness that had descended on him when he'd dropped his hand lamp. Profoundly relieved that things hadn't turned out as badly as he'd feared, he still regretted ever having gone to the Star Garden. Neos had sounded like a madman, not just during their recent flight through the Enclave, but earlier when he'd visited Zowan in the infirmary. Zowan had not wanted to admit it then, invested as he was in the hope of getting away. Now he could not escape the horrifying realization that he'd been tricked.

After a time he sat up and groped around until he found his hand lamp, then switched it on to look around, the beam noticeably weaker than it had been. He sat in yet another narrow, rock-walled tunnel, though this one was at least high enough he could stand up in it. Mindful of the hand lamp's failing battery, he switched it off and settled down against the wall to wait. Silence pressed about him so profound the rasp of his own breathing sounded loud. The rankness of Neos's unwashed flesh lingered in his nose, and he could almost feel the trembling, too-hot hand upon his arm. He was getting thirsty, too, and had no idea where he might find water. . . .

*Led here by a madman. What an idiot you are,* he told himself. But then, maybe he was also mad. . . .

Eventually he drifted into sleep, where Andros called to him again. *"They've got me locked up in a dark cell down here. Please, Zowan, come and get me out. I don't know what they're going to do to me!"*

*"Why would you think they're going to do something to you?"* Zowan asked him.

*"Because I can hear them talking about it. It's your fault I'm here, you know. You have to come and get me out!"*

Guilt seared Zowan's heart. *"I don't know where you are, Andros! I don't even know where I am right now."*

Andros did not reply.

*"Besides, I have to wait for Neos to come back. . . ."*

Again, only silence. Andros spoke to him no more, and somehow Zowan knew his friend was annoyed with him.

He awoke to the same dark, dusty corridor he'd fallen asleep in with no idea how long he'd slept. Neos had not returned and Zowan's thirst was stronger than ever. He was getting hungry, too.

How long should he wait? What if, in creating his diversions, Neos had been caught? What if they'd made him tell where Zowan was and were coming for him now? Or worse, what if Neos had been caught and taken to that place where the experimental subjects were kept? What if he wasn't coming back?

He wrapped his arms around bent knees as horror consumed him. For a time he sat nursing bitter self-recrimination. Then a sound made him look up, and he glimpsed a gleam of light on the rock walls of the corridor ahead of him, just where it took a turn. He sat forward in sudden hope. "Neos?" he called.

*There!* Another gleam. He leapt to his feet, switched on his hand lamp, and soon reached the place where the corridor turned and angled upward, arriving just as the person ahead of him disappeared around the next corner. "Neos!" he called, louder this time. "I'm down here!" Neos must have come back, after all, and not seen Zowan sleeping in the darkness beside the hole.

Now Zowan hurried up the sloping corridor, expecting his brother to reappear around the corner at any moment. But he did not. When Zowan reached the corner himself, he saw the light shining down a rugged rocky wall from above. Hurriedly he climbed after it, speculating that Neos wasn't speaking for fear of drawing the attention of Enforcers. But as the mysterious man with the lantern continued to lead upward, never letting him draw close enough to see more than a robed figure with a light, he began to think it wasn't Neos at all.

Instead his thoughts returned to the voice of I Am, who had told him during his time in the infirmary to leave the Enclave, to come out of the darkness. . . . Was that who was leading him now? A new eagerness seized him, a sense of something greater than he could imagine. He hurried along narrow passages that had turned from solid rock to earth and rock together, his shoulders brushing the walls, the top of his head sometimes brushing the wooden supports that held up the tunnel. Intersecting passages offered alternative paths, but he ignored them, his eyes fixed on the light ahead. The passages gradually grew wider. At one point he passed a small room and found a dusty striped mattress on a metal frame, a blanket folded at its foot, a not-so-dusty bucket sitting beside it—as if someone might have lived here for a time.

Soon after that, he felt the faint draft of drier, warmer air, and his pace quickened yet again. Then his guiding light winked out, and he stopped in astonished dismay. Darkness pressed around him like black wool. He thought of all the side spurs he had passed, how hard it would be to return. Yes, he still had his hand lamp but . . . how would he know the way?

The draft caressed his face, carrying an odor reminiscent of the goats' grotto. Maybe he could follow the direction of that air current. . . .

Heart pounding with new hope, he started onward, and slowly, perhaps as his eyes adjusted, he became aware of a faint glow ahead. It wasn't enough to make out forms, but it was light. At the next corner, it grew subtly brighter as the passage leveled off and took a series of short turns, each new vantage showing more and more illumination. The temperature was rising, as well.

For the first time it occurred to him that he had no protective suit, no brown-lensed goggles for his eyes. . . . All the terrifying warnings he'd ever heard about walking unprotected on the surface flooded his mind, and he came to a stop. Neos said it was all a lie, that the world had not been poisoned, that people *could* walk its surface and live. But Neos had left him alone in the darkness for who knew how long, failing to keep his promise to return. How could he trust Neos?

His thirst had grown into a monstrous craving, and going back would be a long and difficult journey. Maybe there would be a quiet pool ahead, like in the goats' grotto.

Besides, it was not Neos who had led him this far. It was the light of I Am.

He continued on and soon turned into a short passage, which clearly led to the surface. A grating stood in the opening, but even so the light was so bright he flung up an arm to shield his eyes.

The opening was so small he had to crawl on hands and knees to get through it, and the grating turned out to be a dead tree, whose sharp thorns and rough branches tore at his skin and cotton tunic as he pressed through it. Finally, though, he escaped its clutches and stood upright on a sloping, rocky surface. At first he had to clench his eyes shut and hold an arm up against them. Even then, the brightness flared white and yellow against the back of his eyelids. But after a while it didn't seem so bad, and he pulled his arm away just a bit, slitted his eyes open, and peered around.

The space was horrifying. He stood at the midst of an expanse of heat and whiteness that sucked at him from every angle until he felt as if he would explode away into it. The brightness, the barren ground, the space, the heat . . .

Panic swooped upon him and he fled back through the dead tree's thorny, grasping branches, wriggling through the hole, then running down the first passage and around the corner into the second—into the blessed velvety darkness from which he'd come. He fumbled on the hand lamp—which seemed a puny light indeed after what blazed on the surface—and kept going. He passed the bed on its metal frame, ducked under the straining wooden supports, and on down the increasingly narrow passages, his hand lamp flashing off a succession of oblong glowstones that guided him steadily downward. And all the while he felt the pain mount in his head, as his throat and lungs burned worse with every breath.

Neos had lied, not Father! The surface was everything the Elders had said it was: barren, burned, and poisoned. And now, for his foolishness he was dying. Unless he could get back to the infirmary before the poison spread and his organs began to shut down. . . .

He reached the small chamber where he'd slept, clawed his way through the crawl tube, and rammed into the steel plate and metal drum that blocked the tube from the pump room. Hysterically he threw himself at the plate, smashing into it with shoulder and hands, toes dug into the rock floor as he shoved with every ounce of his strength. When it didn't give an inch, he collapsed in despair, weeping bitterly. But as he regained his breath, his fear exploded again, driving him to shove himself at the plate, again and again and again.

How could he have been such a fool! Neos was dead. He'd obviously imagined all of this, made his way to the surface somehow. He'd gone out unshielded, and now the toxins were slowly frying him from head to toe.

*I'm going to die!*

Out of his mind with fear, driven by desperation, he kept on hitting and shoving at the plate. Finally it gave, just a bit. He shoved some more—shaking, sweating, his toes blistering from the repeated need to grip the rock and push, push, push.

Finally he'd moved it enough to slide his hand out and get hold of the plate's edge. Slowly he worked it sideways until he made an opening large enough to squeeze through and wriggled out onto the pump room floor. Once he'd caught his breath again, he stood and hurried past the red- and blue-lined pipes, still using the hand lamp, heading toward the door at the far side. Beyond it lay another room, then another door and another room. But finally he pressed through a third much heavier door and staggered into the light of a small finished corridor. He'd made it!

And then he realized he still had no idea where he was.

Thirst clawed at his throat and glued his tongue to the roof of his mouth. He sagged against the wall, feeling dizzy and cheated. All that work for nothing. They would never find him in time. His lungs were on fire. His heart was beating so fast he thought it would come bursting from his chest at any moment. His vision was blurring, and the paralysis was setting in. . . .

He began to weep. "Oh, Father, what have I done? *What have I done?*"

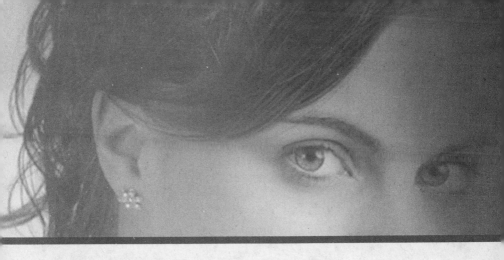

PART TWO

# Chapter Twenty-Four

On Wednesday morning Cam sat in his usual place at Swain's table, surrounded by a cacophony of breakfast chatter, with not one remark directed toward him—though many were undeniably about him.

It had been like this since Monday morning when he'd walked into the dining hall and found himself greeted with such coolness from his co-workers, he feared his new alliance with Rudy had already been discovered. It was almost a relief to learn of the Saturday night fight he'd supposedly had with Manny Espinosa wherein he'd murdered the postdoc and dumped his body in the desert.

Since it was more or less what Swain had predicted the rumor mill would produce, Cam wasn't too concerned, knowing the arrival of Manny's letter of resignation would set things straight.

Except it hadn't arrived. Despite Cam's faithful return Sunday night, Swain had not only withheld announcement of his "receipt" of the letter on Monday, but had been "forced" to notify the police of their missing postdoc after twenty-four hours.

The police had come to investigate that same Monday, questioning Cam in his glass-walled lab office in full view of his subordinates. Though completely innocent, he'd been so nervous and lied so poorly, his questioners left the interrogation convinced he was involved. But with no witnesses, no evidence of foul play, and no body, they could bring no charge of murder. Especially since Manny's car and personal belongings were missing, too. And since he'd certainly had motive to quit his position and walk away, they could only agree he'd likely done so. Until something more turned up, that was how they would leave it.

But as of Wednesday morning, with the absolving resignation letter still missing, Cam was being avoided like the plague. His arrival inevitably cut off conversation and usually cleared the immediate area within five minutes. Swain himself hadn't said one word to him, though they had shared every meal at the table in front of the stage for two days now. In fact, the director had never even looked at Cam, treating him as if he didn't exist. The rest of his Inner Circle followed suit, except for Nelson Poe, who couldn't seem to stop himself from answering Cam's questions, even if his answers were mumbled monosyllables and he never made eye contact.

Since Cam knew Swain could have generated that letter whenever he wished—or released his incriminating video from the Vault's loading dock the night Manny disappeared—it was obvious he intended this as punishment. Discipline for Cam's having missed the director's special Sunday afternoon security meeting, and for leading the blue Honda Accord nearly to Mexico before heading back to Kendall-Jakes. Cam suspected there was also the crime of telling Lacey McHenry the truth that night in the Madrona Lounge: her sudden transfer out of Cam's department and into Gen Viascola's on Monday morning had come as a genuine shock.

She worked on the sixth floor now, in Gen's suite of offices and cubicles, developing a project for Swain. Should it be acceptable, the project would serve as her doctoral thesis in an adjunct mentoring arrangement K-J had allegedly made with the U of A Genetics department. Cam had found that notion so irregular, he'd called the university that same Monday to corroborate with the department head, a personal friend. Unfortunately, he'd been sent straight to voice mail, and as of yet, no one had returned his call.

With the exception of the brief walks she'd taken around the campus each morning, Lacey's new project had claimed her every waking moment. According to Jade, she divided her time between her new office and the staff library on the fourth floor, while living off vending machine food. And Cam couldn't help but notice that not only had

Swain isolated her, he'd used her hope of fulfilling her abandoned dreams of gaining her doctorate to win her loyalty.

That he'd so swiftly pulled her into his web of influence might have been solely to ensure she didn't guess the truth of what he was doing to Cam. Or it could be something else entirely. Rudy had said Swain seemed to be stepping up operations in various locations, so perhaps there was some overarching timetable driving the director's actions.

Across the round table, Swain was pontificating to Slattery, Oscar Orozco, and Maia Ahmed-White, his immediate neighbors, about the importance of the open house set to begin in two days. Gen, who sat to Cam's right, was in deep conversation with her other seatmate, Lee Yuen, while to Cam's immediate left, Nelson Poe methodically ate his scrambled eggs, bacon, and whole wheat toast, his normal melancholic mien downright gloomy today. His monosyllabic answers to the few questions Cam asked him soon discouraged further attempts, leaving Cam free to entertain his own thoughts.

With McHenry out of his reach for the moment, and his movements too closely watched to make snooping feasible, he'd used the last two days to reintroduce himself to the ziggurat and its grounds, taking every reasonable opportunity to follow routes he'd not yet traveled, or explore outbuildings and floors he'd not yet visited. He'd been careful not to make so great a change in his habits and activities as to draw undue attention, and in that regard was grateful for the rumors and false accusations, since they justified his avoidance of the more populous places he usually frequented.

He made a point now of noticing details of his environment he'd not before, and over the last two days, the hyperawareness he'd cultivated during his time in Afghanistan had returned with surprising ease and speed. Already it was almost second nature to note the positions of air vents, corridor intersections, camera positions, the locations of various supply and electrical closets, the people who used them, the routines of the service staff, and of the others with whom he interacted. He took note of the lay of the land in an active, inquiring way, noticed the relationship between roads and buildings and the surrounding hills and arroyos, even the weather and the vegetation, a myriad of details to be filed into his memory for potential use later.

Beyond this general reconnaissance, the only one of his goals currently achievable was snatching one of Swain's eating utensils. Having decided on a fork, Cam had concluded it had to be taken at breakfast, that being the meal after which people—particularly Swain—were least likely to linger. He had picked up an unused replacement fork from one of the outlying tables at dinner last night. It now rested in the front right side pocket of his lab coat, awaiting the best combination of events to be put into play.

Crucial in that combination was that Swain leave before the servers cleared his place. Though yesterday he'd sat and talked long after they'd done so, this morning Cam hoped—and prayed—he would adhere to his regular routine and leave swiftly. Having already gobbled down most of his breakfast, Cam dawdled now over his last few bites of pancake, sipping his coffee thoughtfully. Once the director left, Cam's greatest challenge would be getting around the table to Swain's place before the servers swooped in.

Feigning obliviousness, he listened intently as Swain went on about the various financiers crucial to K-J's operation, who must be courted during the open house, a task he now assigned to Slattery, Orozco, and Ahmed-White. As the director's words and tone wound down, Cam set down his coffee cup. Swain asked for questions. When no one spoke, he gave his underlings a nod, said good-bye, and left.

Immediately Cam grabbed his files and the used napkin they rested on and skirted the table. He reached the place a step ahead of a busboy, barging in front of the young man and laying his folders and napkin atop the fork he meant to take.

"Director Slattery," he said as the assistant director laid his own napkin beside his plate. "I was wondering if I might have a word? This requisition order is only for—"

"Not now," Slattery cut in, standing abruptly. "I have a security meeting."

"It's about my new frogs. I—"

But the AD was already turning away. "E-mail your concerns to Deena," he said over his shoulder.

When Cam turned back to the table, he found himself being self-consciously ignored by his tablemates. Some were bending to pick up purses or briefcases, while others hurriedly arose to walk away, everyone keeping their eyes off him. Perfect.

He scooped up his folders, grabbing Swain's fork through the napkin, stepped back quickly, and turned to walk away. To his horror the tablecloth came with him—glasses tumbled in fountains of water and leftover orange juice; plates and flatware slid away; coffee sloshed across the white linen and onto several of his tablemates. He let go of the tablecloth, napkin and fork, the latter falling to the floor. Immediately he bent to retrieve it as people swore in annoyance and the service staff came running. Somehow he managed to pocket the napkin-wrapped fork and drop to the floor the one he'd stolen earlier before he was pressed aside by those trying to clean up his mess.

As he backed out of the chaos, he realized his little escapade had drawn every eye in the room. Embarrassment blazed in his face as he headed for the door and snickering arose in his wake.

*Could you have been more inept?* he asked himself as he left the dining hall. *What was Rudy thinking? What was I thinking to imagine I'm up to doing this sort of thing anymore?*

He entered the men's room just outside the dining hall, gave thanks that one of the two stalls was empty, and pushed into it. As he latched the metal door, a wave of trembling overtook him, and he sagged against the panel, waiting for it to pass.

After a few minutes, he stood upright again. Drawing a deep breath, he set his folders on the floor and with shaking fingers pulled one of two long, narrow manila collection envelopes from the breast pocket of his lab coat. He squeezed it open, reached into his side pocket and, using only two fingers, pulled the fork gingerly out of the bigger pocket and dropped the implement tines-first into the envelope. The fork was just a bit too long for him to seal the flap, so he had to leave it open as he dropped it back into the front side pocket.

When he returned to the corridor outside the dining hall, he ran into Gen Viascola coming out of the women's room, the front of her white blouse wet and faintly stained with coffee. She glared at him. "Cameron, you are such a klutz! Don't you *ever* pay attention to what you're doing?"

He stared at her, the fork in its envelope seeming to quiver and bulge from his lab-coat pocket so that he was certain her gaze would be drawn to it any moment.

But it was not. And when he only stared at her blankly, she rolled her eyes and huffed exasperation. "Well, I'm glad I've run into you, anyway. We need to talk about Friday's unity meeting."

Relieved and feeling silly for his unwarranted paranoia, he couldn't help but wonder why she'd not simply talked to him at the breakfast table. "You really think I'll still be here Friday?" he asked quietly.

Her gaze shifted to someone walking past them in the corridor, and she stepped toward the wall, tugging him with her, out of the way. "Why would you not be? Do you have plans otherwise?"

"No. But if that resignation letter doesn't show up soon, the police'll come back. I hear Espinosa's parents are pushing them to search the campus and surroundings for a grave."

She tossed her hair, which she'd worn down today in a tumble of loose red curls. "Parker would never allow that. Not without some shred of evidence there would be anything to find. And there isn't." She paused, then said, "Now, for Friday: I want to explore an issue that has been perplexing many of your co-workers of late—how you can be a working geneticist and yet hold to an archaic belief system that not only defies reason but rejects the foundational concepts of our discipline."

Cam chuckled his incredulity. "Come on, Gen. You can't really expect me to believe that my view of evolution is the curiosity of the day. Right now the only thing anyone wants to know is how I killed Manny and why."

She shifted the shoulder strap of her large red bag and made a face. "Oh, come on. No one really believes Manny's dead. We all know that sooner or later he'll send that resignation letter—we've e-mailed, texted, and called him repeatedly. It's not like he can ignore us forever."

She spoke her assurances with such conviction, he wondered if she might not know the truth. If Swain really had kept the incident close as he'd promised. Cam hadn't seen any of the guards who'd been involved since Monday, either, and he'd been looking. . . .

"Are you listening to me, Doctor?"

Gen's words broke into his thoughts. "Yes, of course. You were speaking of Friday's meeting."

She frowned and smoothed a curl of red hair behind one ear. "Do you have *no* idea of the power I hold over your advancement in this institution, Cameron? Can you possibly be that obtuse?"

He blinked at her.

"Parker would've brought you into his Inner Circle months ago if not for me. Do you know why?"

Cam took her question as rhetorical, but when it seemed she'd not go on unless he answered, he finally said, "No. I don't."

"Because I don't think you're worthy of us. Because I don't trust you. Because to be one with us, your highest allegiance must be to Parker and to his vision, as ours is. He doesn't take your religious beliefs seriously. I do. He thinks you'll abandon them in the end. I think you'll abandon us first."

He said nothing, surprised by the depth and accuracy of her perception, but having no idea what to say.

"You see, I don't think you can reconcile your views with the vision we have here," she went on. "But Parker believes you should be given the opportunity to explain yourself, so I'm giving it to you."

He cocked a brow at her, thinking surely she wasn't serious.

"Come now," she prodded. "Doesn't your Bible command you to be ready to answer anyone who asks why you believe? Doesn't it order you to witness to the atheist evolutionists all around you? Isn't it your duty to warn us? To save us from our sinful ways?"

And now he saw that she was very serious, though not at all about understanding what he believed or why. This was not a chance for him to explain and be heard, but a chance for him to be humiliated. "Why not give me the podium one evening at dinner?" he asked dryly.

She snorted. "As much as you detest the limelight? No. We wanted to offer you the chance to explain yourself in a safe environment."

Safe environment. Right.

She tilted her head at him. "You know, if I only wanted to humiliate you, I could've blindsided you with this Friday. But I didn't."

"Well, thank you for that."

"You want to know why?" And this time, when he looked at her

242 — KAREN HANCOCK

without response, she answered anyway. "Because I don't think you have the guts to stand up in front of people and face me! Because when it comes down to the last hour, I think you'll get another titration going and 'forget' to come. Again."

"Maybe I should, given what you've told me."

"Maybe you should indeed. If you do, you can give up any hope of ever sitting on the Circle with us."

She shifted the shoulder strap of her bag again, then strode off, the click of her six-inch heels on the vinyl flooring echoing sharply in a corridor that finally stood empty.

He watched her go, chagrinned, though he had no idea what he could have done or said differently. When she'd disappeared around the corner, he stepped away from the wall and headed in the opposite direction, threading the maze of corridors and open spaces that would take him to the Madrona Lounge and the service elevator accessing the animal facility.

As he walked, he chewed on the implications of Gen's challenge. He would have suspected it all her doing, except for the unmistakable marks of Swain's hand in it. That quote from the Scriptures for one. The opportunity to speak of something so deeply important to him, for another, presented as if it would be something stimulating and pleasant when it would be anything but. Part of him *did* want to bow out. But the way she'd set him up, how could he? Besides, she was right about the command to be ready to give an answer, and if one of the reasons God had brought him here *was* to witness to these people, he could hardly bypass so obvious an opportunity to do so.

The elevator doors opened into the animal facility, and he stepped into the quiet, a now-familiar uneasiness washing over him. With Manny's disappearance and the Institute's continued failure to find a replacement, the task of caring for the animals had ironically fallen to Cam—likely also Gen's doing—and every time he set foot on the floor, he wondered if Frogeater would be waiting for him.

The halls were empty, though, as was his small lab. With the door shut behind him, Cam laid the fork in its envelope atop a stack of similar envelopes, then set up a series of electrophoretic gels. On the last machine, he flipped an ancillary switch installed by one of Rudy's team members. In two minutes it would start a video loop that would override the existing surveillance feed. The loop would run for half an hour before the normal feed resumed. In that interim, the janitor would come in to pick up the envelope.

Leaving his lab well before the two minutes was up, Cam headed for the prep room, where he washed his hands, then decided to go for broke and investigate the stairwell down which he'd chased Frogeater. He'd been considering it as a diversion from events that would be taking place in his lab but feared jeopardizing his standing with Swain should he be caught. After Gen's talk of how gutless he was, though, he felt the need to act in opposition to that label. Besides, the chance was great no one would even notice unless they were actively watching him 24/7. Normally places of infrequent use went unmonitored, the recording devices triggered by a motion detector, their stored images reviewed only in the event of some abnormal occurrence.

If Swain did call him on this, he figured he had a reasonably believable excuse for his curiosity and then he'd know for sure the level of surveillance they had him under.

Entering the stairwell, he descended to the locked pump room door, where he was not surprised to find the thumb pad gone and an electrical socket installed in its place. The card-key reader remained, and he debated trying his master keycard but decided against it.

Overhead the fluorescent light flickered, pulling him from his thoughts. Realizing he'd seen pretty much what he'd come to see, he started back up the stairs. Behind him the light flickered again. It went out altogether as he rounded the first turn and started up the second flight of stairs, his way now lit by the landing light in front of the AnFac door. He picked up his pace, was rounding the third turn, when movement down between the railings in the darkness below caught his eye. He stopped to look more closely, but whatever it was had stopped, as well. Listening hard, he thought he heard the sough of someone breathing. Nape prickling, he started upward again, more rapidly.

Still the sense of another presence coming up the stairs behind ate at him. He started to sweat. The edges of his vision began to flicker. He quickened his pace yet again, rounded the fifth and final turn, and stepped into the full illumination of the landing light, the AnFac door still propped ajar as he'd left it. He continued upward . . .

And found himself striding across the barren, sunbaked yard of a dusty mud-and-rock-walled compound on the other side of the world. Rudy walked at his side as they followed a man wearing bone-colored robes and a rolled-wool Massoud hat, a trio of barking mongrels dancing at their heels in protest of their passage. A few dirty sheep huddled in the lee of the building ahead: a one-story, flat-roofed structure also made of mud and stone, with a raised porch on which sat several men in robes similar to those of their guide. Beyond the building and the compound walls loomed the barren, rocky slopes of the Hindu Kush, shearing skyward at a breathtaking angle. From this vantage he was too close to see the snowy peaks of Mt. Noshaq, the landmark that had served as the orientation point for the last five days of their journey.

Rudy took the lead as they followed the man up the stair and across the porch, where the others lounged in the sun, soaking up the heat that the thin, cold air could not hold. They watched the Americans with dark, hostile eyes glazed from drug use. "Christian devils" he heard one of them murmur in Farsi as their guide pushed open the wooden door.

Then he stepped after Rudy into the building's warm, dark interior, rank with the stench of body odor, urine, and the smoke of opium. The robed men who lay there were hardly conscious, and though a few glazed eyes watched them pass through, none said a word. At the back of the room their guide led them into a narrow stone corridor, the beam of his flashlight probing the darkness ahead.

Soon the corridor opened into a small chamber, where together they descended numerous flights of concrete steps to a heavy, steel door. Their guide turned a key in the door's ancient lock mechanism and pulled it open. As it swung back with a squeal, Cam gasped at the sense of another mind brushing his own, at the voices murmuring on the moving air, welcoming him, praising him, demanding he come *now* and free them.

"*Where's the girl?!*" one grated.

This one was so different from the others, so grating and loud it dissolved the images around him. He stood once more in the stairwell, midway up the final flight of stairs below the AnFac landing, his hand on the railing.

"I want the girl!" the voice rasped again from somewhere in the shadows below him.

Though distorted by the roughness, it was so sharply familiar, Cam's heart nearly stopped in recognition.

"Does *he* have her?" the croak continued.

"Who are you?" Cam demanded.

"Does Father have her?"

"Who's Father?" Cam turned to the speaker behind him but found no one there. Through the space between the railings, he glimpsed a flicker of movement along the bottom flight of stairs. The rattle of the pump room door closing told him not to bother giving chase. As the silence flowed back around him, he stood in shocked replay of what he'd heard.

The words still made no sense. But the voice had unquestionably belonged to Parker Swain.

# Chapter Twenty-Five

On Thursday, Lacey arose before dawn, put on shorts, T-shirt, and walking shoes, and set out around the asphalt path that encircled the Kendall-Jakes campus. Since this was her third day of the new walking regimen, she trusted her intent this morning of waylaying Cameron Reinhardt on his way back from his run wouldn't be totally obvious to anyone who might be watching.

With the sun still below the horizon, the morning air was cool enough to be comfortable, fresh with the smell of the damp grass. Birds chirped and twittered in the oak and mesquite trees around her, and on the quiet, deserted walkway—except for the two black-uniformed security guards patrolling some distance behind her—she relished the time to move and to reflect.

She still couldn't believe what they'd done to Cameron Reinhardt.

After three days of working like a maniac on her proposal, due this morning in Swain's office at 10:30, she'd deemed it close to where she wanted it to be and had broken her self-imposed exile to go down to the dining hall for dinner last night. There, for the first time, she'd heard how the Sunday rumors of Cameron Reinhardt's alleged Saturday night murder of Manuel Espinosa had blossomed into a suspicion strong enough that the police had come out to question him. Even now, though there was still no body, the fact that no resignation letter had yet arrived prompted talk of implementing an air search of the surrounding desert.

She'd listened to Jade's recounting of the tale with mounting horror. For Lacey had seen Frogeater, seen the mutilated frogs, the overturned tank, the weird words scrawled across the wall. *His eyes are over all his creation.* She had heard from his own mouth that he had done it all for her, and knew he would be very unhappy she'd been replaced by Manny.

Of course, right now the tales were just tales. The only real fact was that Manny was missing. It would be just like Espinosa to walk off in a snit and refuse to send word of his whereabouts or intent. It was also possible he'd been injured or, like Lacey herself, merely been in the wrong place at the wrong time and seen what K-J officials didn't want him to see. Maybe they were holding him somewhere under sedation until such time as they could work out an appropriate story.

She hated the ease with which the last notion had come to her, and tried to put it aside. Better to believe that Espinosa had quit like a spoiled child and the rumor mill had eagerly seized on Reinhardt as a target for scandal. Jade had confided that many didn't like K-J's only Christian researcher and would be delighted to see him fall.

Lacey believed it. She well recalled them last weekend after Friday's unity meeting, pecking away at Reinhardt's lack of response to Gen's question regarding his problems with PTSD. Jade said that once Manny disappeared, rumors erupted about Reinhardt's "checkered past," which included not only his divorce and failure in the military, but drug addiction, black market ties, and even doing jail time for assault. When Lacey expressed strong doubt that he was guilty of any of those crimes, Jade assured her they were quite reasonable.

But then, Jade knew nothing of what had been going on in the AnFac recently, nor of the eagerness of Institute authorities to cover up things they didn't want others to know about at the expense of their employees' reputations.

Lacey was particularly troubled by the realization that at the same time Reinhardt's reputation was being ground into dust, she'd been pulled out of circulation, held captive in her little office by her deadline, and sedated by visions of earning her doctorate. Visions whose potential still exerted their influence—even now it was nearly unbearable to consider the possibility her grand opportunity was nothing but a ploy to ensure her silence about what might truly be going on with Espinosa and Reinhardt.

Her uncertainty had disturbed her sleep last night, and she'd awakened early, tossed, turned, fretted, and finally arose to meet the day. It put her out for her walk a little earlier than usual, and thus introduced the possibility of waylaying Reinhardt at the end of his morning run. If Manny *had* walked off in a snit, and the rest was all rumor, Reinhardt would have nothing to say and she could put her doubts to rest.

By the time she'd completed her three circuits of the path, a passel of workers had arrived and begun setting up booths for the open house around the park, the erratic pounding of hammers and the whine and growl of various drills and screwdrivers having shattered the morning's quiet. With so many people around, she was seriously considering abandoning her plan of meeting with Reinhardt when she spied a runner in a red baseball cap, black shorts, and white muscle T-shirt jog up over the crest of the south berm and head down into the basin following a service road.

Though she lost sight of him behind the service buildings and trees, by her estimate of his rate of speed and her own, she figured she'd reach his point of emergence onto the outer walking path about the same time he did. Torn between continuing on, and turning around to avoid him—what if he didn't tell her what she wanted to hear?—she compromised by slowing her pace. Eventually he emerged from the oaks onto the asphalt path just about where and when she'd thought he would. He turned to jog toward her, white iPod earphone cords dangling from his ears, and even though Lácey knew it was Reinhardt, it took her a moment to recognize him.

He was in considerably better physical condition—and far more muscled in the arms and chest—than she'd have guessed. Even more out of character, he sported a tattoo on his left shoulder: A scimitar above a word in . . . Arabic? Hebrew? She wasn't used to seeing him without his glasses, either, nor sheened with sweat, which inexplicably added to his appeal.

Seeing her, he moved to the side of the asphalt, nodding as he approached. *I can let him go by and keep myself in ignorance. . . .* She almost did. Then, at the last second, she stepped into his path and asked if he had a minute.

He stopped in surprise, looking down at her with an expression that did not make her eager to continue.

"I, um . . ." She trailed off, heart suddenly pounding. With a gulp she tried again. "I wanted to talk to you about . . . last weekend."

His stony look turned scowly.

"You said the walls have ears," she added, "so I thought . . ."

"Yes. And the windows have eyes. Very long, keen eyes which are no doubt fixed upon us right now." He glanced up at the ziggurat behind her. She resisted the impulse to turn and look, as well. "And if you don't mind," he added, "I've had quite enough talk of last weekend."

He started around her.

"I know you didn't kill Manny," she said softly, stopping his motion. "I think what they're doing to you is unconscionable."

He glanced at her sidelong. "Well, if the payout is at all proportionate to what you're experiencing, it might turn out to be worth it," he said.

That stung. For a moment she could hardly believe he'd said it. Then her face flamed, and she had to look away. It was only as he started to move on that she recalled her objective and blurted, "I was also wondering if Manny is really dead."

He froze. "Perhaps you should ask your mentor."

"I may. But right now I'm asking you." She stepped closer to him and lowered her voice. "*You* might actually tell me the truth."

He cocked a brow at her, and again turned his gaze down the path at her back. She recalled the guards who had been following her, who should have caught up by now and hadn't.

"You shouldn't be out here," he said.

"Even with my entourage back there?"

"They're probably hoping you'll bait him out."

Him. *Frogeater,* she realized.

Reinhardt turned to face her and pulled the iPod cords from his ears. His expression was deadly serious, his voice low but intense. "I know everything looks bright for you right now, Ms. McHenry, but . . . believe me, it's not as bright as it seems."

His words knocked the wind out of her. She wanted to call him a liar and run away, but something made her stand her ground and say, "That's why I stopped you." She gestured up the path. "Will you walk with me a bit?"

He frowned, glanced up at the ziggurat behind her yet again, then at the guards. Finally he shrugged and turned to walk at her side.

"So you think this graduate degree arrangement I've been offered is just a distraction, then," Lacey said, startled at how hard it was to say that in an even tone, and how violently she'd begun trembling. "A way of buying my silence."

"In part, yes." He paused. "I put in a call to the Genetics department head at U of A when I first heard of it on Monday. Finally heard back from his secretary yesterday. She knew nothing about it, and could neither confirm nor deny because Dr. Essex and the whole department's on vacation while a new ceiling is being put in. No one will be back for two weeks, at least. Which I find just a bit too convenient given what's going on."

"She didn't give you a contact number?"

"Essex is backpacking in the Sierra Nevada. His phone sent me straight to voice mail, and so far, he's not responded." Again he hesitated. "I'm sorry to say I also find it extremely doubtful anyone at the U of A would risk their reputation by entering into any kind of arrangement with Parker Swain."

"But we'll learn the truth in two weeks, so what would be the point?"

"I'm not sure. But Swain's obviously seeking to pull you into his orbit." He glanced over his shoulder as if he'd heard something, then stepped to the side, pulling her with him as a third security guard, this one in a small electric cart, wheeled silently past.

She'd heard not even a creak of its approach, though given all the racket made by the booth workers, that was hardly surprising.

Reinhardt stepped back to the middle of the path, and she moved again to his side.

"Did you read the articles I left you last night?" he asked.

"I didn't get any articles."

"They're on a disk. I put them in a manila envelope with some other stuff. Left it on your desk, under the proposal."

She didn't recall it. "I must've thought it was one of mine."

He grunted. "Well, you should read them."

"All right." Her thoughts turned to why she might not have noticed the new envelope, and a wave of guilt rippled through her. "For what it's worth, I had no idea they were saying all these ridiculous things about you until last night. It wasn't like I was just ignoring it."

He said nothing at first. Then, "Even if you'd known, would it have made any difference? Would you have backed out of Swain's offer?"

"Well, no. But I sure would have protested. . . ." She trailed off, knowing how little good that would have done.

"What if I told you Manny really was dead and they're covering it up?" He glanced down at her. "Would you go in there today and tell him you want to leave?"

"*You're* not leaving."

"It's not that easy for me."

"But it would be for me," she said dryly, "because I'm not the great Cameron Reinhardt with the fancy career."

"You're not the one who's being framed for murder," he said quietly.

She stopped in the path. He kept walking, though, and after a moment she hurried to catch up. Coming up beside him, she reminded him quietly, "There is no murder without a body."

"And as soon as one turns up, there is."

She felt as if a chill wind had blown through her flesh, separating each cell from the other, and that any moment now they would all collapse in a heap on the path. "Oh, sweet Lord . . . *Is* there a body?"

Instead of answering her question, he said, "We need to talk, Ms. McHenry, but not here, and not now. Maybe we can meet up tomorrow night at the open house. There'll be plenty of people around, so it shouldn't look too conspicuous. . . ." He glanced up at the zig now looming ahead of them as they'd come round the circular path. "I hope you'll read those articles before then. They'll give you some context for what I'm going to suggest. Oh, and when you're done, destroy the disk."

"Destroy it?"

He nodded. "And since they haven't found your frog-eating friend yet, I'd suggest you stick with the weight room treadmills for your exercise. That may not be totally safe, either, but it's better than this. Good day, Ms. McHenry."

With that, he broke into a jog and pulled swiftly away from her. Soon a bend in the path took him behind a screen of trees and out of sight. She followed more slowly, struggling to process what he'd said. His articles would give her context? What kind of context? And what was he going to suggest? Why did he tell her to destroy the disk? Why had he not answered her question about Manny, yet made all those comments about his maybe being dead. Did he really mean to imply Swain was *hiding* Manny's corpse somewhere in order to blackmail him? For what purpose?

Far from resolving the issue, their conversation had only left her with more questions. She wished she'd never spoken to him at all.

Upon returning to the zig, she considered going straight to her sixth-floor office to look for the envelope he'd supposedly left there last night. But her ambivalence was so great in the end she stuck to her routine—returning to her room to shower, then going to breakfast with Jade. When she finally did reach her desk, she decided to focus first on putting a few final touches on her proposal.

Thus it was a good two hours before she found the envelope hidden under some pages of scribbled notes she'd tossed upon it last night, having indeed assumed it was one of her own. She pulled its sheaf of papers partway out and fanned through the top edges, finding Reinhardt's disk sandwiched between stacks of gel readouts and research abstracts. Pulling it out of its cardboard sleeve, she slid it into her drive. The directory listed various files of old stories from the *Tucson Citizen* on the disappearances of Andrea Stopping and five other girls, all associated with the Institute. The dates on some of them, though, were close to eight years ago, when Frogeater would have been only a boy and could not have been responsible for their fates. So, if not Frogeater, who? Swain? Reinhardt *had* remarked about the director trying to draw Lacey into his orbit. . . .

Suddenly queasy, she removed the disk from her drive and

considered shredding it right there. The articles were old news. Why torment herself with the doubts and nasty suspicions they would surely sow?

But she couldn't make herself toss them outright. *I'll read them later,* she told herself, *and then decide.* For now she returned the disk to its sleeve, slipped it back among the gel readout pages, and shoved them all back into the envelope. Pushing it aside, she went back to fine-tuning her proposal.

At 10:15 a.m. she rode one of the atrium elevators to the ninth floor, filled with trepidation and hope.

An hour and a half later, she floated back, struggling to believe all that had just happened. He'd approved the project! More than approved it, raved about it. Leapt up from his chair to pace about before her in his excitement, gesticulating his wholehearted endorsement of the potential of an investigation into the effects of HGH on cloned baby mice. To hear him speak, this was the greatest project to ever come along, one that would unlock myriad mysteries and generate a boatload of innovations.

Besides that she'd done a "smashing" job on the proposal. So good he'd need only tweak a word or two before faxing it off. Most likely that very day. And though Dr. Essex at the U of A had unfortunately just left on vacation, Swain was absolutely sure he would approve it when he returned. "Only a matter of time, my dear," he'd said with a wide grin. "Only a matter of time."

He was so confident of that development that at lunch he introduced her as K-J's newest independent researcher and their first doctoral candidate actively pursuing her degree under K-J's auspices in arrangement with the University of Arizona. In the midst of the general light applause, Jade and the other research assistants with whom Lacey had been sitting cheered wildly, whistled, and a couple of them even pounded the table. After all the grief she'd endured, it was a sweet moment.

"Well, I guess you won't be sitting with us peons anymore," Aaron teased when she was back in her seat.

She shook her head. "The whole thing still has to go through all the channels at the U of A, so it'll be a while. In the meantime I'll split my time between assisting Dr. Viascola in Human Resources and working on the nuts and bolts of supply and requisition for my research, so I don't think I'll be changing tables anytime soon."

They were interrupted by Doctors Slattery, Poe, and Yuen coming by to congratulate her, followed by a steady stream of others. Dr. Reinhardt was conspicuous in his absence.

Since Swain had given Lacey the rest of the day off and a free pass for the health resort across campus, she went directly there—worked out at the gym, sat in the steam room, and got a massage. By the time she left, she was so relaxed and sleepy she took a shuttle back to the zig, wanting nothing so much as a long and well-deserved nap.

Cutting through the atrium en route to the basement elevators off the Madrona Lounge, she ran into Jade, who told her Manny's resignation letter had arrived. Director Swain had spoken with him by phone and was flying out that afternoon to Guadalajara, hoping to win him back. "It's just what we all thought," Jade said, shaking her head in disgust. "He walked out on us like a first grader. Frankly, I hope he turns down the director's offers. We really don't need the likes of him around here."

Lacey agreed they didn't, and wisely ignored her friend's "we knew all along" remark. In truth, after all the fear and speculation, her relief was so great it was almost more than she could handle in her present state of fatigue, and the last thing she wanted to do was talk about it all. Thus she excused herself and hurried off, hoping Jade hadn't noticed how the tears had welled in her eyes.

When she neared the basement elevators across from the Madrona Lounge, she was still so rattled she nearly ran into Dr. Reinhardt as he left the lounge's coffee bar. He swerved to miss her, and thankfully only a little of his coffee sloshed onto the floor.

After apologizing profusely, she lingered to say, "I just got the news about Manny's letter. You must be a happy man!" She lowered her voice. "You have no idea how relieved *I* am to know you didn't actually see a body." She chuckled a little at her foolishness.

His already somber expression went completely stony. "I'll bet you are," he said dryly. "I'd feel better if someone besides Swain had spoken to him."

The words hit her like a slap in the face.

He leaned closer. "As for the meeting in Guadalajara, for all we know, Swain could be taking a two-day vacation in his penthouse."

Her shock gave way to irritation. "Director Swain is right," she said sourly. "You *are* paranoid. Why can't you just let this go?"

He cocked a brow at her. "So you *did* ask him about Manny this morning."

"Why would you say that?"

"Why else would Swain tell you I was paranoid?"

She frowned at him. "He said the idea Manny was dead was ridiculous and that you may have some serious mental problems. That you have a history of them, actually."

"Naturally he'd say that."

"He mentioned Dr. Essex being on vacation, too, by the way."

"Of course. He knows I called over there, and probably guessed I told you of it this morning."

She felt her frown deepen. "I can't believe the contortions of logic you go through to make this into something sinister and covered up."

"Contortions of logic?" He snorted. "I'm not the one contorting logic here, Ms. McHenry. He's given you a stake in his vision now, and you just don't want to believe the truth  when you more than anyone should be able to see how it works: the problem never lies in what is actually happening, only in those who have the misfortune to see things they shouldn't. Suddenly they become mentally unstable, sleep-deprived, stressed-out. Paranoid." He paused. "Did you happen to notice which way that telescope in his office was pointing when you were up there?"

When she only glared at him, he shook his head ruefully. "He's played you perfectly, Ms. McHenry. I just hope you come to see that before it's too late." With that he stepped around her and strode off down the walkway.

# Chapter Twenty-Six

*"He's played you perfectly, Ms. McHenry. . . ."*

Reinhardt's words echoed through Lacey's mind as she watched him walk away, her irritation swelling into outrage. How dare he say such a thing! It was not only ridiculous, it was insulting. Both to her and to Dr. Swain. Did he think she was an idiot? Did he have *that* low an opinion of his employer? *Played me perfectly, indeed!*

"Was Dr. Reinhardt harassing you again, my dear?"

She startled at Dr. Viascola's voice sounding directly behind her and turned. Her supervisor had apparently just left the coffee bar's cash register and now stood before her, cup in hand. Slattery was paying for his own coffee in Viascola's wake. They must have come from the same meeting Reinhardt had.

"Harassing me?" Lacey asked.

"You looked angry speaking to him," said Viascola. "You look angry now."

"Oh." Lacey shrugged and smoothed the irritation from her expression. "We just had a difference of opinion."

"I heard about how he tried to persuade you to go alone with him to Tucson last week," Viascola added, "even though you didn't have leave."

"That was just a misunderstanding on my part," Lacey assured her. "Besides, *I* stopped to talk to him just now."

Slattery came up behind Viascola and stood at her elbow sipping coffee from his cardboard cup, watching Lacey with his electric blue eyes.

"You don't need to cover for him, dear," said Viascola. "I outrank him by several degrees."

"I know, ma'am. I'm not covering."

Viascola regarded her speculatively. "Well, if he bothers you again, you let me know and we *will* deal with it."

"Of course I will, ma'am."

"Enjoy the rest of your day, then, dear."

They walked off with their coffee, leaving her more out of sorts than ever. She didn't like it that they'd been watching her so closely they'd seen she was angry. Nor that Viascola had offered to deal with Reinhardt. Nor that Reinhardt's paranoia seemed to be rubbing off on Lacey herself.

She continued to the basement elevators and finally reached the sanctity of her small dorm room, where she dropped her gym bag onto her bed. As she started toward the bathroom, her eye caught on the manila envelope she'd left on her desk earlier: the one with Reinhardt's disk full of articles. Anger washed through her again, and she turned away from it, determined to shred it as soon as she finished in the bathroom.

But his words continued to surface, niggling her conscience. *"Did you happen to notice which way that telescope in his office was pointing . . ."*

Which of course she had: positioned at the western window wall, the scope was precisely where it would need to be for Swain to have watched her and Reinhardt on the path.

It burned her that he'd been right about the telescope, and even more that he'd predicted correctly Swain's interest in their conversation. The director had pounced the moment she'd stepped through his door, wanting to know all about it and why she was talking to Reinhardt at all. He'd startled and unnerved her, especially when he'd gone on to condemn Reinhardt as volatile, paranoid, and quite possibly a murderer, and urged her to stay away from him.

Moreover, it was only now as she actually thought back to the early part of their meeting that she realized Swain had blown off her questions about Manny and Frogeater altogether and countered by asking if Reinhardt had given her those ridiculous ideas. When she didn't answer, he'd nodded smugly, repeated his warning about the man, then assured her Manny had simply walked out on them.

She hadn't had the chance to ask him why he was so interested in keeping Reinhardt on if the man was as volatile, paranoid, and dangerous as Swain claimed. The words had been on the tip of her tongue when he'd switched subjects and asked her to present her proposal. Caught completely off guard, she'd given a disjointed presentation with a dry mouth and trembling voice and was horrified to find herself almost babbling in her attempts to answer his questions.

As he'd skimmed through the written material afterward, she was sure he'd suggest she take an extra week to work on it. Instead, he bowled her over with an onslaught of praise, and she'd forgotten all about the business with Manny and Reinhardt. Suddenly her dream was all but being handed to her by a man who was telling her she was brilliant, valuable, pretty, and a very nice and principled girl, to boot.

For all the euphoria those words had generated in her, they'd also planted a sense of obligation and a strong resistance to thinking ill of him who had praised her so highly.

*"He's played you perfectly. . . ."*

Was that why she'd gotten so angry with Reinhardt? Because he spoke the truth?

Her eyes went again to the envelope with its disk full of copied articles on the disappearances of six girls. Beside it sat her black cube, more or less ignored since last Sunday night when she'd played her silly Magic 8 Ball game with it. There'd been no answer in the window— there was no window at all—but there *had* been an answer. For right after she'd handled the cube, the idea for her HGH effects on cloned mice had come to mind. Wasn't that exactly how Dr. Viascola said it was supposed to work?

She picked it up, marveling anew at its silky feel and calming weight—and at the way it completely absorbed the light. Not a glimmer of reflection showed in its flat surfaces, no matter which way she turned it, or how close she held it to the lamp. As she sat down on the side of her bed, the cube drew her into its darkness, melting her

THE ENCLAVE — 259

tension as it chased away her confusion. Before long, she felt renewed, more clearheaded, and increasingly inclined to believe Swain over Reinhardt. And why not? She was a nobody, barely worthy of working at Kendall-Jakes. Swain didn't have to do any of this, and Reinhardt's claims just made no sense.

The next thing she knew she was being jolted out of a very strange dream by the clacking of the door lock and the sudden tumultuous entrance of her roommate. Jade had indeed noticed Lacey's weepy reaction to learning of Manny's resignation letter and wanted to know what was going on. Lacey passed it off as fatigue after a week of frantic work and intense emotional seesawing. She wasn't sure whether Jade bought her claim or not, but her friend let it go.

Later, after dinner and the Thursday evening musical enrichment series, she begged off an invite to join the Lab 500 workers in the resort cantina and returned to her room. This time she put the black cube in one of her drawers right away, then sat at the desk, powered up her laptop, and reluctantly slipped Reinhardt's disk of articles into its drive.

The most recent of the articles was on Andrea Stopping, who had wandered into the mountains last January never to be seen again. Given the rough terrain and the many ravines into which a person could fall and never be found, she was thought to have died of natural causes, though the *Citizen* article did note she had suffered from depression.

One other girl had likewise vanished while hiking in the mountains; she was believed to have been swept away by a summer flash flood, though her body had not been found, either. Of the other four, one died in a fiery car crash on Highway 77; another committed suicide by carbon monoxide poisoning in her own vehicle in K-J's parking garage; a third ran off with her married supervisor; and the fourth left without forwarding notice only three weeks after arriving. . . .

In addition to the articles, Reinhardt had included a list of Swain's international research facilities—in Asia, the Middle East, South America, and Micronesia—along with the two hundred young women associated with them who'd also died or gone missing over the last ten years. Most of these had not been actively employed by Swain, had merely lived and/or disappeared in the vicinity.

When she had finished reading all the disk's contents, she returned it to its cardboard sleeve, then sat for a time, reflecting.

It all made her terribly uncomfortable, and Swain's accusations of Reinhardt's problem with paranoia and conspiracies kept coming back. She hadn't seen Manny's body, after all. But neither had she seen Manny alive. And she *had* seen Swain's telescope. And Frogeater. And been accused of paranoia and hallucinations herself.

Then there was the whole two-week vacation thing with the U of A Genetics department and the resultant absence of official confirmation of Swain's arrangements for her there—a wrinkle that wouldn't stop nagging at her.

Maybe it was time to see if she could prove any of this stuff on her own. With that in mind, took her laptop to the bed and sat with her back against the wall. It didn't take long to confirm that Swain was involved with the research facilities cited in Reinhardt's report, but there wasn't much online about any of the disappearances. She couldn't even access the *Citizen* articles without signing up and paying, something she wasn't in a position to do.

Frustrated and perplexed, she was about to abandon the effort when she recalled the special security code and password Gen had given her last week to access classified K-J files. Might they also access personnel records? To her pleased surprise, they did.

She called up the archived files of each of the six women mentioned. They were all attractive, young, athletic, bright, and well recommended. Four of them had dark hair like she did. The other two were redheads.

One had served as a personal assistant to Swain, two as lab assistants, and the other three had come from universities across the country, two with master's degrees, one with a doctorate. That was Andrea Stopping. Except for the dead girls, all were still considered missing persons, though their cases had long grown cold, and only the personal assistant had been remotely close to Swain.

Would Lacey's code get her into any of his personal files? She spent about twenty minutes trying various search words and file names, but in the end was not surprised when her access was denied. She was also denied access to the personnel files of all eleven of K-J's highest-level personnel; but she wasn't denied access to Cameron Reinhardt's record. She hesitated before opening it, knowing it was a breach of conduct. But he'd read her file, so she figured turnabout was fair play. Besides, she wanted to see for herself how many of those checkered-past rumors were true, and—more importantly—if there was any official diagnosis of paranoia. Or PTSD.

She was surprised to learn he'd grown up in Tucson, graduated from Rincon High School with straight A's, and had gotten the second highest score in the city the year he took the SATs. His PSAT scores were good enough to win him a National Merit Scholarship and full-ride scholarships to all the in-state schools. He was also offered partials at Stanford, UCLA, and Johns Hopkins.

Instead he joined the Army, Special Forces. In fact, he didn't even enter as an officer but as an enlisted man. He also married shortly before that, not even nineteen years old.

She sighed and shook her head, relating far too well.

His first deployment was a year in Kuwait, during which his daughter was born. After Kuwait came Afghanistan, about which little was said, which she found odd in light of the scary thoroughness of the rest of his dossier. It did note that his daughter died of Leigh's Syndrome during his tour there and that he came home right before her death, staying stateside for a couple of months afterward.

By the end of his four years in Afghanistan, he was discharged for medical reasons stemming from his service. The file gave no official details regarding symptoms, treatment, or duration of his condition, nor was anything said of the incident which caused it. The K-J investigator suspected PTSD, despite the fact Reinhardt's military assignments were characterized as primarily administrative, and speculated that it could have been a strong contributing factor—along with the death of his daughter—to Reinhardt's divorce shortly after his return to the States.

A year later he finally capitalized on his stellar test scores, entered the U of A on the GI bill, and did spectacularly. Graduating in three years, he went on to postgraduate work and earned his PhD from Stanford at the age of thirty-three. Following prestigious postdoc positions—first at Cold Spring Harbor, then Johns Hopkins—he secured a fellowship at Stanford, where he was about to be discharged for insubordination when he quit and came to Kendall-Jakes. In all this there was no further mention of any kind of mental problems, including paranoia.

The K-J evaluator noted that Reinhardt was highly intelligent, though a bit absentminded, perfectionistic, athletic, and was most likely to have engaged in covert/intelligence-type activities during his military service. He continued to practice regularly with handgun and rifle and had supplemented his running regimen with weight training and tae kwon do. The file also documented his sports history, his artistic tendencies—he dabbled in acrylic painting and pen-and-ink—all major medical procedures he'd undergone, allergies, and health risks, including his possible post-traumatic stress disorder. It even noted his current vision prescription.

His conversion to Christianity occurred sometime during his military service, languished following his discharge, then rebounded with "*the sort of fanaticism one sees in those who have been most desperately injured, physically or emotionally,*" said the evaluator. "*Reinhardt claims affiliation with the Seaview Bible Church in Seaview, Virginia, which encourages almost daily worship, a practice he has been faithful to for over ten years. It will likely not be easy to sway him from his beliefs.*"

She frowned, her uneasiness edged with indignation. Reinhardt's religious practices might be a bit odd, but was this the sort of thing that belonged in a company profile? Were not one's religious beliefs out of bounds as an area an employer might seek to alter?

In addition to his church's street address, the file listed its Web site, which also seemed not right, even as she recalled that a similar designation must be in her own files. Reinhardt had read there that she had her own local assembly and apparently knew where it was.

She typed in the Web address for Seaview Bible Church, and the Web site appeared, listing what turned out to be hundreds of lessons. Nor were they your usual readily accessible titles: *The Shekinah Glory. The Circumcision Made Without Hands. The Angelic Conflict. Positional Truth and the Resurrection.*

Heavy theological studies. But then, Reinhardt was known for his intellectual ability, so why be surprised he would pursue his spiritual life in the same sort of vein?

She was just about to click on *The Shekinah Glory* when the lights flickered and the Web site vanished behind a screen of solid blue. She frowned, wondering first how the battery could have died in the brief time she'd used it, and next if someone at K-J had deliberately jammed her wireless connection. That would have left her screen intact, though, not crashed the entire computer. Then again, with computers, who knew what might happen? It probably *was* the battery.

She set the machine aside and was unfolding her legs when a soft knock sounded at her door. She froze. Who would be knocking on her door at—she glanced at the clock—one in the morning? Dr. Reinhardt? Jade would have her keycard, of course. . . .

Another soft knock.

She sat forward slowly. When the locking mechanism clicked and the latch turned slightly, she exploded upward in alarm and flung herself at the door, slamming the security dead-bolt lever into place. "Hello?"

Silence followed her words. She'd hoped to hear the staccato thump of running footfalls, but there was nothing. Whoever it was, he stood on the other side of the door, waiting for her.

Maybe it *was* Reinhardt, coming at a time when he thought he'd not be spotted by the walls that had eyes and ears. She grimaced at the creepy mental image that thought produced and realized his coming to her room now would be more suspicious than ever. No, it wouldn't be Reinhardt.

She swallowed and peered through the peephole, her fingers trembling as she pressed them against the wood. Outside, the narrow, dimly lit hallway stood empty. She peered for a long time, moving this way and that, wondering if maybe he had stealthily withdrawn out of the peephole's range. There was a dark shape that could be either a man or a door. . . . Though the more she stared at it, the more she thought it was a door.

Finally she pushed back and glanced around at the bed, where her laptop still sat with the blue screen. Surely she hadn't imagined it all. . . . Her eyes strayed to her desk, where lay her bound proposal, the envelope of research abstracts and sleeved disk, and the pill bottle of Valium.

"I didn't imagine it," she said firmly, looking again through the peephole. Nothing had changed. Whoever had been out there was gone. Still, it was some time before she could make herself open the door and confirm her suspicions. . . .

The hall did, indeed, stand silent and empty.

There was, however, a small royal blue tree frog positioned on the tile floor directly in front of her door's threshold, looking up at her with bright black eyes.

# Chapter Twenty-Seven

## New Eden

Shortly after Zowan collapsed in the physical plant sector sometime Tuesday afternoon, he had been found by two workers who'd revived him and brought him to the infirmary. Certain the clinicians would bring out their toxin sensors to see if he'd been contaminated in his wanderings, Zowan was surprised when they did not, and was further surprised when he was diagnosed as suffering only from dehydration, given fluids and a few crackers, and handed over to the Enforcers who'd shown up shortly after he'd arrived.

Surprised that Gaias wasn't one of them but not about to complain, Zowan had freely admitted that Neos had grabbed him in the Star Garden when the lights went out and told them pretty much everything as it had happened, leaving out only the parts relative to the hidden crawl tube and his solitary trip to the surface. Since he'd been in the dark the whole time, it was no lie to claim he'd had no idea where he was or how long he'd waited for Neos after being abandoned.

His interrogators had given no sign they thought he might not be telling them everything, and when done had sent him back to the goat barn, where his youthful assistants had made a muddle of things during his absence. He'd spent the next two days putting things to rights in the barn and continuing to train the eldest as his replacement, since in spite of everything—or maybe because of it—he was still being reassigned at week's end. Rumor suggested it might be kitchen duty, janitorial services, or even the furnace room again.

Now, Friday morning, a week since he'd been exposed to the toxic wind surge in the goat ravine, and three days after his unshielded venture to the surface alone, he lay on his back atop the third tier of the three-man bunk he shared with Parthos and Erebos, and stared at the cement ceiling of their narrow sleeping cell arcing less than a foot above him. To his right, a sliver of access space separated him from the opposite wall, where cubbies for each occupant's belongings burrowed into the stone. There were no windows, only a doorless entry beyond the head of the bunk bed, where a metal ladder dropped straight to the cell block's central walkway—along with eleven other ladders from the block's eleven other cells. Arranged six on a side in offset rows of three, the cells could accommodate thirty-six residents, though currently only held thirty.

Zowan had awakened at the alarm with the other twenty-nine young men who shared the cell block with him, but had stayed in his bed as the others went down to the sanitation facility without him. He could hear their boisterous voices now amidst the rhythmic flush of the toilets, the sounds muted by distance and location, so that he lay in a well of relative silence. His cell's one lamp, set flush in the center of the ceiling curve and governed by motion detectors, had dimmed after the departure of his cell mates, leaving him in a semidarkness that encouraged reflection.

His not going down with the group began on Wednesday morning when he'd held back for fear of what he'd find in the mirror—the bloodshot eyes, fiery red face, and bleeding gums that were early signs of toxin exposure. Only after they'd all gone off to breakfast did he go down to look at himself, amazed and relieved to find nothing amiss. He'd done the same on Thursday, and though he'd held back this morning for the same reason, his fear of toxin poisoning was fading.

He ran his tongue along the back of his teeth, not one of which had yet come loose. He fingered his hair, growing back in a fine stubble after being shaved off in the decontamination process, when it should have been falling out. His fingernails had not turned black, nor was he coughing up blood, and his appetite was fine.

Though he'd said nothing of his true concerns, the others had applied their own perceptions to his situation and were treating him gently, mindful of all the things that had been dumped on him this last week—the public condemnation, punishment, and death of his best friend; his exposure to the toxic wind surge in the goat grotto from which he was still recovering; and finally, Monday night's blackout, the stress of which had allegedly triggered the delusion that he'd been abducted by his dead brother, Neos, which in turn had sent him wandering through the darkness and chaos all the way to the physical plant before collapsing from dehydration.

When he'd first heard this official viewpoint of his blackout escapades he'd understood immediately why the Enforcers had so easily accepted his story—they'd believed he'd been hallucinating. The unnerving part was that Zowan couldn't be sure he hadn't been. Yes, everything about his time with Neos had seemed solid and real—except maybe for the parts where he'd heard Andros's voice and followed the light of I Am—and he still mostly believed it had happened as he'd experienced it. But he'd also been assured by Enclave authorities that there was no moveable panel, nor any behind-the-scenes network of spy passages in and around the Star Garden. No one else had seen Neos, who was still supposed to be dead. Moreover, the fact that Zowan had shown no ill effects from his alleged trip to the surface could itself be the proof he *had* hallucinated it all, never having been contaminated in the first place. Perhaps restoration of the Enclave's power and lights— so shocking after hours of darkness—had been translated by his then drug-tainted mind into a blast of light from the surface. . . .

Perhaps.

He could rationalize it both ways. The only way he'd know for sure was to go back to the physical plant. If he couldn't find the crawl tube in the pump room, he'd know he had imagined it. But if he *did* find it and the upward passage it emptied into, then he could return to the surface to see if it was really as bad as he'd first thought.

He knew he'd been bowled over by the brightness, the heat, the space, and the endless folds of barren land rolling into a blue haze of mountains. But over the last couple of days, bubbles of recall had floated in his awareness: there *had* been plants—not just the prickly tree he'd had to push through, but shrubs growing on the slope at his feet; if he'd seen mountains in the distance, the air couldn't have been choked with dust; and yes, it had been hot, but not enough to sear his lungs or blister his face as he'd been warned.

He was pretty sure he could find his way to the hole in the pump room once he got to the physical plant. The problem was *getting* to the physical plant. He couldn't just walk up there without a good reason, and waiting until after curfew would only make him look more suspicious. There was no way he could re-create Neos's trek through the ductwork, and with no means of contacting his brother, he'd run out of options.

Frustrated, he gave up thinking about it, turned on his small reading lamp, and pulled his red hardback *Edenite Catechism* from the crack between his bunk and the wall. Opening it to the partial chapters of the *Key Study* he'd glued into it, he read again about the one called the LORD God who had called the light out of darkness, formed the waters and the land and made a garden called Eden, where he'd placed the first man and woman. How He'd given them the freedom to eat from all the trees save one, and how the talking serpent had deceived the woman into doing so with his subtle lies. "You really won't die," he'd told her. "God's just afraid if you eat the fruit you'll become like Him." Despite the fact it made no sense for God to have put such a tree in the garden were that truly His fear, the woman had believed the deception, persuaded the man to follow her lead, and both had eaten. But instead of becoming like God, they'd only become aware of their nakedness and guilt.

And then there was all that talk of seeds . . . the serpent's seed, the woman's seed, the enmity between them . . . Zowan didn't understand any of that, but the use of the word *seed* caught him, because seeds were so important to the Edenites. Indeed, the one story he did understand was that of the Flood, so similar to New Eden's history of a catastrophic destruction, complete with an ark of salvation. Noah had built only one very large ark, designed to float and to carry two of every animal, whereas New Eden's six much smaller arks only carried the genetic information of the Earth's plants and animals, the "seeds" that one day the Edenites would sow on the resurrected Earth. . . .

It seemed a desperately glorious mission—man's and Earth's last hope of survival—and most Edenites embraced it and sacrificed for it all their lives. Now he wondered if it was as much a lie as what the serpent had told the woman about the fruit of the Tree of the Knowledge of Good and Evil. What if the surface was not a wasteland of death and there was no mission? What if New Eden was not an ark of salvation at all, but a prison, as Neos claimed? One where a person's every move was watched and controlled. Where questions were discouraged and prisoners were forced to say an affirmation of thanks and praise to Father every single day. Where, despite being Earth's last repository of human thought and history, they were burning books.

He wondered, too, where his *Key Study* fragment had come from before it had been tossed into the burn bin. If there were no people left except those in the twelve enclaves, who had either entered with Father from the first or been born there, then who had brought the *Key Study*? It had to have been one of the Elders, for they were the only ones who could have had access to books Father disapproved of. But why would an Elder bring a heretical book into the Enclave during those last terrible days? And why had it been here for twenty-five years before being slated for destruction?

The rattle of conversation in the space outside the sleepcell and the soft pat of footfalls alerted him to his fellows returning from their morning ablutions. He turned off the reading lamp, rolled onto his side, and slid the book into its place between the wall and mattress. Shortly, the muffled clang of feet on the ladder outside his cell heralded the arrival of his cellmates. They crowded into the small space, smelling of soap and deodorant, but he kept his back to them and said nothing, listening as they shrugged into their tunics and trousers.

After a time Parthos said, "The block's pretty cleared out now, if you want to take your turn."

"Thanks," Zowan said to the wall. He didn't move.

"You sure you don't want us to wait and go with you?" Parthos asked.

"Yes." Zowan rolled onto his back and glanced around at his friend. Parthos stood in the doorway, a tall, dark shadow, with Erebos at his side. Both watched Zowan warily. He smiled at them. "Thanks for asking, though."

For an awkward moment no one spoke.

Finally Parthos turned away. "See you at breakfast, then. We'll try to save you something good."

"Thanks."

They descended the ladder, passing out of his sight. He waited until their footsteps faded to silence before rolling out of his bunk and heading down to the deserted, water-splashed Sanitation.

His reflection showed him exactly what it had shown him the last two days: his own face, completely healthy and normal. He didn't usually spend much time looking at himself, but it struck him now, with the fine blond stubble of his returning hair barely visible, how much he looked like Gaias. In an Enforcer's robe, with the hood up to obscure his lack of an oculus, he could probably pass for his brother, at least long enough to get into the physical plant. In Enforcer robes he wouldn't even have to observe curfew.

In fact, now that he thought of it, Neos had come to him wearing such a robe. And Parthos worked in the Enclave's laundry room. Perhaps he could put one aside. . . .

At breakfast Parthos had saved him a place near the back entrance in the crowded cafeteria, and a plate of food, as well. Erebos moved aside as Zowan stepped over the bench to squeeze between them. Helios sat across the table, and beyond him one table over, Terra sat among her screaming charges. She caught his glance with her soulful brown eyes, held it briefly, then looked away, leaping to grab the arm of the small blond boy beside her before he could toss his biscuit at another child.

Having earlier noted Gaias seated at a table behind him, Zowan knew his brother was watching their interaction closely. Thus he turned to his plate and, as the others resumed their conversation, wolfed down the eggs, soy bacon, and cheese biscuits Parthos had saved for him.

He was nearly finished when Parthos leaned against him and said quietly, "There's talk you went to the surface last Monday night."

Zowan froze, half-chewed biscuit in his mouth.

"That you know a way out of here," Parthos continued. "And that's why they're sending you away."

Zowan forced himself to resume chewing and, when he had finished, swallowed hard before turning to look at his friend. "They're sending me away?"

"To New Babel."

He felt as if Parthos had slugged him in the gut with a two-punch. Panic beat at the doors of his soul, but he held it back with the observation that Parthos didn't truly know Zowan had been to the surface or he wouldn't have asked. And the part about his being sent to New Babel had to be just rumor. . . .

"Is it true?" Parthos pressed.

Zowan looked at Helios, eating unawares across the table. Then he turned to Parthos, his friend's dark, handsome face sober. "If it were true," he said, "wouldn't I be in the infirmary now?"

"One would think so," Parthos agreed. "And I'm guessing that's why you've been waiting until everyone leaves the cellblock each morning before you go down to Sanitation. Fearful of what you'll find in the mirror."

Zowan gulped as panic flared again. Had he been *that* transparent? A glance at Helios showed he had, or that Parthos had at least confided his suspicions. Zowan had no answers for them. None he was willing to utter in such a public place, at least. Instead he asked, "How do you know they're sending me away?"

Parthos shrugged. "I overheard some Elders talking. Father's coming in today to make the announcement."

*Father? Coming today?* For a moment the room whirled and Zowan had to force himself to breathe. "Do *they* think I went to the surface, too?"

Parthos shook his head. "I have no idea."

Zowan recalled Neos's warning about the secret lab where terrible things were done and to which Zowan would be brought if they knew where he'd gone. But if they knew, why hadn't they taken him away already? Because they wanted Neos, too?

Over the Enclave's sound system, a chime rang softly, and the familiar voice of Elder Sophia announced it was half an hour until the morning Affirmation.

"When's Father supposed to arrive?" he asked.

"In time for the Affirmation. He may be here now."

Zowan stared at him bleakly, his capacity for thought frozen in the face of this sudden disaster.

"They'll have to have a going-away party, though," Helios said. "They always do."

"Probably tomorrow night," Parthos added. He gave Zowan a long, intense look, as if he waited for him to realize something important.

Zowan tilted his head in question and shook it slightly, hoping for a clue. But Parthos only flashed a grim look over his head at Erebos. "We'll talk more tonight," he said, pushing up from the table.

Zowan followed him from the cafeteria and into the mall, where they walked together toward the mouth of the ramping corridor that led up to the Sanctuary of the Glorious Father where the Affirmation was held. Two lines, one male, one female, were already moving past the four-faced statue of Father and up the ramp toward the entrance. Zowan stepped into the line for the men, Parthos, Erebos, and Helios behind him. Terra used to pair with him for this morning entrance, but since her transfer to the crèche, she'd had to enter last with her charges. Thus Zowan walked with a girl he barely knew.

As with all the Enclave's corridors, this one's ceiling just brushed the top of his head as he walked. Surrounded by the rustle of clothing and the soft slap of felt slippers on the polished stone floor, they moved slowly toward the open doorway at the top of the ramp, and before long were stepping into Father's Sanctuary, the Enclave's largest and brightest chamber.

Ranks of fat white cement columns of increasing height marched the length of the rectangular chamber toward the altar at the end. There one of the Enclave's six golden arks stood upright against the wall, framed by twists of golden ivy and bundled sheaves of wheat. Sky prisms pierced the pale ceiling, flooding the chamber with shafts of light. On account of the ark, the Sanctuary was one of the few places in the Enclave where the air was dry and crisp and cool.

A raised platform accessed by three front steps stood immediately below the golden ark, flanked by two long linen-draped tables. They were set with various sizes of white crystalline singing bowls that the choir would use for the service. Protocol dictated worshipers sit in the order they entered, and today Zowan ended up on the central aisle of a middle pew—the last place he'd have chosen. Especially today. As he sat down, Parthos, Erebos, and Helios headed to the outside end of the pew behind him.

Once the Sanctuary was filled, the white-robed choir marched up the aisle in two columns, which split at the front, each side moving around behind their respective tables to assume their places at the bowls. Once in place, they moved their hands around the delicate rims and a long, harmonious chord eased into the silence, calling the Elders to advance in their blue cloaks, with cowls cast back and golden keys hanging round their necks.

Because of Father's attendance today, all twelve High Elders participated. They entered in two groups of six, those of highest rank leading. Elder Sophia, with her deep red hair and heart-shaped face, looked a lot like Terra, and Elder Apsu bore a marked resemblance to Andros—tall, thin, gangly, with a long nose, a pocked face, and a perpetual air of melancholy. The resemblance had never seemed so strong to Zowan as it did today. As Apsu walked stiffly by, his jaw clenched, his eyes straight forward, Zowan heard Andros's voice again faintly: *"Come and get me out of here, Zowan! You owe me."*

For a moment Zowan was so surprised his attention left the procession as he chased after the location of the voice—but as before he did not find it. When he returned to the moment, the High Elders stood facing the tables and the ark. As the bowls' song turned bright and celestial, everyone stood for Father's entrance.

Taller by a head than any of the others, Father was a magnificent man. Beneath an ankle-length cape of golden satin, his white sleeveless tunic revealed bronzed, muscular arms. Golden hair flowed over his shoulders, restrained by a golden circlet on his brow. His blue eyes were clear as water, piercing as eternity, and his bronze features were a study in perfection. He looked so much like Gaias before the oculus, it was uncanny.

As Father approached, those along the aisle reached out to him, murmuring praises, enraptured by his nearness. Once Zowan would have done likewise, overwhelmed as much by the aura of his presence as by the power of his reputation. Today he stood devoid of feeling, unmoving except as he was jostled by those at his back, pressing against and around him to reach for Father.

He watched the man draw near, the awe-generating aura sweeping over him with almost aversive effect. As Father's gaze came forward from supplicant to supplicant, it caught on Zowan's and held, and though Zowan half expected to see fury blazing in the blue eyes, he saw only a benevolent blankness. The gaze touched him briefly, then moved on to the worshipers ahead, as if Zowan were no more than an extension of the pew. Father walked past him, followed by the last three pairs of Elders, and on to the altar, where he ascended to the platform and turned to face his people. Shimmering in the light of the sky prism shining down on his head, with the golden Ark of Life as his backdrop, he held out his arms as if bidding his supplicants come to his embrace. The worship bowls sang a harmonic tone and the choir led everyone in singing the First Praise.

On Zowan's every side, New Edenites wept and raised their hands and sang with unbridled passion. Zowan watched them as if he were somewhere outside the Sanctuary, immune to the emotion and thus able to see as he had not been before. Not just the loss of reason on the part of his fellow Edenites, but the smug superiority with which Father drank it all in. It made the back of Zowan's neck crawl. How had he never seen that look of amused contempt before?

The First Praise was followed by the choir's Chant of Loss and New Beginnings as corresponding images undulated across the Sanctuary's white walls: a great blue sky, purple mountains, tree-cloaked hillsides; birds and beasts and gleaming white cities; men filling the arks and carrying them into the enclaves. . . .

The music shifted to a minor key, and the chants grew deep and guttural. Huge waves curled on the walls now, smashing down on those same cities, sweeping away buildings and bridges and roads; boats and carts and flying tubes; animals and people struggling vainly to keep their heads above water.

As the images changed to the flickering orange flames and belching smoke of the Inferno that was now their world, the choir sang of death and then rebirth. They would bring back the life. The Father would show them, and they would do it. And one day, all that was lost would be regained.

During the last lines of the song, Enforcers marched up the aisles, center and sides, to take their stand, their watchful eyes ensuring none would shirk his duty. Gaias, of course, positioned himself alongside Zowan, watching boldly as the Affirmation began.

> "Our Father who walks among us, wise and holy are you.
> Your kingdom has come, your will be done,
> Now and in the age of awakening to come.
> Strengthen us against temptation
> Deliver us from the evil of selfishness
> Bring us together in unity to make our world home again.
> For you are the answer and the strength and the only righteous
>     one forever."

Having said those same words every day for eighteen and a half years, they'd become a chain of meaningless syllables Zowan could recite by rote. Which was exactly what he did now, all his awareness focused on Gaias— who watched him so closely—and on the hard, hot knot of bitter anger that had formed within his heart.

The official portion of the ritual completed, Father now addressed them regarding recent events, assuring them that New Eden's atmospheric integrity had not been breached, that all the damage created by the power failures had been repaired, and that despite the problems, they must keep their focus on their very important task, one entrusted to only the best and the brightest. Some of those best and brightest he would honor today.

He called up a man who had worked hard to restore the power after Monday's blackout, then another who had labored twenty-four hours straight to ensure the Enclave's seals were indeed secure against the outside toxins. Third was the block leader who'd held his poise under pressure and kept his people calm and safe.

Finally he called up Zowan and, after introducing him to the gathering, announced, "I will be taking him with me when I travel to New Babel on Sunday."

*Babel,* Zowan thought irreverently. *That's a name from the* Key Study *stories, too.*

"They have had illnesses there, and need skills such as Zowan here can provide," Father was saying, his hand warm on Zowan's shoulder. "He will do an important service there in furthering our glorious—"

Suddenly another's voice overlaid Father's, strong and firm and compelling: *Go from this place, Zowan. Go from your people, and from your Father's rule, to the land which I will show you. Come out of the darkness and into the light. . . .*

Father was still speaking, but Zowan hardly heard him; the voice was so close and clear the speaker might have stood in Father's place.

"But how do I get there? I don't know how to get back to the physical plant without getting caught," he murmured.

The voice did not answer. Instead, the memory of being alone in the tunnels following someone with a light flashed into his mind. And with it came the inexplicable assurance that if he obeyed this command, he'd be shown the way to go.

# Chapter Twenty-Eight

Midmorning Friday, Cam was surprised to look up from his work at a tentative tap on his open office door and find Lacey McHenry standing in the doorway. The last time they'd spoken was yesterday afternoon, when he'd told her bluntly that Swain was playing her, and she had *not* been happy with him.

The remark had been as much impulse as calculated risk in hopes the truth might startle her out of the cocoon of euphoria Swain's promises had spun about her. Perhaps it had worked, for she did not seem angry now, though she was unquestionably agitated. As often of late, some high emotion had flushed her cheeks, the rosy glow making her dark eyes luminous and drawing attention to her high cheekbones and long elegant neck. Realizing suddenly that he'd been staring at her far longer than was polite, he averted his eyes and waved her in, unnerved at the intensity of his attraction to her.

She surprised him further by closing the door behind her and stepping toward his desk. "I probably shouldn't even be here," she said, "but with Dr. Viascola closeted for the day, I decided to take the risk."

With Swain still in Guadalajara supposedly meeting with Manny Espinosa, his Inner Circle had announced at breakfast that they would be in an all-day meeting on the ninth floor and unavailable until late afternoon. Though Gen had made sure to tell Cam they'd be back in time for the unity meeting.

His eyes fixed on the small manila collection bag that McHenry now held out to him.

"What's this?" he asked, taking the bulging bag from her. She let him pull back the flap and see for himself: it was a blue plastic tree frog.

He looked up at her quizzically, and she explained how she'd come to have it.

By the time she finished, he was chilled, recalling his own recent interaction with the frog eater, who'd questioned him in the stairwell outside the animal facility on Wednesday morning. Clearly he'd found out where—and who—"the girl" was. "So why did you bring this to me?" he asked.

"Who else could I take it to? I didn't even see him this time, only the door latch turning. And that." She gestured at the envelope in his hands. "I thought maybe you could get fingerprints or something."

He arched his brows in surprise. "Because *I* have an in with the police now, after their lengthy questioning of me, coupled with my recent exoneration?"

Her blush deepened, and he was relieved to see genuine chagrin fill her face. "I didn't think about that. I just thought . . . you'd want to know who he is as much as I do, and you might know who to give this to. Maybe through your friend at the U of A Genetics department . . ." She paused, then asked in a quiet voice, "Did you really see Manny's body?"

Cam nodded.

"Was it Frogeater?"

"I believe so."

She turned pale and sank onto the chair before him, her eyes big and troubled. "What is going on here, Dr. Reinhardt?" she whispered. "Who is he? Why is he still out there? And why are they covering all this up?"

"I'm not sure yet." Though he did have a couple of ideas, they weren't something he was willing to share here. He decided then that their need to talk freely was too great, and that with Swain off doing whatever it was he was doing, Cam had better seize this God-given opportunity while he could. "Are you still game to go with me to the open house tonight?" he asked.

She frowned, her dark eyes full of uncertainty. "I don't think Director Swain would like that."

"Probably not."

He reached for a pad of sticky notes and scribbled on it—*Atrium pond, 6:45 tonight?*—then pulled off the sheet and stuck it atop one of the file folders sitting on his desk, as if he'd just thought of something irrelevant to their conversation.

"I'm not sure I want to do a lot of walking, either," she said. "I still haven't recovered from the blisters I got at the theater last week."

"I understand. There *would* be a lot of walking." With his eyes he directed her to the note he'd just slapped onto the folder. She glanced down, seemed to read the words, then met his gaze again. He wasn't sure if she nodded or not, but given the fact their conversation was probably being recorded, he would just have to hope she got the message. "I doubt I'll be in the dining hall tonight, is all," he said, "given what's likely awaiting me in this afternoon's unity meeting."

The girl's eyes widened. "Oh, that's right!" She looked genuinely distressed. "Viascola is really going to go after you in that. I've heard her plotting. She's even got one of her assistants serving as your substitute while she launches all her arguments."

"I'm not surprised." He made a show of looking through the stacked folders, then pulled one out and opened it.

"She's going to have half the Inner Circle there, and other people, as well. They've already decided to change the venue for lack of space in our original room. Now they'll be holding it in the common area on the fourth floor."

"Well, I did ask her to give me the microphone and the podium at dinner one night," Cam noted ruefully, closing the folder and moving it to the top of the stack, where it covered his sticky note.

"She's not going to let you speak, you know. She only wants to make you look like a fool."

He shrugged. "I've rejected the doctrine of evolution. That makes me as vile a heretic as ever came along, and you know what happens to heretics when they meet the true believers."

She cocked her head at him. "You make light of it, but they're going to tear you apart. I don't understand why you've agreed to this."

"Because part of the reason I came to K-J was in hopes of giving the gospel to these people. And now, thanks to Gen's vitriol, the crowd has expanded. There just might be someone among them who is ready to receive what I'll say. Even though they might not know it right now." He burrowed through his files and papers again, just to make his earlier actions look more convincing.

"What are you going to say?"

"Whatever the Lord gives me."

"And if He gives you nothing?"

"Oh, I doubt that'll be the case. He set this whole thing up, after all." Though of course it could only be to give the people at Kendall-Jakes the chance to hear the truth and then reject it. Noah had preached one hundred twenty years, after all, without a single convert.

She leaned forward as if to go, then said, "Well, good luck with it."

He looked at her in surprise. "Thank you."

After she left, he dropped the bagged frog into his pocket and wondered if Rudy might be able to get anything off it. Probably not, but he'd give it a try. Anything to shed light on why exactly Frogeater had sounded so much like Swain. It could be he was one of the man's many illegitimate sons, out for justice. Or it could be some weird Dr. Jekyll and Mr. Hyde situation. The latter in particular would account for why the voice in the audio recording of Manny's murder had been so rough and deep—someone had distorted it so as to hide any connection to the director. There was one other thing it could be, but he wasn't willing to seriously consider that one. Let them rule out the more reasonable possibilities first. Any prints on the frog would go a long way to either confirm or eliminate his theories.

As he turned back to his computer, he pressed the small transmitter button he'd affixed to the underside of his keyboard tray. About ten minutes later, the fluorescent bulb in the fixture near his office door began to flicker.

Eventually he called maintenance to have someone up to fix it, and when Rudy showed up, Cam spoke to him sharply, because it was the third time he'd allegedly fixed that bulb.

"I'm beginning to think you're just putting the same bulbs back into the fixture," Cam complained. Which was *exactly* what he had been doing.

The elderly janitor insisted he was not and set down his toolbox to arrange his ladder beneath the fixture. While he did so, Cam surreptitiously slipped a small, oddly bulging manila collection envelope into the sheaf of work orders stuffed in the toolbox.

⊷⊷⊷

At precisely 5:00 that afternoon, Cam arrived at the changed venue for the Department of Applied Genetics's weekly unity meeting, moved from the Desert Vista room on the third floor to the fourth-floor common area open to the atrium. As Lacey had predicted, a sea of people clogged the carpeted common area in anticipation of his arrival. The organizers had pulled over every available chair, bench, and sofa, but even that wasn't enough, forcing many to sit on the floor. The gathering included a number of familiar faces from the Inner Circle, including Nelson Poe, Maia Ahmed-White, Oscar Orozco, and Lee Yuen.

Gen sat in one of the two wing-backed chairs Cam had last seen in the reading area on the other side of the atrium. The second chair, separated from her by an end table, waited for Cam.

As the attendees became aware of his presence, the rumble of conversation damped swiftly, making the trickle of the waterfall and the echoing shrieks of the parrots from the atrium seem loud and close. Cam threaded a path through the gathering, feeling surprisingly calm, despite the hostility radiating around him. Not until he reached the empty chair did Genevieve look up from reading the typewritten paper in her lap.

"Ah. Dr. Reinhardt. Right on time. Guess I won't be needing this." She waved the typewritten sheet at him, then tucked it into her red straw bag with the yellow flowers sitting on the floor at her feet.

Her hand emerged from the bag with a black cube, which she set on the end table, and uneasiness invaded his calm. "What is that for?"

"I thought it might exert a calming influence, considering our subject matter for today." She smiled, then let her gaze sweep over the others as she addressed them. "As most of you know, we're tackling the very ticklish subject of religion this afternoon, one that must be

282 — KAREN HANCOCK

approached with the utmost civility and tact. I would like for this to be more a conversation than a lecture, so if you have questions or comments, please feel free to interject. But I also want all of you to remember that just because someone holds an opinion different from your own, they must still be treated with respect."

Cam spotted Lacey McHenry out in the audience, seated on the floor at Aaron's feet beside Jade and Mel. As he made eye contact, she flashed him a quick smile and he immediately felt a little less alone.

Viascola went on: "I am sure that Dr. Reinhardt, being the man of science that he is, has many excellent reasons for his beliefs. We should respect his willingness to share them with us." She turned to him. "So tell us, Dr. Reinhardt, how *do* you reconcile the truth of evolution with your belief in the Bible's story of a seven-day creation?"

"Actually, I don't," he said, turning toward her, "seeing as they are two antithetical belief systems that cannot be reconciled."

Hisses of indrawn breaths greeted this statement, followed by irate mutters.

"The theory of evolution is not a belief system!" Maia Ahmed-White declared derisively. "It's proven fact."

"Is it?" Cam turned his gaze toward her. "How many of us, not being paleontologists, have actually seen the evidence that allegedly proves it? The way I understand it, the bulk of the theory rests on a slew of hypothetical ancestors the fossil record does not begin to support. But even that I don't know for sure, since, again, I'm no paleontologist. I must take the respective experts at their words. Which is another way of saying 'by faith.' "

His conclusion was met first with shocked silence, then sputtering outrage.

"That's ridiculous!" cried Ahmed-White. "Humankind's breadth of knowledge is simply too great for any one person to have intimate experience with all the evidence. If we don't take the various experts at their words, no one would ever get anything done."

"Which is my point," Cam agreed. On the table to his left, the black box quivered as if it were made of gelatin rather than hard plastic—but only if he wasn't looking right at it. Far from exuding calm, it stood his hairs on end and filled him with restlessness.

"Science builds on the work of other scientists," said someone. "There's nothing wrong with that!"

Cam pulled his mind back to the discussion. Searching in vain for the speaker, his glance caught on Nelson Poe, who sat hunched in a chair not far from Lacey, seeming inexplicably tense as he studied his hands folded in his lap. It wasn't Poe who'd spoken, though; Cam would have recognized his voice.

"I'm not saying it's wrong," he said, giving up on a direct answer. "I'm just saying it involves faith. I can put my faith in the word of various scientists and in the assumption that they and their predecessors have properly assembled, evaluated, and reported all the relevant evidence regarding the origins of our world, or I can believe what God has told us about such things in His Word."

"First you have to believe the Bible *is* His Word," said Dr. Orozco.

"No!" interjected Ahmed-White. "First you have to believe that God exists at all, and frankly, I don't know how you can be involved in science and believe that."

"I don't know how you can be involved in science and not," Cam countered. "So maybe the real question here is not why don't I believe in evolution, but why *do* I believe in God? And why do many of you present today choose not to?"

Beside him the box edged forward and closer to him, quivering ever more frantically, as if demanding his attention. He shifted position to put it out of his field of sight, and turned his gaze toward those seated right of center.

"Well," said Gen, "it has always seemed obvious to me there is no God. Just look at the chaos and suffering in the world."

"God is just a human construct," said Ahmed-White, "left over from an age when people did not understand the underpinnings of our world. God worship gave them answers to the questions of where they came from and why they are here."

"And now that we've found the answers for ourselves," said Gen, "we don't need it anymore." She shook her head in puzzlement. "You're a man of learning, Cameron. I should think this would be obvious to you."

"You like the answers your conclusions give you, then?" Cam asked.

284 — KAREN HANCOCK

"That we came from slime, a random accident, and there is no purpose for our lives?"

"We make our own purpose."

"Ah." He let the silence draw itself out.

Then, seemingly out of the blue, Aaron Stiles blurted, "It's part of religion's purpose to blind people. That's why it always goes after the kids. If you're raised in a particular belief, when you grow up you can't break free." He glanced down at Jade, who'd turned to look up at him as he spoke, and gave her a triumphant smile. For winning the bet on whether he'd have the courage to bait his boss, perhaps?

"My parents are unbelievers," Cam said. "I was not raised in any church. I believed in Christ on a dark desert plain in Afghanistan when I was twenty-one."

"Before you went to college," Gen noted.

"Nothing I've learned in university has changed what I believed that night in the desert." His restlessness was deepening into outright anxiety, and his pulse pounded in his ears as a high-pitched whine now wrapped itself around his head, making it harder and harder to hear anything else.

Gen drew the conversation back to reasons why she didn't believe in God, and there followed a lively interchange among the crowd, which he only partially heard, where various members of the meeting voiced their objections to blind faith, magical thinking, superstition, and the other usual protests.

"Where is God when we have all this misery and suffering?"

"If the Bible says we're to pray for whatever we want and we'll get it, why haven't all the cancer patients been healed?"

"If He is love, how can He allow wars and famines and serial killers . . . ?"

Increasingly distracted by the quivering box and the mounting whine, Cam was caught off guard when the diatribe finally ran down and their attention returned to him. Having affirmed their mutual beliefs in materialism, facts, and their own flawless logic, they defied him to say anything about God that could possibly fit into those three criteria.

The waterfall in the atrium had grown into a roar, as if trying to drown out the box's whine. It didn't help that a voice at the back of his mind derided him for his anxiety. Here was his chance to proclaim truth. He knew what he believed. He knew he wasn't what they thought, that his reasons were not without logic or basis. Yet he shook like a whipped dog and said nothing. *Gutless* is what Gen called him.

She prodded him. "So, Doctor, what do you have to say to all of that?"

He looked at the people around him, tried desperately to haul his mind back to the issues, and prayed for words. And amazingly, they came: "There's too much complex order and design in the natural realm to think otherwise."

"Order and design?" Gen cried. "What about all the chaos and suffering?"

"Suffering and chaos are mostly products of the free will of sinful men."

"Tsunamis? Earthquakes? Mudslides? Those are the result of sinful men?"

"Those are evidence that the world is fallen along with the people that live in it."

"I thought you just said there was order and design in it all."

He stared at her, wondering if she really couldn't understand what he'd meant or just didn't want to.

"And how can the *world* be fallen? Natural processes don't have . . ."

The whine surged, drowning out her words. He concentrated harder, trying to hear past it, but she stopped talking before he could figure out what she'd said.

"Are you all right, Doctor?" Gen was regarding him curiously.

"I'm fine. The point is, you cannot prove the existence of an immaterial being if you demand that proof be made in material terms." He wasn't sure that was the point at all, since he'd forgotten what he'd been trying to get across and had no idea what she'd just said in rebuttal. But his statement *was* the crux of the matter.

"Hah!" Gen cried in exultation. "You admit, then, that He doesn't exist."

"I admit that One who is spirit by definition cannot be measured by empirical means. But rationalism *can* logically deduce His existence from what we see that He has made—the detail, the complexity, the inherent purpose in biological life and systems alone show that."

"That is an inference, not a proof."

"And what is evolution but the conclusion to a string of inferences?" he asked, somewhat testily.

She ignored him, turning her attention to their audience even as she pretended to speak to him. "You refuse to admit defeat, even though you've just conceded the fact there is no proof for God's existence." At her fingertips the box was literally jumping about now, seeming to fly at him every time he looked at it. Yet none of the others appeared to notice, all of them staring hard at Cam.

"There is no more proof for God's existence than there is for fairies," Gen declared. "Or unicorns. Or flying spaghetti monsters . . ."

Maybe the box wasn't flying at him. Maybe it was actually drawing him into itself. . . . Cameron dragged his attention back to her words. "Except that no fairies, unicorns, or flying spaghetti monsters have sent us a communication proclaiming their existence—"

"Communication? You're hearing voices now?"

"I'm referring to the Bible."

She reddened, realizing she'd missed his obvious point and immediately countered with, "The Bible?! That thing is so full of inaccuracies, so full of nonsensical happenings, myths, and magical stories! It's obviously man's creation of his god. . . ."

The box leapt off the table at Cam and pulled him into it.

Suddenly he was riding in a small electric cart along the narrow, roughhewn stone corridor that led to the tomb hidden deep beneath the highest peaks of the Hindu Kush.

"Have you ever heard of Nimrod?" asked their guide, the Afghani archaeologist Dr. Sayid Khalili.

Rudy said they hadn't, but he was lying.

"Great-grandson of Noah, grandson of Ham," said Khalili. "King of Akkadia and the builder of the Tower of Babel. You know. In your Christian Bible."

The cart's head lamps showed that the tunnel opened into a larger chamber up ahead, their glare reflected off a pair of closed stone doors.

· "We think this may be his tomb."

"Why would the tomb of the builder of the Tower of Babel in Iraq be all the way up here in the Hindu Kush?" Rudy asked.

"We aren't sure," said Khalili as they entered and crossed the vast room. "But the friezes are consistent with what we know of him." He slowed the cart as they approached the huge double doors, which were maybe forty feet high, and came to a stop in front of the smaller human-sized opening that had been cut into one of them. A metal door painted to match the stone covered the opening, and now Khalili got out and unlocked the padlocked chain that held it shut. The door squealed open, and he led them into the long, high-ceilinged hall beyond.

Electric lights on tall metal stands lined both walls, their illumination barely glinting off a ceiling some fifty feet above them. At the gallery's end hung a second pair of closed gargantuan doors, these adorned with bas-relief friezes of fish and ocean waves. The walls themselves were also lined with friezes, these of thirty-foot-tall warriors carrying swords, shields, lances, and other implements that looked more like bazookas or automatic assault rifles in stylized form than ancient combat gear. Cam eyed them curiously as he followed the others, footfalls echoing around them.

Their faces were handsome, stern, heavy-browed. Their eyes caught the light as if gems had been placed in the stone. They glowered down at the buglike intruders, and he could almost feel their disdain. Could almost hear their muttering in the air currents that sighed about them.

In one of the great doors at the hall's end, another small opening had been cut out and sealed with a painted metal door. Again they waited while Khalili unlocked the chain and pulled the door open. This time they had to stoop down to step through the revealed opening. As Cam came in after Rudy and straightened up, Dr. Khalili turned the light switch, and the immediate area brightened as several standing lamps blazed. The spacious chamber before them was empty but for a single chest-high pedestal about twenty-five feet long, atop which rested a giant, stony, podlike object. Black crystalline cubes littered the floor around it.

*"Ah,"* said one of the constantly muttering voices, *"you've returned. Now come and let us out."*

Behind them, Khalili flipped more switches, and four parallel lines of standing lamps revealed themselves, lighting in dominolike cascade to illumine the arena-sized chamber beyond the entry alcove. It was so large Cam wasn't sure he was seeing all the way to the end, and it was filled with sarcophagi, each as large as the first. And each of them, it seemed, had a voice, all demanding that the intruders come and release them.

He took a giant, gulping breath and returned abruptly to the common area outside the atrium, still seated in the chair, staring at the startled faces of his co-workers. His heart raced; sweat dribbled down his sides and trickled from his brow. Confusion amplified the terror that already gripped him, and he flinched hard at the sudden squawk of a parrot from the atrium.

Beside him, Genevieve leaned over the end table. "Dr. Reinhardt? Are you ill?"

Pain in his fingers drew his attention to his hands, gripping the chair's arms like vises. He looked down at his hands but saw the box instead, resting right beside his left hand, practically touching it. Aversion and horror exploded within him as he realized what it was and knocked it violently off the table, so hard it sailed out into the midst of his startled audience. He stared up into scores of pale, wide-eyed faces, trying to figure out who these people were and why they were here.

He drew a long, calming breath and felt his muscles unlock. As the panic bled away, he realized he'd had another flashback, right in front of everyone.

"Doctor?" Gen repeated.

He drew another breath and said, "No. I'm not ill."

"Another one of your episodes?" She leaned back, an almost-smile on her face. "I thought you were over those."

He turned away from her, embarrassment rushing in to replace the fear.

The others were glancing around now and shifting uncomfortably in their seats.

"Just exactly what *did* happen in Afghanistan, anyway?" Gen pressed.

"I counted a lot of beans," he said dryly. His eyes fell then on the black box, which was being passed forward by those in the audience on its way back to Gen, and sudden horror filled him. Was it mere coincidence that Swain would have chosen as symbol of his institute an object that exactly matched the cubes associated with the sarcophagi?

"Is that what drove you to your faith?" Gen's words intruded on his thoughts. "Whatever happened there?"

He stood. "I think our time is up, Gen. Now, if you'll excuse me, I have a lot of work to do this evening."

She looked up at him with a smug smile. He turned and walked to the elevators.

# Chapter Twenty-Nine

At 6:50 that evening, Lacey stood in the atrium dressed in shorts, a blue tank top, and sturdy tennis shoes, ready for a warm evening of walking about. She stared at the tiny red tree frog crouched on a branch at eye level as tour groups and a never-ending stream of smaller parties trooped around her, all wandering the portions of the zig that Swain had opened to the public for the weekend's open house.

Parrots squawked overhead and soared from branch to branch, the rush of the stream and waterfall damping the echoing chatter of the visitors. The frog, which appeared to glisten with moisture, did not move. As it had not since she'd arrived ten minutes ago, but that was not unusual for tree frogs.

She glanced around at the *ping* of an elevator car. Its doors rattled, disgorging passengers, but Reinhardt wasn't among them. As the waiting tourists pressed into the car, she wondered for the fiftieth time if she was being stood up and should just go over to the dining hall while there was still time. The degree of her disappointment at the possibility he wouldn't show surprised her. Though after what he'd endured in the unity meeting, she could hardly hold it against him.

Experiencing a post-traumatic flashback was bad enough, but doing so in front of a hostile audience had to be mortifying. At least he'd done little more than go stiff and pale, clutching the padded arms of his chair as his gray eyes widened at the sight of horrors no one else could see—and, coming out of it, knock Gen's black box off the table as if it were a suddenly discovered cockroach. Her heart went out to him.

But she still hoped he'd come. She hadn't told him about the note attached to the blue plastic frog left outside her door because she'd feared being overheard: *My father is not what he appears to be. Meet me in the Vault tomorrow night, and I will show you.*

When she'd first brought the frog to him, she'd hoped—prayed—there'd be some way for her to talk to him privately. So when she'd heard him say they needed to talk—and how about tonight?—she could hardly believe it. She frowned at the unmoving red frog, and decided to give him five more minutes.

A repeating cascade of notes finally penetrated her musings, and she realized it was her cell phone. When she answered she had to plug one ear to hear over the rush of the waterfall. "If you're waiting to see that little guy move," said Reinhardt's familiar voice, "you'll be there a long time. He's plastic."

"Oh!" she exclaimed. "It's you! You can see me here? Where are you?" She looked around.

"Don't gawk about like that. We're trying to be discreet here."

"We are?"

"There's a shuttle leaving for the campus overlook right about now. See if you can get on it. If not, take the next one. I'll meet you up there."

"A shuttle?"

"They're running every fifteen minutes tonight. Don't say any more—just go. I'll watch till you're on."

"Okay." She flipped the phone shut and left the atrium, heading across the crowded main lobby, a cavernous, high-ceilinged chamber whose west wall was a mosaic of glass panels—clear, opaque, and reflective. Reinhardt was probably watching through one of them. She didn't let herself look up, though, and concentrated on threading her way through the milling crowd, dodging around the little knots of people who'd stopped to look at the various freestanding displays or huddle over their visitor's guides to see which way they should go. When she finally reached the front doors, the sky-blue shuttle van was just pulling away.

Disappointed but resigned, she waited by the sign that said Overlook Shuttle Boarding. It wasn't long before a second shuttle drove up, unloaded its few passengers, and she got on. A handful of visitors joined her, and within five minutes they were on their way.

The van followed the paved road through a gap in the man-made berm that rose on the campus's north side, hiding it all from the highway a half mile away. Once through the berm, the road curved westward in gentle ascent through a landscape of chaparral and juniper, following the berm and then rising above it with the natural landscape. At length they reached the crest of a tall ridge, where a series of covered stone-worked ramadas were scattered along the eastern slope between stands of oak and madrona. A narrow, paved service road continued on, looping round the property and giving access to outlying campus installations.

The shuttle drove around the small but very full parking lot and pulled up to a curbed sidewalk to let off its passengers and pick up those waiting to return to the campus proper. Lacey had been told that in cooler weather the Institute held cookouts and parties at the overlook as part of their social enrichment program.

She stepped off the van into the baked atmosphere of what was still late afternoon in June, though it was nearly 7:30. Not seeing Reinhardt, she joined the swarms of people meandering the looping path between the four ramadas and the parking lot. Most went straight to the walled overlook for a quick scan of the campus, then returned to the shuttle pickup site to go back.

She strolled slowly, stopping to read the identifying signs for local vegetation and spending a good amount of time at the overlook, picking out the various buildings according to the large metal map bolted to the wall. It offered an exceptional view of the ziggurat, whose many mirrored surfaces were just now catching the rosy glow of the setting sun so that it gleamed like a jewel against the rumpled purpling hills behind it. From the overlook she could clearly see the long downsloping water channel that traversed the stairstepping levels and ended in the waterfall that greeted visitors arriving at the front door. It also served as imitation of the great stairways by which the ancient priests ascended to the tops of the original zigs, to offer sacrifices to their gods.

Suddenly her stomach growled so loudly it drew the attention of the woman standing next to her. Embarrassed, Lacey moved on. She circled the loop twice, then climbed up to the farthest and highest ramada, where a cement table and benches stood empty on the platform. By now ravenously hungry, she settled on one of the benches to wait, her back resting against the edge of the table.

Her position offered a good view of the overlook area, as well as the campus, the latter scattered with a lot more outbuildings and fenced car parks than she'd expected. There was even a helipad complete with orange wind sock on a pole and two parked choppers. Though she could not see it, she knew a third chopper sat atop the zig for Swain's private use.

"Sorry I'm late." Reinhardt's voice startled her so badly she jumped, then turned as he hiked out of the brush from the ramada's south side.

He wore a black baseball cap, a khaki-colored army T-shirt, and jeans over hiking boots. A gray daypack hugged his back, and a pair of binoculars dangled from his neck. He wasn't wearing his glasses—had probably exchanged them for contacts again—and in the ruddy light of the setting sun his gray eyes looked almost hazel. "I hope you like burgers and fries," he said, lifting the thermal bag he carried in his right hand. "I picked some up at the Resort Café before I left. They gave me the bag to carry them in, so hopefully they're still warm."

"You brought dinner!" she cried in astonished delight. "That's awesome! I don't care if they're stone-cold, I'm so hungry!" She swiveled her legs over the bench to face the table as he set down the bag and slid off his pack.

"I've got a salad in my pack, if you'd prefer that," he said, sitting down across from her.

"Can we have both?"

He pulled a boxed salad from the pack, followed it with bottles of cherry-pomegranate juice, napkins, and utensils.

"You've thought of everything!" she exclaimed. "I'm amazed."

"I'm not always on total disconnect," he said with a sheepish grin.

As they ate, he got right to business, relating his experience Saturday night in the animal facility when he'd chased Frogeater down the stairwell to the locked pump room door. She listened in horror as he recounted the details of his subsequent arrest by Institute security, their discovery of Manny's body in the frog tank, and his private interview with Swain, during which he was shown the surveillance video of someone dressed like him loading a body onto a gurney at the Vault's rear loading dock.

"He really *is* keeping the corpse in the Vault, then?"

"That's what he said."

"But why would he want to blackmail you into staying? To hear him talk—in private, anyway—you're an unstable, paranoid psychotic."

Reinhardt grimaced as he plucked the last French fry from the orange paper that had wrapped his hamburger. "For one thing, that sort of talk is primarily designed to get you to distrust me so he can advance his plans for you unhindered. As for why he's blackmailing me . . . ?" He popped the fry into his mouth and chewed, fixing his gaze on the ziggurat at her back. A gentle breeze kicked up around them, rustling the oak trees and the grass, and carrying snatches of conversation from the visitors meandering about on the ridge below them.

Finally he swallowed, sighed, and shook his head. "I honestly don't know. Could be part of his plan to break me from my Christianity, his desire to own my soul, or something else entirely." His gaze returned to her. "Did you read the articles?"

"About the missing girls?" She reached for her juice. "I did. And then I tried to confirm online the information in that report on the international sites, and I have to tell you I found nothing."

"That's because the report is a copy of a top secret government document. And I do hope you've shredded that disk like I asked."

She stared at him, struggling to get her mind around what he'd said. *Top secret government document?* "Are you a spy?"

He looked pained. "It's a recent development."

"Who sent you? CIA? FBI?"

"Hmm." He seemed bemused. "I'm not really sure. Could be either one, or Army Intelligence . . . And they didn't exactly send me, they positioned me. Then let me know what they'd done."

The K-J evaluator *had* mentioned he'd likely done intelligence work when he'd been in the military. "I thought you had a medical discharge."

"I did. They said I'd gone mad from my exposure to the elements after an extraction mission gone wrong. I was the lone survivor, and at first I *was* quite insane. Raving, terrified, unable to sleep, unable to trust anyone. Whatever I said about my experience, no one believed. Of course, the mission had been officially expunged from the record by then, so there was no hope of confirmation. They just wanted it all to disappear. Including me.

"They gave me a medical discharge. Blamed it on my daughter's death and the problems I was having with my ex-wife . . . At least that way I had benefits and they paid for my treatment."

He paused and drank from his bottle of juice. "Once I got the notion to go for the genetics degree, I just shut the door on my past, like it was someone else's life."

"But now you're having flashbacks again."

"After ten years of being 'clean.' " He crumpled the hamburger's paper wrapper and stuffed it into the bag. "The first one hit about twenty minutes after I'd taped up the cut on your arm in the prep room last week. The most recent was a couple of hours ago in the unity meeting, as you saw."

She nodded, thinking back to this afternoon. "Is that why you knocked Gen's box off the table? Because of something in the flashback?"

He grimaced. "Yes. In fact—"

She watched his thoughts jump track as he speared her with a gaze of horror.

"You have one of those boxes, don't you? From last week's meeting." He went on before she could answer. "You've got to throw it away. As soon as you get back to your room. And don't just throw it in the trash. Throw it out the window."

"I don't have a window. I'm in the basement, remember?"

"Then take it to the dumpster."

"Why? What is it?"

"Dangerous. You haven't heard any voices, have you?"

"Voices?"

"Or been troubled by strange dreams?"

She frowned at him. "You're starting to sound paranoid again, Dr. Reinhardt."

"I'm probably going to sound worse before I sound better. Just remember before you condemn me what everyone thought of you when you claimed there was an intruder in the AnFac that night. And you never even got to the part about his taste for frog legs."

Her frown deepened. "All right. I'll throw it away. But can you at least tell me how it's so dangerous?"

"It's . . ." He paused, seeming reluctant. "It's some sort of mind control device."

"A *mind* control device?"

"Just promise me you'll get rid of it."

"I'll throw it in the dumpster as soon as I get back tonight."

He accepted that, and they fell silent—his sudden fanaticism about the box leaving them adrift in a sea of awkwardness. She wanted to return to the subject of his flashbacks. What was he seeing? Was he remembering what had happened in Afghanistan? And why now? What could some military extraction mission in the Middle East twelve years ago have to do with Swain and Kendall-Jakes?

She had just worked up the nerve to reopen the subject when he suddenly stiffened, eyes narrowing as they fixed on something in the parking lot. She turned to see a shuttle disgorging yet another load of visitors, among whom he'd apparently seen someone who interested him. Indeed, he now picked up the binoculars that he'd set aside on the table and focused them toward the milling group.

"I think I've seen that guy down there in the red hat back at the zig. In a security guard's uniform. You ready for a little hike?" He lowered the binocs from his eyes and slid the carry strap over his head, then stood and stepped over the bench, reaching for his day pack.

"As long as it's not too far," she said. "I meant it about the blisters."

"We'll just go up the ridge a bit. There's a rock formation there that'll give us a good view of the sunset." He pulled a dark blue ball cap and a dark denim shirt from the day pack and told her to put them on. As she did, he zipped up the pack and swung it onto his shoulders, in the process of which she was shocked to glimpse a pistol grip protruding from the back waistband of his jeans.

They gathered up their trash, threw it in the garbage can, and then he led her south along a dirt path up the ridge. She followed him with acute uneasiness, trying to convince herself that the pistol wasn't what it had looked like, when she knew very well that it was.

# Chapter Thirty

After a few minutes, the trail ran out, and Reinhardt led Lacey down
the ridge-side, then up along its western face, climbing steadily until
they reached an outcropping of rocks where they could sit out of sight
of both the ziggurat and the picnic area. Below them, rolling grasslands dotted with stands of brush and trees stretched off to the west,
where the sun was dipping behind a fringe of clouds hovering over
the horizon.

As he swung off the pack and settled beside her, she said, almost
accusingly, "You have a *pistol* stuck in the back of your pants!"

"Yes."

She stared at him, openly horrified.

"Snakes," he explained. "They like to come out this time of day."

Which was reasonable, she supposed, but she didn't believe that
was the only reason he'd brought the gun. She thought she should feel
worried, out here alone with a man who was carrying a gun, and whom
her employer told her was borderline psychotic and dangerous. But
they'd been through enough together, she trusted him, despite Swain's
efforts to prevent that, and recalled from his file that he'd kept up his
practice with firearms over the years.

They sat in silence, watching as the sun dropped behind the clouds,
rays of light spearing across the pale mauve sky. From their position
she could see the asphalt service road below them, arcing around the
property. A red Jeep Cherokee sat to the near side of it, facing their

way. She asked if it was his and he nodded. Except for that, the road lay deserted. As they sat there the rays of light faded, grayness returned, and then the red orb of the sun slid past the gap between the thunderheads and horizon. Suddenly the clouds were turned to blood and the rumpled grasslands at their feet looked as if they were on fire.

It was breathtaking, but ephemeral. All too soon red and gold gave way to gray and purple again, highlighting the slice of moon that hung high in the western sky, attended by a single bright star. As a slight breeze kicked up around them, she finally turned her mind to the reason she was sitting here alone with her former boss, a man she barely knew.

"So what is this all about?" she asked. "You said you had something to suggest to me that the articles would give me context for. Do you want me to play spy for you, then? Serve as bait in another possible abduction?"

"I'm not sure 'bait' is the right word, but yes."

"What if he just kills the girls after he abducts them?"

"We don't think that's what he's doing. We don't even think the girls who supposedly died are dead."

"So what *do* you think?"

"Twenty-five years ago Parker Swain was obsessed with human cloning, which he saw as a means of attaining eternal life. There are reports he achieved viable cloned human embryos well into the third trimester, but could never bring the fetuses to term. That was twenty years ago, though, and if he'd had any real success you'd think we'd have heard of it. On the other hand, given the controversial nature of such a project—not to mention the potential profits to be made—maybe not."

A horrible, stomach-curdling suspicion bloomed in Lacey's mind. "To the third trimester means he had to implant his embryo into a surrogate."

"Exactly."

She gaped at him in equal measures of disbelief and horror. "You can't be serious."

"Why not? You could go online right now and sign up to be a surrogate with some fertility clinic. Women do it all the time."

"Then why abduct them? Why not just pay them?"

He sighed as if in frustration and shook his head. "I don't know. The secrecy of the project? The fact he's a megalomaniac? Maybe he didn't abduct them. Maybe they went willingly. He certainly has a way with women."

She thought of Parker Swain's charisma, the way all her discernment seemed to leave when she was in his presence.

"It's only a theory," he added.

One that made a kind of appalling sense, unfortunately. She considered for a moment; then, tucking a windblown lock of hair behind one ear, she said, "So if you're right, and I agree, there's the potential I could be impregnated with a cloned embryo." She spoke quietly, and kept her voice even, though horror churned in her stomach until she thought she might vomit.

"Ideally, we'd extract you before it got that far."

"Ideally." The breeze swirled around them again, carrying errant snatches of voices from the picnic area and even the brief distant sound of a steel band playing down in the campus bowl. She blew out her breath. "I'm sorry, Dr. Reinhardt, but this is just too . . ." She trailed off, overwhelmed with aversion. "It's too weird. Kendall-Jakes is a respectable institute. What you're talking about sounds like a bad science fiction movie."

"I told you it would sound worse before it sounded better."

"When is it going to sound better?"

"I don't know."

"Well, I don't think I want to be your bait."

He nodded but said nothing, turning his face toward the west, where darkness swathed the land, broken here and there by the distant twinkle of isolated lights. Overhead, a nighthawk wheeled in the air beneath the partial moon and star.

She frowned, kicking at a knob of rock near her feet. "I really don't have a choice, though, do I? Since he means to take me anyway." It was very hard to swallow the notion that this had never been about her researching ability or her aptitude for science.

He shifted beside her. "We can extract you right now and put you under government witness protection if that's what you want."

Government protection. That would mean she'd have to change her name, never see her mother again, and forget about a genetics career or anything high profile. "I wouldn't have to pay back my debts, though, would I?"

He smiled slightly. "I wouldn't think so, no."

Again they fell into silence. She didn't want to disappear. But then, she didn't want any of this. "Wouldn't Swain think it terribly odd if I just disappeared?"

"It would impact our operation here, certainly."

"But you have similar investigations going on at the other sites, right?"

"I don't know." He glanced at her. "Given the way I was recruited, I doubt it. One of the reasons they approached me was because Swain was already after me, and they hoped as a respected and well-known geneticist I might break through barriers that so far had been closed to them."

"Getting onto the Inner Circle, you mean."

He nodded. "You'd do us one better, though."

She tucked the errant lock of hair behind her ear again. "What would I have to do?"

"Mostly just be our eyes and ears. Keep in contact. Let me know what's going on. We might wire you if it starts to look like he's going to move."

"Which would be before the U of A Genetics department returns from their vacations next week, no doubt."

He nodded.

She gazed blindly across the twilight-cloaked landscape, sick with fear. The moon and star had dropped behind the pile of clouds by then, a rough marker of the length of time they'd been out here. Probably too long . . .

Again the wind shifted, and they heard voices from the picnic area, then car doors slamming and engines roaring to life.

When she'd said nothing for a time, he pulled a head lamp from his pack's external pocket and suggested she should probably get back to the zig. He'd see her back to the picnic area so she could take the shuttle, then go back to his car and drive around. When she agreed, he stood, slid on the pack, and offered a hand to help her up.

She took it, then stood staring up at him, her hand still resting in his. "I'm scared," she said softly.

"You should be," he said. He'd put his hat on backward and positioned the head lamp, but had not yet switched it on, which made it easier for her to see his face, softened and shadowed in the dim light. "We both should be. But I think God brought us both here for a reason. Put us both in the position we're in. For a reason. We have to believe He'll take care of us through it."

She looked at the ground, embarrassed and suddenly uncomfortable. "I don't think I have enough faith for that anymore. God's done so very little for me over the years."

After a moment of silence, he lifted her chin with a finger, forcing her to meet his eyes. "He might not have given you everything you want, but He's given you life. You're healthy and whole—" he paused, his eyes roving her face—"beautiful and brainy, and a pretty nice girl, too. I don't think you can fault Him. Especially when you consider He's done all that knowing you'd turn your back on Him."

She frowned at him, not sure she liked his assumption that she'd turned her back on God. Even if it was true.

He seemed to read her thoughts, for he smiled slightly. "He's given you the opportunity to make choices, as well. And the time to change your mind, if some of those choices don't turn out to be very good ones."

"You mean like bad marriages?"

"Actually, I was thinking more of bad attitudes. The way we ignore God and run off after our own plans, then blame Him when they don't work out." He said it with such irony, she thought he must be speaking from experience.

Even so the words burrowed like arrows into her heart. For she *had* run after her own plans. But after the debacle with Erik, after all those years of trying so hard to do the things she was supposed to as a good Christian girl, only to fail so miserably, in both her marriage and in her personal life, why should she not go her own way? Why should she trust Him to work things out when He never had before? Especially now, when once again everything was falling to pieces around her—in the most bizarre manner possible.

Unwilling to say any of that to his face, though, she averted her eyes and said nothing.

Finally he stepped back and released her hand, was just starting to speak when a head-sized rock sailed through the air where he had been, cracking loudly into the cliff behind them. It was so close, the wind of its passage whooshed into her face. She blinked at him in surprise and the next moment he'd pulled her to the ground with him, hunkering behind a mound of rock.

After a time, when no more rocks came flying, he drew her down along the cracks and gaps in the outcropping until they reached the grassy slope at the bottom. Then, without a word, and without turning on his head lamp, he led her at an almost run across the open ground, heading for a nearby copse of trees and brush. Dashing from cover to cover, they reached his Jeep without further incident.

He jammed the key into the door, unlocking it, and she scrambled in as he went around to the driver's side. There he tossed his pack and binoculars into the back and got in beside her.

"Why were we running like that?" Lacey said as he switched on the engine and lights.

"You think that rock just hurled itself into the cliff on its own?" he asked grimly, throwing the SUV into gear and pulling onto the blacktop.

"What? Are you saying it was thrown?" Now that she had time to think it through, she realized that was the only way to explain its trajectory.

"I'm guessing it was Frogeater, though it surprises me he'd come all the way out here."

"Oh no!" she cried in sudden chagrin. "I meant to tell you earlier—there was a note attached to the frog he left me. He wanted me to meet him tonight at the Vault."

"He wanted you to *meet* him?" Reinhardt took his eyes off the road for a moment to flash her a horrified glance.

"Well, it wasn't like I was going to. But, yeah. I didn't tell you in the office because I was afraid we'd be overheard."

He faced the road again, one hand on the steering wheel, the other still covering the stick shift. "Well, no wonder he's—"

A basketball-sized rock slammed into the hood, rolled into the windshield and off as Reinhardt stomped on the brakes and cranked the wheel leftward. As the SUV went into a tight, leaning U-turn, Lacey screamed and gripped the armrest in terror, certain they were going to roll. . . .

But they didn't. As they straightened out, heading back the way Cameron had originally come, he up-shifted as rapidly as the transmission would allow. As the minutes slid by along with the roadside vegetation, she began to catch her breath, shaken, but unhurt.

And then a boulder the size of a small chair slammed into the pavement directly ahead of them. Reinhardt swerved hard right to miss it, then left to stay on the road. Again the Jeep tilted precariously, its right wheels clipping the dirt shoulder. Barely were they square on the pavement, when a small uprooted tree fell into their way. Again, Reinhardt swerved around it and kept going.

"How could he have caught up with us so fast?" Lacey cried.

Cameron didn't answer as boulders now rained upon them. Like a race-car driver, he dodged and swerved between them. Then, as suddenly as it had begun, the assault ended, and for a moment the road lay clear. She was just daring to hope it was over, when a man in a green hooded sweatshirt appeared square in their path. Cameron wrenched the wheel to the right; they swerved again onto the shoulder—

And the engine died, the lights with it. Lacey was aware of Reinhardt struggling with the steering wheel as the Jeep fishtailed; then the ground dropped out from under the right front tire and a dark wall of vegetation reared up before them. She slammed hard into her shoulder harness, the force of impact snapping her head back against the headrest and driving the breath from her chest.

Stunned and disoriented, she was fighting to drag some air into her breathless lungs when her passenger door vanished in a deafening squeal, and a horrible smell engulfed her. Then her seat belt was torn away and she was yanked out of the car. She heard Cam shout as she was hurled over her abductor's shoulder and carried away.

*It's Frogeater!*

He ran, twisting and jumping through the grass and spotty woods, Lacey bouncing over his shoulder. Where his bare hand gripped the backs of her upper legs, it felt like hot coals pressed against her skin. The *wop-wop-wop* of a helicopter somewhere in the distance ahead of them brought him up short. He stood listening a moment, then turned and fled back the other way. By then she'd regained enough of her senses to fight him—twisting, hitting, and struggling futilely to get free.

Suddenly a deafening *boom-boom* thundered in the night, and he stumbled badly, losing his grip on her. She slid off his shoulder and slammed into the hard, prickly ground. Urgency screamed at her to get up and run, but her lungs had locked up again, refusing to take in air, despite the fact she was close to passing out.

When she was finally able to breathe, Cameron was kneeling over her. "Are you all right? Where does it hurt?"

"Everywhere," she gasped, pushing herself up on one elbow. "Where did he go?"

"Off into the darkness." Reinhardt gestured vaguely in the direction Frogeater had fled. He seemed disoriented. Blood ran from a cut on his brow and she noted that the bulb of his head lamp had been crushed.

"Did you hear those two booms?" she asked. "Right before he stumbled? It was almost as if someone . . ." She trailed off as thought caught up with words and she remembered he had a gun.

"Shot him?" Cameron supplied. "Yeah. That was me."

"You *shot* him?!" She sat upright, outraged. "I was hanging over his shoulder! You could've hit me."

"I was aiming at his legs. I'm pretty sure I hit him, too, 'cause that was right when he stumbled."

She realized he was right, but before she could say any more, the formerly distant chop of the helicopter's blades grew loud and immediate. In milliseconds the aircraft came whooshing over the ridge, its spotlight slicing the darkness before it. For a moment it bathed them in blinding brilliance, then flashed on as the helicopter swooped past, buffeting them with the wind of its rotors.

They scrambled to their feet, dust and debris settling around them as the sound faded—only to be replaced by the roar of several SUVs

306 — KAREN HANCOCK

speeding down the service road just to their west. The vehicles turned off about where Lacey and Cam were standing, heading further westward over the rough terrain, searchlights spearing wildly through the night.

"Was it him?" She turned to where Cameron had backtracked and was peering at the ground. He stooped to pick up something shiny.

"I think so," he said. "He was wearing that hood, so I couldn't see his face much, but the form looked like his." He kept his eyes on the ground and stepped back, though with the meager light from the partial moon and stars, she didn't see how he could find anything and wondered why he didn't turn on his head lamp—then recalled its smashed bulb.

"I didn't see his face, either," she said. "But he seemed bigger than before. And stronger."

"Much stronger," he agreed grimly. "And I don't think he liked it that you stood him up."

She frowned at him. "At the Vault, you mean? How can you stand someone up if you never agreed to a meeting in the first place?"

Amazingly, he found what he was looking for, stooped and picked it up. "It doesn't have to be logical. He invited you and you rejected him." He approached her, and the starlight reflected off the two shiny brass bullet casings resting in his palm, right before he pocketed them.

"And instead I met you out here in the desert alone." Her words sparked the sudden realization that he could still be out there. It seemed he'd been running from the chopper, which was circling not too far away. As fast as he moved, he could easily swing back. . . .

Evidently Cameron had the same thought, for he suggested they return to the Jeep.

When they got there, however, they found that more had gone wrong than simply an engine stall and a trip into the ditch. Though the vehicle had a winch with which Reinhardt had hoped to pull it back onto the road, he couldn't turn it on. Nor would the Jeep's engine turn over. The dome lights did not come on, either, and turning the key wouldn't even bring up the dash lights.

"Is it the battery?"

"Probably," Cameron said, pulling his pack out of the rear seat and slipping it on. Then he reached for his binoculars, shut the door, and turned to her. "Come on, let's get you to that shuttle pickup before anything else happens."

"Won't it give away the fact we met up here if we ride the shuttle back together?"

"I suspect that fact has already been given away, but I won't be riding with you." He looped the binoculars strap over his head. "There's a path at the picnic area that leads down to the resort. I'll take that."

"Do you think it will be safe?"

He cocked a brow at her. "The shuttle? Or the path?" When she only looked at him in growing uneasiness, he held out a hand to her. "You okay?"

"Not really." But she was glad to take his hand and walk beside him.

They'd not gone far when a flash of white flared around them, trailed by a tremendous boom that shook the ground beneath their feet. Turning back, they saw great orange tongues of flame licking upward into a cloud of black smoke.

"Was that the helicopter?" she whispered.

"Most likely," Reinhardt said grimly. "Come on. I'll feel better when you're back at the Institute."

## Chapter Thirty-One

Halfway up the side of the ridge, Cam turned back to survey the crash site. The smoke of burning oil and fuel made his eyes water and his nose burn. Thanks to the binoculars and the circle of klieg lights set up around it, he could see things quite clearly. The flames were smaller now, but smoke continued to churn upward from the chopper's crumpled fuselage—though the only way he knew it *was* the helicopter was by the single main rotor standing at a rakish angle beside it. A fleet of Institute SUVs and vans surrounded it, including several larger emergency vehicles with lights still flashing. The area swarmed with people, and along the outer ring of the mayhem lay a handful of tarp-covered bodies.

The most disturbing aspects about the scene, though, were the lights of the searchers moving about in the chaparral beyond the crash and the distant barking of their search dogs. Frogeater was still at large, and it was highly likely he had brought down the chopper now burning before them. Given what Cam suspected Frogeater had done to his Jeep, this wasn't entirely surprising, but he shuddered to think what that meant about the nature of his abilities. And their range.

Turning from the site, Cam led Lacey to the top of the ridge, where they were met with the surreal sight of the gargantuan zig aglow with its golden night-lighting. It loomed over the bowl-shaped park at its feet, which was itself ablaze with light and activity. Festive white twinkle lights garlanded the many booths set up for the Open House Expo amidst which visitors thronged. The steel band's music was considerably louder and more persistent now, the whole picture a bright and happy contrast to the grim scene of destruction at Cam's back. If the attendees down there had any idea what had just happened less than two miles over the ridge from them, they'd be stampeding to escape.

Rather like the visitors to the overlook must have done not too long ago. The picnic area now stood dark and deserted, its parking lot empty, the gate closed at the entrance and locked. "They probably cleared everyone out when they sent up the choppers," Cam said as he and Lacey considered the scene.

Since there would obviously be no more shuttles, they set off down the dirt path toward the campus proper, their way lit by the golden ziggurat. It pleased him that she hadn't seemed too upset with the prospect of walking with him, despite her earlier discomfort with his "trust God" spiel. Though he didn't regret what he'd said, he didn't blame her for rejecting it, either. Given the magnitude of the problems she faced, it had probably sounded more like a platitude than sound advice.

Though after their most recent adventures, perhaps she'd be willing to give God another chance, seeing as they were both still alive. And still together.

Again he relived those terrifying events, ending with the moment when he'd shot Frogeater's leg squarely out from under him, yet only made him stumble rather than bringing him down. As the strange youth had regained his balance, Cam had been milliseconds from firing again, when Frogeater looked over his shoulder and the gleam of something in his forehead stopped Cam's hand and triggered another memory from Tirich Pazu: the monsters had broken through a wall, and though thick clouds of rising dust obscured their forms into mere silhouettes against the flames behind them, the third eye on the leader's forehead had been unmistakable, glowing like a bright red ember as he searched out his prey. . . .

By the time Cam shook the memory off, the youth had disappeared into the darkness. Though at first Cam had assured himself he'd seen only the glint of starlight reflecting off the boil in the boy's forehead, now he wasn't so sure. The creatures Cam had encountered in Afghanistan were huge and violent, and Frogeater was obviously not one of them.

But he seemed to share a measure of their abilities, and according to Rudy, Swain had acquired his own collection of sarcophagi. Had he used some of their DNA in his modifications of Frogeater?

"Tell me more about that note," Cam suggested abruptly. "The one attached to the bottom of the plastic frog."

She thought for a moment, then said, "It was taped on. I left it attached and unfolded it with tweezers . . . so if there were prints or something I wouldn't mess them up. I hoped you would have seen it without me having to say."

"Well, I didn't," he said, annoyed with himself for that oversight. His new habit of noticing details was clearly not as comprehensive as he'd thought. Of course, he did have something of an excuse, given how distracting her presence often was to him. "So you read it, then?"

She nodded and told him what it said.

"Meet him in the Vault? You're sure?"

She nodded.

"What could he show you there that would discredit Swain?"

"Manny's body, perhaps? Although I'd think that would discredit Frogeater more than Swain, since Frogeater's the one who killed him. . . ."

Cam heard her words without really comprehending them, for the mention of Manny had shone a sudden new light on what Cam himself had done tonight, and it appalled him. He had known Frogeater was after Lacey—he'd heard the words Frogeater had spoken to Manny on the audio record, seen what he'd written on the wall in the frog room, and been questioned by the young man himself not three days ago in the basement stairwell. Yet knowing full well Frogeater's obsession with her, Cam had brought her out here anyway.

He stopped in his tracks and turned to face her. "I'm sorry," he blurted, cutting off whatever it was she was saying. "I had no business sending you up to the overlook with him in the picture."

She was still wearing the baseball cap he'd given her and now blinked up at him from under its brim. "How could you know he'd come all the way out there?"

"I knew he was interested in you. I knew he was angry enough over your replacement to kill Manny over it. And I knew that at least once he's fled the Institute and disappeared into the desert. I should have thought it through better."

She raised a skeptical brow. "And where would that have led you? We needed to talk. And that was a good place for it. You couldn't have known Frogeater would be there." She took his hand and squeezed it. "Actually, I think you've been rather amazing tonight."

He felt the heat of embarrassment surge into his face.

"So have you," he said quietly, making no move to release her hand. "A lot of women would've been reduced to hysterics by now. You're just trooping along like nothing's happened."

"In case you can't tell from my shaking hand and sweaty palm, I've been a jittery mess ever since that first rock almost took your head off. And I was so relieved not to have to ride back alone on that shuttle without you, I could hardly speak."

He frowned at her. "You give me too much credit. I'm no more protection against the likes of Frogeater than the next man."

She tilted her head at him. "Oh, I think you *are*. You got me free of him, didn't you?"

He could think of nothing to say to that, except the million things he'd done wrong tonight, which she clearly wasn't interested in listening to. *Well, fine.* He knew he would have a hard time protecting her, but in the end it didn't matter because God could. Which was obvious from the fact they were both still alive. *You really do have my back, don't you, Lord?*

Lacey smiled up at him and reached to touch the cut on his brow. "You might want to clean this up, though, before we go walking around other people. And take off the broken head lamp."

He pulled off the head lamp and stuffed it into his pocket. Though the blood had dried, he rubbed as much of it away as he could, then reversed the hat so its bill shadowed his face. "That better?"

She said it was and they continued down the track. After a moment she spoke again. "Why *would* he come out here, though, when he told me to go to the Vault?"

For a moment he didn't know what she was talking about. Then, "You mean Frogeater?"

"Shouldn't he have been waiting there in the Vault?" she asked. "And if he was, how would he know I'd gone to the overlook?"

"I don't know."

"Unless he was watching to see if I'd go to the Vault in the first place. Fast as he moves, he could do that, couldn't he? I mean, you were watching me down there in the atrium. Why couldn't he? Then he could run over to the Vault before I got there."

"I guess that makes as much sense as anything." It unnerved him to think the young man might have been watching them the entire time they'd been out there. And, for all he knew, might be watching them still.

Not until they passed the first group of the resort's casitas, and the dirt road transitioned to asphalt with sporadic streetlights, did Cam begin to relax. Even then it was a very alert state of relaxation. Letting go of her hand for the first time since they'd started back, he swung his pack around, drew his cell phone from the front pocket, and flipped it open to call the campus garage.

The Institute switchboard operator answered, and when he explained his need for someone to pull his Jeep out of the ditch on the service road southwest of the overlook, she informed him the garage was closed for the night and wouldn't open until 6:00 a.m. tomorrow. She suggested he call a towing service.

He'd known the garage was closed, of course, but thanked her anyway. Then he called his insurance agent and left a message informing him of the accident, giving considerably more detail about the situation than he'd given the operator, including his need for a tow truck. He tucked the phone into the front pocket of his jeans, knowing Rudy would have gotten both messages, since his station monitored every call that went in and out of Cam's BlackBerry. Hopefully he'd not only send a team out to inspect the vehicle ASAP, but would also set up a face-to-face meeting without Cam's having to ask directly.

It wasn't long afterward that Lacey stepped nearer to him and slid her hand into his again. "Do you mind if we walk around the expo booths for a while?" she asked in an almost sheepish tone. "I know it's late, but . . . Jade's probably not going to be in till the wee hours, and I just don't want to go back to that room yet."

So they walked past the resort to the bowl, where the crowd was still moderate and the steel band was still playing. Wandering among the different booths set up along the park's pathways, they checked out the various offerings, sampled some of the food, and picked up free pens, snack bag clips, brochures, and other advertising oddities. Fortunately, most of their co-workers were at the resort bar by that time, so they didn't run into anyone they knew.

At 10:30 the steel drum band stopped playing and the first explosion of fireworks began. Since there weren't supposed to be fireworks until Sunday, Cam suspected these were being shot off to cover the significance of the earlier explosion when the chopper went down. This view was confirmed shortly by an overheard snatch of conversation between two booth vendors.

When the fireworks show ended fifteen minutes later—and the steel drum band was packed up to leave—he took her back to the zig. There in the elevator lobby off the dark and deserted Madrona Lounge, she pushed the Down button and the elevator doors opened immediately. But instead of boarding she turned to face him, as if still reluctant to leave. Having no idea what to say, he said nothing, which made for a spell of awkward silence.

"Oh!" she exclaimed. "Don't want to forget to give you back your hat...." She took off the cap and handed it to him as the elevator doors rumbled closed again.

When he took the cap from her, she rested her hand on his forearm, her dark eyes meeting his with sober intent. "What you asked me to do earlier?" she said softly as she drew closer to him. "When we were on the outcropping?" She paused, drew a steadying breath, then said, "I'll do whatever you want. Or . . . umm . . ." Her face flamed as she apparently considered more carefully whom she was going to be involving herself with. "Within reason, anyway. I don't know what's going on, but I know it's not good. And if he really is kidnapping young women for . . . whatever reason, well . . . I can't just walk away and let it keep happening."

He wanted to tell her to do just that. But he didn't. Instead he brushed a smudge of dirt off her cheekbone, smoothed the tendril of hair behind her ear. "It could be more dangerous than . . . what we spoke of."

Her eyes never left his. "For you, as well. And *you're* not leaving."

He frowned down at her, then pulled one of the freebie expo pens and a brochure from his shirt pocket. "Here's my cell number," he said, scribbling it onto the back of the brochure and handing it to her. "Call me anytime. Even if it goes to voice mail, someone will get the message real time and take action if need be." He paused, then added, "It might be that we'll figure all this out before he makes his move to take you. That's what I'm hoping, anyway. But let me know what's going on."

She nodded, stood there a moment more staring up at him, then stepped back to push the Down button again, reopening the waiting elevator's doors.

"You sure you don't want me to go down with you?" he asked.

He saw her force the smile. "You can't go with me everywhere. If he was waiting down there, surely security would know by now. I'm hoping, though, that with all those men and cars and dogs up there they finally caught him. I mean, how could they not?"

"They probably did," he agreed. Though both of them knew very well how easily Frogeater could have evaded them.

The doors closed between them, and he left the small lobby, returning to the deserted atrium to board one of the glass-walled elevators. But instead of going straight to his room—he knew he wouldn't be sleeping anytime soon—he took a detour by way of the ninth floor, wanting a look at the crash site from the viewing gallery there to get a sense of how things were progressing with the search.

Located on the floor's west side, just north of Swain's complex of offices and suites, the Golden Saguaro viewing gallery hosted many of Kendall-Jakes's high-level receptions and cocktail parties. No matter which way one went from the elevators, it was a long walk around the atrium to reach it, and seemed especially so now, the corridor dark and deserted. With no sign of even a security guard around, he was surprised when he reached the short hall leading to the darkened gallery and heard voices coming from within.

Cautiously he continued forward and soon realized there was

only one voice—Gen Viascola's—engaged in a one-sided conversation, probably on a cell phone.

"Thank God!" she said. A pause. Then, "Sedated?! Are you mad?"

Cam stole to the gallery's open doorway and peered into the spacious room beyond. The window wall directly across from him provided views of the western landscape at higher elevation than he and Lacey had enjoyed at the overlook outcropping. In the darkness beyond he saw the klieg lights still arrayed beyond the service road.

His interest now, however, centered on the two people standing in silhouette before the window about thirty feet to his right. One was Gen; the other—tall, gawky, with a hook nose and dark, disheveled hair—looked like Nelson Poe.

"Yes, but at the rate he's developing, he could come out of it and—" She broke off, having obviously been interrupted.

"I understand that," said Gen, irritation sharpening her voice, "but if you're wrong, he—"

Again she was cut off, her responses limited to "uh-huh" and "yes, of course." Cam eased through the door and leftward around one of the potted faux saguaro that dotted the gallery. He settled on a loveseat in the shadows against the wall.

"Well," said Gen, "you'll do as you think best, of course, but I hope you're right. He's caused us more than enough trouble already."

After another silence she said good-bye and flipped the phone shut with a sigh. "They've got him," she said to Poe. "Tased him and wrapped him in Spiderline."

"And the chopper?"

"No one knows why it crashed. The copilot survived, though. He might be able to tell us."

"He'll only tell us what we already know," Poe grumbled, sinking onto the chair beside him. "And then Parker will find some way to make it mean what it doesn't."

Gen put a hand on one hip and looked down at him. "What's that supposed to mean?"

"Nothing."

"They've got him back in the lab. Lee's prepping him now for the tests. Parker said his phenotypical transformation has been phenomenal.

The crest is almost fully realized, bone and muscle mass have nearly doubled since his escape, his hands and features have coarsened, and get this"—she sat in the chair beside him—"he's formed an *oculus*. One that actually seems to function in some way. Parker says it has a glow to it, seems to track targets, and was very hot when they brought him down."

"Oh, Lord, help us," Poe muttered.

Gen flounced back in the chair. "Well, of course *I* think we should terminate him, and just do a full autopsy. The results so far have gone beyond our wildest dreams—"

"More like nightmares," Poe grumbled.

She huffed and shook her head. "Why must you always be the voice of doom?"

"I don't know. Why do *you* always go along with him, even when you don't agree? Even when you know he's pushing far beyond anything that's reasonable?"

"If he didn't push beyond what's reasonable, we wouldn't be here." She leaned toward him again. "Look around us, Nels. Look how far we've come since that rickety houseboat with the cockroaches in Costa Rica."

"Maybe it would be better had we not come so far."

She stared at him silently for a moment. "You're still upset about D-210, aren't you?"

"His name was Andros."

"D-210 didn't have a *name*. You've got to let that go. We did nothing wrong, and the project must move forward."

"We killed him."

"And we made him in the first place, which gave us every right to terminate him when we deemed the time was right. He was obviously degrading and would've only gotten worse. Look at this debacle with A-118. And it looks to me like A-432 is going off, as well. Those earlier lines just aren't stable, as I've said from the start."

At first Cam had thought she was referring to Frogeater as the one they'd terminated, even though she'd said earlier that he wasn't. The more she talked, though, the more he realized he had no idea what she was talking about. But the mention of subject numbers, termination, and "earlier lines" made his blood grow cold.

"Listen to yourself, Gen," Poe said, speaking with more passion than Cam had ever heard from him. "We *made* him? We terminated him at the *proper* time? I just—" He fell silent, shaking his head. "This playing God stuff is not right."

"We're not 'playing God,' " she rebuked him. "There is no god. We're just doing what's best for everyone."

"What if you're wrong?"

"I'm not wrong. How can you argue that this all won't lead to better things for everyone—ourselves and the whole world?"

"I meant about God."

In the electric silence that followed, Cam could almost feel Gen's shock. She was probably about to pop.

"Reinhardt made some good points in that meeting today," Poe said. "Much of what we believe *is* based on faith. Including what we believe about where all this"—he gestured vaguely around them—"is going. . . ."

Another protracted silence followed, and finally Poe said, "You're not even going to respond to what I said?"

Gen sighed wearily. "You're obviously depressed. I'm going to see about getting you some vacation time. Come on. We've seen enough here."

She stood, and Poe did likewise. As they threaded their way around the couches, loveseats, and faux saguaros, Cam held utterly still, his eyes focused downward lest an errant gleam from them betray his position.

Thankfully they left without noticing him, and he continued to sit there afterward, mulling over what he'd heard, trying to put the pieces together, and knowing there were still some crucial parts missing. "*We made him . . . and then we terminated him. D-210 was not a person. . . .*"

But there *was* a special lab somewhere. And, apparently, additional frog eaters, as well . . .

# Chapter Thirty-Two

New Eden

Zowan expected to meet up with Parthos in the lozenge-shaped mall in the commons Friday night, but it was Terra who sought him out. Freed of her charges for the evening, she came up beside him toward the end of the group walk-around—a nightly mall ritual. Not everyone walked every night, but everyone walked at least once a week. The Enclave's community organizers piped in music or Enclave news, changed the lighting, staged art shows, and held occasional contests to keep things interesting for the walkers.

Tonight, though, they just walked, strolling along the mall's long central island of trees and plantings, past its pools of fat, glowing orange fish under their lily pads and luscious white flowers, past its stream and waterfall and the big cage of brightly colored birds, then around and through the Tangle Grid that stood at its far end, the maze of lighted blue and purple bars. And all the while, Gaias watched them from the post he had taken up near Father's statue at the base of the Sanctuary's ramped entrance.

"Did you hear Father toured the crèche after lunch today?" she asked him.

"Yes."

"And that there was a Winnowing?"

He frowned down at her. When one of the children sickened or displayed some anomaly or weakness, they were winnowed from the crèche—for treatment, the other children were told. It was only last year that Zowan learned they were being killed. "Terminated" was the official word. Or perhaps they were being sent to that experimental lab Neos had mentioned.

"It was Fyver," she said softly. Fyver was a five-year-old boy with whom Terra had bonded the first day she'd worked in the crèche.

He found her hand and squeezed it. "I'm sorry." Mindful of Gaias's gaze, he released her immediately.

"We're not supposed to care, I know," she said, brushing away her tears. "But it's hard. There was nothing wrong with him," she said as they approached the lighted Tangle Grid at the far end of the island. "He was just an active little boy who had trouble settling down. He reminded me a lot of you at that age."

"How could you remember me at that age?"

"You used to pull my pigtails. And you always made me laugh when I was supposed to be listening to the story. That's how Fyver was. Smart, active, always getting into mischief, yes. But his heart was good. He wasn't mean. Just curious and fun loving."

None of which were qualities Enclave Elders valued, Zowan observed. "Smart," "curious," and "active" were not traits that inclined one to the docile, unquestioning submission they clearly preferred.

"Father was so sweet to him today," Terra went on. "Called him over, invited him up onto his lap, gave him a honey drop, told him what a good boy he'd been . . . then sent him off to be put down." Her voice cracked, and she shuddered. "How could he be that cold? How could he lie so easily? And then that charade with you this morning! All that talk of your promotion to New Babel, when we all know it's no promotion. Babel is the poorest of all the enclaves. The place where everything always goes wrong and people die. Oh, but *you're* going to turn it all around." Her voice took on a tone of bitter sarcasm and choked off. She drew a deep, almost groaning, breath. "I hate it that we have to live like this!"

They walked on, entering the archway that bisected the Tangle Grid. Halfway through it, she looked up at him and grated between clenched teeth, "Zowan, if you know the way out, take it before he sends you away!"

He gaped at her in alarm. "Why would you think I—"

"I was sitting in your lap after the blackout Monday night, remember? So I felt it when you were jerked out from under me. I felt the draft of the panel opening and smelled that awful stench. Parthos smelled it, too. It was how we realized our first suspicion—that Gaias had taken you—was wrong. I only know one person who smells like that: Neos."

They came out of the Tangle Grid and headed back around the island in the opposite direction, Gaias now directly ahead of them. Horrified she was talking about this right here in the mall, he looked around to see who might have heard them and hissed, "Neos is dead, Terra!"

"You know he is not," she said firmly. "As do I. And don't worry—they don't watch us nearly as much as we've been told that they do."

"Gaias has been staring at us since we got here. And I was *in* the spaces around the Star Garden," Zowan began. "I know—"

"Which is why we're talking out here in the open," she cut in grimly. "And don't worry about Gaias. He can't hear us. He's only trying to intimidate us."

"Can't hear us? What about the oculus?"

"Neos says they don't work nearly as well as we've been told. In fact, he doesn't think they work at all."

Zowan frowned at her. "How would he know that?"

"He's been evading Enforcers for the last six months."

"You've talked to him?!"

She nodded.

"Since Monday?"

"It was a couple of weeks ago."

Zowan exhaled a deep, shaky breath, rocked as much by the content of Terra's disclosure as by the fact she'd chosen not to tell him until now. "Why didn't you say anything?"

"I guess I didn't think you'd believe me."

The music stopped, and having completed their twenty laps of the island, they settled side by side on the freestanding bench, a little way off from the Tangle Grid, with the entire length of the mall separating them from Gaias.

Zowan's eyes swept the high mirrored window that stretched the length of the mall, overlooking all of it. The reflective surface created a sense of airy space where there was only a narrow vault—and hid the rooms where Father's wives lived. Father had visited them today, before he'd toured the crèche. They could see out, but no one else could see in. In fact, no one Zowan knew had ever seen any of the wives. They were even more imprisoned than the rest of the Edenites.

He wondered, as he often did, if his birth mother was among them, and why he'd never been allowed to meet her. . . .

At his side, Terra spoke softly, breaking into his troubled thoughts. "Parthos is convinced the New Babel reassignment is a ploy and that you'll never leave New Eden alive. He's certain once the departure ceremony is over, they'll whisk you away to the termination facility and do the same to you as they did to Fyver."

He shuddered and didn't even try to argue with her.

"Which is why you have to leave now," she said.

Well, he'd pretty much decided the same, so he couldn't argue.

"And why I want to come with you," she added firmly. "Parthos, too."

He looked at her aghast. "I don't know if anyone can live up there, Terra. It was bright and hot and—"

"So you did go up!" she whispered, suddenly awed. "You *have* seen it!"

He frowned. "I have. And it didn't look very habitable."

"Neos says it is."

"Neos is dying."

Her brown eyes widened.

"I also think he's more than a little insane," Zowan added. "He says they did something to him in some secret deep-level lab. He doesn't know what. But it looks like he's forming an oculus."

Her surprise gave way to ferocity. "And you don't think that will be you in six months if you don't flee now?"

He sighed and fell silent. Then, "I have to get to the physical plant to find the hole I went through, and I can't just walk up there without a reason. Not to mention the problem of getting in, since the physical plant is restricted to anyone who doesn't work there."

"You could go as an Enforcer," she suggested. "Parthos has a robe. With a bit of smudge on your forehead, you could pass for Gaias if no one looked too closely."

A shiver crawled up his spine. It was the very idea he'd entertained himself. And Parthos had apparently acted upon it. "When did he get the robe?"

"Today."

This time the chill rushed over his whole body as he recalled the assurance he'd felt in this morning's Affirmation that if he sought to obey I Am's command to leave the Enclave, he'd be shown the way.

"He also has a couple of Elder's robes," Terra added with a smile. "I could go as Elder Sophia, and he as Elder Horus."

"Absolutely not! Bad enough that I would masquerade as Gaias—I'm already slated to be removed. But if you or Parthos were caught—"

"How could it be any worse than what we're already living?"

"Didn't you hear what I said about that secret deep-level lab? Besides, I meant it when I said I don't know if we could survive up there. It was hot, dry, empty. Where would we find food? Or water?"

"Neos says it's up there. And I'm willing to take my chances. So is Parthos."

"Okay. I understand that. But there's no reason for you to rush. Let me go up and see what's there. We might need to plan this more slowly, stockpile food and water. If we all go . . . everything will be thrown into turmoil and they'll hunt us down."

"If you disappear, the first people they'll come to will be me and Parthos," she said bluntly.

And he knew she was right.

A competition of acrobatics in and off the Tangle Grid started up then, and the crowd closed around them, blocking off their view of Gaias as it blocked off his view of them. Moments later Parthos squatted before them.

"Did you ask him?" he asked of Terra.

She nodded, then summarized their recent discussion, concluding

with Zowan's insistence on going alone. "He's worried we'll get ourselves into trouble."

"Just being your friend has already done that," Parthos said, affirm-
ing Terra's earlier words. "And we're happy about that, so don't try to
spare us from it. If you use the robe, I'll be implicated. If you don't,
you won't go anywhere. Besides, they'll be looking for you, not us." He
smiled. "They would never expect us to be so audacious."

Zowan frowned at him.

"How do you plan on getting into the physical plant once you get
there?"

"I don't know," Zowan said. "Though Neos did say that as Father's
son, all he had to do was hit the lock plates and the doors would open.
I don't see why that wouldn't happen for me, as well."

"He could do that *before* he kidnapped you and took you to the
surface," Parthos pointed out. "Those plates have undoubtedly been
reprogrammed by now, and while I suspect they'll still work for you,
they'll also surely signal security so the Enforcers will know where
to look. Since I'm betting Elder Sophia's touch will also be accepted
without the stigma, Terra should be the one to push the lock plates.
For as you are one of Father's sons, she is surely Sophia's daughter."

He had a point.

"Here's what I'm thinking," said Parthos. "We leave tomorrow night
during your party, right after Terra returns to crèche duty. Helios and
Erebos will distract Gaias while you slip away. I'll leave shortly after."

They'd meet in the orchid room, where Parthos would already
have hidden the robes. Once those were donned and a blot of grease
dabbed on Zowan's forehead to serve as the substitute oculus, they'd
head out through the food storage areas and into the main corridor
leading up from the commons. Surely "Elder Horus" and an Enforcer
on a mission of great haste and importance were unlikely to be stopped
and questioned.

Terra would meet them in a small court near the physical plant
and access the lock plates to let them in.

When Zowan again sought to argue against her going, the other
two refused to listen. "Elder Sophia is second only to Father," Parthos

pointed out, "while Horus is several ranks lower and doesn't have the range of access she does. We need her."

Zowan continued to frown from one to the other, deeply annoyed that all their ideas made so much sense and that, not only could he think of nothing to refute them, he lacked a reasonable alternative. But what if he couldn't find the hole? What if he *had* hallucinated? What if they were caught? There were so many risks. . . .

Terra squeezed his hand and leaned against him. "There's another compelling reason for me to go I haven't told you about," she said grimly. "Gaias. He's put in a request for a union with me."

A mix of horror and intense anger nearly choked him. She was too young. She was a crèche worker. She was unwilling. . . .

But Gaias was an Enforcer and one of Father's sons, as well, and with Terra only a week away from turning eighteen, Zowan knew the Elders would not deny him his choice.

"I will *die* before I submit to that," Terra hissed beside him.

"Heads up," said Erebos, whom Zowan noticed now for the first time. He'd taken up a lookout position at Parthos's side, facing away from the conversation so he could watch the mall. "He's on his way."

"That'll be Gaias," muttered Parthos. "Are we good on this plan?"

Zowan heaved a breath of resignation. "Okay. We'll do it your way."

Nodding, Parthos stood and, taking a sudden strong interest in the contest at the Tangle Grid, slipped away into the crowd. At the same time, Terra released Zowan's hand and slid off the bench, leaving him to sit alone, contemplating what he'd just set in motion. The destruction of his friends' lives might not stop with Andros, he realized. For if Parthos and Terra had guessed the hole to the surface originated in the physical plant, surely the Enforcers had, as well. What if all this ended with him leading his best friends to their deaths?

*But what if it leads you all to freedom?* The question brought with it the awareness that only minutes ago he'd had no idea how he might get to the surface again, and now he had a plan, with the disguise and access he needed provided for him, along with two—no, *three*—co-conspirators. Could that possibly be the work of I Am? It certainly wouldn't be hard for a being who had created the Earth and destroyed it with water to take care of such minor details in Zowan's insignificant life, but would He?

Zowan wished he had more of the *Key Study*. When God had told Abram to leave, he'd obeyed, but Zowan had no idea what had happened after that.

He stood up just as Gaias pushed between the wall of people surrounding Zowan and stopped before him. The Enforcer frowned, eyes flicking from the empty bench to the backs of the immediate bystanders, all of them focused on the Tangle Grid contest and none of Zowan's closest friends among them. Frustrated, Gaias scowled darkly at him, then shoved him aside and continued through the crowd as if he had not been watching Zowan at all.

## Chapter Thirty-Three

Cam's cell phone rang early Saturday morning, rousting him out of a deep sleep and then out of bed as he groped across the bedside table trying to find the phone. From the way the light blazed around the cracks in the bedroom's blinds, he judged it well past his normal hour for rising. But when he'd fallen into bed around 3:00 last night, he'd planned to sleep in. For the second Saturday in a row.

Finding the phone, he answered with a groggy hello. Immediately the person on the other end apologized for a wrong number and hung up. By then awake enough to remember the calls he'd made last night, Cam waited, and after a moment an encrypted message appeared on the screen. He pressed the key to decrypt and read: *"Frog prnts & bld smpl = PS. EMP fryd Jp."*

As soon as he'd read the words, the message vanished, erased by the BlackBerry's automatic security function. Even so he stood there, staring down at it, struggling to get his sleep-fogged brain around what he'd just read: An electromagnetic pulse had fried the Jeep's electrical system, and the prints off the plastic frog and the blood sample were . . . Parker Swain's? But Cam hadn't taken a blood sample from Swain, only whatever saliva was on the fork he'd pilfered.

Finally he realized that the prints and DNA profile Rudy's lab had gotten off that fork matched the prints off the frog on the one hand, and the blood on Lacey McHenry's lab coat on the other.

Which meant either Director Swain was indeed some kind of

modern-day Jekyll and Hyde or . . . Cam drew a deep breath as the pieces fell into place.

Frogeater wasn't Swain's son; he was his *clone*. As incredible as that was, it was the only explanation that answered all the questions, particularly in light of the conversation he'd overheard last night in the Golden Saguaro viewing gallery. Somehow Swain had succeeded in producing a human clone of himself that had survived to adulthood. More than that, he'd succeeded in subsequently introducing genetic modifications into that clone without immediate catastrophic malfunction. Modifications which had resulted in "phenomenal phenotypical transformation" and given him terrifying abilities. Like his extraordinary strength and speed. Like the wielding of the electromagnetic pulse that had fried Cam's Jeep.

Light suddenly flared at the edges of Cam's vision, and he gasped as the flashback swept him back into the depths of the Hindu Kush. With his three remaining teammates on his heels, he raced into the tomb's vast outer chamber, where the hundred mighty warriors glared down from their seventy-foot-tall panels—clubs, swords, spears, and stylized bazookas raised to annihilate all intruders.

A roar of fury erupted from the inner chamber Cam and his fellows had just exited. The ground shuddered as static crackled in his headset and everything went dark—the gallery's twelve standing lamps and the men's head lamps alike. Acutely aware of the approaching roars from behind, Cam pulled a handheld flare from one of his side pockets and lit it.

"Run!" Cam yelled to the others. *"Run!"* And they ran. The ground shuddered again as a sharp wind buffeted them. The rock around them groaned, followed by a series of earsplitting cracks as fissures parted the gargantuan panels. Still in the lead, Cam was halfway down the vast chamber when the first piece bowed out from the wall and flung itself at them. He put his head down and sprinted, leaping and dodging debris as the chamber itself assaulted them, hurling jagged shards of itself into their path.

Choking dust rose up around them, obscuring the meager light of the few remaining torches. The dark hole of the tomb's exit yawned ahead, and he sprinted harder. Suddenly a strong downdraft pummeled him and he seemed to rebound off a wall of air as a huge piece of panel, broken into a spearhead shape, planted itself directly in front of him. It was part of a man's face, the eye of the warrior glaring at him, so strangely alive he expected a sword swing to come in the next moment.

It didn't. Instead he raced around the self-embedded shard and sprinted all out for the doorway lost somewhere in the smoke and dust ahead, wondering how they would ever survive. . . .

He drew a deep, shuddering breath and blinked as his present reality returned. His apartment lay around him—quiet, clean, aglow with the light of a new day. Yet he trembled, and sweat slicked his underarms; he tasted dust and smoke, and his stomach churned. He'd forgotten the deep sense of evil that had filled that tomb. And the hatred the creatures trapped there had for him and all his kind. The Afghanis had released six of them. Though he could not remember how they'd done it. Or even how he knew they had.

He forced himself to take a deep breath. Those were all dead now. Killed. Vaporized. Incinerated. He didn't know how they had perished, either, only that they had. Along with all the sarcophagi in that vast chamber. Which didn't matter anymore if Rudy's new information was true and Swain really had found more monsters in the tombs of the Bekaa Valley and elsewhere.

Cam went to the bathroom and drank a cup of water, then sat on the side of his bed and checked his voice mail. There were two messages. The first, sent at 4:55 a.m., was from the campus garage. "We have your vehicle," the mechanic's voice informed him. "Unfortunately, we had some trouble getting it out of the ditch, and it has sustained a small amount of additional damage."

The second, sent at 6:00 a.m., was from Deena Flynn, informing him that Director Swain would like his company at 10:00 a.m. in the resort's poolside restaurant for an early brunch. It was a summons he'd anticipated, and a meeting he didn't expect to enjoy. Swain had to know he'd met privately with Lacey McHenry last night, and that alone would anger him. It was also possible he knew Cam had a firearm, in violation of K-J's rules forbidding staff members to keep a weapon on-site. As closely as security had been tracking Lacey, someone could well have heard the shots Cam had fired at Frogeater. His one hope was that Swain wouldn't confront him openly on it, since that would lead to the question of what Cam had been shooting at, which Swain probably didn't want to answer.

He left his apartment at 9.30 and headed for the resort by way of the garage to see about his Jeep. As it turned out, the "little bit of additional damage" was a complete flameout of the engine and interior. Something about a gas leak and a spark from the cables against a rock. He could translate that easily enough: they'd discovered the engine had been fried and deliberately torched the car to hide the evidence.

After calling his insurance agent again to provide the latest news on his car, he strolled across the campus to the resort's restaurant. There the maître d' directed him to Swain's table in the sunny back room beside a long poolside window. Talking to him was Lacey McHenry. She stood with her back to Cam and was apparently just leaving, if the mostly empty plate across from Swain was any indication. Indeed, in moments she turned and headed up the aisle toward where Cam stood waiting. *It can't be good,* he thought, *that Swain's booked appointments with both of us back to back.*

Watching her approach, though, he felt the same warm tingle he always did in her presence. It was a sensation intensified this time by the way her eyes lit up at the sight of him. As she drew closer, however, her expression grew troubled.

"Good morning, Dr. Reinhardt," she said softly as she reached him.

"Good morning, Ms. McHenry," he replied, adding as she started past him, "Are we in trouble here?"

"I don't know," she said, "but *I've* just been invited to be his date for tomorrow night's reception." And with that she was gone.

Stunned, even as he knew he shouldn't be, Cam reluctantly forced his attention to Swain, who was conversing now with the server refilling his coffee cup. As the server left with Lacey's plate, Cam strode up. But other than gruffly telling him to have a seat, Swain ignored him, focused on adding sugar and cream to his coffee.

Then, after sipping from his cup a couple of times, he leaned back and said quietly, "You disappoint me, Cameron. Here I offer you a prime position with our most important program and you let me down like this."

Even last week, Cam would have been thrown completely off guard by the man's sudden and open hostility. Today he was braced for it. "Sir?"

"You know how I feel about drunkenness. My disgust for it is matched only by my disgust for those who betray my trust."

"Drunkenness? Betray your trust?" He must be referring to last night, but . . . "What are you talking about, sir?"

"Oh, come, Cameron. I know about your evening tryst with my graduate student up at the overlook last night. I and everyone else."

Cam leaned back in his chair. "Ah."

"Have you no sense of propriety at all?" Swain asked with quiet intensity. "No concern for the lady's reputation? You, the so-called devout Christian among us?"

"Sir, I assure you I was not drunk, and—"

"You ran your Jeep right off the road, boy! The dispatcher told me your voice was slurred when you called last night."

"Sir," Cam said quietly, "you know we did nothing remotely along the lines you are implying." But he understood now that this was the story being used to cover the real reason for his crash, and to dish out a little punishment on the side.

Swain glared at him, unable to deny what Cam said was true, unwilling to let go of his anger, anyway. "The bare bones of what you did was unseemly," he said finally. "Whether you actually had relations with her or not is irrelevant. As I keep telling you, the truth doesn't matter. It's only what's perceived to be true that matters. And it's all over the campus now that you and Ms. McHenry were indeed having relations last night out on the rocks above the overlook picnic area."

Cam met his angry gaze with fortitude, knowing there was nothing he could say.

"You could've at least had the decency to rent a hotel room," Swain hissed. "We have plenty."

He fell silent, tapping at the tablecloth and glaring at Cam. Then he said, "You'll have nothing more to do with Ms. McHenry, neither during work nor afterward. And should you decide you don't want to abide by that rule, please recall that no one has yet actually seen or spoken to our Argentinean Rhodes scholar. If anyone were to investigate, however, they'd find his resignation letter was composed on *your* office computer." He leaned back in the chair. "Have I made myself clear?"

Cam sat at rigid attention. *On* my *computer?* "Yes, sir, you have."

Swift and painful as the strike of a snake, the dressing down was over. Swain seemed to forget it entirely, as if they'd been discussing the weather rather than murder and blackmail. "So. What do you think of the efficacy of continuing your investigation with the frog mitochondria? Ian Trout has already been asking about it, and I want to tell him where we stand in our meeting this afternoon." He glanced over Cam's shoulder and gave a nod to someone there.

Cam pointed out Swain had already agreed the preliminary results had not been as good as they'd hoped, and for a few moments they discussed the pros and cons of proceeding. Then the server showed up with a plate of eggs over-easy, Canadian bacon, and half a whole wheat Belgian waffle, along with coffee and juice. "I took the liberty of ordering breakfast for you," Swain said. "Just to speed things along a bit. I presume you haven't yet eaten today?"

"No, sir."

"Well, then"—the director gestured with his cup toward the food—"dig in."

And Cam did. Meanwhile, Swain's eyes drifted to the window and the pool with its bikini-clad beauties, and for a time he sat lost in thought, nursing his coffee.

Cam was nearly done eating when, seemingly out of the blue, the director said, "Taking death out of the equation would really put a kink in your beliefs, wouldn't it?"

"Excuse me, sir?"

"Without the fear of death, how could you Christians bring people into the fold? If death were vanquished, there'd be no need for Christianity."

*Oh. This again . . .*

Cam speared the last square of his waffle and ran it around the plate, mopping up the remaining syrup. "Of course there'd be a need, sir," he said. "We'd still be estranged from God. Still be in these present bodies, governed by the desires of the flesh." He paused to eat the syrup-laden bit of waffle, and then, since Swain was giving him the opportunity, added, "Frankly, I'd prefer not to spend eternity in my current body with all its limitations. I'd rather have the new one God has promised me."

Swain set down his cup and leaned forward. "But don't you see, Cameron? The point is, we *will* overcome the limitations. With science we don't have to trust in the claims of some old book of dubious origins. We can believe what we see and feel. We don't have to wait for a new body we know nothing about; we can transform the one we already have."

They paused as the server came and refilled coffee cups. As he left with Cam's empty plate, Cam said, "That's a fine dream, Director, except for the fact that we can't *do* any of it. Which makes it as much a matter of faith as believing in a resurrection."

"*Yet.* We can't do any of it *yet.* And yes, it does require faith—but faith backed up by concrete facts of science that lead logically to the next step." He steepled his fingers and cocked his head at Cam. "Sometimes I wonder if you really want to be part of that next step. If you think our quest to extend longevity is as futile and unnecessary as you claim, why pursue it?"

"Maybe I want to prove that death and aging cannot be stopped."

Swain cocked a brow at him. "That's an unprovable hypothesis."

"But each new effort proven false may help people to look toward the true solution."

The director grimaced with displeasure and leaned back. "Not good enough, Cameron. It's negative. It's passive. . . . It's depressing. I told you last week I wanted your loyalty, not so much to me as to my vision. I'm beginning to think perhaps you can't give that to me. Because my vision is all about finding a fountain of youth you've pretty much admitted you don't believe exists."

"If I do my work to the best of my ability, why does it matter what I believe?"

"It matters profoundly if your bias compromises your ability to evaluate the data fairly. For example, the mitochondria project. I think the preliminary data has promise; you think it has none. Why? Could

THE ENCLAVE — 333

it be your bias is blinding you? That the evidence is right in front of you, but you can't see it because you have already decided it's not possible?"

Cam's indignation kindled. "Excuse me, sir, but why would I want to compromise my professional integrity in such a way? I'd only end up looking the fool."

"I'm not saying you'd do it consciously. It's just a built-in blindness produced by your world view." Swain let his steepled fingers interlace. "Then there's the lack of fire and passion for the search. If belief forms the reality—as I believe it does—then your doubts will inevitably disrupt our progress."

Swain regarded him almost smugly, and Cam realized that Swain had not finished with his dressing down after all.

Sure enough, the director hit him again from an entirely different angle: "You're doing a very poor job of persuading us of your sincerity and commitment, son. That little stunt last Sunday when you stood us up at the security meeting and drove almost to Mexico, knowing I had people on you . . . I could forgive you that, knowing you were distraught. But then there was that embarrassing fiasco in your unity meeting yesterday, where you offended almost all your co-workers with your silly accusations. And finally the profound lapse in judgment you used in connection with Ms. McHenry last night." He shook his head. "After all that, is it any wonder the others remain skeptical? Even *I* am having my doubts." He leaned forward again. "Do you really want to be with us, Cameron? Or are you just here to convert us all?"

"Sir, you knew who I was when you brought me here," Cam said. "And one of the reasons I came was because of the freedom I thought you were offering me. Freedom to pursue the truth. But I see I was wrong." He paused, then added, "I'm not going to renounce my faith for this, if that's what you're after."

"No?" Swain leaned his forearms on the table to lean close. "I hold an awful lot of power over your life, Cameron Reinhardt."

"You hold nothing God has not allowed and cannot take from you in a moment."

Swain's chin jerked up. His mouth tightened, and Cam saw anger flash in his blue eyes. "I can't just let you leave, you know."

"Do you want to reassign me to the animal facility, then?" Or did he have something else in mind? A sudden disappearance? A faked death? Or perhaps a death not faked at all?

"Think it over for a couple of days. Consider how much you want to pay for what you believe."

"I could say anything to get you to bring me in. And mean none of it."

"You could." Swain smiled. "That's really all I'm asking you to do. Show the others you're willing to offer them a hand of partnership. Since you had the public meeting to air your views on the origins of our world, I think it only fair you give us a public renunciation of those views. And your full and enthusiastic endorsement of our vision."

Even if everyone knew he didn't mean it, it would still be a capitulation. It would still prove that some things were more important to Cam than his loyalty to Christ. To his beliefs. Doing what Swain wanted would tell them his beliefs were just beliefs. Interchangeable with any other beliefs. Not truth. Not life. Not who he was. And certainly not something worth losing his position for. But if he didn't, he'd be out . . . and then what?

"You have until Monday to give me an answer," Swain said. His gaze slid off Cam to someone behind him, and his expression changed dramatically, from sly and calculating, to a warm smile. "Ah, here is Mrs. Lederman. Looks like she's early. You don't mind cutting this short, do you? I think we're finished here and I don't want to keep her waiting. She's been a very faithful supporter of our work."

Cam, of course, took his leave, though not before being introduced to Estelle Lederman, who was remarkably well-preserved and well-put-together for a woman of eighty-four. At least he'd been able to finish his breakfast; he'd gotten the distinct feeling Swain would have asked him to leave even if he hadn't.

As he left the restaurant and crossed the resort's main lobby, his BlackBerry vibrated. A quick check showed a message from his insurance agent. The adjuster would be out at 3:00 to photograph the Jeep and investigate the crash site, and a tow truck would arrive at 4:00 to haul the demolished vehicle into town. Either the adjuster or the tow-truck driver would be his contact.

## Chapter Thirty-Four

Following her breakfast with the director, Laccy went up to her office and tried in vain to work. Though she opened the first of the research abstracts she planned to peruse, between the events of last night and her momentous meeting with Swain, she was hopelessly distracted.

She'd awakened way too early this morning, then couldn't go back to sleep, already beset with second thoughts about her decision to help Cameron Reinhardt find the lost girls and expose whatever it was that Swain was up to. Twisting and turning in her sheets, she'd tormented herself with the horrors of what she might be getting herself into, only to realize if she stayed and did nothing, she would end up there, regardless.

Then the whole breakfast-with-the-director event had swooped down on her like a bird of prey, snatching her out of her nightmares and plunging her into a world of golden opportunity. Once again the power of Swain's personality and words, combined with the constant emotional stimulation of his delightful praises and possibilities over-rode thought. It was like some sort of bizarre interactive performance that always sucked her in and carried her along until he was finished with her.

He'd said nothing about last night, other than to ask if she was enjoying the open house, then moved on to inquire about her satisfaction with her present office space—because if she desired something else, he would certainly see about accommodating her. From there he conveyed with great enthusiasm his expectations and plans for her as a graduate student and beyond—heady visions that far exceeded the fulfillment of her simple dream of earning her doctorate.

Sometime in the midst of all that, he'd flashed his charming smile from where he sat across the table from her and, with a mischievous sparkle in his gorgeous blue eyes, asked her to be his date for the VIP reception to be held in the zig's tenth-floor Hanging Gardens tomorrow night.

Her mouth had dropped open as much from surprise as from the horror of having Reinhardt's nasty suspicions confirmed. Then she'd blushed furiously, so uncomfortable she'd wanted to crawl out of her own skin and vanish. What would be next? An invitation to the penthouse?

*I will* not *go to the penthouse,* she told herself firmly.

Then Swain laughed and assured her he was only kidding. "It's not the sort of affair one brings a date to," he explained, "but I'd be honored if you'd be my guest for the evening. There are a number of folks I'd like to introduce you to—being K-J's first and thus far only graduate student."

Profoundly relieved, she'd let him carry her along again, wanting desperately to believe everything he said was true—that the reception invitation really was nothing more than the manifestation of his commitment to helping promising young researchers advance. That it really would dramatically further her career to be at his side tomorrow night at the biggest function of K-J's year, meeting all the movers and shakers in the field.

"If you work this right, your place in genetics will skyrocket," he'd assured her. Then he'd grinned again and this time urged her to use her pretty face to advantage. "I'm not suggesting anything immoral, just advising you to make use of all your assets. It's amazing the power feminine charm can have on some of these old, crusty scientists."

She'd laughed with him, and it was impossible to feel anything but flattered and honored under his admiring gaze.

But the moment she'd turned from his table to see Cameron Reinhardt standing in the archway at the juncture of the restaurant's two sunny rooms, she'd known it had all been an act. She couldn't dismiss the things that had happened to her over the last two weeks, and especially not what had happened last night. No, everything Swain had just done only proved the truth of Cameron's suspicions.

The director was pursuing her, and if she "worked this right" and "used her feminine charms," she'd be well rewarded. . . .

Though Reinhardt had looked more exhausted than she felt, and the knot on his forehead was beginning to bruise, the sight of him there in the breakfast room had ignited in her a swell of strong affection. She wished now it had been Cameron who'd asked her to the reception instead of Swain, but then, even as senior staff, he probably didn't get to invite whomever he wished to the affair. At least his senior status meant he'd be there, too. She wondered if he was as good at dancing as he was at driving and shooting. . . .

Her computer screen turning off from disuse startled her out of her musings, and she frowned at her seventh-grade thoughts. Telling herself sternly to get to work, she pushed all thoughts of Cameron from her mind and twitched the mouse to wake up her PC. When the darkness held sway, she twitched the mouse again, frowning now as she heard voices apparently coming from the screen itself. Not only that, but vague shadowy shapes were lurching across it. She peered at them intently, wondering if the screen was broken or the system was crashing—

Suddenly the darkness pulled her into a place that was eerily familiar. As before, she smelled the sweet fragrance of jasmine on damp air and followed the voices ahead. This time, though, the darkness dissipated rapidly, revealing walls of huge-leaved foliage on either side. Stalks as big as her waist rose around her, some supporting bright blue daisylike flowers as big as sombreros.

She walked barefoot on a white spongy pavement through the foliage. It was warm and moist, and she wore only a white Grecian-style shift made of thin, exquisitely soft silk. The garment fell halfway to her knees, and though she wore nothing underneath it, she wasn't the least bit cold.

The path's curve prevented her from seeing the people who were walking ahead of her, but she could hear their voices clearly—two men and a woman, speaking a language she didn't recognize. Finally, though, she came to the edge of the forest, where a wide plaza stretched out before her. A huge white building stood at its midst, but she noted it only peripherally, her attention drawn to the motion of a chariot lifting from the pavement. It held the three people she'd been following and was pulled by two winged, horselike creatures up into the misty sky before her.

She watched them with pleasure, knowing somehow that she'd seen them many times before. Only when they had disappeared behind the mist did she return her attention to the building, where she was headed for her appointment. It had a wide porch, lined with Grecian columns and fronted by a rank of wide steps.

Crossing the plaza, she ascended the stair toward the huge open doorway at the back of the porch, feeling increasingly averse. The door led into a bright and airy rotunda, illumined by high clerestory windows. A shoulder-high counter ran along the inside wall, above which various panels blinked with lights and graphs. To the left a riot of plants grew in small dishes under glowing orbs. Some had green leaves. Others had purple and yellow and bright orange foliage. There were odd lumps of pink puttylike material balanced atop small, shallow cones, these latter illuminated beneath red orbs.

A man stood on the far side of the chamber, working at a space on the counter where there were no plants. He stood over seven feet tall and the simple white knee-length wrap around his hips exposed his marvelously muscled upper body. Smooth, unblemished skin glowed like warm, rich cherrywood, and his hair fell like a river of spun gold to his waist.

At her tentative hello, he turned, and she was frozen in place, bowled over by his heart-stopping, godlike beauty: the angled strength of his jaw and brow, the narrow, straight nose, the long-lashed, neon blue eyes. Just the sight of him made her bones go soft and her mind turn giddy with rapture.

"Ah, you're here," he said, though not in English. In fact, she was pretty sure he was speaking the same language as the first group of people she'd encountered, but for some reason now she could understand his every word.

"Climb up there on the table. This won't take long."

She hadn't noticed the massive table, though it stood in the midst of the room. Carved of white marble, its surface stood level with her shoulder.

He turned back to the counter and picked up what looked like a white pipette with a pale purple blob in its tapered tip. This he fitted into a tubular silver frame with multiple prongs at one end. Each implement, though perfectly scaled for his use, was as big as one of her arms.

"You can drop your gown there before you climb up," he said, gesturing at her feet. "Usually impregnation is bloodless, but sometimes we spill a drop or two."

He smiled, and suddenly he terrified her. Whirling, she fled back through the gargantuan doorway and into Ma's kitchen at home. Swain was fixing hamburgers at the yellow-tiled counter and turned to ask if she wanted cherry juice with them. When she told him about the giant who was chasing her, he only patted her shoulder, told her everything would be fine, and turned her about.

Whereupon the godlike man poked his white pipette with its cloned embryo through her belly button and into her womb. All the while Swain patted her shoulder, assuring her it would only be for nine months and well worth the trouble. . . .

She jerked awake in horror, lurching violently in her padded desk chair as she stared wide-eyed at the computer screen, which was still in hibernation mode. It had all seemed so real! As if it were a real place, a place she'd actually been. She was trembling and gasping, and her belly button even ached. Compulsively she ran her hands over her stomach. But it was only a dream. There was no embryo. She'd not been impregnated. . . .

Then she saw the black cube sitting on the desk to her right, atop a small stack of manila folders. It had not been there when she'd sat down. In fact, she didn't know how it had gotten into her office at all, since the last time she'd seen it had been in her room Thursday night, when she'd put it into her bottom desk drawer. It might be someone else's cube. Either that or she'd mindlessly brought it up here herself.

With a chill, she recalled Cameron's urgent words in their conversation at the overlook last night, ordering her to throw her box away the moment she got home. He'd asked then if she'd been hearing voices or having strange dreams. Said it was some sort of mind control device. But in the trauma of Frogeater's attack and its aftermath, she'd forgotten all about the box.

Abruptly she stood, snatched it up, and walked down the hall to the lounge with its small balcony overlooking the eastern berm. Thankfully, she had the place to herself and wasted no time tossing the object over the rail. It sailed out in the morning light and plummeted to the roof of the ziggurat's first main level, three stories below. As soon as it hit she lost sight of it. Hopefully it had shattered on impact.

"What are you doing out here?" Gen Viascola's suspicious voice intruded into her private moment, and she jerked around guiltily.

Her supervisor stood in the opening of the sliding glass door, frowning at her.

"I got cold," Lacey said. "So I came out to warm up." Which wasn't far from the truth. Sometimes the Institute's air-conditioning worked *too* well.

Viascola continued to frown. "I thought I saw you throwing something."

"It's against the rules to throw things off the balconies, Dr. V. I know that."

The assistant director stepped out onto the balcony and looked over the railing. But since the box was far too small to be picked out from this distance, she saw nothing and grunted. "Must've been the reflections, I guess."

Then, to Lacey's intense dismay, she lingered. "The heat does feel good out here, doesn't it?" She surveyed the sweeping eastern berm for a moment, then said, "You must be thrilled that Parker has asked you to the reception."

Lacey's wariness instantly doubled. "I'm . . . overwhelmed by it, to tell the truth," she admitted. "Last week I was cleaning up after rats and frogs, after all."

Gen gave her a smug smile. "I told you your circumstances would change dramatically before too much longer. You had only to be patient." She laid her red-nailed hands on the copper railing and lifted her face to the sun, its light accentuating the gold strands in her deep red hair.

Lacey was thinking about excusing herself and going back inside when her companion said, "I heard you had a secret rendezvous with Cameron Reinhardt up at the overlook last night."

"It was hardly a rendezvous, ma'am. I just took the shuttle up to see the view and ran into him while I was there."

"I was given to understand he brought you dinner."

Lacey almost gasped. Cameron was right. They *had* been watching her—far more closely than she'd ever dreamed. "He brought his own and shared it with me," she explained.

"Ah. Of course." Gen looked at Lacey sidelong. "You do understand what this invitation means, don't you? The director has his eye on you. He won't like it if you start flirting around with Reinhardt."

"It was just a conversation," Lacey said. "And why should the director care if I did flirt with him? I'm just his graduate student."

Gen snorted. "Oh please, my dear. Not even you can be that naïve. You don't *really* think he made you his graduate student out of the goodness of his heart? It's a favor he'll expect you to return."

Her reply struck Lacey mute—not because the truth she'd already suspected had been confirmed, but because Viascola admitted it so blatantly.

The other woman gave her a small, mean smile. "I'm sorry to burst your bubble, dear, but we all know the director's vices. The nice thing is, now that he's chosen you, he'll do very well by you."

*Like he did by Andrea Stopping?* Lacey wondered.

"Frankly, I can't imagine why you'd be giving Dr. Reinhardt a moment of your time under any circumstances. The man's a loser, Lacey. You *do* know he's been arrested at least once for assault?"

"Actually, there's no arrest cited in his personnel file, ma'am. That's just gossip."

Gen regarded her narrowly. "Perhaps you should read that file again. He also has problems with paranoia and a tendency to see conspiratorial plots where none exist." She paused. "I say this only out of concern for your well-being, dear. Your ability to judge a man's character hasn't been the best, you know. . . ."

*Am I supposed to say thank you for that?* Lacey wondered.

They stood there in awkward silence. Then Viascola pushed back from the railing. "Well, I'd best get back to work." She started toward the doorway, then turned back. "By the way, Parker's taken the liberty of having a gown sent up from Tucson for you. It should be here this afternoon, so you'll want to look for that. If it doesn't fit, let Deena know ASAP so we can have a new one sent out."

And with that, to Lacey's relief, she left. A few moments later, Lacey followed her, returning to her office and forcing herself to attend to the abstracts she needed to read.

# Chapter Thirty-Five

Rudy showed up at 3:00 p.m. disguised as Mr. Mallory, the insurance adjuster, perhaps surmising there wouldn't be much reason for Cam to talk to a tow-truck driver, since the car had been effectively totaled even before the fire. He'd dyed his shoulder-length hair black and wore it oiled and loose around his face. A black goatee, horn-rimmed glasses, and a very well-applied latex nose—which Cam noticed only because he knew it was Rudy—radically changed the look of his face. A wrinkled suit two sizes too big and worn a day too long, with the tie loosened and askew, and a gaudy ring on his right hand completed the disguise.

Cam met him at the garage, where he was already in conversation with the head mechanic beside the blackened, crumpled remains of the Jeep Cherokee. The moment Cam came up and introduced himself, Mr. Mallory informed him that according to the garage man, his vehicle had been found already burned. Cam frowned at the garage man. "They told me it burned when they tried to remove it."

"No way!" said the mechanic. "It was burned like that when we found it."

"I thought security found it."

"They found it—we pulled it out of the ditch."

"So how *did* it burn, Dr. Reinhardt?" Mr. Mallory asked.

"I told you on the phone, we left it because it wouldn't start and headed back to campus on foot to—"

"So you're saying you don't know how it got burned?"

"Yes, that's what I'm saying." He frowned at the mechanic. Mr. Mallory looked to the latter, as well.

The garage man continued to insist the Jeep was already burned when they found it, and after several moments of back and forth, Mallory suggested he and Cam drive out to the accident site.

They got into Mallory's dusty, dark blue Volvo and belted up. Then he started the engine and pulled out of the parking lot onto the campus drive. The air-conditioner blasted hot air at them as it labored to bring down the temperature. "While we drive over, why don't you tell me what happened," Rudy said, pulling a small recording device out of his coat pocket and balancing it on the cup holder between them. Except it wasn't just a recording device, for on its readout screen a bright green circle flashed dead center: the car was clean of listening devices. Rudy glanced at it, then at Cam, and said, "Well. Guess they aren't as suspicious of you being a spy as I feared. I thought they might slip a bug in while we were talking to the mechanic. Go ahead and debrief."

So Cam told him and the recording device all that had happened since Sunday, ending with his poolside breakfast with Swain and the director's demand he make public renunciation of his faith or lose his position at K-J. "There's no way I'm going to do that, Rudy," he concluded.

"But he's given you until Monday, right?" They were approaching the overlook area by then, which was once more milling with visitors. Cars overflowed its parking lot, lining the service road on both shoulders, forcing Rudy to slow as he threaded his way between them.

"Yes, until Monday morning," Cam confirmed.

"It may not matter anymore by then. . . ." He glanced at Cam. "I don't think he seriously suspects you of being a spy. You just made him mad when you went out with McHenry last night. We should probably chip her before tomorrow night's reception. Do you think you can get her to go for it?"

"I'll try. Though with Swain's ban, it'll be hard for me to actually do the chipping."

"One of my team can do it. See if you can set up a time and place."

THE ENCLAVE — 345

They passed out of the clog of cars, and Rudy sped up as they headed westward, gradually turning south to parallel the ridge. Ahead, thunderheads towered over the Catalinas in great billows of white.

As they drew even with the outcropping south of the overlook, Cam gestured to the side of the road. "There. They've moved all the boulders onto the shoulder."

"And look at all the potholes and cracks in the pavement that have been newly filled. . . ." Rudy slowed the car. "Backhoe tracks on the shoulder . . ." He turned his gaze up the road again. "Where'd you crash?"

"Up there a bit." Cam gestured toward the opposite shoulder, still ahead of them.

Rudy eased the Volvo to a stop and turned off the ignition. "Let's have a look, then."

They got out of the car into the humid oven of midafternoon before a storm. A chorus of cicadas buzzed loudly around them as they walked up and down the road and Rudy took measurements, photographed skid marks and tire tracks, and found the charred spot in the ditch where the Jeep had come to rest. He put a few soil samples into small manila collection bags and tucked them into his shirt pocket.

"Where'd you shoot him?" Rudy asked finally.

Cam gestured farther up the road. "That's where the security vehicles took off into the desert, too." He pointed southwest. "The chopper crashed out there."

"You said you thought you'd hit him? There should be blood spots, then."

"I don't think so."

"Let's have a look anyway." Reaching the clearing where Cam had shot at Frogeater, they searched both ground and grass for blood but found none. They did, however, find the two slugs Cam had fired—both of them flattened from contact with something. Rudy put them into a collection bag.

"I have to say I'm glad they've got him," Rudy remarked. "It's a bit unnerving to think something like that was out here running around free."

"You saw them get him, then?"

"No, but we did see them bring someone back in a body bag from the search area west of the crash. They slid it right into one of the emergency vehicles and immediately rushed it back to the campus—not to the clinic, but to the big hangar on the south side. The truck drove in and they shut the doors, and we have no idea what happened afterward."

"Gen told Poe they had him in a lab. Maybe the entrance is in that hangar."

"Maybe. Or maybe it's at the Vault. Does McHenry have any idea what Frogeater wanted to show her there?"

Cam looked at him in momentary surprise, then recalled that Rudy had known about the note on the bottom of the plastic tree frog hours before Cam had. "No."

"I had a man stationed there last night," Rudy said, "but obviously Frogeater never showed up."

"Shall I go and have a look?"

"No. You have no reason to, particularly in light of your stated views on the matter of extending longevity. You've already irritated Swain enough, though I seriously doubt he'll send you away just because you won't renounce your faith."

"And why is that?" Cam asked as they headed back to the road. When Rudy did not immediately answer, he added, "You still haven't told me what this is about. Why he's after me in particular."

Rudy continued to walk along in silence for a bit, then said, "About five years ago a huge underground explosion and a violent electromagnetic pulse occurred near his Ecuador research facility. Supposedly no one was seriously injured, nor was the facility significantly damaged. They claimed not to know what the source was. Many regarded it as a natural earthquake, assumed to be the site of a new fault line."

"Well, EM pulses have recently been associated with earthquakes—thought perhaps to be precursors of some sort."

"How did you know that?"

Cam shrugged. "I have an interest. . . ."

Rudy scowled at him sidelong, then faced forward, shaking his head. "You really are a geek at heart."

"So you don't think it was an earthquake, then."

"No, all the measurements that came out of Ecuador are startlingly close to what happened at Tirich Pazu. Even more significant ... immediately after the destruction of the facility, there were stories among the natives of a giant golden-skinned monster ravaging the local villages. Then a fleet of helicopters flew in and gunfire echoed through the mountains for a few days, after which the choppers flew away and no one saw the monster again.

"Not long after that, Swain's people hacked into the DOD, looking for information on Tirich Pazu and delving into your file specifically. Of course, there's nothing in it about that mission, but even so, he started making discreet inquiries at the various institutions where you'd worked."

Cam frowned at the pavement before him, heat radiating from the black surface. "So you think they opened a sarc, the monster ran amok for a few days, and somehow they managed to recapture it without losing their entire team?"

"Well, as I said, it's speculation, but yes."

"And what does that have to do with me?"

Rudy eyed him sidelong. "Actually, I was hoping you might tell me." He paused. "Have you had any more flashbacks?"

Cam nodded. "They seem to be coming pretty regularly. Just yesterday I recalled the day we were shown the Tomb of the Thousand Warriors. Remember all those black cubes that had piled the floor around the sarcophagi pedestals?" He paused, feeling his pulse rise. But much as he wanted to derail his thought train from the direction it was headed, he pressed on. "I think Swain's meditation boxes and Institute icons are modeled after them. In fact, I think some might even be the real thing, because yesterday Gen Viascola brought one to the unity meeting and it's what threw me into the flashback right there in the middle of everything." He paused. "Have your people examined any of them yet? To see what exactly they are?"

Rudy regarded him, deadpan.

Cam frowned. "You already know what they are."

"So do you," Rudy said. "You were in Garzi's lab that day, before we'd even seen the tomb, remember? When he explained all about them."

Cam shook his head, pressing his mind for a memory of what Rudy was describing.

"We were all standing there beside the sarc they'd brought in to examine, and while he was speaking—"

As he spoke, an image of the sarcophagus overlaid the reality of the roadside, and Cam stood again in the cavernous main laboratory of the Tirich Pazu facility in Afghanistan. The sarc lay on a steel examining table amidst the gathered group of foreign scientists, lab technicians, and other interested persons. It was some twenty feet long and five feet high, and in the bright white light of the fluorescent ceiling lights it looked like a gargantuan dried seedpod. Its nubby, wrinkled surface was brown veined with green, and studded with black three-sided points.

Dr. Ahmed Garzi, the US-born and -trained Afghani cell biologist who was heading the examination, informed them that the pods had been laid out in ranks in the tomb, each on its own pedestal, some with what appeared to be weapons at the foot of those pedestals, as if they were some sort of army. Wood and metal fragments from those weapons had dated the chamber to four thousand years ago.

Barely had he said those words than the whole pod expanded, as if it were drawing a breath, sending all the spectators jumping back in alarm.

Garzi chuckled at their reaction. "Yes," he said. "Despite its age this vessel is living, biological material, though like none we've ever encountered. This pod has so far been impervious to cutting, piercing, tearing, burning, and all other methods of dissection. It gives before the pressure source—saw, needle, scalpel, arc welder—for a time, then flings it away with what we think is a kind of magnetic pulse. Any implement involving electronics is immediately fried, and sometimes half the lab, as well.

"Just obtaining enough samples to study has been a major challenge, and mostly we've had to use aged cells on the verge of sloughing off. Still, we've obtained enough to learn that on the cellular level, as one would expect, they are also unique. The nuclei are exceptionally large and robust, the chromosomes triple the usual number. Cellular organelles include the mitochondria and Golgi apparatus standard to Earth life-form cells, in addition to several other structures whose purpose we've so far been unable to determine. The cell walls are exceptionally strong and resilient, and allow respiration, yet have formed an airtight, watertight outside surface. It's unclear whether waste products are excreted or recycled, but if the latter, then these cells have essentially lived off themselves for millennia. There is also some electrochemical process we are still identifying.

"This electrical activity manifests in an emanation similar to our brain waves, but at much higher and lower amplitudes than ours." He paused, frowning. "We suspect they are capable of interacting with the environment—turning lights and instruments on and off, and even, some think, communicating with receptive humans. Several technicians have experienced visions and hallucinations when working in their proximity. Others reported the relocation of objects and instruments around the lab that no one can account for, and we've actually recorded sounds and voices whose source and even identity we cannot pinpoint."

He paused again. "We have concluded they are not native to Earth but have come from—"

He was cut off as the pod shivered and a deep groan echoed through the room, sending the entire group leaping back in unison. The shiver traveled over the pod's surface in a way that only a rubbery outer skin would have accommodated. At first they all stood in rigid, alert silence, but when nothing further happened, they began to relax, and Garzi continued with his presentation.

They had found 1005 of these pods in the temple of Nimrod. Why they had been put there, he did not know. What they were, likewise he did not know, though in the year since they had discovered the things, they had observed not only the groaning and shuddering but also the curious expulsion of obsidianlike cubes. In fact, he pointed out one of the larger three-sided spikes that poked out of the pod before them. "That one is probably very close to expulsion now," he said. They'd been examining it for six months before the first one was expelled. A second cube had come out three months later, but none since. There were many more found in the tomb. Piles of them, in fact.

The count had been something like five thousand, he'd said. As of yet, they had no idea what the cubes were. "Perhaps an accretion of waste. Whatever it is, we've been unable to cut it, break it, dissolve it, X-ray it, or really, analyze it in any way."

"Perhaps they're seeds," Cam suggested.

The Afghan scientist shrugged. "If so, none appear to have germinated." He paused. "Like the pods they come from, they do seem to have odd mental effects on those who handle or work around them, so we keep them all in a lead-lined vault."

Rudy asked if the pods had been X-rayed or otherwise scanned in an attempt to determine the contents. Garzi said they had been X-rayed, but results were inconclusive. Seeming suddenly ill at ease, he turned the discussion back to the black cubes—which, like the pods, generated low-level electricity.

*"Come and help me."* The voice sounded clearly in Cam's head, startling him. Not in his ear, but in his head. He glanced around, but no one looked at him, everyone staring at Garzi or the pod with varying degrees of attentiveness.

Another shiver convulsed the pod and he saw one of the black points jut outward from the elastic hide, then fall back again, and then once more press forward.

"Ah," said Garzi. "Here it comes now."

Cam stood transfixed as the pebbled surface contracted and released and the three-sided point grew ever larger. Then in a burst of thick viscous fluid, it broke free and fell to the floor—not a triangular pyramid, but a solid black cube, its faces slightly bigger than the palm of his hand.

"So now you've seen how it works," said Garzi.

*"It is time to let me out. . . ."* the voice commanded again.

A current of panic blasted through Cam—

And abruptly he stood once more at the side of the service road south of the overlook picnic area, sweating in the 105-degree heat, his heart hammering at his breastbone. From over the mountains, thunder rumbled.

He looked up at Rudy, who was watching him closely. "You all right?" his friend asked.

"I remember now," Cam answered. "That was the first time they spoke to me."

Rudy's dark eyes narrowed. "And have they spoken to you here?"

"No."

He walked to the side of the car and pulled open his door, waiting until Rudy went round to the driver's side and got in first. Cam followed him, and a window of silence ensued as they fastened their seat belts. But instead of starting the engine, Rudy asked quietly, "You're sure. Because if they have, maybe you shouldn't—"

"They haven't."

But for a moment his friend continued to study him, searching his face. Finally he seemed satisfied and faced forward, turning the ignition key. The engine roared to life, and Rudy did a tight U-turn, heading back for the Institute's main road, the half-cool air-conditioning blowing in their faces.

After a few minutes, Cam said quietly, "You still haven't told me why Swain would be interested in me."

"We think he wants you because you are apparently the only person to survive the opening of a sarc."

He glanced at Cam repeatedly, as if expecting him to remember something again or in some way confirm his words.

Cam grew aware of his heart thudding dully in his chest and throat and ears, too rapid to just be a result of the heat and the walk. Images flashed through his mind—a massive puddle of blood pooling out of the dying Garzi, who clutched at his sleeve and sought to speak a warning. . . .

And then it cut off as completely as the flipping of a switch. He swallowed. "I don't think I was present," he said finally, frowning at the tremor in his voice. "But why would it matter if I was?"

"Because then you'd probably know how to open them."

# Chapter Thirty-Six

After returning to her desk, Lacey waited until she heard Gen leave the area before accessing Cam's file. Sure enough, there was a notation of his having been arrested for assault while he was at Cold Spring Harbor three years ago and an additional psychiatric evaluation that noted his problems with paranoia, particularly when it came to the government and authority figures. He had repeatedly accused his superiors—or various arcane objects—of trying to control his mind. They speculated it was a result of his ongoing problems with post-traumatic stress disorder.

There was also an addition to the comments about his faith and the church he attended, noting that some had accused the organization of being a cult because of the way adherents were encouraged to attend daily and submit to the pastor "as if he were some kind of god."

Not one of those notations had been in his file the first time she read it, and she was absolutely certain of that because she'd been looking specifically for references like them. Thus, like the addition of her new scar, attributed to a beating from Erik, Cam's file had been doctored just as hers had. But for what purpose? So Gen could direct Lacey's attention to them in an attempt to get her to distrust him? Or—more likely—part of the plan to frame him for Manny's death . . . ?

Of course, for the moment, Manny's death remained officially a disappearance and the whole matter seemed to have fallen off the radar. Swain had returned in the wee hours of Friday morning from his meeting with the disgruntled postdoc in Guadalajara, and they'd heard nary a word from anyone about it. Which wasn't surprising given Swain had already warned everyone against discussing the matter with the public, and with the public currently inundating the campus, there was precious little opportunity to say anything. Besides, everyone was more interested in the events related to the open house and expo.

But she couldn't help wondering if, when Monday came and all the booths and important people had gone away, Manny's body would show up somewhere and Cameron Reinhardt end up the chief murder suspect again.

"Ms. McHenry?"

The unfamiliar voice drew her around to find a campus delivery-man standing in the doorway of her office holding a large, flat brown box. "That's me," she said.

"This came for you," he said, handing over the box. "I have another."

She set the package on the desk and used her letter opener to slit the packing tape. Meantime the deliveryman came in with the second box. At her direction, he set it on her chair.

Inside the first package, she found a white dress box with an embossed Ann Taylor logo on it. Inside was a sleeveless, knee-length cocktail dress of dark blue silk georgette. A deep V neckline plunged to the satin band at its empire waist, the skirt a wonderful fall of draping silken folds. Subtle gathers at the bust and shoulders added interest and a soft femininity. She drew it out of the box with a feeling of awe. When she'd heard Swain was having a dress sent, she'd been annoyed. She hadn't expected to like it, much less love it at first sight.

Never in her life had she worn anything so . . .

"Ah," said Gen, who had once again snuck up on her. "I see it's come." She stepped into the room and shut the door behind her. "Well, try it on. Let's see how it fits."

And so Lacey did. It fit perfectly. And except for the neckline, which was deeper than anything she'd worn in her life, it felt wonderful. Cool and light and swirling, it was the perfect weight and style for a party that would be held outside in mid-June.

Though there was no mirror in her office for Lacey to see for herself, Gen pronounced it lovely. "He got it right the very first time," she said. "As always, it seems."

The other box held a pair of metallic sandals with crisscross straps over the toes and three-inch heels. Also a perfect fit and a perfect complement to the dress. "There'll be jewelry, as well," Gen informed her. "We'll have that for you tomorrow." She smiled, and then offered Lacey use of her own apartment on the seventh floor as a place to dress before the reception. "That way we won't worry about theft, and you won't have to traipse all the way up from the basement, risking snags or a broken heel or what have you." Though her suggestion was perfectly reasonable, it also reminded Lacey of the low station from which she was being raised—as she suspected it was supposed to.

In any case, when Lacey didn't object, Gen packed dress and shoes back in their boxes and took them up to her apartment, leaving Lacey in a state of disquiet once again. She really didn't want to spend any time with Gen Viascola at all, much less prepare for tomorrow night's festivities with her. There was something creepy about being primped and prepared by the former mistress of the man who was to be her escort.

It was late afternoon when the front desk called to tell her that Dr. Reinhardt's insurance adjuster was in the main lobby, wanting to talk to her about the accident last night involving Reinhardt's Jeep Cherokee. Uneasy with knowing she was probably going to have to lie, Lacey went down to meet him.

A disheveled man with horn-rimmed glasses and stringy black hair, Mr. Mallory shook her hand as he introduced himself, and immediately wanted to know how much Cameron had had to drink before he'd crashed the Jeep.

"A bottle of cherry-pomegranate juice," she replied, instantly annoyed. "He wasn't drunk."

"So why did the Jeep run off the road?"

Suddenly she had to avert her gaze, unnerved at how the truth was going to sound. "There were a bunch of boulders on the road. A rockslide, I guess."

He asked her to describe the boulders, then asked where she thought they might have come from, seeing as there weren't any cliffs or even steep slopes near that stretch of the road. She said she didn't know.

Frowning, he made a few more notes, then asked how the fire had started. She had no idea what he was talking about, and when he explained, assured him there was no fire and that the Jeep had been fine when they'd left it, except for its crumpled front end and the fact it wouldn't run.

"Could Dr. Reinhardt have come back later and—"

"No!" She cut him off, more annoyed than ever, and explained that Reinhardt had walked her back to the expo, where they'd roamed around until closing—during which time he'd called the garage about getting it towed back in the morning. Still, Mallory pressed her—had she heard an explosion, perhaps, after they'd left the vehicle? Seen a light flaring in the sky behind them?

Which of course they had. "That was more to the southwest, though," she said. "Where the fireworks went off. We assumed it was one of them, firing early."

"You're sure it wasn't the Jeep? It *was* dark, after all. And you were in the middle of the desert."

Bristling, she assured him she hadn't been the least bit confused as to where everything was, and the boom they'd heard was not from the Jeep. He made some more notes on his pad, then thanked her for her time and gave her his card. "In case you remember something more about it all."

She frowned after him, then dropped his card into the pocket of her lab coat and pulled out her cell phone to call Reinhardt. He didn't pick up, so she left a voice mail, telling him she'd just talked to his agent and that she hoped she hadn't caused him too much trouble. "I don't lie well," she admitted. "I don't think he believed me."

By then it was 4:30, and her late night having finally caught up with her, she went over to the Madrona Lounge to get an iced mocha from the coffee bar. There she was surprised to find Reinhardt sitting alone at a table by the window, reading from a fat file of documents. A cardboard cup of coffee sat on the table beside it.

As she approached, he ignored her, his attention fixed on the documents.

"That must be mighty interesting reading," she commented as she sat in the empty plastic chair across from him.

He looked up with an attentiveness that told her he'd been feigning his preoccupation. "The DNA and prints came back on Frogeater," he said without preamble. "They're a match for Parker Swain."

The words were so far from what she'd expected him to say, it took her a moment to make sense of them. And when she did, she struggled to get her mind around their implications.

He helped her along: "I think he's Swain's clone."

Then he looked back down at the paper he'd been reading while she stared at him. "He's got to be close to twenty years old," she protested. "How could they have kept him secret for so long?"

"I don't know. But from what I heard last night, I fear he's not the only one. And there *is* a secret lab. They caught him and have taken him there."

He fell silent, allowing her to digest that information, then said, still keeping his eyes on his reading material, "Swain's ordered me to stay away from you, so I'll have to go soon. We'd like to chip you before the reception, though. Are you game?"

"*Chip* me?!"

"Insert a radio frequency ID chip. It looks like a grain of rice and goes in under your skin—on your arm, hand, back. You won't even notice it's there. That way we can keep track of you wherever he takes you."

She stared at the table, choking on the sudden horror of being wholly in Swain's hands to be taken wherever he wanted.

"It shouldn't take long," he went on, eyes still on his reading material. "Maybe tomorrow afternoon—"

"I'll be at the resort salon most of tomorrow afternoon, getting my hair and nails done."

"That could work." He paused, as if he sensed her disquiet. "Unless you've changed your mind?"

"I'm not sure I want a radio-whatever-you-said chip under my skin." *And I'm really not sure I want to do any of this.*

"It's harmless. We'll extract it when this is over." Finally he looked up at her, his expression grim. "Well?"

She met his gaze. "I'm a geneticist, you know. Not a police-woman."

"I know." He didn't press her.

She knew she could back out right now if she wished. He'd offered to extract her from the situation last night, so surely he could do it tonight. And yet nothing had happened since then to make the situation any different than when she'd agreed to help. In fact, his news made Swain's machinations seem even more diabolical.

Frogeater was indeed a clone, and human clones needed a surrogate to be born. The girls were still missing. If they were being held against their will, Lacey's choice could buy them their freedom. Did she really want to live the rest of her life knowing she'd refused to help them?

"Okay," she said finally. "I'll do it."

Exhaling softly, he gave her a sober nod, then closed his file folder, picked up his coffee, and left her sitting there dazed and irrationally hurt by his cool, businesslike attitude.

Of course he *had* said Swain had ordered him to stay away from her, and she didn't doubt that was true. Gen had essentially mirrored it in warning Lacey to stay away from Cam so as not to provoke the director's jealousy.

*"Now that he's chosen you, he'll do very well by you."*

*Oh yes. Promise me everything I've ever wanted, and reel me right in under his spell.*

Anger swelled within her, eclipsing the fear, and her determination to stand up to him—however she might do that best—solidified.

## Chapter Thirty-Seven

New Eden

Zowan was right to fear that Enclave authorities had guessed his route to the surface lay in the physical plant. On Saturday night, when he, Terra, and Parthos arrived as planned in their respective disguises at the small court just below the plant's entrance, they found two black-robed Enforcers guarding its doors.

It was Terra in her gray Elder's robe who took the lead, turning from the plant and heading back down the narrow corridor she'd just come up. Stopping at the third door they came to, she slapped its lock plate with practiced authority, and Zowan held his breath, half-expecting to hear the blare of a restricted access alarm. Instead, the locking mechanism clacked, the green admittance light blinked on, and they stepped into a dusty tunnel so narrow Zowan's shoulders brushed its sides. The door swung shut behind them, and Terra's hand lamp chased off the utter darkness as she switched it on.

"Do you have any idea where you're going?" Parthos whispered.

"I took some of the older children to the library today," she said softly over her shoulder. "While we were there I studied a map of the physical plant." Her smile was sly. "My thumbprint gave me unlimited access to the computer files. . . . Anyway, I figured the front door might be guarded, so I looked for alternate entries. I checked out this route on the way to meet you, just to be sure it works."

She led them along the dark, dusty access tunnel, where thick bundles of wires garlanded the too-low ceiling, and heavy cables snaked along the floor. Soon the tunnel dead-ended, and the cables left the floor to join the bundled wires as they fed through a hole in the wall. Reaching over a small ledge in the back wall, she pushed away a panel beside the hole, an opening just large enough to wriggle through.

On the other side was a small rough-walled chamber filled with humming cabinets. Varicolored lights blinked on the front of them and bundles of colored wire snaked here and there. He had no idea what the cabinets did, nor what the great bulbous machines in the adjoining room did, but it didn't matter—Terra was just passing through.

"I only explored this far," she said, "but I think my recollection of the floor plan will get us the rest of the way."

She led them up a narrow tube on a metal ladder, through an unlocked metal door, and into a larger chamber full of aluminum boxes some twenty feet high, whose metal sides rattled with the constant rush of moving air. Ducts snaked away across the ceiling and down into the floor. They seemed to be sucking air from somewhere above—the surface, maybe, as Neos had claimed?—and channeling it below.

More narrow passages led them to a chamber filled with tanks of swirling water, the stench so bad they ran across the suspended platform that traversed it. More tunnels greeted them on the other side, but eventually they came to a room full of pipes, the smaller branching from the larger and each running off into the darkness.

Though they'd obviously reached the pump room, the intersecting pipes all looked the same, and for a while Zowan led them aimlessly, hoping to stumble onto an arrangement that looked familiar.

Doubts battered him. It could take all night and half the day to find the crawl tube this way. Worse, what if there was no crawl tube to find? The longer they wandered, the worse it got, until he was on the verge of abandoning the plan altogether.

And then, after a seeming eternity, they followed yet another pipe to where it dove into the ground by a wall, and this time found the metal drum not far away, with the metal sheet behind it. Quickly Zowan and Parthos moved both; then they all stood staring at the revealed opening in shared amazement. "It really *is* here," Terra breathed.

After a moment Parthos gestured at the drum and metal plate and asked Zowan, "Was all this pretty much how you left it?"

"I think so."

"Shall we go on, then?" Parthos asked.

But now Zowan stepped in front of the hole and turned to face them, frowning. "I told you it doesn't look very hospitable up there."

"We've been through this, Zowan," Terra said.

"Not quite. They found me in the physical plant, remember? The guards at the door prove they know the exit is here somewhere. Even if this isn't a trap, once they find out we're all three gone, they'll come here immediately and search. And since no one will have stayed behind to push back the plate and the drum, they'll see where we went and be on us before the day is over."

He paused. "It's still night. You can both go back without being missed. Let me go up alone now and see what's there."

"You've been up there and lived," Terra said. "That's all we need to know."

"That doesn't mean the surface isn't dangerous. You've seen the histories. There could be wild beasts . . . even Enforcers."

"I'm not going back," Terra said firmly. "I told you Gaias has asked for me—"

"Yes, but he'll be busy the next few days searching for me, and by that time you'll be out." He looked from one to the other. "All I'm asking for is a day or two. They're sending me to New Babel. So if *I* disappear they'll think I fled because of that. They can even tell everyone I left early in the morning with Father and no one would think anything of it. If we all go through now, with no one to cover our tracks, and three gone instead of one, we'll stir them into a frenzy. We may find ourselves with our backs against a wall we don't even know is there."

His words fell into silence as his friends considered.

Finally, Parthos said gruffly, "I don't like it."

"No," Zowan agreed. "But we need more than just an escape hatch. We need a place to go that's safe once we're out."

"This is crazy!" Terra protested. "We already agreed all three of us would go! I'm *not* staying behind, Zowan! Stop trying to protect me! We'll meet the new world together."

"I'll stay," Parthos said, drawing Terra's angry glare. "He's right. Someone needs to cover the hole."

She scowled at him. "Do you remember how to go back the way we came?"

Parthos looked stricken. His gaze turned from Zowan to Terra.

She exhaled in exasperation. "Then I guess you'll just have to go with us."

"Terra—" Zowan began.

"You two are acting like old crèche mothers! When we get to the top, let's just keep walking!"

Seeing see she would not be swayed, Zowan gave in. They crawled through the tube and emerged in the small room where he'd waited for Neos to return. But now a new worry assailed him: What if he couldn't remember the way up? After all, the first time he'd followed I Am's mysterious light, and that wasn't here now.

His concern turned out to be baseless, for at first there was only one way to go. Then even when the other passages began to intersect the main one, many of them angled back and downward, away from the path to the surface, obviously not the right choice. And with the few that were not clear, there was always, stuck to the wall of the right path, one of the oblong glowstones he'd unconsciously followed in his panicked trip back down. Glowstones like the ones he'd seen in the spy passages outside the Star Garden, which Neos must have placed to mark the trail.

Confidence began to build in him, and when they found the gray-striped mattress on the metal bed frame, with its folded blanket and empty bucket, he had to stop and take a deep breath. Excitement warred with trepidation.

"Are we almost there?" Terra whispered.

With a nod, Zowan moved on. Soon he felt the draft of warm, dry air, fragrant with the tang he now firmly associated with the outside. He turned a corner and the passage leveled off before bending into the final series of doglegs. Then, just like that, they strode into the small chamber before the exit hole. Zowan switched off his hand lamp in triumph, then frowned in confusion, wondering why the room was so dim.

He approached the hole and the tree, dropped onto his knees and started through it, his friends following on his heels. He pushed out into the branches, pressed a couple of branches back, and realized it was nighttime. The only light they had was from the stars. . . .

Excitement flooded him, and he started to press on through the tree, then recalled something else and turned back to his friends. "It might feel strange when you get out there. There's so much space. Standing in it makes you feel like you're going to fly apart. But you're not."

"Come on, Zowan," Parthos said. "Stop talking and let us see for ourselves."

So they fought through the tree and stepped out onto the hillside beyond. It was much easier emerging without having to contend with the blast of the midday sun, first and foremost because he was able to see. The air was warm and moist, and a slight breeze occasionally rustled the sparse foliage about him. The sensation of the space pulling at him was still unnerving but no longer overwhelming.

He gazed upward, awed by the hugeness of it all, the starry heavens expanding above him, filled with uncountable points of light. Some were tiny, others large and bright. Some flickered as if they were alive. And there were so very many. The Star Garden hadn't even come close to reproducing this.

After a while he sat down on a rock and the others joined him, the quickness of their actions indicating that, while they weren't as traumatized as Zowan had been, they weren't entirely comfortable either. Terra boldly pressed herself against him and slid her hand into his.

He reveled in the tang of the air, in the fresh, bracing power of it. The way it cleared his mind and energized his flesh. He couldn't take enough of it in. They sat for some time, watching the stars overhead, frozen in mind and body by the magnitude with which their world had shifted. Gradually the stars began to fade, and a rosy glow seeped into the fabric of the night sky above the crest of the long hill that paralleled the one on which they sat.

With the growing light, Zowan saw that trees and small shrubs did indeed scatter the slope on which he sat, the growth thicker in the bottom drainage, all alive, even the tree that covered the opening.

Now birds began to call, a sweet succession of coos. Under one of the nearer bushes he spied a rabbit nibbling leaves.

There was plant life. There was animal life. It was not a poisoned wasteland. But it was also devoid of any sign of water or people or real shelter. In a few hours they would be found missing and the search would begin. How long before the Enforcers arrived?

He was contemplating that question when Terra hissed, "Someone's coming." She pointed down the draw, to where a man had rounded a fold in the land on the opposite slope and was running up the drainage in their direction. He wore something on his head, and at his waist. An Enforcer's protective suit?

"Both of you! Back into the hole, now!" Zowan commanded. "Quietly!"

"What are you going to do?" Terra asked.

"I'll come when you're in. I want a closer look at him, and we can't all stand outside the opening, showing him exactly where it is." He feared she'd keep on arguing with him, but apparently she realized the need for stealth.

He crouched down by a nearby bush, watching the approaching figure, who no longer looked like an Enforcer in protective gear. In fact, he looked like no one Zowan had ever seen. He wore scandalously short trousers, a big sleeveless tunic, and a strange red cap with a stiff flap pointing off the front of it. A black belt bulging with mysterious implements hung at his waist, and long white wires flapped from his ears.

Hoping the man might know where to find food and water, Zowan stood his ground, fear battling curiosity, need, and something more: the sense that he was meant to meet this man, that in him he would find the answers to his most important questions.

It helped that the stranger did not appear to be pursuing anyone— his pace was easy and relaxed—and that he seemed to be following a path along the opposite slope. One which, not too far upstream, turned to cross the drainage and ascend the side of the very slope on which Zowan crouched. If the man continued to follow it, he would loop around to head back in the direction from which he'd come—

and in so doing, would pass below Zowan's position by no more than twenty feet.

Fear urged Zowan to retreat to the hole with his friends. How did he know the man was not an Enforcer? Maybe when Enforcers went to the surface they didn't dress as they did in the Enclave. . . .

Still, he felt the inner nudge to stand his ground, a promise not unlike the one he'd received in yesterday's morning Affirmation, when I Am told him to come out of the darkness.

When the man disappeared into the foliage in the drainage's heart, Zowan picked his way down to the trail's edge and took cover behind a large shrub. As the runner emerged from the thick vegetation and started up the trail, Zowan trembled at what he was about to do. Finally, the fellow mere strides away, Zowan stepped around the bush into his path.

The man pulled up, his mouth dropping open, the whites of his eyes showing in the astonishment of his stare. A moment later he plucked the wires from his ears and glanced up the hillside behind Zowan and then around him, before stepping forward, slowly. Warily Zowan held his position until they were face-to-face. The stranger, he saw now, was sweating slightly, and the wires were attached to a small white box on his belt. He had a freckled face and honest, friendly gray eyes.

"Who are you?" Zowan blurted. "Where have you come from?"

The stranger arched a brow. "I'm Cameron Reinhardt. And I work over at the zig." He gestured toward the crest of the hill at Zowan's back. "Who are you?"

*Zig?* Zowan had no idea what that was, though he looked over his shoulder to see if something was there he'd not noticed earlier. Would there be food and water there?

"You can't see it from here," the man said. He stared at Zowan intently, brows drawn together in puzzlement. His gray eyes traveled over Zowan's form, fixing finally on his felt slippers, which were in striking contrast to the thick-soled shoes he wore himself. "Who are you?" the man repeated.

"I'm Zowan," Zowan said. "How long have you been outside?"

Again this Cameron Reinhardt seemed bemused. "Outside." He glanced down at a strap on his wrist. "About forty minutes." He looked at Zowan again. "You aren't the fellow who's been breaking into the zig, are you?"

It was more of a statement than a question, so Zowan did not answer. "Are you an Elder?"

"An Elder?" The other's puzzled expression deepened, and he shook his head.

"Do you serve Father?"

Zowan had expected some sort of reaction to that. Either affirmation that he did, or a firm declaration that he did not. Instead Cameron Reinhardt's puzzlement continued. "Who is Father?"

A sudden rattling of brush at Zowan's back drew the man's eyes up to where Terra and Parthos were now emerging from the hole. Again, Cameron Reinhardt's mouth dropped open as he watched them descend the hill to stand at Zowan's flank. And still he stared at them, his eyes roving over the three of them in wonderment. Finally he stepped back, wiped his palms on his white shirt, and murmured, "By all that's holy! He actually did it."

"You are not an Enforcer?" Parthos asked.

Which was obvious, Zowan thought, since he had no oculus.

"What is this zig place where you work?" Terra asked.

The man's gaze flicked to her. "You even *sound* the same!"

They stared back at him, and Zowan wondered if he might be suffering from the same instability of mind that Neos did. But then Cameron Reinhardt shook off his wonder and gestured ahead. "If you'll let me by, I'll show you."

Zowan let the man pass, and the three of them followed him up the side of the grassy slope. Just below the crest he bade them crouch and ease their way up until they could see, to avoid drawing the attention of those on the other side.

Zowan's heart began to pound. *Others*? Was this a trap, after all?

He eased forward and up through the prickly grass, and gradually a huge terraced structure made of glass came into view, top first, getting larger and larger the more he saw of it. On the far side what looked like a huge pool of water gleamed in the growing light. And there were people! Dressed in trousers and tunics, moving about on foot or in small self-moving carts.

Overhead a bird floated high in the sky, wings not moving as it dipped and soared against the mauve background, and Zowan's wonder knew no bounds.

Everything Neos had said was true.

Everything!

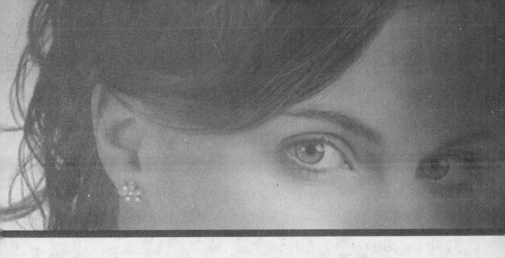

# PART THREE

# Chapter Thirty-Eight

"That big stairstepping building is where I work," said Cam. "We call it the ziggurat because that's what it looks like—an ancient ziggurat." He wondered if these three strange people had any idea what an ancient ziggurat was. "Zig, for short."

All three stared at the campus and the zig with an open astonishment that probably resembled Cam's own when he'd seen the three of them for the first time. Having missed his run yesterday, he decided to make up for it today. And while he didn't often come out on Sunday morning, the last thing he expected to see was three young people dressed like medieval peasants robed in gray or black, emerging from a hole in the ground, two of them with skin so white and unblemished, it looked as if today was the first time sunlight had ever touched them. Even now they squinted in the dawning light as if it hurt their eyes, and though they spoke English, they seemed like people out of time.

Then there was the fact that Zowan not only *looked* exactly like Swain, he sounded and moved like him, too. There was no question he was the director's clone. Nor had Cam missed the significance of his name: *Zoan* was Latin for a creature developed from a fertilized egg. . . . An odd thing to name one's son. Unless one was a geneticist interested in reproductive cloning.

The girl was an exact—though younger—replica of Gen Viascola. It was eerie seeing them and talking to them, youngsters who looked exactly like people Cam knew and yet were not at all the same persons.

What were they doing here in the predawn hours of this day, in the middle of the desert, unaware of the ziggurat just over the hill?

Might they be more escapees from Swain's secret lab?

"Let's go back now," Cam said. "It wouldn't be good if you were seen up here." And with the telescope in Swain's office, there was every chance of that happening.

He withdrew down the slope on his belly a bit before he stood and descended to the juniper from which the girl and the black youth had emerged. Approaching it now, he saw the hole in the ground at its base, and the scuff tracks the clones had made passing through it.

"Why were you hiding in that hole?" he asked as they came up around him.

"Because you came," said Zowan, who couldn't be twenty years old but already stood at least as tall as Cam. "You don't look like anyone we've ever seen before."

"But how did you find the hole in the first place?" Cam pressed, for it did not look at all a likely hiding spot.

Again they looked at one another. "It is where we came out of New Eden," said Zowan. "We have run away to the surface, and we feared you were one of the Enforcers come to bring us back."

"New *Eden*?!" The situation grew more bizarre by the moment. "What is that?"

"You have never heard of New Eden?" the girl asked in astonishment. "It is the first and largest of all the enclaves."

"There are more than one?" Cam asked, aghast.

"Twelve altogether. All over the world."

"Or so we've been told," Zowan interjected bitterly. "For all we know, New Eden's the only one there is."

Casually, Cam drew his phone from the holster at his waist and held it up toward them. As he suspected, not one of the three seemed to have any idea what it was. He took several pictures. "Do the rest of you have names, too?" he asked.

"I'm Terra," said the girl. "He's Parthos." She pointed to the third youth.

*Terra* was obvious in its reference to the earth. *Parthos* he wasn't so sure about, his knowledge of ancient mythologies sketchy at best.

No doubt it had some sort of meaning, though. All of it smacked of Parker Swain. . . .

"Nice to meet you," Cam said. "You say you're runaways?"

The story came out helter-skelter from Zowan and the girl—how Zowan's renegade brother, Neos, had claimed the surface wasn't poisoned as they'd been taught and had taken Zowan up to show him, but the Elders had found out because Zowan had just been reassigned to New Babel. Only, they feared he was really going to be taken to the special lab where the Elders did terrible things to people, and so they had all three fled together.

Cam listened with growing horror, not only because of their predicament but because it was becoming clear that Swain had created an entire community that for at least twenty years had been completely cut off from the rest of the world. A community as restrictive and repressive as any communist or religious regime he could name.

His first thought was that he had to move them before the Enforcers they feared showed up. Or worse, campus security. With the fleet of SUVs K-J had, plus the dogs and choppers, these clone children stood little chance of eluding the kind of dedicated search operation Swain's people could mount. Given their pale skin, flimsy clothing, and useless shoes, a cross-country trek would be out of the question. With the Jeep wrecked, Cam had no means of transporting them, yet with every moment of delay the temperature rose, the sun's intensity increased, and the likelihood of their discovery mounted.

"Was that supposed to be the Tower of Babel?" Zowan's voice broke into Cam's musings.

He stared at the young man blankly. "What?"

"That building you showed us. Where you work. Is it supposed to commemorate the tower in the story where all the men on the Earth came together at Babel and the LORD confused their languages?"

"You have access to the *Bible*?" Cam exclaimed. He could not believe that Swain, for all his pilfering of biblical names for his sick experiment, would actually allow his subjects to read the Bible. And maybe he hadn't, for Zowan's fellow clones regarded him with puzzled looks.

"What story are you talking about?" Terra asked. "I've never heard of a Tower of Babel."

Zowan kept his focus on Cam. "I don't know about any 'Bible.' My book is called the *Key Study*. Or maybe Gen-ee-sis. I only have a portion of it. It flew out of the furnace one day when I was working there and landed at my feet, and the pages opened to a place where the words caught my eye: 'In the beginning God created the heavens and the earth.' "

Cam stared at him. " 'And the earth was formless and void, and darkness was over the surface of the deep. . . . ' "

Now it was Zowan's turn to stare. "You *do* know it!"

"We pronounce it Genesis," Cam said. "It's the first book of the Bible, which is the Word of God."

"Only the first book?" Zowan's blue eyes widened.

Cam sensed Zowan would have gone on to ask him more questions, and Cam had a number he wished to ask, as well, but Terra was growing impatient.

"We can't stand here all day," she said. "It won't be much longer before somebody realizes we're gone." She turned to Cam. "Do you think you could take us over to your ziggurat?"

"I could, but . . . This Father of yours—does he look a lot like Zowan here?"

"Oh yes. Zowan is one of his sons."

"Well, your Father also happens to run everything that goes on in the ziggurat and on the campus surrounding it. He is not my father, but he is my employer. His name is Parker Swain, and what he has done here with you is profoundly illegal, morally reprehensible, and . . . Well, let me just say, if the authorities found out what he was doing, they would put a stop to it at once and haul him off to jail.

"Which means it's very important to him that they not find out, and thus he'll be searching for you three with every resource he has. I'm afraid the best thing for you to do is go back down, cover that hole, and make like you know nothing about Zowan's disappearance."

"I'm not going back," Terra said.

"You are as much at risk as Zowan," Cam told her. "Because your . . . because Swain's second-in-command up here looks just like you. Everyone in the Institute knows her. One look at you and they'll know exactly who you are."

"Then let's just leave this place." She gestured northward down the draw.

"You wouldn't last an hour out there."

"Why not? And don't tell us because the air is toxic."

If the girl wasn't so young, Cam would've sworn it was Gen herself, she was so feisty. He frowned. "How about we all go back into the hole while you work all this out? Someone could come over that hill at any moment."

His observation startled Terra out of her assertiveness, and without another word the three of them scurried beneath the tree, disappearing one by one into the hole. Cam followed Zowan in and discovered it to be the collapsed mouth of an abandoned mine.

"The air's not toxic," he said, taking up the conversation where he'd interrupted it. "But the sun is very hot in midsummer. It can make you very sick, especially if you're not used to it. That's why I'm out here running now instead of later. Besides that, your shoes wouldn't last to the end of the draw, and you have no water. No, the safest place for you right now is down below."

They turned to one another and began to argue. Zowan had apparently already advanced the plan Cam was putting forth, but Terra had rejected it. She continued to reject it and wondered why they should trust Cam at all.

"If Father does rule up here like he says, how do we know he wasn't sent out here to get us back?"

"Why would he have told us he worked for Father if he was sent to get us back?" Zowan asked. "I think Cameron is telling the truth."

"You don't know a thing about him."

"He knows the words in the *Key Study*." Zowan turned his gaze to Cameron. "I think he knows I Am."

"You are what?" Terra demanded. "You think he knows you are what?"

"I'm not talking about me. I'm talking about I Am. It's a name. He's also called God and the LORD God."

Terra clearly had no idea what he was talking about, so Zowan explained to her about the voice he had heard in his head, speaking words like the ones from his fragment of the Bible, telling him to leave and that he'd be shown the way to go.

Cam could hardly believe what he was hearing.

"And I *was* shown," Zowan concluded, telling them about the mysterious light he'd followed up to the surface after Neos had abandoned him. "Now I think part of why I'm here is to meet him." He looked around at Cam.

A chill crawled up the back of Cam's neck. All this time he'd thought he'd come to witness to the scientists at K-J, when it was this young man he'd been sent for. Suddenly the hand of God upon his life had never been clearer.

He glanced down at his watch. "It's five-thirty," he said. "When do you need to be back to avoid discovery?"

Immediately Terra went all stiff and stubborn again. But Zowan pressed her. "Come on, Terra. It'll only be for a day. To buy us all enough time."

At length Terra reluctantly agreed, but with the warning that they'd probably just get lost trying to go back.

"It's marked," Zowan told her. "But I'll take you down to the pump room."

"I'd like to go with you," Cam said. "I want to see this pump room, at least."

His request produced yet another round of protest and hesitation, but finally it was agreed he'd go, and they set off down the dark passages, past the striped bed on its frame, under the groaning wooden supports, through the rock tunnels, down the steep slope, and through the crawl tube. At least, Parthos, Terra, and Cam did—Zowan stayed on the other side, waiting while Cam had his look.

Having brought up the rear, Cam was last to wriggle out of the tube into the damp, musty confines of the shadow-cloaked pump room. He crawled out on his hands, got his feet under himself, and stood, surveying the array of horizontal pipes and pumps and thinking it looked like a regular pump room. Maybe a bit bigger than most. One that might service only the Institute and its campus. And while he thought he'd kept a good sense of direction in their underground jaunt, and thus believed they had come a considerable distance from the campus, he didn't know for sure.

Parthos shifted uneasily, and Terra said, "If we really are going back, we need to do it now."

Cam pulled out the BlackBerry, took a few photos, both by natural light and with the flash, then reholstered the phone. "Remember," he said, "after you secure the drum, make sure you brush away the footprints."

They nodded, and he turned toward the hole he'd just come out of. Abruptly another mind brushed his own, catapulting him back to the Afghani lab with Dr. Garzi. The other visitors had left, and Rudy, in his guise as a potential buyer of one of the pods and financier of the project, was pressing the biologist about the X rays that had been taken of the thing, wanting to know what exactly had been found.

Garzi grew visibly disturbed, rambling on about the difficulty of penetrating the covering, the question of whether what they'd seen might be a reflection, the general inconsistencies of subsequent X rays, and other objections until Rudy cut him off.

"Dr. Garzi, what do you *think* you found?"

"Bones. There are bones inside."

"Human bones?"

"Oh no. Not human."

"Then what?"

Garzi's dark eyes flicked away. "We aren't sure. . . ."

"And is it alive?"

"The outer covering is, most definitely." Garzi paused. "But is the inside alive? We don't know."

"But you *think* it might be."

"The bones do seem to shift position, but that might be a result of the outer covering, the way it moves when it expels the cubes."

"Dr. Garzi," said Rudy, "give us your best guess. We need to know."

Garzi frowned, rubbed his beard, and said, "We think whatever these things are, they may somehow be trapped inside their pods. Workers report hearing voices commanding them—sometimes pleading with them—to come and let them out."

"Let who out?" Cam asked intently, having heard the voices himself.

"It's always just 'me.' 'Come let me out.' But some hear multiple voices, especially when in the tomb, and aside from the pods themselves we can't pinpoint anything else that might want letting out. . . ."

The loud rushing-air sound of the ventilation system overwhelmed Garzi's words, and Cam heard the voice again.

*"It's about time you got here. Come down now, little mouse, and let me out."*

With a gasp Cam returned to the moment, the hum of water pumps around him replacing the rush of the Afghani ventilation system. The voices, however, came with him:

*"Why are you standing up there?"* it rebuked him.

*"I know you hear me, grasshopper!"* a second voice intruded. *"Come and release me."*

*"I will make it worth your while,"* said a third voice. *"Whatever you want is yours—just come now."*

"Oh, my Lord!" he murmured.

Parthos and Terra were staring at him in consternation and some alarm, and he had the feeling they'd been speaking to him while he'd been in the flashback.

But he had nothing to say to them, only turned and scrambled back through the tube as they positioned the plate across the hole behind him, the metal drum clanging softly as they pushed it against the plate.

It was only as he emerged into the room on the surface side of the tube that he realized he'd cut his hand—most likely on the edge of the steel plate as he'd entered the tube. He stood beside Zowan, regarding the red blood welling out of the ragged cut on his left palm while panic pushed at the edges of his mind.

"Are you all right, Cameron?" Zowan asked, watching him wide-eyed.

Folding his thumb across his palm to close the cut and slow the bleeding, Cam said, "Let's get out of here."

# Chapter Thirty-Nine

When Cam and Zowan returned to the exit chamber at the top of the tunnel passages, they found it much brighter and warmer than when they had left it. Here Cam finally sat down to examine the slice in his palm. The blood that had flowed from the wound as he'd walked had cleaned it fairly well, so he just wet a spot at the bottom of his T-shirt and wiped the skin clean on both sides of the cut. Then he pulled some bandages from his fanny pack, intending to use them to hold the cut's edges together.

Unfortunately, he was so hampered by his shaking hands, he could hardly get the bandages out of their wrappers, much less peel off their protective backings.

"Let me help you," Zowan said, reaching out to take the one Cam was mangling.

"No! I'm okay."

But as the shock of hearing the ancient warriors speak to him waned, memory of their words crowded more insistently into his mind. *"Why are you standing up there? Come and release me. I'll make it worth your while."*

Nausea clawed up the back of his throat, and the exit chamber grew so white he had to drop his head between his knees so as not to pass out. All this time he'd never truly believed they were here. At one of Swain's other facilities, perhaps, but not here. *Not here.* God wouldn't do that to him again.

*No, of course not "again." You're not the same person you were the first time. I've brought them back so you can see that.*

*No!* Cam prayed. *Not again! I can't face them again.*

"Please," Zowan said, breaking into his distress. "Let me help you." He laid a hand on Cam's shoulder, jolting him out of the dark fog of fear into which he had blundered. Fear was a sin. Fear was an insult. He had no reason to fear, not if he really believed *I will never leave you nor forsake you.* Besides, hadn't Rudy said he had a team to go in? That Cam was eyes and ears only?

Cam drew a deep, shuddering breath and straightened, nodding for Zowan to go ahead with the bandages and telling him how to place them when he got them out of the packages.

As he pressed the first one into place, Zowan asked, "Do you know about the seeds, Cameron?"

"Seeds?" A myriad of horrifying meanings raced through his mind, all involving the sarcophagi and their mysterious black cubes.

"In Gen-ee-s . . . er . . . Genesis. Where it talks of the seed of the serpent and the seed of the woman . . . How the first will bite the heel of the second—"

"—and the second will crush the head of the first," Cam finished for him, his mind glomming on to the topic as a welcome diversion from his inner horrors. "It's a prophecy." He drew a shaky breath. "You know of the Fall, then."

"The Fall? No. I just . . . Our mission as citizens of the Enclave is to eventually reseed the earth. We have protective arks carrying all the seeds of every plant and animal in the world hidden away in New Eden's depths. Seeds are very important to us. So that part caught my eye, and I wondered what it meant—seed of the serpent, seed of the woman. But what is this Fall you refer to?"

"When the serpent tricked the woman into eating the fruit of the Tree of the Knowledge of Good and Evil, then getting the man to eat it, too."

"Oh. I know about that." Zowan tore open the second bandage, frowning. "So . . . did the woman fall out of the tree, then? I thought she just picked the fruit off, but sometimes the sentences are confusing to me."

Cam chuckled. "No one fell out of the tree. But when they ate, they disobeyed God's command not to and were changed." He paused, trying to think of the best way to describe it to someone with no frame of reference. "Not only would they one day die physically, but at that moment they had died to God, to I Am, as well. That deadness has been passed down to all their offspring—including you and me—except one: the seed of the woman. The seed is one of her descendents."

Zowan applied the second bandage to Cam's palm. "So her descendents are separate from the man's?"

"No. The seed of the woman didn't come from the man." He fell silent again, realizing he wasn't making any sense. Suddenly he was overwhelmed with all that Zowan most likely didn't know. Best he just keep his explanation very simple. "The seed of the woman had no human father, because His father was God himself."

"His father was God?" Zowan murmured. "You mean he is the son of I Am?"

Cam grimaced. "More or less. Yes." No way would he try to introduce the concept of a triune God on top of everything else.

"And the seed of the serpent?"

"That would be all those who follow the serpent's ways."

Zowan's blue eyes narrowed.

"The way the serpent hated God and lied about Him to deceive the woman into disobeying," Cam explained. "He's still around today, though not in serpent form. Still deceiving people into disobeying God, and fighting against Him. Those are the serpent's ways, and those are what drove the people who crucified Jesus."

Zowan looked up from peeling the backing of the third bandage, his expression one of utter incomprehension. "Who is Jesus? What is 'crucified'?"

Well, of course the young man had never heard of Jesus, nor of His crucifixion. Swain would have no place for such a tale in his world. . . .

"Jesus is the seed of the woman," Cam said. "People plotted to kill

Him, and He let them do it so He could take the punishment God demanded for our disobedience. God's totally perfect and righteous. You see . . ." He trailed off in frustration. That wasn't the way to go, either. With every attempt to explain, he just made things worse.

He watched as Zowan applied the last bandage to his palm and then breathed a sigh of resignation. "The bottom line is, if we believe in Jesus Christ and what He did for us, we'll be saved . . . er . . . God will give us new life that can never be taken away."

He fell silent, praying the Holy Spirit would take something in all that jumble and make it clear to the kid, because right now Zowan looked completely lost.

Cam gathered up the discarded wrappers and backings and stuffed them into his fanny pack. "Maybe I can explain it better tonight. For now, I have to get back to the zig before someone comes out to look for me."

"You're *leaving*?!" A note of real panic sharpened the youth's voice.

"Just for the day. You'll be okay. I'll have to make arrangements for supplies or a vehicle, neither of which can be delivered until dark. With the crawl tube secured, this is the safest place for you. It won't be pleasant, but these'll help." He handed over his water bottles—one full, the other half—then followed them with two Powerbars, a package of dried fruit, and a sack of salted nuts.

"Okay, then. I need to go." Cam moved to the hole and dropped to his knees.

"Cameron? Does I Am ever speak to you?"

Cam looked back over his shoulder. "Not with words I can hear like I hear you. But inside, yes, He does."

"He told you to come here, didn't He?"

"I think He did."

"And now He's telling you to go."

"Well, I hope so. I believe so."

Zowan nodded. "I haven't slept all night. I think I'll go down and use that bed."

"Good idea. I'll see you, once it's good and dark again. Don't get concerned if I'm not here right away."

With that, Cam turned and wriggled through the hole. Crawling out from under the juniper, he stood and immediately texted an encrypted message to Rudy asking for a face-to-face ASAP. He did not include the photos, just said he had something to share.

Back in his apartment he showered, then doused the slice in his palm with hydrogen peroxide and antibiotic ointment and closed it up with superglue and butterfly bandages. He brewed up some coffee in the machine in his room as he dressed, then poured himself a cup and went to stand at the window, staring down at the campus as he reflected.

He knew he should go down to breakfast soon. That was why he'd cut off the conversation with Zowan, after all. But now that the prospect loomed before him, he didn't think he could face all those people and maintain the façade that nothing had changed. The immensity of what they had done—were *doing*—overwhelmed him.

Poe was right. They *were* playing God. Or at least Swain was, creating his own little world, populating it with people who had no normal family ties and relationships, who had no choice but to believe whatever he told them was true. They were his slaves. Worse than slaves, if Gen's remark about their not being human was indicative of the attitudes of most of those in the Inner Circle Were *they* Zowan's vaunted Elders? Was this the fold Swain yearned for Cam to join?

For a moment he was so angry he couldn't breathe, and it shamed him that he'd ever responded to any of Swain's offers. In it he saw his own arrogance, not just in thinking he could come to Kendall-Jakes and be above it all, but in his desires for success and approbation, and in his frustration with the constant hindrances of the academic bureaucracy. He'd chafed at their pettiness, their small-minded rules and silly procedures. Swain had offered him deliverance from all that, or so he thought—even knowing the old adage that whenever something seemed too good to be true, it usually was.

And yet . . . and yet he didn't believe he was entirely out of God's will in all this. He'd asked for guidance, after all, the doors had opened, and it seemed pretty clear now God had brought him here, in part, at least, to free Zowan and his friends—and not just from Swain, apparently. Zowan's self-initiated desire for God in a place where no one had ever mentioned God's name amazed him, and the story of how he came to have the fragment of Genesis amazed him even more. *Almost as if there is a God,* he thought wryly.

There was the matter of the warriors in the sarcophagi, as well: beings at least 4000 years old whom he believed to be the Nephilim referenced in Genesis six, the unlawful offspring of fallen angels and human women.

He stood there, fear fluttering up in him as he touched again the notion that God really did want him to face them. . . . He could almost consider it now, knowing that if it were the case, God would see him through it.

And if he could face the Nephilim, he could surely face those people in the dining room. Which, seeing as he'd finished his coffee, he'd better get to before it was too late.

Still, it wasn't easy. His first sight of Swain—looking exactly like Zowan—ignited his outrage all over again. And having to sit there as if nothing was wrong—giving civil answers to Gen's questions about the day's schedule, watching the director chat lightheartedly with his subordinates—took every shred of self-control he possessed. Then it got even harder when Swain addressed him directly, asking about his Sunday run, mocking him with suggestions that his injury was a sign of God's displeasure for Cam's having neglected Him, and finally getting round to ragging on his obsession regarding his daily Bible studies.

"I mean, do you have to listen *every* day? Do you ever actually take a break?"

Cam scraped up the remains of his cheese omelet and piled it onto his fork, then looked up at Swain. "Do you ever take a break from eating?"

Swain's blue eyes flashed. "Is that supposed to be some sort of equivalent?"

"Food for the soul and spirit." Cam slid the forkful of omelet into his mouth.

Swain held his gaze levelly, and Cam knew he'd succeeded in

irritating the man, even as he wondered why he did so. Or was he simply not seeking to avoid it anymore?

"You're a fanatic, Doctor," Swain snapped.

"It goes with my paranoia." Again the words just popped out. Maybe it was the shock of having a man he'd admired for years exposed for the monster he really was.

"Indeed it does," Swain said. "What? Are you afraid you're going to forget what you believe?" He paused as the others snickered. "Or is it your only hedge against all those terrors and disappointments of your past?" He smiled smugly, for he'd certainly nailed part of the situation. "You keep trying to convince yourself that God won't let those haunting inner voices touch you, when what you really need to do is just listen to what they're trying to tell you!"

It was as if Swain had physically pushed Cam into another reality. Suddenly he could *smell* the pump room again, hear the hum of the motors as the Nephilim's words whispered through his mind. *"Come down now, little mouse. . . ."*

With a gasp he slammed his mental doors against the voice, fumbling his fork into his plate as he tried to set it down.

Everyone at the table watched him wide-eyed. Except Swain, whose gaze had turned intent, the smugness gone, blue eyes glittering. *He did that on purpose,* Cam thought. *Does he know I've heard them here?* He recalled Rudy's theory that Swain believed Cam knew how to open his pods and shuddered. *But I don't know. And even if I did, I'd never do it for him. I'd never do it for anyone. . . .*

To Cam's relief, Swain's cell phone beeped and he was pulled away from the table. A moment later, Cam left, too, not caring if the others saw him as a dog fleeing with his tail between his legs. As he walked out of the dining hall, he checked his voice mail. Rudy had responded to his request to meet face-to-face; he should go to the library after breakfast and wait near the books on wind power. Someone would contact him. He was texting a response that it needed to be Rudy, not "someone," when he nearly ran down Lacey McHenry in the hallway.

"Oh, excuse me, Doctor!" she exclaimed as she bounced off him.

"I'm sorry," he blurted simultaneously, stopping to face her. "I didn't see you."

She didn't look terribly unhappy about their collision. For a moment they stood staring at each other. And though he sought desperately for something to say in order to prolong the moment, nothing came. She glanced over his shoulder, then gave him a smile and said, "See you tonight."

He watched her walk away, transfixed, fire rushing up from the soles of his feet to the top of the head. He had not been so strongly attracted to a woman in years. Maybe ever. Was it the bonding they'd experienced through the ordeal with Frogeater? Or was it more than that? He'd read her file. There were many parallels in their lives, many areas of rapport, even beyond their mutual interest and training in genetics. . . . And her courage on Friday night had impressed him greatly.

"Geez, Reinhardt, you could at least try not to drool openmouthed," came Fred Slattery's voice at his shoulder. "Everyone knows she's the director's, anyway."

And in that moment Cam realized—they no longer needed Lacey to penetrate Swain's operation. She could get out. She should get out. He should go and tell her to leave now. . . . No, he'd meet with Rudy first.

Fifteen minutes later, Cam was on station near the wind power books at the back of the fourth-floor library when the lights went out. Rudy arrived shortly thereafter wearing a baseball cap and rimless glasses. He opened a door in the wall and they crowded into the small electrical closet behind it. With the door closed and latched, Rudy set a portable lamp on the floor and switched it on. "We have ten minutes," he said as the lamp buzzed and flickered to life. "What do you have?"

As Cam related the morning's events, he showed Rudy the pictures on his BlackBerry. He finished with a shake of his head. "I'm still struggling to get my mind around it. Especially how Swain could have constructed an enclave that extensive and no one know of it."

"Well, that I *can* answer," Rudy said. "After you brought up the possibility of there being additional levels beneath the zig's official floors last week, I put out some feelers. Something came in last night: Seems old Mr. Kendall purchased this property back in the sixties during the nuclear scare and built a bomb shelter on it. Designed it to support thirty people, with means of processing air, water, sewage—even had some rooms to grow food hydroponically. He kept it secret because he didn't want others trying to get in when disaster hit and because he'd spent a *lot* of his company's money on it.

"When he died, they closed it down—moved out the useful stuff and left the rest. All the info's here—pics, blueprints, etc." He dropped a flash drive onto Cam's palm. "This is huge, Cam. After all this time, we finally have our in."

Cam grinned. "I figured you'd be happy. Before you send your guys in, though, I want to go back and get those kids out. They're meeting me in the hole tonight, so I'll need a vehicle and supplies—food, water, clothes. You saw what they're wear—"

"Cam—"

"Oh, and I want Lacey out of here, too, since we don't need her anymore. This afternoon, if you can swing it."

"She's all set to attend the reception tonight. We can't just pull her out."

"Then pull her when it's over."

"And if Swain means to take her to the penthouse afterward?"

"All the more reason to get her out before he can act."

Rudy frowned at him.

"Come on," said Cam. "If this little episode hadn't destroyed my car, I wouldn't be asking. But it did. So I am. Why are you still frowning at me?"

"Because we can't just blow our whole operation for a few innocents."

"I promised them."

"You're not responsible for them. And we have other considerations. This mission was never about rescuing kidnappees, nor the illegality of Swain's experiments. There's something far greater at stake."

All of Cam's forward-racing thoughts halted. "The sarcs," he murmured.

Rudy nodded. "You say you were inside. Did you sense anything? Have another flashback?"

Cam said nothing.

His friend went very still. "They spoke to you?"

Cam released a long, resigned sigh and nodded. "At least three."

"They spoke to you?!" Rudy frowned, stepped half away, then turned to face him again. "You've got to go in."

"You said I was eyes and ears only! You said you have a team."

"I just want you to find them, Cam, not open them. We need recon before we can send the team. And we have a window here that's going to close very soon."

"Your team doesn't have its own recon?"

"The team's not all here yet. It'll take a day or two to assemble."

"A day or two? I thought you said last Sunday that your team was in place! We've suspected since Monday that Swain could move on Lacey anytime."

Rudy looked perturbed. "First of all, as I said, rescuing McHenry was never part of the mission objective. And second, I didn't expect an underground installation of this magnitude. I thought it would be a single lab, maybe multiple rooms, but this . . . from what you've learned today it obviously taps into the network of old mine shafts, so we'd have no idea of its configuration. *You* not only have a way in, you have some tour guides. Which you'll surely need, since I doubt those old plans will reflect the reality."

"I promised those 'tour guides' I'd get them out tonight," Cam said.

"They'll be out by morning. I'm only asking you to take advantage of the situation that's presented itself. Just go down and check things out."

Cam scowled at him. "You said eyes and ears only," he repeated stubbornly.

"You know how this business is!" Rudy muttered. "Flexibility is the name of the game. You know what's at stake, too. Are you really going to just walk away?"

Cam said nothing as the inevitability of the moment overtook him. Finally he sighed again. "I'll do it on one condition: that you get Lacey out of here tonight. *Before* I go in."

Rudy sighed, massaged his temples with thumb and fingers for a time, then dropped his hand with a grimace. "That's gonna be problematic, Cam."

"Then deal with it. It's the only way I'll do it."

"All right. In the meantime get me a list of the things you'll need. Tools, ammo, clothes, whatever. You should have a lot of it already. . . ."

# Chapter Forty

Dressed in her borrowed finery, Lacey came to a stop at the edge of the reception patio in the Institute's famed tenth-floor open-air garden. Somewhere an unseen string quartet played Mozart as monkeys and parrots shrieked in raucous accompaniment from the surrounding trees. On the patio before her, a throng of elegantly dressed people mingled around white linen–draped tables, a lighted white obelisk spearing dramatically into the dark heavens behind them. Stunning in its own right, the obelisk was nevertheless dwarfed by the formidable glass-and-granite edifice of Swain's two-storied penthouse rising out of the garden's jungle to the right.

Abandoned in Gen's apartment half an hour ago when the assistant director left to attend to some last-minute details, Lacey had arrived unattended and self-conscious. And while looking at the other ladies' gowns made her more thankful than ever for her lovely dress and the diamond necklace and earrings she'd received this afternoon, she still couldn't shake the sense of being a doll someone else had dressed for their amusement.

A sense which only added to the dread she'd carried with her since it had awakened her at 5:30 that morning. Quivering in her belly like a hive of angry bees and flooding her mind with various dreadful endings to this evening's festivities, it had eventually driven her out of bed and up to her darkened sixth-floor office. There she not only read her Bible for the first time in months but listened to the message Cam's online pastor had given that very morning—on the faithfulness of God.

That couldn't have been an accident, and while listening she'd been terribly excited. It was as if God himself assured her He knew exactly what was going on and would protect her. But later, at the salon, and then as she'd dressed in Gen's apartment, and especially now as she stood alone, trying to think what to do, He seemed as indifferent and far away as ever.

"Ms. McHenry?" A swarthy-faced servant with an East Indian accent bade her follow him through the crowd toward the obelisk. She glimpsed not one person she knew until they reached the dais set up before the obelisk, where she was delighted to see Cameron Reinhardt deep in conversation with Swain and several other men. Cameron alone stood facing her, and dressed in suit and tie as he was tonight, he looked far more the dashing spy than the absentminded professor, a thought that almost made her giggle.

As she approached he glanced up at her, then did a double take to stare in unabashed appreciation. Seeing his reaction, Swain turned and immediately blazed with an approving smile.

"Lacey, my dear," he cried, stepping forward to take and kiss her hand, "you look even lovelier than I had imagined you would. The gown is perfect."

She flushed, uncomfortable all over again, though Swain seemed not to notice. Eagerly he introduced her to the other men in their conversational circle: the deep-voiced billionaire, Ian Trout, who was so integral to K-J's funding and direction; a U.S. Army general in civilian clothing; the CEO of a weapons manufacturing company; and a high-powered investment broker. To say Lacey was out of her element was an understatement. Thankfully, after only a few moments of conversation, Swain whisked her away to meet a new round of overachievers—except for her, it seemed there was not one regular person here.

Within ten minutes she was so completely intimidated and demoralized she could hardly speak. It didn't help that people made no attempt to hide their opinion that her attendance had nothing to do with her professional achievements. Some of the guests, especially the older women, made her want to fold up and crawl away.

She and Swain returned to the head table as dinner was about to be served, where she was profoundly disappointed to find that Cameron not only wouldn't be sharing their table but had, in fact, disappeared. Not until then did she realize how much she'd craved his company, a balm of sorts to the battering her self-confidence was taking. She feared it was going to be a very long evening.

Standing behind his chair as his guests settled into their places, Swain tapped his wineglass with a fork. As the rumble of conversation died away, he welcomed his guests with great affection, then drew everyone's attention to the table centerpieces, each of which showcased one of K-J's genetically engineered marvels—either a bioluminescent tree frog in a small octagonal terrarium or a glowing starburst protea blossom floating in a shallow glass water bowl. The head table was graced with the latter, but Swain cited both as "examples of the artistic and aesthetic potential of the amazing field of genetic engineering."

Finally he called for the feasting to begin, and as the first-course salads were set before them, the general who sat beside her wondered aloud if the food had been genengineered, as well.

Genengineered or not, it was fabulous, and Swain turned out to be the consummate gentleman—attentive, complimentary, even funny. Despite her rocky start and all the dread she'd brought with her, Lacey ended up enjoying herself. In fact, Swain was so courteous and proper, she began to think all her fears about his plans for her were baseless.

Until the meal ended and a servant appeared at his side to whisper something in his ear. Whatever the servant said turned him stiff and tense. He frowned darkly across the patio, then nodded to the servant and immediately turned to Lacey, all sign of his previous animosity completely masked by his charm. "There are some new arrivals I must greet," he told her. "Please come and let me introduce you."

He led her not toward the elevator but away, off the back of the dais to a gate in the greenery that led to the penthouse's immediate grounds. There three men in Middle Eastern garb awaited him, watching the partygoers with obvious disapproval, Swain's lighted swimming pool glowing in the inner yard behind them.

Despite his earlier displeasure, Swain greeted them with his usual warmth and enthusiasm. He drew her up beside him, introducing her with obvious pleasure. Intense and aloof, the men showed not the slightest interest in her. After a few moments of attempting to make polite conversation, and failing, Swain turned to her with an easy smile. "Would you excuse us for just a moment, my dear? I'm afraid these gentlemen have business that will not wait. Perhaps you'd like to explore the gardens in the interim. I can have one of my people show you around if you like—"

"Oh, that won't be necessary," she assured him. "I'll be fine."

He gave her a nod. "That's my girl. This shouldn't take long. I'll no doubt be with you by the time you make it to the orchid house."

With that, he and his surly guests passed through the gate and around the swimming pool, disappearing into the penthouse to do their business. Which left Lacey standing there, uncertain whether she'd been abandoned or freed. Would it be permissible to leave? Probably not. He'd promised to rejoin her. And in exploring the gardens, at least she wouldn't have to meet any more CEOs, Nobel laureates, or other luminaries to whom she had nothing to say. If she was really lucky, she might even run into Cameron.

She'd just exited the lovely enclosed orchid garden and was admiring the jaguars in their naturalistic enclosure when a server approached her with a tray of chocolate candies in fluted paper cups. "Would you care for a truffle, ma'am?" he asked.

He was very neat, very professional, with very short blond hair, blue eyes, and a snappy black waitstaff vest. He also seemed very familiar, though she couldn't think where she'd seen him before.

At her request he identified the varieties of confection on his tray. Then, as she chose a mocha truffle, he said casually, "Dr. Reinhardt is enjoying the view at the south end of the garden's west wall if you'd care to join him there."

Her head jerked up in surprise. "Now?"

"Yes, ma'am." He left her and went to present his tray to a group of glittering dowagers not far away. Lacey glanced around. Swain was still nowhere to be found. Dare she risk being found in Cameron's company? Absolutely.

Separated from the reception patio by the atrium, the garden's west side lay virtually deserted. She strolled southward along the waist-high wall as far as she could go but didn't find him. Disappointed, she stood under a tree and stared across the campus, wondering what to do. The bowl was still bright with lights and bustling with activities on this last night of the expo, but the rest of the grounds lay blanketed in stillness, the hangars and storage buildings standing as lonely outposts, bathed in cones of light from their security lamps. It was humid and still warm. Over the mountains, clouds flickered with intermittent lightning, accompanied by the lagging rumble of thunder.

He came up beside her without a word and put a finger to his lips for silence the moment she looked at him. Then he slipped around behind her and she felt the kiss of his fingertips on her nape as he unfastened the clasp of her diamond necklace. He lifted it off her chest, laid it carefully on the flat stone atop the wall before her, then removed her hook earrings and laid them with the necklace. Finally, he covered all with a twelve-inch square of gray jeweler's cloth and, taking her hand, led her away from the wall into the jungle behind them. He stopped in a shadowed bower, where a toolbox and watering station were concealed in the greenery and light from the penthouse's decorative lamps filtered dimly through the trees. There he turned to face her, still holding her hand.

She thought he'd ask about the chip that had been surreptitiously inserted under her shoulder blade at the salon that afternoon or how things had gone with Swain, but he just stood there, staring down at her.

"What?" she finally asked.

He shook his head. "You look amazing. It was all I could do to get my mouth closed that first time I saw you. And whatever I was going to say to General Lader flew right out of my mind." He paused and his lips quirked. "Kinda like now."

After an evening with Swain and his easy praises, his effusive warmth and supreme confidence . . . she found Cam's awkward but honest manner not only refreshing but endearing. She stood there for some time, happy just to gaze up at him, feeling safer than she had all day.

Abruptly he seemed to reorder his thoughts, then pulled out his BlackBerry, pushed at it a few times, and handed it to her. A years-old photograph of Swain, Genevieve, and the diamond merchant from the Ivory Coast she'd met before dinner glowed on its screen. "Where in the world did you find this?" she asked. "It must be forty years old. They look like children."

"They *are* children. And I took it this morning beyond the eastern berm."

"*You* took it?" She stared at the screen, thunderstruck. "This *morning*?"

"They're living, breathing clones—of Gen and Swain, at least. The other one I don't recognize."

"He's Mr. Abuku from the Ivory Coast. I met him tonight. "

He slipped the phone from her fingers and back into its holster. "There's a whole village of them down there. Where they call Swain Father and have to say a worshipful affirmation of their gratitude every morning."

As the implications of Cam's discovery slowly solidified in her thoughts, she began to feel sick and light-headed. Clones. Real, live, nearly adult clones. They proved Swain's need for surrogates, possibly egg donors, as well. . . .

Suddenly all the fears with which she began the day came surging back. Once again, she'd fallen for the Swain Effect, her emotions bedazzled by his charm, her mind shut off, her fears dismissed Even after she'd seen him put on his happy face with her own eyes tonight. He was going to ask her up to the penthouse; all his amiable platonic behavior had merely served to get her to lower her guard.

As she stood in jittering shock, Cameron told her all that he'd experienced that morning. "I'll be going back in tonight. The good news, though, is that *you're* out."

She gaped at him. "Out? What do you mean?"

"We have our way in now." He drew a breath and shook his head. "You don't have to play his games any longer. In fact, my friend is set to get you out—"

"Wait a minute. I was willing to help before when it was just missing girls. Now it's a whole slave factory, from what you're telling me, so why shouldn't I—"

"Because there's no need, and the risk is too great." He caught her hand and squeezed it. "You can leave all this behind—with your reputation intact, if all goes well."

She looked up at him, wondering why it felt more like she'd had the rug pulled out from under her than that she'd been delivered. "Will I ever see you again?" she asked, mortified by the pitiful tone threading her voice.

He stared at her wide-eyed, then swallowed and said, "I don't know. Would you even want to?"

"Yes. Very much."

She seemed to have stunned him into wordlessness. Then a crackling of leaves drew her attention suddenly and guiltily toward a man now standing in the path not ten feet from them. It was the blond server, minus his tray of desserts.

She looked at Cam in alarm. "What's he doing over there?"

Cameron smiled slightly. "Standing guard."

She frowned at him, then at the server. "Is *he* the one who's going to help me?"

"Yes."

She looked at the server again, and suddenly she knew who he was. "Is that Mr. *Mallory*? Your obnoxious insurance adjuster?"

"Not anymore." Cam grinned and shook his head. "He'll be disappointed you recognized him. He puts great stock in his chameleon abilities."

"Well, I probably wouldn't have if he hadn't been so annoying yesterday, accusing you of being drunk and going back to burn your own car."

"Yes, he said you were quite defensive of me."

"And there I was worrying I was getting you into trouble."

"Not then, but you probably are now."

"Hey, *you* invited me."

He smiled at her. "You didn't have to come."

Her frown deepened.

"I'm glad you did, though, because now I'll know you're safe." Quickly then, he outlined the plan they'd devised to get her out. She was to leave the reception as soon as she could and return to her room to change clothes. At 12:11 there'd be another blackout, during which she'd take the outside stairwell to the ground floor and wait at the exit for a Broadmoor's catering van. "That'll be Mallory," he said. "You got all that?"

After she repeated it back to him to his satisfaction, he returned her to the spot where he'd first met her. Uncovering the necklace and earrings, he carefully put them back on her, the mothlike touches of his fingers on her ears and neck and shoulders shooting tingles throughout her body. When he was done, she turned to face him, and he stood watching his hands as he adjusted some of the stones in the necklace, fingers trailing lightly upward along its edge and up the side of her neck to her jaw. Then, almost inevitably, his palm cupped her cheek and he was kissing her. It was a gentle, tentative kiss, as if he wasn't sure of her response, and he withdrew after only a moment.

She stood with her eyes closed, reveling in the touch of his lips along the edge of her jaw, his breath in her ear. He kissed the bend between her neck and shoulder, and she trembled as his hands slid down her sides to rest on her hips. Then she turned her face to his to kiss him again, and this time his lips were not so restrained. Her arms slid up around his neck as he pulled her against him and waves of heat surged through her with increasing magnitude. It had been so long since she'd been in a man's arms, she'd forgotten how it felt, how completely, deliciously overwhelming it could be.

Finally, he pulled his mouth from hers, kissed her forehead, then stood there, holding her. She laid her head against his shoulder, wishing the moment would never end. But of course all moments ended, and at length, with a sigh of resignation, he released her, stepping back wordlessly as he slid his palms down her bare arms to take her hands.

"*You be careful,*" she mouthed.

He smiled crookedly, gave her fingers one last squeeze, and walked away.

And as she watched him go, it felt as if he were taking some vital part of her soul with him. She pressed her hands against her cheeks, aghast at the sudden, powerful sense of loss she felt, at the almost overwhelming desire she had to run after him, to go with him, to never be apart from him again. . . .

She swallowed, then laid her palms flat against the cool stone on the wall and stared blindly at the night-cloaked campus before her. *What is wrong with you? You're thirty-three years old and you're acting as giddy as a teenager. You can't be in love with him. You don't even know him.* . . .

For a few moments she stood there, trying to talk herself out of what she was feeling, then dropped it all in horror as she recalled that she was supposed to leave the reception as soon as possible. With Swain still detained by his business associates, there was no better time than now. Pushing away from the wall, she hurried back through the gardens, beset with the irrational fear that she'd started too late and he was going to get her after all. . . .

She was almost to the elevator when she ran into Swain's East Indian servant, bearing Swain's invitation for her to rejoin him. She nearly refused, but common sense prevailed. Why fight him now when she was so close to getting free? Better to endure for a few more minutes than jeopardize that chance. Thus she followed the servant back to the reception patio and past the dance floor at its far end, where a number of couples already swayed to the strains of a Viennese waltz.

Swain waited at its fringes and broke into his marvelous smile as she approached. "Ah, here you are! I understand you've been exploring my gardens."

"I have," she said. "They're incredible. I'm amazed at all you've done up here."

He grinned. "Wait until you see what I've done with the penthouse."

It was as if one of the musicians had struck a sour note. *Oh, Lord, please, not the penthouse.*

He snagged two flutes of champagne from a server's tray and handed her one. She took it reluctantly but did not sip from it, searching madly for an excuse to escape. Rattling on about the architect he'd contracted to design his living space and the world-renowned interior designer who'd helped him decorate it, he guided her inexorably toward the lighted swimming pool glowing behind the penthouse-grounds gate.

"How about I give you a private tour?" he suggested, touching

THE ENCLAVE — 397

the lock pad beside the gate to open it. "We could go for a midnight swim later."

When she couldn't keep her dismay from showing, his face fell. "Not tonight, eh?" His tone carried an unsettling edge.

"I'm sorry, sir. It's awfully late."

"Late? My dear, it's barely midnight The night has just begun."

"Perhaps for you, sir. But I'm just the frog girl. I'm not used to all this excitement and wine and fancy food."

He regarded her bleakly. "Is this my punishment for having left you so long in favor of attending to my business?"

"Of course not."

He cocked a brow at her.

"I would never do such a thing, sir. In fact, I'm immensely grateful you invited me as your guest tonight." She went on to pour out her appreciation for all the people she'd met, all the things she'd learned, the food, the gardens, the incredible evening she'd had. "But I'm turning into a pumpkin here, sir," she lamented. "Some people may be able to get by on four hours sleep a night, but I am not one of them."

"There are beds in the penthouse, you know. And I am quite skilled at massage. A little wine, a little downtime . . ."

She couldn't hide her horror any better than her dismay. "I'm sorry, sir, but that would be *most* inappropriate."

"Not for me," he said, grinning. He sipped his champagne, then leaned close and whispered, "A lot of these people are judging you for being with me, it's true. But only because they're bitterly jealous that I chose you instead of them."

She had no words to respond to that and was reduced to praying for deliverance.

Like everything else she'd failed to hide, he must have seen her distress, for he backed off. "Very well, I'll take a rain check for now. But rest assured, I'll be back soon to collect."

"Thank you, sir. I'll look forward to that." Did he hear the tremor in her voice?

He motioned to the black-uniformed security guard standing near the gate and told him to escort her to the elevator. Nodding, the man turned and led her back toward the south side of the penthouse to a golden door in the granite block.

"I thought we were going to the elevators," Lacey said warily.

"This is the express elevator, miss," said the guard as the door slid open. He stepped in after her, slid his key into a small hole beside the door, and the car rose gently.

"Why are we going up?"

The guard didn't answer, for already the car was stopping and the door on the opposite side was sliding open. Beyond lay a cathedral-like entry area with a wide curving stair and flowing waterfall. "Please exit the car, miss," said the guard.

She stepped like an automaton into the penthouse's entry.

"The director will join you shortly," the guard said. "In the meantime he wishes you to make yourself at home."

# Chapter Forty-One

After leaving Lacey by the garden's west wall, Cam walked directly to the elevators and descended to his sixth-floor apartment. The first thing he did was exchange his formal wear for the black running shorts and T-shirt he normally wore to bed, and after that moved restlessly between his three rooms.

Parting with Lacey had been difficult. He still couldn't believe he'd actually kissed her, struggling in the aftermath to recall whatever had possessed him to do such a thing. It was not the time, nor the place, nor remotely sensible, but somehow his desire had gotten the better of him. She had been so heart-stoppingly beautiful. Swain had surely chosen the dress to have exactly the effect it did, though perhaps he'd not intended the effect to play out in Cam as it had. . . . One moment he'd been standing there, reveling in her nearness, her scent, her creamy skin beneath his fingertips as he'd adjusted the necklace, and the next he was laying his lips upon hers.

Even more unbelievable was how she'd responded. Thinking of it still made the heat rise and his fingers tremble. In fact, one of the reasons he'd left the reception so abruptly was out of fear he'd run into Swain and be reminded of what the director intended for her. Every time he even came close to touching that possibility, the passion of his desire transformed itself instantly to a passion of fury.

And the last thing he needed at that moment was passion of any kind. He needed to be cool, calm, and in the moment, doing his job, undistracted by worries for her safety—or memories of holding her in his arms, her warm lips moving against his. . . .

He flung himself up out of the chair into which he'd mindlessly collapsed a few minutes earlier and forced himself to attend to preparing for his mission—filling water bottles, getting out running shoes and socks, and collecting it all with fanny pack and head lamp in a pile beside his bed. At ten minutes until the blackout, he turned off all the lights save the lamp at his bedside, and climbed into bed, where he pretended to read his Bible as he waited.

The moment the lamp went out, he jumped out of the bed and made a quick circuit of the room, extracting from their hiding places the various implements Rudy had given him that first Sunday they'd met and adding them to the fanny pack: the fat ballpoint pen that worked like a pen but wasn't one, a flash drive disguised as a heart-rate monitor, his special iPod, the Taser, and the pistol along with five magazines of shells.

When the lamp relit, he was in bed again, feigning sleep, and had only fifteen minutes to wait before the BlackBerry beeped and he snapped it up to read with profound relief the decrypted, translated text message:

*Package received and home safe. You're good to go.*

He texted a *copy that* reply, slid the cell phone back into his fanny pack, then turned out the lamp for good and went to bed. There he tossed and turned, rucking up the bedding into a long ridge beside him in hopes that whoever was monitoring the surveillance images after the next blackout would be unable to distinguish the rumpled bedclothes from his body, at least until daylight.

It wasn't hard to feign restlessness. Waiting was always the hardest part of any mission, but with this one it was especially difficult, given what he feared he would encounter down there. *But you're just eyes and ears. Just finding out where to send the team. You won't have to make contact.*

With a sigh, he turned his thoughts to God, praying for direction and protection, reminding himself just who God was and that He was certainly stronger than anything Cam might find in Swain's lair. . . .

The vibration of his watch jerked him out of a half-sleep, and he opened his eyes as the hum of the air-conditioning silenced, and the illumination under the door vanished. He punched off the watch alarm, reset it for thirteen minutes, and rolled out of bed. Shoving his feet into his running shoes, he tied the laces, then donned head lamp, water harness, and fanny pack and stepped into the silent, pitch-black corridor outside his room.

Four minutes later, he exited the east stairwell into the cool, starlit night and started up the east berm. By the time his watch vibrated again, giving him a two-minute warning for the re-illumination of the campus security lights, he'd crossed over the berm's crest and was moving upstream, following the familiar path by starlight. He found the black bag Rudy had left for him under the bush they'd agreed upon—a bit put out, not only that it was a duffle bag rather than the day pack he'd requested, but that it seemed to be filled with rocks—and continued to the mine shaft without incident. He stood quietly beside the juniper for a few minutes, seeking any sign he'd been followed. When none came, he shoved the duffle under the tree and crawled after it.

As he stood upright in the darkness beyond the entrance hole and switched on his head lamp, Zowan leapt up from the rock on which he sat waiting.

"Where have you been?" the boy cried, sounding so much like Swain, Cam worried for a moment it really was Swain and that he'd been horribly deceived.

"I told you I'd be late," said Cam, squatting beside the duffle bag to unzip it.

"Is that all the supplies and clothing?" Zowan asked.

"There's been a change in plans." Cam glanced around. "Where are Parthos and Terra?"

"I don't know. I've been down and back three times now. The drum hasn't been moved. I'm afraid they've been caught."

"The Elders are probably all in a tizzy after your disappearance. Security may just be tighter than usual." Cam pulled open the duffle. Right on top was the set of tan technician scrubs he'd requested.

"We never should've talked them into going back," Zowan moaned.

"We did the right thing," Cam assured him as he tore open the plastic packaging.

"But now they're stuck down there," said Zowan. "Or worse."

"And you and I are going to go and get them." Cam shrugged out of his T-shirt and donned the tunic.

"You and I?" Zowan asked. "What about your friends? The ones you said you'd bring?"

"My friends'll be here later. First I have to find out where they're supposed to be going."

Zowan looked at him aghast, and Cam saw the fear of betrayal sweep across his face. "I haven't betrayed you, Zowan," he said hastily. "But security is very tight at the zig." He would have stopped there, but God nudged him to go on. "And there's more at stake than you know. Swain's got something down there that could destroy us all. I have to find it."

"The secret lab," Zowan said, nodding.

"Or worse." Cam pulled off shoes, fanny pack, and belt, then stripped off his shorts and replaced them with the scrubs' trousers.

"If the Enforcers catch me," Zowan said presently, "they will kill me."

Cam looked up at him, seeing suddenly how young he was, how innocent. How could he even ask the kid to do this? He wasn't a trained soldier. He sighed. "Okay, don't go, then. But do you think you could draw me a map?"

Zowan said he could, and Cam handed him a note pad and pen.

As Zowan sat down on the rock and began to draw, Cam put on the gray leather walking shoes Rudy'd supplied with the scrubs. Then he examined the other things that had been slipped in under the clothing: compass with clinometer and small laser range finder designed to connect to the BlackBerry; a tiny computer with miniature keyboard and flip up screen; several packets of light-duty explosives; a half dozen smoke grenades, and . . . ah. There was the reason for the duffle bag instead of the pack: Rudy had supplied Cam with an assault rifle, a dozen clips of ammunition, and a good two dozen hefty packages of

C-4. No wonder the bag had been heavy. He frowned at it all, filled with foreboding. What need had he of all this just to look around?

His eye caught upon a corner of paper sticking out from among the blocks of explosive. It was a handwritten note from Rudy:

*I fear the mission is unraveling out of my control. Do what seems best to you. And trust no one but God.*

Cam stood up slowly, reading the note repeatedly, more alarmed than ever. The mission was unraveling? What did that mean? Was he already compromised? No. Rudy would have called him off if that were so. Wouldn't he? Then what was this stuff about "trust no one but God" and "Do what seems best to you"?

"I can't do it," Zowan exclaimed in despair, breaking into Cam's frantic ruminations. "It's too complicated. They're not all on the same level, and I don't know how to draw it in a way that keeps them all straight. Plus I have no idea how to draw the way out of the pump room."

Cam reached for the pad and flipped through the several pages that Zowan had marked on. He was right; it was a chaotic jumble. "I guess I'll have to wing it, then," Cam said, closing the pad and tucking it back into the duffle. *What in the world are you doing here, God?* He zipped up the bag, looped its handle-straps over his shoulder, then tossed his shorts, shirt, and shoes into the corner.

As he started down into the mine's twisting passage, Zowan said, "Maybe I'll come with you, after all." When Cam turned to him in surprise, he shrugged. "I have to know what happened to Parthos and Terra. Maybe I can help them."

"Fair enough," Cam said, stepping aside. "You want to lead?"

They descended swiftly through twisting passages to the crawl tube, where, not surprisingly, the metal drum and plate were still in place. Cam went through the tube first, kicking the drum away from the hole with his feet, then sliding out into the dimly lit pump room. As Zowan scrambled out after him, Cam waited tensely for the Nephilim to make contact again.

Sure enough, there came the rushing wind of voices, then the

404 — KAREN HANCOCK

imperious commands to come and free them. After the initial onslaught, though, when he didn't respond, they backed off.

Only then did he realize one of the voices was actually Zowan, muttering at his side. "I can't, Andros. I don't know where you are."

Cam laid a hand on his shoulder. "Zowan?"

Zowan blinked up at him, disoriented by Cam's intrusion. "It's my friend Andros," he said finally. "He needs my help."

"Andros?" That was the name Poe had given to one of the clones in his conversation with Gen in the viewing gallery—when Gen had rebuked him for thinking the clones were persons. "Isn't he the dead one?"

Zowan's gaze skewered him with sudden intensity. "How do you know of Andros? Is he in the zig?"

"I heard some people talking about him the other night. Who is he?"

The young man's intensity bled away. "He is my friend. They put him in the Cube last week because he wouldn't say the Affirmation, and it killed him. Or so they said. I think he might be in the secret lab, though, because he keeps calling to me, asking me to come and free him."

"How do you know it's Andros?"

Zowan frowned. "I'm not sure. Maybe because he says I owe him. And I do."

"Does he say where he is?"

"No. Only I should come and free him."

Cam exhaled grimly. "Listen, whoever's speaking to you, it's not Andros. Are there more voices than just his?"

Zowan's frown deepened as his gaze turned inward. "I don't know. It didn't seem like it." He paused. "But if it's not Andros, who is it?"

"A vicious and violent monster you do *not* under any circumstances want to free," Cam said firmly. He turned to the plate and drum. "Help me push these back in place and we'll get going."

He soon saw why Zowan had despaired of drawing him a map of the pump room. For a time, Cam feared they might never get out of it, as the kid kept leading them to dead ends. Eventually, though, he found his way and they passed through a series of dark, cramped rooms and narrow walkways to a corridor that was not only taller and wider than the others, but the first with walls finished in painted concrete.

Zowan informed him they were now in one of the Enclave's main corridors and offered to take him down to the central commons. Cam followed him downward, increasingly aware of the unnerving press of rock and earth around him as panicky memories quivered in the backstage of his mind. At least the Nephilim's vague whispers had subsided, almost as if they'd lost interest or fallen asleep. He knew they'd be back but appreciated the reprieve.

"Here we are," Zowan said finally, stopping behind a pillared doorway.

Cam peered around him into what looked like a miniature shopping mall, its central island of trees, bushes, and gurgling stream positioned crosswise to their vantage, its vaulted ceiling startlingly higher than anything Cam had yet encountered. Beyond it stood several doors that Zowan identified as entrances to the library, the cafeteria, the public meeting room, and the Star Garden. "The Sanctuary's up there," he said, gesturing leftward to where a small court at the island's end lay at the foot of a narrow ramp.

Cam pointed to the high mirrored panel running the length of the mall's far wall just under the vaulted ceiling. "What's behind that?"

"Father's wives."

*Father's wives?* He was about to ask if Zowan had ever seen any of them, but two figures in cowled gray robes emerged from a door to their right and strode toward them. Cam and Zowan flattened themselves against the wall as the robed ones walked by, their voices carrying clearly in the night silence. Cam recognized both.

"We can't let the Saudis down here, for crying out loud," Fred Slattery protested indignantly. "That would be insane!"

"You're way too suspicious, Fred," said Gen Viascola. "With a billion dollars on the line, why wouldn't they want to see what they're buying?"

"They have the videos! Why do they need to see the things face-to-face?"

"You can put anything you want on a video. . . ."

As they moved down the mall their words grew muffled and indiscernible. Cam glanced at Zowan and mouthed, *"Elders?"*

When Zowan nodded, Cam stepped to the opposite side of their corridor and peered around the edge, watching the pair ascend the ramp. As soon as they disappeared into the Sanctuary, Cam hurried after them, Zowan in his wake. At the frosted-glass doors atop the ramp, he paused to listen and, hearing nothing, cautiously pulled one open. Giving the chamber behind it a quick scan and finding no one, he slipped inside.

Like the rest of the Enclave, the Sanctuary was surprisingly small, and cramped—except for the altar up front, where the ceiling soared to twice the height it was at the back of the room. Sounds from the right side of the sanctum drew his attention to a small door at the head of the side aisle, but then breath hissed against his teeth as his gaze snapped back to the altar, realization having caught up to what his eyes had just shown him.

Raised upright and fastened to the altar wall was a great golden sarcophagus at least twenty feet tall, gleaming in the focused light of a single ceiling lamp. As Cam approached to study it, though, he realized it was only a likeness cast in gold. *The real ones must be somewhere else.*

"This is one of the arks," Zowan said, coming up beside him.

"The things you said carry all the seeds? For restoring the ruined earth?"

"Yes." Zowan snorted bitterly. "I guess they aren't so precious after all."

"Where are they? The other ones? And how many do you have?"

"They're under safeguard deep in the Enclave's bosom." More than that, Zowan didn't know. "I think only the High Elders would know such a thing. The arks are regarded as too precious for everyone to know where they are."

Cam asked, "Were those two who just passed us High Elders?"

When Zowan nodded, Cam hurried to the side door he'd assumed Gen and Slattery had passed through earlier. Hearing nothing beyond it, he was about to press the door's activation pad when Zowan did it for him. "You might set off an alarm. They're keyed to the palms of Father and the Elders."

The door opened without an alarm going off, and they followed the short hall beyond to a small, dark chamber where a heavy wooden wardrobe full of gray and white robes lurked against one wall. The two who had entered were not in the chamber, but the closed door beside the wardrobe, with its adjacent palm panel and retinal scanner, gave Cam a good idea where they'd gone.

He stepped to the wardrobe and began sorting through the robes, for he'd seen at once they'd make a far better disguise than his tan scrubs. Finding one that looked like a good fit, he donned it, then handed a second one over to Zowan.

"Let's head on back to the library and see if we can find some kind of map."

# Chapter Forty-Two

Lacey turned away from the elevator, hugging herself in the penthouse's chill dry air, numb with shock. How could this be happening? Where was God when she needed Him? Here she was just starting to think about coming back to Him, just starting to think she might be able to trust Him after all—and now this!

She began to hyperventilate, half gasping, half sobbing, falling to pieces right there in his entryway. *Get a grip, girl. You can't just melt into a puddle. You have to find a way out.* . . .

*Find a way out.* The objective quenched her burgeoning hysteria and got her thinking again. Drawing a deep breath, she dashed away her tears and took stock.

As the topmost level of the Institute's ziggurat-mimicking architecture, the entire two floors were given over to Swain's private living quarters, and the entry alcove soared through both stories. To her left the great stone stairway curved up to a softly lit loft, while straight ahead, tastefully lit screens and vines sectioned off the private spaces of his abode, all of them steeped in darkness. She'd start there.

But though she went through every room—study, bedroom, bathroom—and in each one found doors and windows leading outside, she could open none of them. And when, in desperation, she tried to break one, the glass refused to shatter. The place was locked up as securely as any prison.

She thought of hiding in wait for someone to come but realized she was probably being watched, and what was she going to do? Go after the guard with a stapler? Even if he wasn't forewarned, she'd never be able to overcome him. *But you could try.*

Maybe there was something better upstairs.

Ascending the great stair to the loft, she found an expanse of cream-colored carpeting bounded on three sides by floor-to-ceiling windows—walls of darkness gilt with the reflections of the interior lighting. Ancient Aztecan stone artifacts mingled with Babylonian treasures, each lit by its own ceiling lamp. Around them stood low, wood-framed Santa Fean couches, end tables, and chairs. In the far northwest corner, where the two window walls came together, stood a leather-and-wicker table set with fresh flowers and two place settings, also spotlighted by a ceiling lamp.

The only interior wall on the entire level ran halfway along the south perimeter. It was hung with huge acrylic abstracts echoing the Aztec and Babylonian motifs, interspersed with a series of inset niches displaying pieces of lighted blown-glass artwork.

An elevator in the far southeast corner was the only exit besides the stairs. Fighting a horrible sense that she was truly trapped, Lacey wandered among the artifacts, noting a curved wooden scepter leaning against one of the freestanding friezes; a spear adorned with eagle feathers mounted across another; a stone-headed club; a massive sword, accompanied by armor that could only fit a giant. . . .

Suddenly the lights went out, enshrouding her in darkness broken only by the intermittent flashes of lightning over the mountains. *This must be the 12:11 blackout!* When she was to leave her room to meet Mallory. When she didn't show up at the pickup point, they'd know Swain had intercepted her. Suddenly she recalled the RFID chip beneath her shoulder blade, and hope flooded her. Knowing where she was, Cam would come for her.

Shortly the lights came back on, and she continued her stroll through Swain's peculiar museum, buoyed by new hope, startling at every little sound in the hope it was her dashing spy, coming to rescue her. But no one came.

At length, she stood before the south wall, examining the blown-glass pieces in their niches, many of which doubled as terrariums for a creepy collection of venomous spiders and snakes: black widows, brown recluse, rattlers, sidewinders, coral snakes, a cobra, and others she did not recognize. All had been genetically enhanced, some with bioluminescent scales, others with featherlike crests or vestigial legs. One rattler even had an intriguing double-helix design running up its back rather than the usual diamond shapes.

"Did you know that some snake venom is regarded as an elixir of life?"

She yipped at Swain's voice sounding suddenly at her back, and whipped around from the red-edged glass bowl she'd been examining.

Swain smiled down at her. "That one's my death adder. Lovely little thing, isn't she?"

Lacey looked at it again, the serpent's flat triangular head lying on the sand near its tail, which cut off abruptly from about three inches in diameter to only a quarter inch.

"Unlike other snakes, it doesn't stalk its victims," Swain told her as he came up beside her, "but buries itself in the sand, head near its tail. Then it lifts up that skinny end and wiggles it around to attract the mouse or bird. . . ."

"Lovely," Lacey remarked, not even trying to repress her shudder.

She moved away from him to the next container, aware that he'd turned to stare at her with an unnerving glitter in his eyes. As she forced herself to look at him, he shook his head as if in awe. "You're thirty-three years old, yet you have the skin of an eight-year-old. Did you know that?"

She blushed furiously, thinking it was creepy being compared to an eight-year-old.

"I'm glad you're letting your hair grow out," he went on, still staring. "I was so disappointed when you arrived with all those lovely locks shorn. Women should have long hair. And yours is especially luscious."

*This is getting weirder by the moment.*

He turned away from the niches, gesturing toward the little table set for two across the room. "Would you join me for dessert? The view up here is striking at night."

He turned down the lights as she slid into the leather seat, and a servant appeared at her side as if he'd popped up from the floor. He set a plate of chocolate mousse on the service plate before her, then placed a napkin in her lap. A second man appeared with a bottle of wine, filling her glass and Swain's.

Lacey picked up her spoon; Swain sat sipping his wine and watching her. Admiring her preadolescent skin, perhaps? *Oh, God, please! Get me out of here!*

Beyond the south-facing window at his back, lightning flickered in the bellies of the thunderheads over the mountains.

Swain set down his wineglass and picked up his spoon. "Tell me, Lacey, do you believe aliens exist?"

Her attention returned to him in surprise. "Aliens?"

"Beings from other planets." He slid his spoon slowly into the mousse. "Do you believe it's possible they exist?"

"I guess."

"What if you found out that they did? How would you fit that into your belief system? I mean, did Jesus die for them, too?"

"I . . . I don't know."

"You don't know." He ate a spoonful of mousse.

"I've never really thought about it."

"You really don't know what you believe, do you?"

"I believe the Bible."

"Ah. Good. You believe that rebellious teenagers should be executed, then. And that your God takes delight in smashing babies upon rocks."

"What?"

"Psalm 137:9."

"That can't be right."

"Yes. No doubt I'm taking it out of context." He shook his head. "You've never heard of that verse before, have you? You claim to believe the Bible, yet you don't seem to know much about what it says."

"I believe Jesus died for me on the cross. That's enough."

He smiled thinly. "If that was enough, why did God waste His time writing a two-thousand-page book? He could've just used a business card with John 3:16 on it."

He was mocking her. Playing with her. Showing her what a fool she was . . . Punishment for trying to run out on him, perhaps?

"You sure aren't doing much of a job explaining to me what you believe. You are not at all a match for Dr. Reinhardt, in this regard. He'd be very disappointed in your performance here. In fact, he will never be truly interested in you if you're not as fanatical about all this Bible stuff as he is. You do know that, don't you?" He paused to languidly scoop up more of the mousse and slide it into his mouth, savoring before he swallowed.

She had no idea how to respond. He was deliberately doing everything he could to distress her. Why? Did he want her to fight back? Or was he just trying to show her who had the upper hand?

They sat in silence for a moment, concentrating on eating their dessert. Swain finished first, licking the spoon clean with a pleasure that was almost erotic. Then he set the implement on his empty plate and looked at her, his blue eyes gleaming in the semidarkness.

He waited until the servant had carried off their plates and spoons, then said, "I know you spoke privately with Dr. Reinhardt tonight, despite my having expressly forbidden him to have contact with you."

She nearly choked on her own spittle. *Oh, Lord! He* did *see us.* Suddenly her heart pounded a mile a minute. "It was I who sought him out," she protested.

"Yet he did not walk away." He smoothed a slight wrinkle in the tablecloth. "And why would you seek him, when I'd already warned you about him?"

She stared at him wordlessly. *He might not have seen everything. It was dark. We were in the shadows. . . .*

Swain slid his hand across the table to cover hers, drawing her attention back to him. "Please, Lacey. I'm only trying to help. Cameron Reinhardt is a very unstable man. I believe you have read his profile. Correct?"

She gaped at him, aghast that he had caught her in that transgression.

"His post-traumatic stress disorder. His episodes of violence. Fugue states. His paranoid delusions."

"I . . . I don't remember any of that. The PTSD, yes, but not the others. . . ."

"Well, it gives me some comfort to know that Gen did not give you everything. He's being treated for the problem, but he keeps going off his medications. When he does, he fancies himself some kind of government spy. Hails back to what he did for the military, I guess, being in Special Forces and all." He paused. "And, of course, you saw him flashback yourself in that unity meeting."

He kept his hand on hers, watching her carefully. She didn't believe a word of what he said, though it made a horrible kind of sense. "Are you saying he's psychotic?"

"Disturbed. Unstable. That's all." He smiled sadly. "You do seem to be drawn to unstable, delusional men."

Indignation flared, burning away the seeds of uncertainty he had sown. So Cameron was unstable and she a poor judge of character? She pulled her hand free of his. "Director Swain, I appreciate your concern, but really, I can live my life without your assistance. I also think there are many things you don't know about Dr. Reinhardt."

"Oh, my poor dear girl. I know everything there is to know about Cameron Reinhardt. Things you can't even begin to guess. Every little dirty secret. I have to, or I wouldn't survive." He paused. "Why do you think he was on the verge of being fired at Stanford?"

His words fell upon her soul like drops of mud, extinguishing her indignation as they sowed new doubts.

"You do know, no one has actually seen or spoken to Manuel Espinosa since he left. His parents have only gotten e-mails, which could've been sent by anyone."

"I thought you went to Guadalajara to speak to him."

"He stood me up." He folded his hands on the edge of the table. "When no one was there, I came back and had my IT people examine Reinhardt's computers. Manny's resignation letter was drafted on Reinhardt's machine."

"If that were so," Lacey said evenly, "why haven't you gone to the police?"

"How do you know I haven't?"

"Because they're not here."

He smiled. "How do you know they're not here?"

She frowned at him, frustrated by his looping obfuscations.

"He's a trained killer," Swain remarked before she could continue. "So it's not that big a jump for him to murder. There was an incident at Cold Spring Harbor . . . a dispute over a young woman. The other man ended up in the harbor with his neck broken. Reinhardt's guilt was never established, but he was questioned at length. . . ."

"I've read his file, as you pointed out earlier, Director Swain. I know none of that is in there."

"You've read his cleaned-up file, my dear. The one we present to our investors and collaborators." He picked up a small DVD player, which the servant had left behind when he came to take away the plates. Flipping up the screen, Swain tapped the touchpad several times, then turned the device so she could see. It was playing the video Cam had told her about, of him supposedly unloading Manny's body at the Vault. Though his face was obscured by shadow, the clothes were right and so was the body shape.

"You're lucky to have survived your night with him in the desert," Swain said quietly. "Now perhaps you understand why I ordered him to stay away from you."

She could find no words to counter his onslaught of accusation, and though she'd drunk none of the wine, her head swam and she struggled to get enough air into her lungs. *I don't believe it. I won't believe it. It was Frogeater who killed Manny.*

Swain watched her like a snake after a mouse, his blue eyes cold and hard. "What did he tell you tonight? That I have a secret lab hidden under the desert where I conduct illicit research projects?"

She opened her mouth, then closed it before she could say more, horrified that Swain had apparently heard everything in their little tête-à-tête. How? They'd taken off the jewelry. Did he have microphones in all the bushes?

"He did, didn't he?" Swain collapsed back in his own chair and rubbed a hand over his face, looking genuinely distraught. "I'm sorry, Ms. McHenry. I . . ." He drew a breath to steady himself and pressed his palms together as if ordering his thoughts. "I confess, for all my fears, I hoped they were untrue. Now I suppose I shall have to move in directions I'd truly hoped to avoid." He frowned at her. "You look very pale, my dear. Are you all right?"

She didn't know what she was. She didn't know what to believe. She only knew that she was with Swain right now, and that being with him almost made her a different person than when she was not. But the fact was, the same could be said of her time with Cam. With no way to independently confirm—or disprove—what either man said, how could she know who spoke the truth?

Yes, Cam had shown her the picture of the clones, but he could simply have uploaded an old snapshot into his phone. Given the sort of man Swain had painted him to be, that wasn't out of the question. Worse . . . *He isn't here.* It hit her suddenly that there'd been more than enough time for him to rescue her, and he hadn't come. . . .

Swain's eyes had dropped to the diamond necklace glittering on her chest, held there a moment, then came up to meet her own. "You know, that thing is quite expensive and it is on loan. I would think with so many stones in it, it might grow a bit weighty." He stood and came around the table to stand behind her. "You won't mind if I take it back now, will you?"

It seemed to her that all Swain did was confuse, coming at her from all different angles, with all sorts of weird topics and suggestions. She was growing weary of keeping up with him, and if he wanted to take back his necklace, why should she care? Indeed, she'd be happy to have him take it.

Thus she shrugged and said nothing as he began to unfasten the clasp—and immediately regretted it when the light touches of his fingers called up the powerful memory of her moments with Cam in the garden, profaning them in the process. Swain's feather-light touches sent such chills of revulsion over her, she was on the verge of standing and walking away when he lifted the unclasped necklace off her chest and deposited it in the velvet box that had somehow come to be set on the table. She removed the earrings herself before he could return and dropped them into his hand, eager to have done with it.

Then, almost in tears, grieving the wreckage he'd made of her newly conceived affections for Cam, she stood and strode to the window, hugging herself as she stared at the view, praying again for deliverance.

He drew behind her, his breath washing across her neck, so near she felt the warmth of his body. If she walked away, he'd only follow. *Oh, God, I've tried to trust you. Not done a good job, but . . . the pastor this morning said you were faithful. So where are you?*

She flinched as Swain's hands settled lightly on her shoulders and rested there, hot and slightly damp. Her pulse thundered in her ears, and part of her screamed for action, urging her to break away, grab something and defend herself. But she felt like the moth she'd just watched writhe in the spider web in one of Swain's terrariums—so wound up she couldn't think straight, so entangled she didn't know which way to turn.

His hands slid over the curves of her shoulders, taking the straps of her cocktail dress with them. She trembled in horror as his fingers walked across her back to the dress's zipper, conjuring up ancient memories of another night and another man she'd let undress her. A choice that had set her life on a ruinous course.

For a moment the comparison was so strong and sharp, she wondered if she might be having a nightmare, or was imagining something that wasn't happening at all. Perhaps he was just picking away lint, or adjusting the dress's lining.

But when his fingers tugged downward on the zipper tab, she jerked aside with a gasp and turned to him. "Please," she said. "Don't."

Swain had a perversely dazed expression on his face. "I can hardly help myself," he told her. "Everything about you is intoxicating. And your innocent sincerity only makes it worse. You stir my heart in a way no one ever has before."

"Please, Director Swain. Don't say such things. You know they're not true."

"You are the one I've been waiting for all my life." Sudden eagerness replaced his dazed expression. "My genetic match. I will make you a queen. You'll have riches beyond your wildest imagination, your every desire fulfilled." He looked at her pointedly. "Your *every* desire. For all of time."

A shudder rolled over her, and she eased back another step. "I don't even know how to respond to that."

He smiled and closed the gap she'd widened, reaching for her hand. "Stay with me tonight."

"Please, sir . . ." She stepped back again, trying to pull her hand free.

He let her go, his face relaxing into a blandness she now knew was deception. "It's him you want, isn't it?" he said flatly.

"I beg your pardon?"

"Reinhardt. After all I've done for you, it's Reinhardt you want."

As understanding dawned, she felt the blood rush condemningly to her face. "You don't understand, sir. It's not that at—"

He cut her off with a roar: "Don't lie to me, girl!"

She flinched backward, but he advanced upon her.

"You thought I was fine when you believed I could advance your career," he railed. "So you strung me along, flirted, made me think you cared. Now that I've promoted you a little, now that I ask only for a bit of gratitude, a few hours of the pleasure of your company, you turn all cold on me. Cast me off for *him*, and shiver at my touch."

She stared at him, aghast. In the blink of an eye he had transformed into another man. A man whose eyes burned with the madness he'd so recently ascribed to Cam. But it wasn't Cameron Reinhardt who was paranoid, delusional, and psychotic. It was Parker Swain.

She wanted to back away from him but feared provoking him further. "What exactly do you want from me, Director Swain?"

"What do I want from you?" He stepped toward her again. "I want these"—he touched just below her eyes—"to see only me. And this"— he ran his fingers through her hair—"for my hands alone. And this"—he drew his fingers down the side of her face and neck—

She backed away from him, but he came after her until she was stopped by the adjoining window wall, the wooden railing pressed against her lower back.

He caught her wrist and held it to his lips. "I want this and this and this. . . ." His free hand wandered across her body, touching her where he had no right, while she stood paralyzed with fright. His palm came to rest finally on her belly. "Most of all I want this."

She flinched back against the window, choking on her own bile. He wanted her for his clone production. A whimper issued from her throat.

He stepped back, releasing her wrist at last. "You were nothing when you came to me, Lacey McHenry. A lost soul wandering about. I will give your life meaning and purpose." He smiled. "I will make you the mother of gods."

Horror exploded into desperation, and she shoved herself off the window, knocking him briefly off balance as she fled. He caught her by the shoulder. She spun and slapped his face, loosing his grip on her. Wrenching free of him, she raced for the stair. Only to have one of his black-garbed guards loom up in her path. She turned back, snatched up the Babylonian scepter from its resting place against the stone frieze, and keeping both men in sight, stood her ground, holding the scepter like a baseball bat. "Let me go, or I'll bash someone's head in," she threatened.

Swain burst out laughing. "Oh, my poor dear girl," he said. "You think I can't take that thing away from you? Even if I couldn't, Buckley here would never let you get by him. I have you. You can embrace your destiny with me and live a wonderful life of pleasure and security, or you can fight it and be miserable. It will happen either way, but I would prefer you accept it willingly."

"Never!"

He shrugged. "Very well. Now, please. Put down that thing and come along."

She set her jaw. "Come and take it from me if you're so strong." But somehow her tongue had gotten very thick and the words came out all garbled.

He cocked his head at her, frowning. "I beg your pardon?"

It seemed he spoke from afar. His face grew blurry, and his eyes gleamed like blue diamonds. "What's happening to me?" But again her tongue betrayed her and the words sounded more like a slurred moan. Then her knees gave way and she collapsed to the floor, bewildered. Somehow he'd drugged her. *Was it in the mousse?* It had to be, since she'd ingested nothing else. But why was it only affecting her now?

Then the room swooped into darkness, and she ceased to think of anything at all.

# Chapter Forty-Three

## New Eden

"Trust no one but God . . . ? What are you doing to me here, Rudy?"

Zowan heard the muttered words clearly as he entered the back room of the Enclave's library. Cameron still sat where Zowan had left him at one of the library's ten computer stations. He'd given no sign of having heard Zowan's approach, and his words were clearly not directed to him; nevertheless, they stoked his already high level of anxiety. It had been hard enough following the man back into the Enclave after he'd spent the day dreaming of freedom. Now that he was back, the last thing he wanted was to find out he'd risked everything to follow someone who didn't know what he was doing.

"Who's Rudy?"

Cameron didn't seem startled by Zowan's words so maybe he'd noticed more than Zowan gave him credit for. "The man who got me into this. The man who got you into this, as well, I guess. Did you find Parthos?"

"No." Zowan had just run down to the sleepcell block, hoping to find him. "I was afraid to awaken Erebos to ask him, since . . . Well, he's been a friend for years, but you never know." Zowan laid the funny retractable "pen" Cameron had loaned him to unlock and lock the library doors on the table beside him.

"No, you certainly don't," Cam agreed sourly, his eyes glued to the screen. When Zowan had left him, Cameron had been studying graphics of New Eden's layout divided into sections of blue, green, orange, and red. The blue and green areas, Zowan had recognized as familiar haunts, but he'd not even known the deeper orange and red ones existed.

Now Cameron was flipping through more detailed floor plans that, from the small red square at the top of each map, Zowan surmised lay within the red sector. He was pretty sure Cameron was searching for the arks—those things he'd said Father possessed that could destroy them all—and felt again the jolt of guilt and fear to think he might be betraying the Enclave's greatest treasures to an enemy.

Then he wondered why he cared, given what Father and the Elders had done to him and his friends. Given all the lies and arbitrary rules and unreasonable punishments. He well remembered Cameron's horror when he'd first learned about life in the Enclave, as well as his talk of topside authorities imprisoning the Elders for what they'd done. No, Cameron was more friend than any of the Elders ever had been.

Then there was the part about I Am, as well. The LORD God . . . When he'd first met Cameron, he'd thought the man would answer all his questions. Instead, he'd only raised new ones, and offered explanations that were . . . mind-boggling. The seed of the woman was someone named Jesus whose father was God? Someone who'd allowed humans to kill Him so people could be forgiven? He was still struggling to grasp the fact that the God of Genesis really did exist and really did speak to people, let alone things like that.

The screen changed to something completely illegible—not words but black fuzzy bars of different widths arranged in vertical columns. The small box at the bottom of each screen described the graphic in words Zowan didn't know. But though they were gibberish to him, Cameron clearly seemed to understand them.

Rather like Genesis, it seemed. Everything was a symbol for something. The serpent's seed bit the heel of the woman's seed. Was that when Jesus let them kill Him? Having one's head crushed seemed a more appropriate analogy for killing, though, so again Zowan didn't understand.

He didn't know why all of this mattered so much to him, but it did. He couldn't stop thinking about it, driven somehow to unravel all these mysteries.

Cameron had connected a small rectangular device with screen and keyboard to the computer with a short cable, apparently transferring the information on the computer to the device.

"How does it look from outside?" he asked Zowan. "Do you think anyone walking by will see us?"

"We're safe, unless they come in, but that's still a few hours off."

Cameron clicked a few keys, and a small window appeared on the screen, the blue progress bar slowly inching across the bar window. "Good. Because we're going to be here for a bit."

He sat back in the chair and turned to Zowan. "Heard anything from Andros again?"

"No. Though I do keep hearing someone whispering behind me, when there's no one there."

Cameron nodded as if this was expected.

"What are they?" Zowan asked.

"The creatures in your seed arks. They want us to come and let them out."

*Creatures in the seed arks?* Zowan stared at him, trying to make sense of his words. "Cameron, why does everything that comes out of your mouth have to be so . . . difficult? It's like . . ."

"I come from a different world? Because I do. Swain and his people have lied to you all your life to keep you here. Why wouldn't the truth seem strange and odd and wrong? Why wouldn't it be hard to believe, when compared to the lie you've grown up with?"

"I guess it would be." Zowan rubbed his finger along the table's edge. "So, assuming you're telling me the truth, what kind of creatures are these?"

Cameron leaned back and folded his arms. "First know this: there are no seeds in those arks. And no plans for reseeding the earth—which, as you've seen for yourself, has no need of it. I've seen these arks before—in a tomb on the other side of the world. Some people think they are special containers for the dead. Except that what's inside isn't dead. Others believe they are protective containers whose passengers should long ago have been freed."

"Which is why Andros—or whoever he is—is trying to get me to come down and let him out."

Cam nodded. "But even he doesn't know how you're supposed to accomplish that."

"*Zowan? Why aren't you down here yet? I'm hungry. I want out of here. You owe me.*"

"He's awake again," Zowan said.

"Yes. I can hear them, too. I think talking about them draws their attention. It's better to focus on something else."

They fell silent, the conversation momentarily derailed. Then Zowan went back to their earlier discussion. "Okay, then—tell me about Jesus and why the people killed Him. 'Crucified Him,' you said."

Cam's brows flew up. "You want even more difficult and unbeliev-able thoughts to wrestle with?" he asked. But he seemed pleased.

"I may not understand all that you're saying," Zowan explained, "but I know this part is truth. And the more I hear of it, the more I know I'll understand."

Cameron unfolded his arms, regarding him with a quizzical look. "You are very wise for someone who has been hidden away, Zowan. You do realize, though, that understanding is not going to come in one or two conversations. The pursuit of God is a lifelong process."

"Yes. But you said we'd be here for a while. And you did promise me a better explanation than what you gave this morning."

Cameron grinned. "I've been thinking about that conversation all day," he confessed. "Trying to figure out a better way of saying it . . ."

Andros insisted again that Zowan free him. Zowan ignored him.

"We're all born disobedient to God," said Cameron. "Unrighteous. And God can't have a relationship with us when we're like that. But *we* can't do anything about it because righteousness demands perfection, and we're not. We're lost, helpless, and condemned to go to a terrible place forever when we die. A place without God. We need someone to rescue us. So God sent His son."

"Jesus," Zowan supplied. Andros, he noted, had completely withdrawn.

Cam nodded, and went on to explain more of who Jesus was, and as they talked, the blue bar on the computer screen crawled slowly across its slot until it reached the end. Yet still they talked.

And sometime in all that, Zowan believed in the seed of the woman, the son of I Am, this Jesus who wasn't just a man but God, too . . . though that part he struggled still to comprehend. It didn't matter. He wanted to know this God who had personally called him out of darkness, who was willing to put aside the trappings of His deity and take on a man's form, to die on a Roman cross in humiliation and suffering for the sake of His creatures—for the sake of Zowan himself—so that they could come to know Him.

When he told Cameron what he had done, the man sat in his chair as if stunned, staring at him without expression, though for a moment it seemed that tears glistened in his eyes.

Then the muffled sound of voices and the not-so-distant clatter of the library's front doors being unlocked jerked them back to the reality of their present situation. Hurriedly Cameron removed the cable and his little device, tossed them and the special pen into the duffle bag at his feet, then closed down the program. Meanwhile Zowan stole into the adjoining room and across it to see who was at the door. He was horrified to see four bald, black-robed Enforcers already striding into the library's main entrance area.

He hurried back to find Cameron stowing the duffle under the far back corner of the table. "Enforcers!" he whispered. "Four of them. I don't know why they're here. It's still early."

He came over to where Cameron was backing out from under the table. "We're trapped. There's no way out from here."

"Yes, there is." Cameron stood, his head lamp back on his head. In his hands he held a small gray canister with a ring on it and an extra head lamp, which he gave to Zowan. As Zowan slid on the lamp, an Enforcer came through the door.

"They're in here!" the man cried.

Jerking the ring off the gray canister, Cam tossed it toward him, gray smoke spewing out of it.

Zowan was standing flat-footed when Cameron pulled him away and into the dead-end sorting room behind the one they had been working in. Only it wasn't a dead end. At the room's far end, a narrow stairway ascended to a door with a palm-panel lock that must lead into . . .

"The Wives' Residence!" Zowan exclaimed. "We can't go in there."

"Hit the panel, Zowan," Cam commanded him.

He did so, and with a series of loud clacks the door opened into darkness. Switching on their head lamps, they raced into a small supply closet, mops and brooms leaning in a tangle against the wall. In passing, Zowan hit one with his foot. It fell to the floor with a crack, but by then he was following Cam into a larger room where girls slept on quilted pallets, already stirring from their slumber at the sounds of the unlocking door.

As the beam of Zowan's head lamp fell on one, she screamed and lurched away from him into the wall. Startled, he stepped back himself and bumped into a wooden screen, which fell over with a crash.

By now almost all the girls were awake, some screaming, others staring about in confusion. As he turned to follow Cam through the room, Zowan's light fell on another girl—brown eyes wide in a heart-shaped face framed by rivers of unbraided red-brown hair—and he stopped in his tracks. "Terra?"

She put up an arm to shield her eyes, squinting at him. "Zowan?!"

Suddenly Cam was back, grabbing Zowan by the arm and dragging him onward as the Enforcers pounded up the stairs in their wake. "You can't help her now," he hissed as he led through the mazelike chambers of the Wives' Residence. He must have seen this when he was looking at the graphics, must have planned out the route in advance, judging from his complete lack of hesitation as they went forward.

Finally they emerged into a wide, low-ceilinged chamber lined with bookshelves and wooden screens and furnished with large floor pillows. Looms and bowls of wool and yarn stood about on a thick, intricately patterned rug, and a huge computer screen hung on one wall. Several more girls slept on quilted pallets, but Cameron ignored them, making straight for the pair of wooden doors on the far side. They were almost to them when the doors crashed open, the lights went on, and three more Enforcers burst through, cutting them off.

"I thought God would help us," Zowan murmured in horror.

"It's all right," Cameron told him. "God decreed this long ago. For our best."

"I don't see how this can be for our best."

Wives stood in the openings between the wooden screens and bookshelves, peering at them curiously, their long hair unbound as was never allowed in public. They all wore sheer, floor-length sleeping gowns, many of them with hugely swollen bellies. Zowan looked at them in added horror, wondering what Father had done to them, and fearing he would do it to Terra, as well. The cry of a small child threaded through the sudden silence as a fourth Enforcer stepped between the others to face them.

"He looks kinda like you," Cameron remarked to Zowan.

"He is my gene brother Gaias."

Cameron glanced at him in surprise. "You know what genes are?"

"I know they're what make us look alike."

A sweeping glare and a flick of Gaias's bald head sent the women in the doorways scurrying back into their beds and those on the floor burrowing into their bedding.

Gaias strode up to Cameron, looking him up and down, while Cameron stared in openmouthed revulsion at the oculus on his forehead. "Take this one to Father," Gaias said to his subordinates. Two of them seized Cam from either side and led him out of the room.

Gaias had already turned his attention to Zowan. "So, little brother. I hear you've been up to the surface—not once, not twice, but *three* times. And brought back some of the vermin there with you."

He'd asked no question, so Zowan said nothing.

"They are evil and corrupt up there. Poisoning their world, as they poison themselves. You have profaned the purity of our enclave by bringing him here. He will have to die, of course."

Zowan swallowed hard. He'd been so concerned for his own safety, he'd not even considered Cameron's.

"Where is Parthos?" Gaias demanded. "Did you leave him up there?" The question was so out of the blue, it drew Zowan's gaze back to him in puzzlement.

"Parthos?"

Gaias was implacable. "I know he went with you. Him and that little vixen Terra . . . ah, but we have her. Oh, she was sweet in my arms . . . her flesh so soft and full, and the way she moved under me . . ."

"Shut up!" Zowan burst out, shocked at his sudden aggression. "If she was moving, it was only in her struggle to escape you."

Gaias drew back in the face of Zowan's sudden ferocity. He stood rigidly, as if fighting some deep emotion, the surface of his third eye rippling like a larvae struggling to burst free of its cocoon. For a moment Zowan thought his brother would attack him. Instead, Gaias relaxed and chuckled aloud. He said something more, but his voice was eclipsed by another's:

"*You must come down now.*" Andros had awakened. "*Kill him and be done with it. Then come and free me.*" The words carried with them a vision of his brother with the eye put out and blood streaming from his slit throat.

"Answer me, Zowan!" Gaias's barked command shattered the gruesome image as he shook Zowan by the arm. For the first time Zowan realized his brother had gotten bigger than he was.

"Answer me!" Gaias shook him again, hard, and Zowan struggled to recall what he'd asked.

"Where is Parthos?" Gaias repeated.

"I don't know." But he suddenly realized what Gaias was asking him, and a perverse joy swelled up. Parthos had gotten away!

He clamped down on his excitement, watching Gaias from the corner of his eye as the oculus swiveled in its socket, gleaming in the pale light from the ceiling lamps as it focused and refocused upon him.

"You're lying," Gaias said finally, his tone one of astonishment mixed with anger. "You're lying to me. Did you think I wouldn't know?"

Zowan said nothing, shocked that Gaias would say such a thing, and almost wanting to laugh. Neos was right: they really *couldn't* read his mind.

"Did you think because I'm new that I wouldn't be able to tell?"

Zowan had no answer for him.

"Where is he?"

"I don't know."

Gaias drew up, scowling at him. "Very well, then. Let us see how the Enclave judges your treachery."

He glanced over Zowan's shoulder to the Enforcers behind him, and they came forward to seize Zowan's arms, dragging him off to his inevitable meeting with the Cube.

# Chapter Forty-Four

## New Eden

Lacey awoke from a nightmare wherein Erik chased her through Swain's penthouse with a baseball bat while people chanted a weird version of the Lord's Prayer in the background.

She lay on a thick, quilted pad in a long, low-ceilinged room. The weak light filtering through a screened opening at the chamber's far end showed ranks of similar pads—all unoccupied—laid out in two parallel rows down the room's length, with a walkway between. An annoying, wheedling music emanated from somewhere outside the opening. From the aroma of coffee and toast she guessed it was morning.

Sorting through her memories, she tried to figure out where she was. . . . The party, the moments with Cam in the garden, the standoff with Swain in his loft-museum. *Ah, that's right.* . . . Swain had drugged her, probably with a tranquilizer dart to the back of her neck as she'd fled. That was no doubt why she felt so muzzy-headed and jittery.

The wheedling music faded to silence, and a man spoke briefly in the other room, something about a trial and that everyone was to meet someplace in two hours. Then he, too, fell silent. After a moment she heard sounds of people stirring and women's voices.

"Well," one said, "I guess that explains last night."

"Except he only mentioned Zowan being on trial. What about the other fellow?"

"I heard they took him to Parker himself."

"I've never seen the other man down there before."

"He was cute, though, wasn't he?"

Lacey sat up to find she no longer wore the blue cocktail dress but rather a set of white cotton pajamas with red and brown embroidery down the front. Pushing herself to her feet, she shuffled unsteadily to the screen and peered around it. A group of young women sat about the room on a thick Persian rug, all dressed in similar pajamas, though in different colors and styles. Several sat tailor-style on pillows and worked at wooden looms. Others spun thread from baskets of wool using ancient drop spindles, while still others embroidered or worked at needlepoint in their laps. A few—hugely pregnant—merely reclined on the large pillows, chatting.

Mirrored ceiling fixtures cast a diffuse light upon the room, where bookshelves stood here and there against three walls, and a large-screen television hung on the wall to Lacey's right, flanked by potted Kentia palms. To the left, a series of carved wooden screens filtered light from what seemed to be a long window on its far side.

The dark-haired girl nearest Lacey stopped her spinning to watch the newcomer closely. She looked familiar.

"Where am I?" Lacey asked her.

"You're in the Residence of Father's Wives."

Father's wives . . . Lacey's eyes fell to the girl's pregnant abdomen, swelling like a basketball beneath her billowy tunic. A quick scan confirmed that nearly every woman in the room was in some stage of pregnancy. Memory returned in a rush: Swain's palm coming to rest on her belly. *Most of all I want this. . . ."*

She'd just spent who-knew-how-many hours unconscious during which they could have done anything to her. Depending on where she was in her monthly cycle, the implantation of an embryo was an easy outpatient procedure accomplished in twenty minutes at most. She could, right now, be pregnant with one of his "gods." Maybe that was why she felt so strange.

Her knees buckled, and she sagged to the floor. *This can't be happening.*

The girl set her spindles aside and came to sit beside her. "I know it's a bit of a shock, but . . . you'll be fine. Really."

"*Fine?!* I've been drugged, kidnapped, am being held here against my will, and you say I'm going to be *fine?* The only way I'll be fine is when he lets me out of here."

The girl looked at her with sympathetic brown eyes. "It's not that bad a life, really. Our needs are more than met, our work is easy, we have fun, and the food is great. They have a great spa, too."

Lacey stared at her as if she were out of her mind. Maybe she was. Maybe that was the only way to survive the ordeal. To live in self-delusion, telling herself everything was great while ignoring reality.

One of the girls pressed a button in the wall near the TV screen, and soft music filled the silent room. The others were all concentrating on whatever work they had, avoiding Lacey's gaze. She returned her attention to the first girl and suddenly realized she'd seen her in the articles about the young women who had disappeared from Kendall-Jakes. "You're Andrea Stopping!" she cried.

The girl smiled sadly. "Sorry," she said. "My name is Isis."

"No, you're Andrea. I'm sure of it. I read all about your disappearance. They said you were depressed and went out to kill yourself."

Now the oldest of the women, almost to term from the look of her giant belly, spoke. "Welcome to Paradise, Eve," she said warmly, as if Lacey had said nothing at all. "We are so glad you have joined us. I am Theia, wife mother. I have borne precious fruit ten times."

Lacey looked over her shoulder to see this Eve, but no one was there. *Is she talking to me?* She turned back to find all the girls watching her. "My name's not Eve," she said.

"It is now, dear," Theia informed her with a smile. "That is the name your husband gave you when you became his wife."

"My *husband*?! I have no husband, and my name is Lacey McHenry. Not *Eve*."

And just like that the women's pleasant expressions turned disapproving, and except for Isis, all turned away from her very deliberately and went back to their work. After a few moments they resumed their conversation, discussing why those two young men had burst into their chambers last night.

Lacey heard them as through thick wool, words she sensed should have meaning, but did not. Her ears began to roar.

Andrea-Isis gave her shoulder a squeeze. "It's hard at first," she whispered. "But it's better if you don't fight it. In the end, Parker's will is done, regardless." She glanced aside, then added, "And it really is an honor to be part of what he's doing."

Lacey leaned away from her, aghast. How could she say such a thing? Accepting slavery as if it were an honor? They *were* insane. Living in denial and sublimation while—

Her thoughts drew up short as she recalled her own forays into that territory. She could have left the Institute right at the start, right when she'd realized they were impugning her mental stability with that false accusation of stress-induced hallucination. Cam had told her to leave, but she hadn't. Even after she knew Swain had lied to her, she stayed on, wanting all the things he'd offered and hoping he was telling the truth.

By the time she'd come around to helping Cam, it had already been too late. But still, even if her own delusions had landed her here, she didn't have to accept it. Didn't have to believe it was "fine" and "an honor," when it was neither. Andrea-Isis had gone back to her spindles, her expression thoughtful, even pensive. . . . Then again, Lacey thought, maybe she didn't believe it, either. Maybe she'd just said what was needed to avoid punishment.

Lacey's hands slid over her abdomen, and she felt a sudden frantic nausea pound at her as she remembered—he'd put something inside her. Some horrid monster, some half-breed mixed with who knew what.

Suddenly it all overwhelmed her. Everything she'd been through— all the deception and empty promises, the perpetual fear and imbalance, the false hopes, the wretched disappointment . . .

She thought of those precious moments with Cam in the garden . . . which Swain had watched and listened to and later profaned in his own disgusting attempt to seduce her. He'd known Cam was going into the Enclave and, given what he must've heard Cam tell her in the garden, probably had a good idea when and where. He had to have been waiting. Which meant Cam could very well be dead.

That realization opened floodgates of emotion that had so far been held at bay by shock and disbelief. She began to weep. From loss and fear and bitter regret, from frustration and horror at her stupidity, from loneliness that only seemed to grow worse—harsh, raw, wretched sobs that would have embarrassed her under any other circumstances. Isis came and wrapped her arms about her, letting her wail until her nose ran and her throat ached and the wild sobbing gradually subsided into quiet weeping, and then just quietness itself. Isis continued to hold her for a time, then gently released her and offered her a glass of water.

Lacey took it with suspicion at first, then realized it was pointless. They controlled everything in her environment. If they wanted to drug her again, they would. What could she do to stop it?

So she drank the water, and Isis handed the empty glass off to the girl who'd apparently brought it in the first place.

"It's the hormones they gave you that are making it seem so bad," Isis said. "To prepare your womb." She paused. "Not that it still wouldn't be hard."

Lacey looked up at her sharply. "Prepare my womb? You mean I'm not—?"

"Not yet." Andrea-Isis smiled.

"Isis, dear," said Theia, "would you come help me with this?"

Andrea-Isis gave Lacey's shoulder another squeeze and got up to obey. As the woman left, Lacey felt as if a huge weight had lifted off her. She wasn't pregnant. Not yet. *Oh, thank you, Lord! Thank you!*

Though no one would even look at her anymore, much less speak, she was allowed to roam freely through the Residence, and did so, hoping to find some means of escape. In addition to the communal sleeping room where she'd first awakened, there were private chambers with closing doors and small bassinets for the newborns, one of which was occupied. Lacey stared at the baby for a long time, comforted that it at least looked normal. In addition to sleeping rooms and a large bathroom area, there was also a library, a music room with a piano, a spa and workout area, a craft room, and a kitchen with an herb garden under lights.

Except for the new mothers' rooms, none of the chambers had doors, and many were simply a result of strategic placement of the ubiquitous carved wooden screens. She found the walking gallery last, stretching along behind the series of screens that separated it from the main room. Its facing wall was a long plate-glass window overlooking a miniature mall, protected by floor-to-ceiling iron scrollwork.

The walking gallery was deserted except for a girl with kinky, waist-length red-brown hair standing at the far end near a recirculating fountain made of three bronze bowls. Her attention fixed on something in the mall, she seemed unaware of Lacey's entrance.

Which was just as well. She probably wouldn't talk anyway.

Lacey stared down at the island of palms and shrubs and water-ways running the length of the tiny mall, where now and then indi-viduals entered and departed. After all the weeping and exploring and the dashing of her hopes for escape, a tide of despair rolled over her. Who was she kidding to think she'd get away? Surely Andrea had fought at first. And here she was, still trapped, still bound to Parker's will.

Another bout of weeping seized her, but it was a quiet flow this time.

Presently a female voice sounded through the speakers out in the mall, announcing that the trial of someone named Zowan would begin in ten minutes and all were to report to the Justorium to render justice. She recognized the name from the women's earlier conversation and wondered what was about to occur.

Moments later a sudden rasping sob drew her attention to the girl at the gallery's end. She stood with one hand flat against the window, tear tracks glittering down her cheeks. When no one appeared from the other room to comfort her, Lacey drifted toward her, realizing only then how strongly she resembled Genevieve Viascola. Was she one of the clones in Cam's picture? The age was right. And even if there might be numerous clones of Genevieve, they wouldn't likely all be the same age. Cam had taken his picture on the surface, yes, but that was yesterday. And Swain would have gleaned information about the runaways from that fateful garden conversation, as well. . . .

Curiosity, guilt, and compassion pushed her down the walkway to the girl's side, where they stood together in silence for a time. Finally Lacey asked, "This Zowan is special to you?"

At first the young Genevieve clone ignored her. But then, just when Lacey was despairing of getting an answer, she said, "We grew up together. We ran away together." She wiped her tears away. "They will kill him now."

"Is that what they do in the Justorium?"

The girl looked at her, startled. "You don't know what is done in the Justorium?"

"No." Lacey marveled at how much she looked like Genevieve.

"You must be from the surface, too, then," the girl said. "Did you come with Cameron?"

"You *are* the girl he met yesterday!" Lacey exclaimed. Then she glanced toward the main room and lowered her voice. "I saw the picture he took of you."

"We should have stayed up there," the girl said. "Now Zowan will be killed, and I don't know what's happened to Parthos. They probably took him to the secret lab."

"Why did you come back?"

"Because Cameron told us we couldn't survive up there. That the Enforcers would come after us. That Father controls the ground there as he controls everything here."

Lacey nodded. "He was right. But he came back last night to get you out."

The girl already knew of that and told her how the Enforcers had cut off Cam and Zowan's escape there in the main room. Cam had been brought directly to Father. "I heard them give the order," the girl said. "Since he's from the surface, they can't very well try him in the Justorium, so I suppose Father will bring him down to the secret lab and do . . . things to him."

"What kind of things?"

"I don't know. Change him like he changed Neos."

Lacey hadn't thought her fear and horror could get any worse, but she was wrong. Cam, changed like Neos had been changed?

"Terra," a voice intruded. "Come away from there. It's time for Zowan's trial."

"I don't want to see the trial."

"Terra . . ."

Wordlessly the girl pushed away from the window and disappeared through the opening in the scrollwork screen, leaving Lacey to stare down at the little mall. *Oh, God, please! I may not have been faithful to you, but he has. How can you do this to him? Please protect him!*

# Chapter Forty-Five

## New Eden

After he and Zowan had been captured by the Enforcers, Cam was taken immediately from the Wives' Residence to an adjoining apartment where Swain was eating breakfast. He must have known they were coming, for he received their entrance without even a glance, finishing up his bacon and eggs while Cam and his Enforcer guards stood waiting. Finally, his plate cleaned, Swain patted his mouth with his napkin, then stood and came around the table to backhand Cam with such force he saw stars.

"I told you to stay away from her," Swain growled. "To keep your hands off her!"

Cam shook his head to clear the dizziness, tasting blood from the cut his teeth had sliced along the inside of his lip. *He knows about our meeting in the garden!* The bug hadn't been in the jewelry, after all. In the dress, perhaps? In the surrounding foliage? From the intensity of Swain's reaction and the words he'd used, Cam thought it likely he'd *seen* that meeting as well as heard it.

And if Swain knew about the meeting, he would have known what they were planning, would've moved to cut it off. *But Rudy called, said they were away.* Had Swain intercepted them after the call? Or had Rudy lied? Was that what he'd meant about the mission unraveling? Lacey might never have made it out of the garden.

Which meant that slender girl on the mat beside Terra back in the Wives' Residence, the one who hadn't awakened despite the crashing of the fallen screen and the screaming of the other girls, the one who had looked for a heart-stopping moment *exactly* like Lacey, even as he'd assured himself it couldn't be . . . really *was* her.

Swain watched him with narrowed, glittering eyes. "She's mine now, of course. I took her last night in my penthouse. She was quite willing."

"I don't believe you."

Swain chuckled. "Of course not." His amusement faded. "You can still have her, you know. You have only to agree to my terms."

"I'm not going to renounce my faith, sir."

Swain regarded him without expression, his eyes hard as glass, waiting, perhaps, for Cam to change his mind. Finally he blew out a breath and leaned back. "You mean to tell me your religious addiction is more important to you than this girl who could well turn out to be the love of your life?"

It was all a lie. Cam knew he would never give Lacey to him. "Why have you brought me here, sir?"

"You were the one who trespassed onto my property, Cameron. I'll ask the questions, if you don't mind. You're lucky to be alive. If it were up to Fred and Genevieve, you'd be having conversations with Manny right now. Oh, wait . . ." He frowned. "I'm not sure Manny's *saved*, so maybe not."

A land-line phone on the wall nearby beeped, drawing his attention. He stepped over to glance at the ID screen, then grimaced and answered the call. "Yes . . . well, he'll have to decide: either he wears the blindfold or he doesn't go down." Swain listened a moment, then sighed. "Oh, all right. I'll come and speak to him." He hung up and gestured toward Cam. "Take him down to EDL," he said to the Enforcers. And then to Cam, "I'll be along in a bit."

The Enforcers led Cam downward along a network of passages to a heavy door with a wide orange bar and multiple locks. Opening it, they guided him ahead of them into the corridor beyond, then shut and locked the door behind him. After a few moments the door ahead opened, and a new pair of guards awaited him whose black uniforms bore the golden ziggurat insignia and whose foreheads did not have extra eyes in them.

They took him down several corridors lined with small rooms whose observation windows showed many who did though. Nor were the oculi the only bizarre modifications. Cam saw a child with a chest of golden scales; another with a snout full of dog's teeth; several young men sporting crests of golden quills rising from the top of their heads and running down the backs of their necks; a girl covered by a thin layer of pale, gauzelike hair; boys with great knobs where their ears should have been.

Finally, having come to the end of one such corridor, his escorts unlocked the last door and ushered him into the cell beyond. Like the others, it was a small, white-walled room with a bed, a table and chair, and a mirror by the door, which was, of course, the observation window for those in the hall.

He had tried not to look too closely—had tried not to look at all, actually—for it was pretty obvious this was the secret lab Zowan and his friends had fretted about. The one from which Neos had evidently escaped.

His fear for Lacey and Zowan had turned to fear for himself. Dying was one thing. Being experimented on was something else entirely. He thought of Neos and realized that at one time the young man must have looked just like Zowan. Until Swain had begun his nightmarish modifications.

Cam sank down on the bed, trembling, light-headed, struggling to breathe. He felt completely blindsided, his confidence in God's presence and protection shredded.

*"Trust no one but God. Do what you think best. . . ."*

What he thought best? Right now that was finding a way to get himself and Lacey out of here. Zowan, too, if he could.

His own words returned to mock him: *"It's all right. God decreed this long ago. For our best . . ."*

*For our best.* A stream of horrific images passed before his eyes, and the panic swelled. He shot off the bed and began to pace, praying for help as he did. *Father, I know this fear is wrong, but I am weak. I do believe. But help my unbelief. . . .*

The thought came then that all these images were of things that might never happen, things that might not be remotely part of God's plan for his life. He knew better than to indulge in such foolishness. Let whatever was decreed to happen, happen, and *then* deal with it.

But just determining to cut off the thoughts wouldn't keep them away. He had to put something stronger in their place. He had to turn his thoughts to who God was. To just how much God loved him. Not the world, not everyone else, but Cameron Reinhardt, individually and personally. *You were the joy Jesus contemplated while He endured the cross,* he reminded himself. *He did it for you, and whatever you face here will be nothing compared to that. Besides, Swain can't do a thing to you without His approval.*

*The question is, do you really believe that?*

He drew a deep breath, and decided that yes, he did believe it. And he would live in it. *Even here. Even now.* For it was precisely when one couldn't see past the desolation of a situation that truth was most needed—and when a man's trust most pleased his maker. It was just that everything about God was always invisible. . . . *It would be nice, Father, to have an occasional voice or something tangible.*

*And bringing you here to meet Zowan, watching him believe in my Son, was not tangible enough for you?*

Cam snorted softly. *Okay, Lord. You win.* He shook his head, still marveling over Zowan. *What would you have me do now?*

*Stand still and watch me deliver you.*

Of course he would be told to wait. Of course. With no clock, no window, no sun, no way to measure the passage of time, and nothing whatever to occupy his besieged mind. To distract himself, he turned to the challenge of reciting all the doctrines and verses he could remember.

He was lying on the bed reciting Isaiah 46 when the door opened and Swain walked in. Immediately Cam sat up and swung his feet to the floor.

"Well," said Swain, pulling the chair away from the desk and turning it around so he could sit facing Cam, "what do you think?"

"About what?"

Swain's blond brows flew up in surprise. "After all you've seen, you have nothing to say to me? No word of congratulations for my accomplishments?"

"All I've seen? I've seen slavery. I've seen people deceived and manipulated. I've seen the human body deformed and distorted in horrifying ways."

"Horrifying!" Swain repeated in a tone of surprised amusement. "You've just witnessed a phenomenal range of genetic manipulation and expertise, and all you can say is you're horrified?" He shook his head. "Well, rest assured, not all see them as horrifying. Including the subjects themselves. My Enforcers, for example, consider their 'deformity' to be a badge of honor."

"Then they are even crazier than you are."

"Don't you even *want* to know how I've done it all?"

"I know it has to be transgenic. I suspect it's something you've derived from that Nephilim you've got hidden away somewhere, but I seriously doubt you have any real idea what you're doing, because the results far exceed existing genetic theory or technology. Have you even mapped the genome of that thing yet?"

Swain ignored his question. "You've always known I'm cutting edge, son."

"This is beyond cutting edge. This is insanity."

"I have you imprisoned, Cameron. I have your friends imprisoned likewise. On threat of death or . . . 'deformity.' I would show a little more respect if I were you."

Cam grimaced and drew a breath to calm himself. "I meant no disrespect, sir." He paused. "*Do* you know what you're doing?"

"Of course I do." Swain settled back into the chair, launching into what Cam knew was one of his favorite activities—lecturing about his own work and discoveries.

The generation of the third eye, or oculus, as he called it, took approximately a year to complete. First the subject received through inhalation the transforming genetic material via a retrovirus targeted to the skull's frontal sinus area. Subsequent injections of a mineral-leeching compound into a small spot in the skull's frontal plate weakened the bone enough to allow the newly forming oculus to create and seat itself into a socket, while simultaneously developing muscle tissue and lid membranes.

Swain was disappointed that, though the oculus exhibited a degree of involuntary movement, as yet the third eye was completely useless— beyond serving as a badge of honor and method of intimidating the general population of the Enclave . . . another accomplishment Swain was unduly proud of. "As a social experiment, it is the largest, the longest, and the most comprehensive ever carried out," he observed. "It has proven all my theories correct."

Cam did not ask him what theories those were. He had a good idea, and they'd been over it before. Nor did he think Swain would welcome his observations that in his experiment, he'd also had people breaking out of the mold, asking too many questions, trying to escape, and even believing in Christ.

Thankfully Swain returned soon enough to the eye, frustrated they'd not been able to induce the generation of an optic nerve to serve it. Of course, he added, it was possible the oculus was not an organ of vision at all, but something else entirely. They would find out for sure when the most recent subject was dissected.

"So Neos is dead, then," Cam observed bleakly.

Swain looked at him in momentary surprise. Understanding cleared his brow. "That's right. Zowan would've told you his name. No, Neos is not dead. We'll keep him alive as long as we can. He's turned out to be an incredibly valuable subject, and one whose development has astonished us all. Alone of all our subjects, his oculus does seem to have developed a function."

He seemed unaware that everything he said confirmed Cam's worst suspicion. That they'd apparently acquired a sequence of genes that would generate the third eye with no real idea what those genes did. Or even what the third eye did. Unless Swain was holding back— entirely likely.

*"Cameron! You must come now!"* His thought had drawn the imprisoned Nephilim's attention. Its voice was distinctly angry, even desperate, as it had not been previously. Suddenly a succession of bizarre images flashed through his mind—the gleam of a knife blade, a man's

bloody carcass, tongues of fire licking upward as someone screamed in a distant hallway.

A sharp pain in his hand drew him out of the vision. He looked down to see that he had pulled up an edge of the glue-sutured slice on his palm, enough that it welled a single bright drop of red blood. A drop that seized and held his gaze with inexplicable power.

The compulsion to stare at it waned as quickly as it had come, and he looked up to find Swain staring at the blood, as well. As if he'd been every bit as caught up in it.

Cam shook off the incident and returned to their earlier subject. "I know about Ecuador," he said. "How your people released one of the Nephilim—"

"Nephilim?" Swain's gaze snapped up to his. "From Genesis six? Is that what you're calling them?"

"It's what they are."

"I thought the Nephilim all drowned in the Great Flood."

"It says, 'The Nephilim were on the earth in those days *and also afterward. . . .*'"

"And, of course, that couldn't be an error."

"When the Jews spied out the Promised Land they found the sons of Anak there, who were part of the Nephilim. Where did they come from if all the Nephilim drowned?"

"Perhaps the sons of God made new ones."

"Or perhaps they made themselves their own individual versions of the ark, in which they planned to ride out the catastrophe should it occur."

"I seriously doubt those in antediluvian times could have produced something as technologically advanced as one of those pods, Dr. Reinhardt."

"Why not? We have no idea what the level of the antediluvians' technology was. Even if it rivaled ours, it would have been completely destroyed in the geologic upheaval that accompanied the Flood. I think it was considerably higher than we give them credit for—a theory the nature of these pods supports."

Swain grimaced at him. "I think you're groping after straws."

"Well, whatever these things are, I know you let one out in Ecuador and it destroyed your entire facility. I also know you went back and got the thing after it began to rampage the countryside. So you know what it can do."

"An earthquake destroyed that facility."

Cam stared at him without argument.

Swain stood up. "But you're right. Our source for the transgenic DNA we've been using is indeed the remains of the first Visitor we released."

They'd frozen him in liquid nitrogen in the same lab where they were keeping the sarcs. Using a personal DVD player, Swain showed him video and stills of the capture operation and of the unconscious specimen wrapped in some sort of white webbing. Surprisingly, it was a very strong Taser that had taken the creature down. Bullets had simply bounced off.

"As you can see," Swain said, "the creatures within those pods are very like humans."

Except for being twenty feet tall, and the thing had the same large brow, crest of golden quills, and third eye that had been slowly manifesting in Neos.

"Their genes are significantly more robust and resilient than human genes, however," Swain continued, "and are consistently dominant when paired with human counterparts. Moreover, the changes they elicit have been exceptionally long-lived. In fact, we've not one instance of regression to the original form."

"What about deaths?" Cam asked pointedly.

Swain shrugged. "Morbidity rates have been high, yes. That's why we need to release one of them. We need to see exactly what it is we're working with."

"I don't know why you'd want to work with it at all. Where's the good in any of it?"

"They haven't died, Cameron. After four thousand years, they're still alive."

Cam sighed his exasperation.

"Yes, I know they're unstable and prone to violent outbursts. But I believe that's a temporary reaction to their long imprisonment and slow starvation. Thus we've devised a system to restrain them using the same material we employed to capture the one in Ecuador. It should hold them still long enough for us to sedate them and feed them for a while by IV."

"How can you possibly know what will sedate them—if anything? Or how much of a dose you'd need? They may be like men, but they're *not* men, and—"

"Well, we'll just have to work all that out. If we lose a few in the process, so be it. I have five of them on-site, so we have room to experiment."

"It's not them you should be concerned about losing," Cam said. "It's everything else."

Swain smiled tolerantly as he pulled open the door. "Shall we go down and see them?"

# Chapter Forty-Six

## New Eden

At last Zowan understood why Andros had been so cowed. Even having been to the surface and knowing the truth, it was hard to hold on to his convictions when standing on the stage of the red-lit Justorium pinioned between two Enforcers—one of them his brother Gaias. He was glad they were holding him, because his knees felt like jelly.

Irrationally he kept searching the upper tiers of the women's section for Terra, even though he knew she was in the Wives' Residence. Maybe it was because he still couldn't believe he'd seen her there—or didn't want to believe it.

He dropped his attention to the High Elders seated in the first three rows before him. He could see the face of nearly every one of them—Elder Horus, Elder Zayus, Elder Amrun, Elder Rhea, Elder Horus . . . He frowned. Wasn't Elder Horus on the other side of that row?

Yes! One of them—likely the one at the very end of the row—must be Parthos! The realization cut through Zowan's fear and energized him like nothing else. Parthos wasn't dead! He wasn't in the secret lab. He was right there!

Silence descended over the Justorium as Elder Zayus arose. In his sonorous voice, he began to speak the History, and Zowan heard it as he had never heard it before: nothing but lie after lie after lie. Worse than simple lying, since by it Father claimed the position Zowan now knew belonged only to I Am. Jesus Christ was the true savior of the world, and Father belittled both His person and His work by claiming that status for himself. By the time the charges were read—rebellion, defiance, blasphemy—Zowan was burning with outrage.

"Do you deny these charges?" Elder Zayus thundered.

"I deny the *History*!" Zowan shouted furiously. "It's all a lie. Father did not save us! He concocted all this to hold us prisoner here. The world has not—"

A tingling, vibrating shock jolted through him, and he stiffened like a pole, his voice choking off.

"Silence!" the Elder commanded, though by then Zowan was completely incapable of speech. The current stopped, and he sagged limply in the hands of the Enforcers.

"You have heard his blasphemy for yourselves!" cried Zayus, voice thundering through the pit-like chamber.

Around him the Edenites exploded with indignant shouts and boos. "Put him in the Cube!" "He deserves the Cube!"

When the sound had died away, the Elder continued: "Father created you, and this is your thanks? He has cared for you, protected you, provided—"

"Father did not create me!" Zowan cried. "*God* created me!"

He braced for the shock that would silence him, but it did not come. For a long moment no one moved or breathed.

"You have broken the most sacred laws of New Eden," said Elder Zayus. "You have defied Father, insulted him, blasphemed against him. For this you deserve death. Repent now. Ask forgiveness that you might live."

Zowan clenched his teeth and said nothing, part of him wondering where in the world this wild obstinacy, this insane courage, had come from.

The Elder glared at him. "Very well."

He gestured for the Enforcers to take Zowan away.

They jerked him sideways through the stage's exit, then urged him down a spiraling, wrought-iron stairway into the basement below, where the black Cube awaited, floating, one corner down, about ten feet above the floor.

*"Zowan, come and free me,"* the false Andros nagged. *"You owe me."*

"I can't wait to see you fry," Gaias said as he propelled Zowan across the rock floor to a spot beneath the Cube's lowest corner. "I'll be laughing with every hop and scream you make, you blasphemous ingrate!"

Once his words would have angered Zowan. Now they seemed irrelevant. The other Enforcer had gone to the control panel on the chamber's far side and now guided the box slowly downward.

Zowan wasn't sure what happened—one minute he was staring up at the point of the Cube, and the next he stood on a mountainside, battered by wind and water, staring down the deep, narrow valley below him. He felt a profound shock at having the wind hurl water through the air at him. It wasn't right. Water didn't fall from the air. And yet it was. Worse, it had been falling for hours, until the ground was saturated, and streams coursed down the hillsides all around him.

Iridescent ovoid aircars were arriving, one every few minutes or so, from seemingly every direction, many of them dashed to pieces on the rocks by the high winds before they could reach the landing plaza carved into the mountainside below him. But it was the rain that captured his attention. The old oracle had been *right*!

"Hurry up!" a familiar voice called from behind him. "We have no time to gawk."

The ground lurched, pitching him off-balance, and the rain and wind disappeared as Zowan returned to the Justorium, where somehow he'd come to be inside the hollow Cube. Balanced with one foot on the meeting of two planes and the other flat in the middle of the third, he straddled the bottom corner where they all came together.

Suddenly the Nephilim called to him, not just "Andros" but many. He heard their voices more clearly than ever before, commanding him to come and free them as the wall in front of him slid downward and the Cube rose into the Justorium. The smoky glass blurred the chamber's concentric levels of spectators into vague shapes of light and dark.

The Cube stopped moving. Zowan held his breath.

A thread of light flickered across the surface of glass, and a shock forced his foot off the crack as he yelped. It was followed by another, which dislodged his right foot before he could find solid purchase for his left. He went down to a knee, put out a hand, as again and again he was shocked and stabbed and burned by the currents—

And was abruptly transported back to the mountainside, the wind-driven rain lashing him furiously. It was not a dream, nor a hallucination, but a memory. Not Zowan's . . . but one of the Nephilim's. Someone named Avalan.

His friend Tumul pulled him around, and drops of water drove into his face. Overhead, the usual covering mist had clumped together into thick, swirling, black-bellied gouts. A flare of light crackled across the angry, churning surface, jolting him. Underfoot, the ground shook ominously.

Urgency beat at him as he hurried up the rain-slicked path, pulling himself along by the handrail. Ahead the Temple opening loomed, a lighted maw in the dark mountainside. Others of his order struggled up the stairs ahead of him and Tumul.

Again light flared and boomed across the heavens, water falling upon him like a river running off a cliff. As he reached the first porch, he came even with his friend, whose golden crest stood upright from the top of his head despite the pounding water, as sure a sign of his alarm as the wide-eyed expression on his face.

Together they dashed through the great arched doorway and up to the black Cube floating in the antechamber, lines of light-power snaking across it. Sidling between those of their brethren already present, they placed their palms against one of the Cube's flat planes, depositing their memories into its depths. Around him, Avalan saw representatives of all three lines—the Three-Eyes, largest of their kind, strong and fierce defenders, the Golden Men, beautiful of face and form, full of grace, bursting with vitality, and the Wisdom Keepers, smallest in stature, but the most driven, the most intense, the ones who led.

As more and more hands touched the Cube's great planes, the lines of light within it increased both in number and in intensity until its form pulsed with red-gold luminescence. Holding his position despite the increased jostling of the crowd, Avalan kept his palm against the glass until the sense of suction eased. Then he stepped back to let another take his place and hurried into the main rotunda.

As he stepped through the door, the air shook and rumbled as once more the floor trembled beneath his feet. He could spare but a moment to note these harbingers of catastrophe, hastening around the raised walkway of the central well toward his life pod, one of the fifty-five prepared and ready. Pod-generation monitors provided a pattern of colorful lighting along the rotunda's curved outer walls.

Reaching his pod, he stripped off his tunic with shaking hands, still hardly believing what was happening. He climbed up the ladder to the platform beside the bright green pod, pressed back the edges of the opening that had been left in it. Then with the acolyte helping to hold it open, he plunged a bare foot into the dark green gel within.

Shivering at the thought of being submerged in the substance, Avalan assured himself he'd be out soon, and congratulated himself for having joined the Order of the New Seeds. At last all the mockery he and his fellows had endured for suggesting the crazy oracle's predictions of calamity might be right was about to fall back on the heads of those who'd mocked.

He grabbed hold of the railing on the far side and plunged his other foot into the pod, the dark gel warm and tingly. Again the ground rumbled, and from the antechamber outside people shrieked about the hillside below exploding in a torrent of water.

With a gulping swallow and gritted teeth, Avalan sat down in the pod. Then taking one last look around, he slid all the way in and the gel seized him. He felt a terrible shrieking pain, the pressure of suffocation, the sense of his body being turned inside out as fire scoured his flesh.

Again Zowan was thrown out of Avalan's memory and back to the Cube, where his body was jittering and yowling and lurching about as hot lines of light scored his skin and rods of fire plunged up the length of his leg bones, burning into his lungs, his heart, his brain. Desperately he shoved himself up in an effort to touch the surfaces around him no longer than he had to, but it was impossible. Soon he would lose strength to keep fighting and the currents would burn him to a crisp.

Then it all stopped and darkness swathed him. He was no longer flesh but color—green and blue surrounded by blackness. He was hungry. Desperately hungry. And he was heartbreakingly alone. When would someone come to let him out? How long could it take to open fifty-five life pods?

That was Avalan again. Not Zowan. And yet his dreadful isolation flowed into Zowan like the thick gel in which he floated, a smothering weight that blotted out all feeling, all hope, all significance. He was cut off, forgotten, cast away. . . . His insides were withering away, his soul shriveling, his heart drying up. . . .

*No, Zowan,* said a new voice. A warm, rich, very familiar voice. *That is not you. That will never be you.*

And the darkness became that which another man had endured long ago, a man who had hung and died on a cross and was cut off, despised and cast away. A man without sin, who was made sin for the rest, so they might live. So that Zowan might live.

He died and rose again so that Zowan would never be alone again. The seed of the woman crushing the serpent's head.

The mind in the darkness of the pod startled out of its self-absorption. *What?* Zowan felt its attention fix upon him, seeing something he did not see. *Died and rose again? Crushed the serpent's head?*

*No. It cannot be.*

*It is,* said the other voice. *It was. It will be forever.*

*Who are you?*

*I Am.*

*"Noooo!"* The creature in the pod erupted out of its dark, sad loneliness into fulminating fury, reaching into Zowan's heart as if it meant to drag him down with it. But the light of I Am merely flicked it aside, blasting away the sticky, gooey darkness, and shattering the Cube that held it, deadly shards of black glass flying outward in all directions.

No longer imprisoned by the Cube's planes, Zowan tumbled through the hole where the Justorium's stage had been into the basement below, slamming into the stone floor and a darkness that knew nothing at all.

A familiar voice speaking his name called him back from it, and he awoke to find an old friend bending over him. "Parthos?"

"Are you all right? You fell an entire story. Can you move?"

Zowan sat up, thinking he felt pretty good for having fallen that far. Was that I Am's doing, as well? His eyes fell upon a dark pile of robes not far off, surrounded by a pool of blood: an Enforcer impaled by a three-foot sliver of glass. He knew the moment he saw him that the man was Gaias.

"Almost all the Enforcers are dead," Parthos told him. "And most of the High Elders. A lot of other people, too . . . What did you *do* in there?!"

"I didn't do anything," Zowan said, getting shakily to his feet and staring up into the ruined Justorium. "God did it."

"God," Parthos said doubtfully. "You mean that I Am person you were talking about earlier?"

"Yes." Zowan looked at his blood-spattered friend more closely. "You seem to have come through pretty much unscathed yourself."

"Maybe, but the Elder next to me was decapitated." He shuddered.

"Come on." Zowan pulled his friend's arm as he stepped across the glass-littered floor toward the spiraling staircase. "Let's go get Terra."

# Chapter Forty-Seven

## New Eden

Lacey found the trial in the Justorium to be one of the most repugnant spectacles she'd ever witnessed. The only thing good about it was Zowan's defiant, unwavering stand for the truth. But when that huge black Cube had risen into view and the lines of electricity snaked about it making the young man inside it writhe and scream, she was appalled. When it suddenly blasted itself to pieces in a flash of light and a boom both heard and felt, she wanted to cheer its destruction—even as she lamented the loss of the courageous young man it had taken with it.

The other women, however, were primarily distressed by the sudden loss of the video signal. Like clucking hens, they pecked about at what might have happened. Was it the camera? The feed? Had the Cube really exploded? No doubt it had been overloaded, what with everyone pushing their lever as far as it would go, but still . . .

It was Terra's wailed "Noooooo!" and her subsequent collapse into inconsolable sobbing that brought them all to silence. Lacey alone moved to comfort her, wrapping her arms around the girl, as Andrea-Isis had done for Lacey not so long ago. It was some time before poor Terra regained her composure, and Lacey could only imagine how she herself would have felt had it been Cam in that Cube.

By then the other girls had worked themselves into a tizzy over what had happened in the Justorium, and why had no one come to tell them about it?

They were all chattering at once when loud clacking sounds erupted from the rear of the residence to silence them. A moment later, two young men burst into the main room, one a dead ringer for Swain—except for his buzzed-off hair—the other a tall black youth who was the clone of Mr. Abuku from the Ivory Coast. They were definitely the men Cam had photographed with his cell phone.

Theia leaned forward imperiously on her pillow. "What is this?! You boys have no right to intrude upon the sacred residence—"

Whatever else she said was lost in Terra's shriek as the girl leapt free of Lacey's embrace and threw herself into the Swain clone's arms, sobbing and laughing at the same time. "You're alive!" she said, over and over. Eventually she stopped to ask how. "We all saw the Cube explode."

And to Lacey's astonishment, he credited his miraculous deliverance to God.

She was further astonished—chilled, in fact—to learn of the large death count that had resulted from the explosion. Zowan said most of the Enclave's leadership had been killed, and many of the Enforcers.

"I have never seen anything like it," Parthos said. "Destruction, blood, glass, bodies. People screaming. We stayed to help for a bit, but there were too many Enforcers."

"And I wouldn't risk my chance to get you out of here," Zowan said to Terra.

"Was Father there?" she asked almost eagerly. "Was he among the dead?"

"How dare you ask that question in that tone, young lady!" Theia interjected. "As if you would be happy to hear of his death."

"I *would* be happy," Terra retorted.

"I don't think he was there," said Zowan. "At least I never saw him, and I had a pretty good view."

Lacey took that moment to intrude with her own urgent questions about Cam.

Zowan looked at her in surprise, then must have reached the

obvious conclusion, for he said only, "I haven't seen him since they took him off to Father."

She was drawing breath to ask where that might be when a second boom shook the floor, and this time the lights went out.

As Lacey's eyes adjusted to the sudden darkness, the dim light that still filtered through the wall of wooden screens drew her into the walking gallery. Despite the power loss, the mall remained partially illuminated by shafts of light spearing down from piercings in its vaulted ceiling. The rooms lining it and the corridors leading off of it, however, had turned into black holes.

Since most everyone had been at the Justorium when the Cube blew and were still involved with the disaster there when the power went off, no one was surprised to find the mall deserted. It wasn't long before the other women busied themselves with moving the screens to let more light into the main room.

As they did, Lacey overheard Zowan speaking to Terra: "We have to leave the Enclave now, while everyone is distracted with the Justorium."

Lacey purposed at once to go with them. Trapped in the residence, she was completely helpless to do anything to help Cam, and wandering about with no idea where he was, or even where *she* was, hardly seemed better. At least up top she might be able to contact his friend Mallory and tell him what had happened.

Suddenly light flickered at the mouth of the corridor feeding into the mall. It quickly resolved into separate narrow beams, and moments later a dozen soldiers in full battle dress burst from its mouth.

"Whoa!" she cried, drawing the others' attention to the newcomers. The soldiers carried automatic weapons mounted with spotlights, which they flashed down the mall and up. Bringing up the rear was a man carrying a handheld tracking device, its green light reflecting off his camo-painted face. Now, at his direction, they all made straight across the mall's island, clambering right over bush and stream to enter the library underneath the residence.

"We need to leave," Zowan said.

But as he spoke, Lacey recalled the RFID chip lodged beneath her shoulder blade, placed there so she could be tracked if Swain took her. Might these men be coming for her?

She'd barely had the thought when the back door of the residence blew open with a bang, and in moments half a dozen soldiers crowded into the main room. The wives screamed and huddled, terrified, into the farthest corner, but the soldiers ignored them, making straight for Lacey. Someone flashed his light into her face, and another said, "That's not Reinhardt. What are you doing, Rudy?"

"That's the girl Swain was after, Lieutenant," said the man with the reader, and she immediately recognized Mallory's voice. Dressed in camouflage fatigues and helmet, with bandoliers of ammunition strapped to his body, he did not look anything like Cam's pseudo-insurance man, Mallory. Nor the trim, tidy servant with the dessert tray. In fact, between the darkness, the face paint, and the helmet, she couldn't make out his features at all.

He continued to squint at the reader, then stepped away from her to squat over the black duffle bag Zowan had brought with him a few minutes earlier. Setting aside the reader, he was rifling through the bag's contents when the lieutenant said, "I thought you were going to chip Reinhardt."

"I was. With everything happening so fast, we never got around to it. So I put it in his duffle." Rudy pulled out a small computer with attached keyboard and switched it on. "Ah, good boy, Cameron. You downloaded the floor plans!"

He stood and turned to Lacey. "Do you know where he is?"

"Some secret lab, we think," she answered.

"In the orange sector," Zowan added.

Rudy tapped the keys on his little computer and images flipped by on the screen.

"What's he got all this C-4 in here for?" the lieutenant asked, now examining the duffle's contents himself.

"To blow out doors if he needed," Rudy said.

"There's enough explosive in here to bring down the whole place. What kind of op are you running here, Rudy?"

"The same one you are. Look here." He shoved the computer before the man's face as he tapped the keys. "See . . . here's the orange sector—obviously some sort of lab. And now the red sector . . . " Screens flipped by, then froze. "Look at the size of this space. That's gotta be where they are."

The lieutenant stepped to the window to eye the mall while Rudy pointed to the lower corridor off the front court and said, "That's the one we'll take."

"Yeah, but where is everyone? It's midday. Shouldn't we be seeing people?"

Lacey told them about the situation with the Justorium, though she didn't know where exactly the Justorium was.

"It's along the upper corridor," Zowan informed them, "the one opposite the lower corridor you are planning to take."

"So we're clear?" the lieutenant said. "Then let's move."

As his team exited the way they'd come in, Rudy hung back to speak to Lacey and the clones. "You all need to get out of here, ASAP. Use the route through the physical plant. We left it open."

The lieutenant's voice squawked out of Rudy's earpiece: "Aguilar, you comin' or not?"

"On my way, Lieutenant."

"What about Cam?" Lacey asked as he turned to go.

"You can't help him now," Rudy said, slinging the duffle over his shoulder. "Besides, he's a big boy. Just get yourselves out—along with as many of these others as you can." With that, he followed his team members down the rear stair, the small computer with its glowing screen of floor plans still in his hand.

# Chapter Forty-Eight

## New Eden

Cam and Swain, surrounded by the four security guards, were on their way down to the red sector when they heard a distant boom. The floor shook and the lights flickered. Cam sensed the Nephilim become suddenly energized by the explosion, as if something dreadfully important had seized their attention, then dealt them a near-fatal blow. He sensed shock, disbelief, and finally despair, the latter quickly swallowed up by a rage that dwarfed all previous manifestations of their frustration.

Swain stopped in the corridor, waiting, perhaps, for an alarm to sound or a call to come in via the land-line phones mounted to the corridor wall nearby. When neither happened, he moved on.

The Nephilim, however, pelted Cam with demands to stop wasting time and let them out, their voices increasingly clear and compelling the closer he got to them. That proximity also seemed to be sparking unwelcome memories—striding out of a crisp fall morning into the Tirich Pazu facility's upper service entrance with the rest of his transport team, while Rudy closed his deal with Dr. Garzi somewhere inside; washing his hands in the sink outside the pod-lab as he eavesdropped on the archaeologist Khalili arguing with someone about Canaanite religious rites; noting uneasily the six pods laid out on the tables inside the lab and wondering who else was purchasing a sarcophagus. . . . He kept shaking the memories off, but they kept returning.

Finally, he, Swain, and the guards passed through the double set of locking doors that separated the orange sector from the red, then followed a short hall into a long, narrow prep room lined with rows of changing lockers and wooden benches. As the guards waited, Swain directed Cam to pull a white Tyvek coverall over his clothing and did the same himself. A second, lesser boom rattled the lockers and shook the floor. But when, as before, no alarms went off or calls came in, they proceeded from the prep room into a spacious meeting area with couches, chairs, and low tables arranged before a large video screen.

As they entered, the people waiting stood to greet them: Gen, Slattery, a half dozen scientists, one of the Saudi guests Cam had observed at the party last night, and most surprising of all, the general he had met at Swain's reception— General Lader, if he remembered correctly—now in uniform and looking quite unhappy.

Swain left Cam by the door as he went around to greet each guest, so, of course, Gen had to come over and taunt him. "Well, if it isn't our great hiring coup, our rising star geneticist. Spy and liar extraordinaire." She shook her head. "I have to say, Reinhardt, the Christian act was a great cover. You almost had me believing you were for real."

He stared at her, deeply dismayed by her words but having no idea how to counter them. Before he could even begin, Swain called for everyone's attention. "You all know why we're here," he said, "and again I apologize for the blindfolds. I assure you, that minor indignity will be more than made up for by what you are about to see."

"Your confidence is awfully high, Director Swain," said General Lader, "for someone who has freely admitted he doesn't know how to open those pods yet."

"Ah, but that's all changed today, General," Swain informed him. "I neglected to mention last night that Dr. Reinhardt here was present during the opening of the pods in Afghanistan eleven years ago. Obviously he escaped that incident. As far as I know, he is the only man who did."

Lader turned narrowed eyes upon Cam. "Reinhardt may have survived, but he remembers nothing. The experience addled his mind."

Cam frowned at him. Lader knew about Tirich Pazu? Knew about his past?

"Only temporarily." Swain turned to Cam. "He's been having a lot of flashbacks lately."

"But not about that," Cam said. "I was there, yes. But General Lader's right: I don't know how to open them."

"I believe you do," Swain countered confidently. "I believe we have only to jog your memory to get the information we want."

"Even if I did remember," Cam said flatly, "I wouldn't tell you."

"No?"

Suddenly the image of the bearded Garzi standing by the giant pod in the oversized cleanroom flashed into his mind. "They were bloody, gruesome rites," Khalili said in his heavily accented English, still occupied with the Canaanites, "but that was not uncommon in ancient times. Man has believed for millennia in the power of blood to restore life, acquire strength, form unbreakable bonds. . . ."

An angry, fearful voice intruded upon Garzi's musings, as memory again gave way to present reality: "You mean you intend to open those pods today?!" one of the scientists demanded.

"Only one of them," Swain assured him. He went on to detail the precautions that had been taken to ensure their safety. The observation booth was well above the reach of anything that might come out of the pod and was reinforced with steel and concrete, its windows made of impact-resistant glass. If at any time they felt uncomfortable, they could easily move back into the prep room, or leave the laboratory entirely, though he didn't anticipate any problems that would require taking such drastic measures.

When he'd finally persuaded everyone that the small risk was manageable, he took them into the spacious observation booth that lay beyond the meeting room's reinforced far door. The observation window encircled the booth on three sides, overlooking a cavernous chamber of cement block walls more than thirty feet high. On the floor stood five massive steel tables, each supporting a monstrous dark green pod, wrinkled and tipped with the black points of the preemergent cubes. For Cam the sight of them was chillingly familiar.

A crane loomed off to the left beside a twenty-foot-wide metal plate set into the cement block wall. Beside it stood the massive cylindrical tank Cam recognized from the videos as the home of the dead

Ecuadoran Nephilim, frozen in liquid nitrogen. All around, heavy chains dangled from reinforced ceiling tracks, used no doubt for moving the heavy pods. A line of steel drums stood against the base of the observation booth's front wall, their top edges some fifteen feet below the booth's window.

The pod Cam assumed would be opened today was surrounded by a cage of stout steel bars. Inside, hanging from a track that ran the length of the cage's ceiling, was a fanlike device with four nozzled flanges, all aimed toward the pod. Outside, a large housing stood beside a cylindrical tank of web-spinning material, hoses connecting it to the nozzle apparatus inside the cage. This, apparently, was Swain's promised method of restraining the awakened Nephilim.

A side gate provided access into the cage, beside which stood an IV stand of heavy-duty stainless steel, several oversized bags of liquid nutrients and attendant tubing hanging from its hooks.

Cam observed all the aspects of the lab while deliberately keeping his eyes off the pods, fearing they'd trigger another flashback. He was certain that was precisely what Swain intended. Indeed the director's eyes darted to him frequently, watching for sign of one. When nothing happened, he took Cam's elbow and urged him toward the booth's side door. "Let's get a little closer," he said, guiding Cam out and down two flights of metal stairs to the lab's floor, his cadre of guards following.

The place smelled of acetone and an unpleasant musk that raised the hairs on the back of Cam's neck. As Swain walked him toward the caged pod, which was the nearest of the five, Cam began to tremble. Tension squeezed his gut and clenched his teeth. The Nephilim calls grew increasingly frenetic.

*His sovereignty rules over all,* Cam told himself. *He will never leave me nor forsake me. And He brought me here for a reason.*

*To open the pods. You are the only one who can.*

*No,* he argued with the Nephilim. *I don't remember how.*

*Yes, you do.*

He frowned then, noting uneasily that the one who argued with him didn't sound like a Nephilim. . . . For one thing the Nephilim had never argued with him.

Suddenly he was back in Tirich Pazu, in the facility's cavernous lab,

462 — KAREN HANCOCK

where six pods now lay on their respective steel tables, awaiting preparation for transport. Rudy had rejoined the team by then, but Khalili had pulled Garzi aside for a private conversation in Farsi, earnestly seeking to change the latter's mind about selling the pods to outsiders, particularly American infidels. Garzi argued that they needed the money and the Americans might figure out how to open them.

"I already know how to open them!" Khalili told Garzi, apparently unaware that most of the Americans in the room at least understood Farsi even if they weren't fluent speakers. Or maybe he didn't care, seeing as, in addition to the American team, there was an army of lab techs on hand to assist with transport, some of whom Cam knew were actually security personnel. Rudy had warned things might go south in a hurry and to be ready.

"You have lost your mind," said Garzi to his subordinate. "We've already tried the blood thing and it didn't work. It has become a bizarre obsession for you, Sayid."

"You've tried pig's blood."

"There is no scientific rationale for any kind of blood being able to penetrate those pods," Garzi pointed out. "This is wild, magical thinking and I cannot—"

"It is not wild. All mythologies speak of the power of blood . . . to bind, to enliven, to free . . . And I don't know how you can throw scientific rationales in my face, when you have no scientific explanation for anything about these sarcophagi. They defy all our knowledge— do things they shouldn't, don't do things they should."

"Sayïd—" Garzi began.

"It would also explain why they always make us think of blood when we are around them. And why we are always cutting ourselves.

Garzi sighed in exasperation. "You have good points, Sayid," he said finally, his tone one of toleration rather than sincerity. "And we will give this idea a more thorough trial once the Americans are gone. But right now is not—"

"Right now is the perfect time!" Khalili interrupted. A knife appeared in his hand, and Garzi lurched back in alarm. But it wasn't Garzi that Khalili cut. . . .

Cam's awareness reverted to Swain's cavernous lab, chains hanging about them like silver lines of rain, shocked to his core.

*It wasn't me!* he thought in wonder. *All this time . . . I didn't do it. It was Khalili!* The terrible guilt he'd borne, not only for being the lone survivor of the catastrophe at Tirich Pazu but because of somehow coming to think he'd been responsible, was not justified. He'd blotted out that memory, perhaps because it was the start of a whole chain of horrors better not revisited . . . but not remembering, he'd feared the worst.

*And now you know otherwise. You also remember how to open them.*

*What?!* He must be mistaken. Surely God did not want these pods opened. The voice must be one of the Nephilim, regardless of how it seemed. They had impersonated Andros with Zowan, so why not God with Cam?

*Do you think I fear them, my son? Do you think I cannot handle them?* The Nephilim *never* called him son.

"Open the gate," Swain said, "so he can enter."

But the voice *had* to be one of the Nephilim. God would never ask him to do such a thing. They would destroy everyone here. Lacey. Zowan. Rudy and the team. It made no sense at all.

*My ways are not your ways, and my thoughts are not your thoughts.*

"Oh, Lord, no," Cam murmured aloud. "This can't be right. I can't do it."

*Will you trust me?*

*This is insane!* But now words from the sermon he'd heard yesterday ran through his mind: *"To find your life, you must lose it. What makes no sense to us is often exactly what He wants us to do. Remember in the Exodus, when the Israelites—two million people with all their goods and their livestock—were told to head away from the Nile into a waterless desert full of tombs?"*

*They had a pillar of cloud guiding them,* Cam noted.

*You have the Holy Spirit.*

*What if I make a mistake?*

*You think I can't handle that? You think I can't make myself clear to you?*

Cam drew a deep breath, his head spinning, his stomach cramping, his mouth dry as dust. How could he do this? If he was wrong . . .

Swain stood on the other side of the bars, staring at him intently. Cam said, "I'll need a knife."

Swain didn't quite smile, but his lips tensed. "How about a scalpel?"

"That'll do." *Oh, Lord, I must be out of my mind. . . .*

*You can't hide from them forever, Cameron. As long as they are safe in their pods, they are a threat. . . .*

At Swain's signal one of the workers hurried off to get the required implement and quickly returned to lay a steel-handled scalpel into Cam's palm. As Cam stepped through the gate into the giant cage, he heard the latch clang shut behind him. Outside, the man at the web-spinner controls flipped a switch, and the nozzles overhead spun into motion, the apparatus moving slowly along the cage-top track but not yet distributing solution.

Cam tore off his left glove and dropped it on the floor, then took the scalpel in his right hand. Fighting past the urge to stop and rethink it all, he retraced the cut that already lay across his left palm, the instrument so sharp he felt nothing. He handed the scalpel back through the bars as dark red blood oozed between the cut's edges. When it started to overflow his hand, he stepped to the pod, turned his palm sideways, and let his blood spill onto the casing.

"Blood?" Swain demanded indignantly. "What is this—some kind of joke?"

Dribbled the length of the pod, the blood stood inertly in uneven drops and blobs for a moment. Suddenly it began to bubble and steam, then sank into the pod's pebbled surface and disappeared.

There was a sudden momentary jittering of the table and the cage bars around them, the technician alert and ready to switch on the feed for the webbing solution. But nothing more happened. The pod sat inert as before, the spinner head whirring and creaking overhead as it continued slowly down its track. Cam's blood dripped from his hand onto the floor.

"Do it again," Swain said.

And Cam did. "It may be dead," he said as he walked the length of the pod. "Or just too weak." Relief washed through him. God had known the thing would be unresponsive.

"Are you sure blood is the way?" Swain asked.

"Yes."

"It can't be dead!",the director cried. "Move out of there and give me that scalpel." He tore off one of his gloves, seized the scalpel from the technician, and unlocked the cage door to press in beside Cam. There he slashed his own palm and dribbled his blood in the place where Cam's had already disappeared.

Right then Cam realized the Nephilim had ceased to call to him. Uneasily, he stepped out of the cage, backed away, and was starting to speak a warning to Swain when for the third time that day a deep boom rumbled from somewhere above. Everyone froze, looking upward as the floor shook, rattling the cage, the steel table, and the observation windows.

One of the techs said, "Maybe there's a thunderstorm going on up top."

A hissing, bubbling sound drew their attention back to where Swain's blood was now smoking and sinking into the pod's leathery surface, just as Cam's had earlier. But as before, nothing more happened.

Suddenly the intercom crackled: "Sir, we're under attack! A military team has broken through the door from the Enclave into the EDL laboratory. They're heading your way." Barely had the voice finished when a floor-level door crashed open in the lab wall, not far from the observation booth's metal stair, and five more security guards burst in. Three raced toward Swain, as the other two covered the open doorway.

Cursing as fluidly and coarsely as any sailor, Swain threw down the scalpel and flew out of the cage to seize Cam by the front of his coverall. "Did you do this?"

"I knew they would be coming eventually," Cam said calmly.

Swain shoved his face into Cam's, teeth bared, free hand clenched into a fist, which Cam thought he might swing at any moment. He was interrupted by a loud ripping sound behind him, as of a huge zipper being worked.

Cam's gaze flashed to the pod in horror. It was now bulging and shivering, as if someone inside was pushing out. Another rip broke the silence; then a long, clawed hand covered with tarry ooze protruded from the pod, groping the air. It was not nearly as large as Cam had expected it would be.

In moments the Nephilim had fully emerged, covered in black goo, a scrawny, bony, stooped-over thing half the height of the pod that had held it—which still made it taller than any man in the room. It leaned weakly against the pod, then took a sudden gasping breath and coughed out a gout of black phlegm. Immediately its crest stood upright; its eyes opened and it turned to look at the people standing around its cage, mesmerized with disbelief.

In that moment Cam realized Swain had left the cage gate open. The web-spinner tech, who had gotten out of his chair when the intercom announced they were under attack, now stood directly in front of the opening. He seemed to realize his peril at the same moment Cam did and was reaching to close the gate when the Nephilim charged out of the cage to seize him and bite away his face. In seconds it had torn off the man's coverall and ripped away an arm, spraying blood everywhere. Cam watched in horror as fat droplets fell onto the neighboring pod, sizzled, hissed, and disappeared.

Swain was already moving for the floor-level doorway beyond the foot of the metal stairway, his security guards closing in around him. The Nephilim, not about to let his food sources escape, dropped the first tech and lunged for a second, tearing off his head. The decapitated body fell spinning, blood pulsing out in long bright streams that fell upon the remaining pods. Meanwhile the Nephilim ignored a third tech, who was seeking cover behind the cage, and went after the group fleeing for the tunnel.

Heart pounding so hard he thought it would burst from his chest, Cam backed slowly away, sidling between the chains in the hope they might obscure him from the eyes of the frenzied Nephilim. By the time he stopped backing up and made slowly for the offside of the observation booth, Swain and most of his guards had escaped, as had all the observers in the booth. The rest—all the techs and a third of the guards—were dead. And now, finally, the Nephilim fell to feeding.

It was shortly interrupted by the emergence of a second and then a third Nephilim, both of whom immediately challenged it. The feeding stopped, and the battle for dominance erupted in a din of bellowing and shrieking. This, Cam knew, was his chance to get around the booth and back to one of the only points of exit. He'd noted earlier that a space large enough to crawl through lay between the line of steel drums and the front wall of the observation booth, but it was as if the sound of the battle held him pressed to the side wall, eyes closed, fighting panic.

By the time he'd nerved himself to move, the contest had subsided. A peek around the corner showed the first Nephilim to be discernibly larger than when it had emerged and clearly distinguishable from the other two—not only by its greater size but by its warm golden skin, the black goo having completely disappeared. It still had most of its kills piled around it, though its two companions had managed to steal a couple for themselves. For the moment the monsters' need to eat over-rode questions of how many corpses each would acquire and keep.

What they had would not be nearly enough, though, so if Cam stayed where he was, he would not survive. The fourth and fifth Nephilim would soon emerge from their pods, both having been sprayed with sufficient blood to initiate the opening sequence. When they came out, he would go.

That moment came sooner than he expected. As the challenging began all over again, he dropped to hands and knees and crawled as fast as he could behind the drums. Reaching the end of them, he dashed across the remaining five feet of wall and around the metal scaffolding to crouch at the foot of the stairway, thanking God he'd not been spotted. Though the whole of the stair support frame now stood between him and the Nephilim, its open slatted structure provided only moderate cover. He couldn't stay there long, and now he had another choice to make: should he bolt across the twenty feet of open floor separating him from the tunnel Swain had disappeared into, or climb the stairs to the almost certainly locked door into the observation booth?

Neither was terribly appealing. *Well, Lord? What do you want me to do?*

Suddenly another great boom sounded, this one the loudest and strongest of all. The concussion blew out the "impact-resistant" windows of the booth above him, shook the walls, and rained glass, dust, and bits of rock upon him. The blast startled the Nephilim out of their quarreling, and to Cam's horror all five turned to stare up at the booth.

Was that Rudy's team blowing the heavy doors between the orange and red sectors? Probably. For a moment he thought to warn them lest they come blundering into the fray and certain death, then realized Rudy would know better. . . .

When nothing further happened, the Nephilim turned back to each other, and the bellowing began anew. Seconds later, seven soldiers in full body armor came rappelling out of the empty front window frames of the observation booth, even as its side door exploded outward. Two more soldiers exited through the latter and raced down the stairway, past Cam and around into a flanking position, firing their weapons as they went. Meanwhile the rest of their team laid down covering fire from the booth, all of which was, of course, useless, as the Nephilim's skin sent the bullets ricocheting every which way.

Cam watched the monsters rise to meet the intruders, the younger ones energized by the entrance of fresh meat yet unclaimed. Then someone from the booth fired a rocket-propelled grenade right at the feet of one of the recently emerged Nephilim. It blew the scrawny, black-coated monster ten feet into the air and backward across the steel tables and their now-empty pods. Knowing there was nothing he could do to help the soldiers, Cam charged up the stairway into the gutted observation booth, pushed through the unlatched door into the meeting room, and pulled up in shock to find Rudy slumped against a wall, bright red blood glistening in a huge splotch across the front of his chest.

"Rudy?" he cried, his voice lost in the chaos of noise.

His friend looked up at him just as the thunderous booming of multiple explosions set the floor jumping and bucking. Cam was knocked off his feet by a powerful blast wave as the prep room disappeared beneath a mound of stone and dirt and the lights went out.

# Chapter Forty-Nine

## New Eden

As Lacey and her companions returned down the tunnel from the physical plant and the familiar form of the mall's island appeared at the end of it, she prayed that Zowan was right about the alternative route through the Sanctuary. And that it had survived the earthquake.

It still irked her to think of all the time they'd wasted trying to convince the wives to leave. Only Andrea was with them, and she hadn't needed persuading. If they'd left when Rudy had told them to, they'd have gotten away. As it was they had just reached the intersection below the physical plant when the world heaved beneath their feet and the tunnel had collapsed before them.

That was when Zowan recalled the small robing room he and Cam had found off the Sanctuary, which he thought might lead up to the surface.

There were more people in the mall now than before, and it was from them Lacey and the others learned that the entire Justorium had collapsed in the tremor, burying all who had been inside. Lacey thought it was a miracle the mall hadn't collapsed, as well, given all the cracks and gaps that now marred its ceiling plaster. As she examined it, she noted the wives standing at the Residence's now glassless window, barely visible in the darkness behind the metal scrollwork, stubbornly holding to their prison.

Zowan led the way up the mall, glass crunching under their feet as they hurried toward the Sanctuary, which appeared to be intact—though the statue at the foot of the ramp had fallen over, and one of its pair of large frosted glass doors hung askew. They told those they passed of a possible exit from the Enclave, but were met with the same hostile obstinacy they'd encountered with Father's wives. Even with their world falling down around them, the Edenites refused to believe there might be something better elsewhere, clinging to the familiar and the comfortable.

Lacey and her group had just reached the front court when the crunch of feet on rock and glass echoed out of the lower corridor, and a bright circle of hand lamps approached rapidly through the dusty darkness. Soon the party was revealed to be a cadre of dust-coated Enforcers and black-tunicked Institute security guards moving en masse around Parker Swain. Swain was much the worse for wear—face and hair spattered with blood, clothing torn and dirty. His expression was one of livid fury.

He and his group surged past Lacey and her friends, heading straight across the court for the upper corridor. Either he didn't recognize any of them—entirely possible given their own coating of white dust—or no longer cared.

Seeing him, though, the others in the mall, mostly older folks and children, cried out with joy, and hurried to meet him. "Oh, Father! At last you've come! We have prayed and prayed for your return!" They told him about the Justorium and all the people killed and trapped.

Swain blew by them all, telling them he had more important things to deal with. He left them standing openmouthed in his wake and was only brought to a stop when he came face-to-face with one of his zig security officers. "The tunnel to the helipad is blocked, sir," the bodyguard gasped. "We can't get through."

Swain swore emphatically, did a half-turn back, then barked, "What of the chopper? Is it intact? Is it flyable?"

"I don't know, sir. We've had no communication with the helipad at all since the cave-ins. The lines are all down. But people in the hall near the Justorium said they were using it to evacuate the injured."

"*What*? By whose order?"

"I don't know, sir. I don't even know if it was true. It's a moot point now if we can't reach the helipad. I suggest you take the Sanctuary exit."

Suddenly Theia and her coterie of terrified wives appeared out of the lower corridor and hurried toward them. "Oh, Husband," Theia cried, "Here we are, ready for you to take us to safety!"

If Swain knew Theia was addressing him, he gave no indication, angling past her toward the Sanctuary ramp. "Keep them all away from me," he commanded his Enforcers. They immediately formed a line between him and the others as he and the Institute security guards stalked up the ramp. Halfway up he turned, lifted the assault rifle Lacey had not noticed he'd been carrying, and opened fire, shooting first into the backs of his Enforcers, then raking bullets across the crowd at large.

Hardly believing her eyes, Lacey saw Theia and all her girls flung backward as the bullets tore into them. People started to run or dive for the floor, Lacey one of them. The moment she hit the ground, someone fell half upon her, and then someone else.

Her ears buffeted by the thunderous reports, she clenched her eyes shut and prayed. The weapon seemed to fire forever, but finally its hideous blasts devolved into a series of clicks as Swain kept the trigger down, though the gun's magazine was empty. Then those, too, stopped, leaving only the cries and moans of the wounded.

Terrified he would reload and start again, Lacey lay where she was, trying to breathe in slow, shallow breaths, feigning death. A sharp pain pierced her right hip, and a warm sticky wetness ran down the side of her face. The body upon her was crushing to the point it stimulated waves of claustrophobic panic. *Please, God, let him leave now!*

Instead, Swain and his guards started shooting the wounded. The moans soon turning to pleas for mercy and screams of terror cut off by short bursts of gunfire. She was shaking uncontrollably now, biting her lip to keep back the sobs of terror that wracked her.

Finally Swain cut it off. "That's good enough," he told his men. "If we don't go now, we won't get out at all." Multiple pairs of boots gritted on glass and rock as the men congregated by the ramp, then moved up into the Sanctuary and faded away. She heard the faint, distant sound of a door opening and closing, then nothing except a soft, rattling moan not far from her. It carried on for a few breaths, then silenced, and she lay there, her ears ringing, afraid of moving, though the body atop her seemed as if it was slowly crushing her.

It was many long, tortuous moments before she dared lift her head. The smell of burned flesh and blood and the sulfur of gunpowder flooded her nose and mouth, and she coughed. That provoked the person lying on top of her to move, and she soon saw that it was Terra, who had been sandwiched between Lacey and Zowan. As Lacey pushed herself to her knees, a middle-aged woman stirred not far ahead of her, wriggling out from under a dead man in a field of bodies drenched in blood and broken glass, dust still swirling gently through shafts of light from the sky holes.

Every Enforcer lay dead, sprawled in the ring they had formed to protect their "Father." Theia and her girls also lay where they had fallen. Poor Andrea Stopping had been shot dead where she'd stood just behind Lacey, perhaps by the same bullet that had skipped along Lacey's ribs. That and the glass cut on her hip from when she'd fallen were her only injuries. The blood on her face was Zowan's, who had a bloody bullet track along his temple and a big chunk of flesh blown out of his upper arm. Terra had come through with no more than a few cuts and bruises.

Parthos had not been so lucky. His body lay almost immediately in front of them, and seeing how badly he'd been shot up, Lacey thought he might well have been the salvation of the rest of them. Finding him, his two friends stood over his body and stared down at it dumbly, as if they couldn't believe what they saw. Terra was first to break, sagging to her knees beside the corpse with a moaned, "Oh, Parthos . . . " Moments later, Zowan fell beside her, wrapping his good arm around her as she wept while tear tracks glistened down his cheeks.

From over by the upper corridor, the middle-aged woman began to wail, drawing Lacey's eyes. She, too, knelt beside the corpse of a loved one, clutching the man as she screamed out her misery. A little ways behind her a young man covered in someone else's blood stood surveying the carnage, dazed and wide-eyed. The fifth survivor of the massacre, and evidently the last.

Seeing the more than thirty bodies sprawled about them, Lacey felt a chill of wonder, astonished and humbled to be alive. Her whiny words to Cam from a couple nights ago ran through her mind. *"God's done so very little for me over the years."*

She could never say that again. . . .

It was Zowan who pulled himself together first, standing and drawing Terra after him. "We can't stay here," he said. "You must have heard Father say we don't have much time to get out."

To which the bereaved woman wailed, "No! I'm not leaving! I'm not leaving."

"If you don't, you'll die."

Ignoring Zowan, she turned to the young man. "Go up to the clinic and get some help for us," she commanded him. He went without comment. She turned a glare on Zowan. "I'm not leaving him. And you can't make me!"

Shrugging, Zowan didn't even try. Instead he turned and picked his way through the corpses toward the Sanctuary's ramp, Terra and Lacey on his heels. But just as they stepped onto its smooth surface, the Sanctuary erupted in a geyser of flame and rock and deafening sound. A hard rolling wall of air knocked them all backward. Lacey fell half on her side and rolled over, covering her head as rock, glass, and who knew what rained upon her. Then the floor trembled beneath her, and though she heard nothing, a thick, choking cloud of dust enfolded her from behind.

She lay in blessed silence for a while, feeling breathless and dizzy. When things had settled a bit, she sat up and looked around. Some of the mall remained intact, but the back part of it was choked with rubble. Palm trees listed off the island and water ran out into the walkway. The sky holes still shone down upon them, though.

It was only as she watched the others stir around her that she realized she couldn't hear anything. After a moment of panic, she realized it was probably only temporary. Indeed, soon after, her ears began to ring and some of her hearing returned. Supplementing the conversation with sign language and pantomime, she discovered all of them had suffered some degree of hearing loss—though that was the least of their problems. Not only was the Sanctuary now a wall of rock and earth, so were the upper and lower corridors.

They stood, staring dumbly around, all escape cut off.

*Surely God wouldn't have gotten us through all He's gotten us through just to end it here,* Lacey thought.

It was Terra who voiced the doubt: "So, after all that, we're to be buried alive?"

"Maybe not," said Zowan. "If it's still standing, there might be a way through the Star Garden."

# Chapter Fifty

## New Eden

As the trickle of streaming dirt and falling rocks died away into silence, Cam heard the hum of a motor starting up somewhere, perhaps an auxiliary generator. If so, it didn't appear to service the lights. Or perhaps the lights were all too damaged to work whether they had power or not.

"There's an extra head lamp in the duffle," Rudy said, his voice dry and rough.

"Where's the duffle?"

"Somewhere off to my left, I think."

Cam groped around for it, then donned the head lamp and pressed the switch.

He turned toward the prep room first, and confirmed that it was completely filled with rock and rubble. There was no way they'd be getting out that way. And with Rudy injured, no point even considering the tunnel that Swain had taken. Especially since Cam was sure that one had been blown as well, Swain's final, but unmentioned, backup provision for keeping the Nephilim contained. Or maybe that was too charitable, considering how quickly he'd fled when things began to go south. Maybe he was simply trying to cover his tracks.

Cam turned to Rudy, the beam of his head lamp illuminating his friend's bloody chest in blue-white light. His swarthy face was gray, cheeks sunken. He didn't look good.

"What happened?" Cam asked, squatting beside him as he pulled Rudy's water bottle from his belt.

"A couple of Swain's security guys were hiding out here when we arrived," Rudy said. "Took us by surprise. We were pretty distracted by the racket coming out of the lab up there."

Cam helped him sip from the bottle, then pulled aside the bloodied shirt to look at the wound. Rudy swatted his hand away. "It's nothing."

"It doesn't look like nothing."

"It doesn't matter. I'm not going anywhere."

Cam frowned at him. "Did you have a medic on your team?"

"Yeah. I think he stayed in the booth, but there's no need . . ."

Cam was already up and striding away. But the three men who'd been manning the booth just moments ago were nowhere to be found. Whether they'd been blown out by the blast wave, pulled out by the Nephilim, or had left on their own, he didn't know. In any case he found no medical supplies, and he could hear the Nephilim eating outside the shattered windows, wet smacks and crunchings intermingled with growls and snorts, all of it far too close for comfort.

He hurried back to Rudy, who looked noticeably weaker even after so short a time.

"Why weren't you wearing a vest?" Cam asked.

Rudy grimaced. "I wasn't part of the assault team, just the eyes and ears, so they didn't figure I needed one. Or so they said."

"So they said? What? You think they set you up to take a round?"

*Things are unraveling,* Rudy's note had said. *Trust no one but God.*

"I don't think they knew those security guys were there, but . . ." Rudy sighed. "Yeah, it probably wasn't an accident *I* was the one without the vest, and also in the lead." He fell silent for a moment, then went on. "When we started this operation, it was about finding the sarcs and destroying them. The big brass deemed them too dangerous to open, and we sure didn't want Swain to have them, given all the routes he could take genetically should he get one out—not to mention the potential of him selling one to the highest bidder. The last thing we wanted was for our enemies to have them. . . . The Saudis at the party last night? That couldn't have been good. . . . And I have no idea *who* Lader's working for, but that was a surprise, too, seeing him there."

"He was here today, too. In uniform."

Rudy grunted, then sipped some more water from the canteen Cam held to his lips. "I think we might be running two simultaneous operations. Or one big one, from which I've largely been excluded. The original plan was that once you'd located the sarcs, we'd send in the team to destroy them. But the group I'd assembled was suddenly called away to a new assignment last week, and when I insisted we had to go in now, they sent me a new team. And new orders—someone up the chain decided we were to secure and recover them after all, rather than destroy them."

He looked up at Cam, pain wrinkling his face. "That's why I was so desperate to get you in last night. I wanted you here with a bit of time to work before they arrived. I figured . . . you'd go ahead with the original plan."

"And that's why you put all that C-4 in the duffle bag."

Rudy nodded, dropping his head back against the wall as he closed his eyes. "I didn't think you'd let Swain open them, though."

"Actually . . . *I* opened them."

Rudy didn't move, didn't open his eyes. He sat there for a long time. "Well, I'm sure you had a good reason."

"I did it because God told me to," Cam said simply, realizing as he did that it might not have been as insane as it sounded.

Another long silence ensued, at the end of which Rudy said, "So you're on speaking terms with Him again, are you?"

"I have been for quite a while."

His old friend and mentor smiled, still with his eyes closed. "Well, that is a wonderful thing to know."

They spoke then of old times, of mutual friends, of events in their lives over the eleven years they'd been estranged, the things God had taught them. And through it Rudy grew weaker and weaker.

Periodically fights broke out among the Nephilim and they trumpeted like elephants, the sound ricocheting off the cement walls, deafening, terrifying, disheartening. . . . Then they'd go back to eating again. Cam occasionally considered going to the window to check their status but never did, not only because of the risk, but because he refused to leave his old friend to die alone.

He thought he understood God's plan now. Released here, there was no way the Nephilim could have penetrated the small corridors of the Enclave, even before they'd been collapsed. Yes, the techs and security men had perished, along with Rudy's recovery team, but all of them had known the risks. Considering all the safeguards Swain had arranged, and how deftly each had been circumvented to result in the present situation, he had to think even that was the hand of God. Now the beasts would eat each other until only one remained . . . and then Cam would take it out.

He remembered exactly how to do that, too. . . .

He didn't hear Rudy's quiet breathing stop, only realized after the fact that it had. He surprised himself when the tears came, for he and Rudy had been so long apart, and he'd carried such bitterness for the man over the years. Unjustly, it seemed . . .

Some time later a sound he could not identify roused him from a semi-doze. Slowly it dawned on him that he could no longer hear the Nephilim. Having turned off his head lamp to save the battery, he kept it so and felt his way into the observation booth and over to one of the blasted-out windows. Were the giants skulking below, waiting for him to emerge so they could seize him? He listened with every fiber of his being but heard nothing. Could they really have fought to the end this quickly? Finally, frustrated, he switched on the lamp and swept the room with its beam.

The lab stood still and silent, spattered with blood and chunks of flesh, the chain tracks pulled half out of the ceiling, steel tables and drums overturned, pods crushed and scattered about. The carnage was such it made him glad he could see only a small bit of it at once. His beam played over two dismembered Nephilim heads, skulls bashed in, brains eaten. But only two. No sign of the other three.

He moved the beam on around the big chamber and stopped, stunned to find that the huge metal panel in the wall to the left had been breached. Cut as with a welding tool, the two edges had been folded back to reveal a room beyond. The squeals of bending metal must have been what had awakened him.

Hurrying down for a closer look, Cam was horrified to discover it wasn't a room, but a massive freight elevator, likely the one that had brought the pods down in the first place. The giants had torn through the car's roof, again bending back the metal to make a hole big enough to squeeze through.

Cam stepped into the ruined car, dread gathering in the pit of his stomach. Cool air washed down from above, but the big shaft was pitch-black and extended farther up than the beam of his light reached. He had no idea how far the climb was, but looking up the shaft, discouragement flooded him. The Nephilim had probably climbed it in moments, whereas it would take him all day, and all the while they'd be ravaging the countryside.

An eerie squealing sounded far above, followed by a gonging sound, a grinding groan, and then a louder squeal, like metal scraping against metal. The sudden sense of something coming at him made him back out of the elevator just as a sky-blue van crashed nose first through the roof, spraying him with shattered windshield glass. He stared at the golden ziggurat on the van's side door, noting at once that there were no people inside it. Moments later a second van fell sideways onto the first and he jumped back. It, too, carried the zig logo, and no passengers. Nor was there any sign anyone had been ripped out of the vehicles.

Did the shaft perhaps terminate above in a garage? Surely Swain would have disguised it, and company vehicles parked on a covering plate would do the trick. The Nephilim's penetration of that cover would explain the falling vans. All of which could mean this lab lay directly beneath the campus, possibly even the zig itself. . . .

The dread in his belly became a sick fear as he stood looking up. It was his fault those monsters were on the loose at all, let alone in a place where there'd be food aplenty. Worse, they wouldn't just kill to eat. He'd sensed the deep and furious hatred they had for his kind. He'd sensed it back in Tirich Pazu, sensed it even more strongly here.

*You knew about all this, Lord, didn't you? And still you let me do it. Why?*

He got no answer to that question, just the sense he needed to hurry—though he had no idea how he'd do anything useful with that endless shaft to climb first.

Suddenly it occurred to him that this was Swain's private and most secret lab. Given the length of that shaft and the size of this car, it wouldn't make sense for Swain to have used it to ride up and down. Was there a smaller express elevator somewhere nearby?

He did a fast sweep of the floor, looking for sign of such an elevator and picking up whatever salvageable bits of the soldiers' gear he could find—mostly weapons and ammunition, including a sniper rifle and a handgun, but also a bullet-proof vest and helmet. He considered breaking the ax out of its glass case by the fire extinguisher but decided it would weigh him down too much. He should be able to find one nearer his point of need.

Hurrying back to the observation booth, he found another door on the far side and used one of the lock blowers in the duffle to get it open. Sure enough, the corridor beyond led to a small private elevator. The only external control was a single keyhole in a panel beside it, so he pulled out his fat black ballpoint pen, pressed a small button on its side with a fingernail, and the end extended. This he inserted into the hole. After a few seconds the latches clacked and the door opened.

The car bore him swiftly upward, and in minutes he stepped out into another corridor, well lit, vinyl-floored, walls finished with painted drywall and topped with acoustic ceiling tiles. It could be any corridor in the zig. He followed it to a narrow stairway, passed through a couple of doors, and walked into the elevator lobby just off the Madrona Lounge.

People huddled there, terrified, disheveled, their faces tear-streaked and some of them bloodied. Among them were many of his co-workers and research assistants: Poe, Jade, Aaron, Melissa. None seemed to recognize him, though. And why not? Covered with dust and blood, dressed in ill-fitting camos and Kevlar vest, and armed to the teeth, he didn't look much like the Cam Reinhardt any of them had known.

The broad window behind them showed the black, threatening

skies of an approaching thunderstorm, and he could hear the chop of a helicopter's rotors outside, then the roar of a Nephilim. He sprinted for the atrium as lightning flashed and boomed outside.

Though he'd thought the giants would avoid trying to push their way into a building not made for their kind, he was wrong. They had easily broken through the two-story glass walls of the front lobby, smashed their way into the atrium, then climbed its balconies to the tenth floor. There they'd punched a jagged hole into the atrium's skylight far above and climbed out into the garden. Huge pieces of translucent acrylic sheeting lay on the ground floor and dangled from the jungle. All six glass elevators had been reduced to piles of rubble at the base of their cables. Thankfully, none appeared to have had passengers when they were brought down.

He hurried out of the atrium and around to the south side, to Swain's penthouse express elevator. It bore him in seconds to the tenth floor, where he opened the inner penthouse door, intent on gaining the highest position possible.

The rhythmic chop of more than one helicopter echoed loud and close. Glass littered the floor of the penthouse's cavernous entry and glistened on the massive stone stairway curving leftward to an expansive loft above. He took the stairs two at a time and shortly glimpsed two Black Hawk helicopters through the loft's surprisingly intact windows. As he watched, one of them came around over the garden from southeast to northwest, raking something in the trees with its machine guns.

As the helicopter pulled up at the end of its run, a narrow beam of red light shot out and hit its tail. Exploding in a fiery ball of orange, the helicopter went down on the northwest portion of the roof, where a secondary explosion sprayed fiery shrapnel across the garden. Flaming metal clanked against the apparently impact-resistant glass of the penthouse's entryway and fell sizzling into the swimming pool below. Out in the jungle of the west garden, flames churned out a thick, black column of smoke.

He suspected the laser or heat ray, or whatever it was, drained its user, seeing as the second chopper remained aloft. Indeed, as it swooped by, it was assaulted with hurled tables and uprooted trees, which would have been almost as effective as the heat ray, had any of them hit their target. He wondered why the Nephilim didn't use their ability to broadcast electromagnetic pulses, for that would have brought everything around them right out of the sky. Perhaps they didn't know what they could do. Or maybe, like their size and strength, and apparently that heat ray, it took time and food to develop.

He continued up the stairway, as out in the garden a renewed wave of gunfire erupted, followed by hoarse, hysterical screams. At the top of the stair, he paused, looking around for the route to the roof and found instead the displayed armor of an ancient warrior not far away, complete with a hefty sword in a wooden scabbard. He ran to it and drew the blade free to be sure it was usable. Just as he'd expect from Parker Swain, it was oiled, polished, and extremely well honed. *Perfect.* He stuffed it hilt up, scabbard and all, between his Kevlar vest and his back, and took off.

A door in the southeast corner led up a short two-flight stairway to the roof, where heavy clouds loomed dark and low and the air smelled of rain. A third helicopter, much smaller than the Black Hawks, sat on a raised concrete helipad about sixty feet away, rotors whirling. Swain's personal aircraft, it was black and gold with a gold ziggurat logo on its side.

A number of people stood about the deck, most of them security, while Swain and Gen engaged in a shouting match not far from where Cam stood. Behind them, lightning flashed from sky to ground, hitting somewhere out past the vault, close enough that again the blast of thunder came almost at once.

The noise interrupting their conversation, Swain's glance lifted from Gen to Cam. Seeing him, the director stiffened, his mouth falling open, blue eyes widening in disbelief. Viascola turned to see what he was gaping at, even as he gestured at Cam and screamed, "Shoot him! Shoot him now!"

But the wind carried his voice away from the guards, and only Cam heard it. Then down in the garden, the Nephilim roared, commanding everyone's attention. Quickly Cam stepped to the wall that encircled the roof and swung the duffle off his shoulder to the ground. As he chambered a round into the sniper rifle, he peered over the edge of the chest-high roof wall.

The three remaining Nephilim stood at the near end of the reception plaza, clustered around the white obelisk. Ranged out behind them through the trees were maybe a score of military and security personnel, most of them flat on their bellies and probably terrified. The garden itself, in addition to having small fires here and there, had been chewed to pieces by the heavy artillery of the chopper attacks. He felt an utterly incongruous lament for the loss of what had been a beautiful sanctuary.

Frowning, he turned his attention back to the Nephilim. Only one of them faced him directly, and he thought it was the youngest of them. Which was unfortunate, but nothing he could do about it. All three were almost twice as big as when they had come out of the pods, and not nearly so frenetic. They were all golden-skinned now, their golden crests rippling in the light, reminding him of similar crests he'd seen on the helms of ancient armor. Oddly, each giant had made himself a loincloth, but other than that, they stood naked, their spectacular musculature on full and intimidating display. Massive, powerful, beautifully formed ... they were, he thought, consummate warriors. The third eyes were their only flaw, though they would hardly think it so.

Resting the barrel of his rifle on the top of the wall, he took aim at his target, lining up the crosshairs on the third eye glowing in the younger creature's forehead. He squeezed the trigger, the gun bucked against his shoulder ... and the Nephilim remained standing. He'd missed the shot, but between the wind and the remaining Black Hawk coming around for another pass, the report wasn't heard.

Drawing a deep breath, he chambered another round, adjusted his aim, then squeezed the trigger again. This time the creature fell straight over backward.

He'd hoped—expected—the remaining two would fall upon him at once and begin feeding, thus ridding Cam of the need to run down and make sure the creature he'd shot didn't revive. Instead, they immediately turned to face Cam, and though he ducked behind the wall, he knew they had figured out where the shot had originated. They were starting to think now, instead of just react.

Swain had come up to flank him, watched as he'd taken his shot, and now swore at him furiously. Turning, he waved two of the guards to come with him and raced for the waiting helicopter. Genevieve ran after him. He leapt into the front passenger seat as the guards piled into the back. Both doors slammed shut just as Gen got there. She banged on the side of the aircraft, screaming at Swain to let her in, but the chopper lifted free of her grasp, leaving her behind, her clothing and hair whipping in the rotor wash.

The helicopter lifted off, heading north just as the first Nephilim climbed over the north wall. The second appeared at the south wall moments later. Both were about the same distance from Cam and focused solely upon him. Dropping the rifle, he pulled the handgun from his belt and brought it up two-handed, aiming at the north target first. Before he could fire, the departing helicopter lowered its nose and raked the Nephilim with a spray of heavy artillery as it flew over him. The massive bullets merely bounced off the creature, ricocheting about the roof and sending everyone diving to the deck. As the aircraft zoomed away, its unfazed target caught it square on the underbelly with a red beam of light, and just like the Black Hawk, it exploded into a fireball and went down.

Gen started screaming, whether in rage or grief or terror, Cam couldn't tell. In fact, he wasn't sure that she hadn't been screaming all along. He'd already abandoned the north target for the south one, the latter heading rapidly for him.

As he raised the handgun, two-handed, fat raindrops began to pelt him. He ignored them, fired off two quick shots, and the creature went down. Immediately he turned to the north target, and right then the clouds opened up with a tremendous flash of lightning and its attendant crash of thunder. It felt more like being in a waterfall than a rainstorm. The droplets, heavy and hard, slammed into his head and face and even his eyes. He couldn't see a thing.

Concerned the handgun would fail if it got too wet, he stuffed it into his pants and ran for the downed south target, hardly able to see it until he was on top of it, the deck already shimmering with a half inch of dancing water. He saw the guards clustered under the tower at the southwest corner, Gen among them. Scanning the empty northwest quadrant, he finally felt confident enough to turn his back on the storm—and found the north target, blundering through the rain toward the position Cam had just abandoned, its back to him and the punishing storm.

Knowing he didn't have a lot of time, Cam drew the heavy sword from out of the scabbard he'd tucked between his vest and back

The fallen Nephilim's third eye was black and oozing where the bullet had entered, but already the ooze was congealing as the tissue prepared to expel the flattened bullet that had penetrated it, impacting the creature's brain enough to stun it, but no more. He lifted the sword and swung hard, once, twice. The head was off. Gritting his teeth, he grabbed it by the crest and tossed it hard over the wall, watching the wind gusts carry it far out over the garden.

Then he turned his attention to the north target. It had finally turned and spotted him and was now heading toward him, face on in the storm—which right then, of all things, suddenly eased up. Dropping the sword, Cam ripped the handgun out of his waistband, praying it wasn't too wet to fire. He raised it, and again, two quick shots dropped the giant in its tracks. Only then did he see the third Neph, already revived, coming up over the wall. It was coming fast, and he felt the mental pummeling of its hatred, its supreme confidence and absolute determination to rip him limb from limb.

He blotted all that out, lifted the gun, and fired two more shots. Then a third when those didn't drop it. It fell almost at his feet and he stared down at it stupidly.

Suddenly he was consumed by the hair-raising, all-over-your-body prickle of an imminent lightning strike. Tossing the gun aside, he hurled himself away from them, crashing onto the raised helicopter pad.

It was like a grenade going off—a flash of white, a deafening roar, then brief blackness and silence. When he regained consciousness, he found that the vest, helmet, and his gray walking shoes had all been blasted off of him. He got to his feet a bit unsteadily and his ears rang, but other than that he seemed fine.

The rain had stopped, the storm had moved on, and the guards had moved out of their shelter to approach him, staring from him to the place where he'd brought the last two giants down. All that remained of them and their headless fellow, who'd fallen not too far from them, were a few shards of blackened bone.

All three had been incinerated by the intense heat of the justice of God.

# Chapter Fifty-One

It was over.

As the rain and the clouds moved northward, he saw that the sun hung low over the western horizon, the hills casting long shadows across the land. Almost twenty-four hours had passed since the reception. The rain had put out the fires in the garden, and the second Black Hawk had completely disappeared.

Gen left her position at the corner tower and joined her three security men beside Cam. The men regarded him with expressions that bordered on awe, and even Gen seemed to favor him with an atypical measure of respect.

"Well," she said, staring up at him where he stood on the raised platform, "I guess you know how to handle yourself in a crisis better than I thought."

He gave her a nod of acknowledgment.

Then she turned abruptly to one of her guards and said, "I want you to get the surveillance records of everything that happened here and earlier, when the aliens came through the lobby, and destroy them all. Do it discreetly. We'll chalk it up to electrical problems generated by the earthquake."

As the three guards hurried off to do her bidding, Cam gaped at her. "You've got to be kidding."

She met his gaze defiantly. "We *can* contain this. The aliens came in through the front entrance and climbed up the atrium, limiting the number of witnesses. Those who did see them are mostly dead. All the damage to the hanging garden we can attribute to the helicopter crashes, fires, and so forth, and the rest can be blamed on the earthquake."

"Earthquake? We don't have earthquakes here!" Cam protested.

"Obviously we do, since we just had one."

"Gen—"

"What else would you have me do, Cameron?" And now her brown eyes met his boldly. "Confess to our nefarious deeds? All the evidence has been destroyed, and most of the people involved are dead. Not only that, the vast majority of K-J's employees have no idea what we were doing, yet they'd be stigmatized for life were it all to come out." She cocked her head, gave him a weirdly strained smile, and stepped around the platform.

"There might still be people alive down there," Cam said quietly. An image of that slim, dark-haired girl curled up on the mat in the Wives' Residence flashed through his mind, but he pushed it away. It wasn't her. Swain had lied, trying to manipulate him. Hadn't Rudy called to say they'd gotten her away?

Gen turned back to him. "I'm sorry, Cameron. But I really don't think there are any. Parker placed those explosives long ago, with the intent of doing just what was done should the need arise."

Nausea swirled in Cam's belly. "Have you no conscience at all?"

She continued on with a shrug. "Very little. The explosives were *my* idea."

He watched her cross the roof, then turned his gaze to the foothills beyond the campus bowl. The lay of the land had changed significantly—a crooked dip in a formerly straight ridgeline, sinkholes and newly formed valleys, and sharp, vertical displacements of earth lay everywhere. Even part of the bowl had collapsed, leaving one of the warehouses slumped to one side. People would believe the earthquake story. Gen would pull it off. And why not? She'd spent a lifetime learning how to manipulate the truth from a master. Still, it wasn't right.

*Do not be deceived, God is not mocked; for whatever a man sows, this he will also reap.*

He snorted softly. *Okay, then, I'll leave it in your hands, Lord. Your retribution will be far more effective than anything I can do. And who knows? She might even believe in you yet.* The woman had a boatload of guilt to carry around with her now, and just because she sought to deny it wouldn't make it any lighter. As Cam knew as well as anyone. . . .

Suddenly bone tired, he picked up the sword, slid it back into the scabbard, then found his shoes and retrieved the sniper rifle and the duffle bag. His phone and the small computer were both inside the bag, carrying numerous pictures of the Enclave as well as the files he'd downloaded of the floor plans. Evidence. But not enough. Besides, as he knew all too well, digital records could be faked. Without someone to back up his story, who would believe him?

He put the sword back with its armor, then went down to the first floor, where people were already sweeping up the broken glass. The dead and injured had all been carried off to the clinic, and seeing as no one was paying him the least bit of attention, Cam decided that if Gen wanted to cover things up, he'd oblige her by making sure there were no loose ends.

Descending once more to the red sector lab, he mined it with the C-4 still in his duffle, then brought Rudy's body back up with him, stripped of its combat gear. As he stepped out of the express elevator, he pressed the wireless detonator. Moments later, the floor trembled beneath him. An aftershock, he thought grimly. One that would undoubtedly destroy the garage in which most of the campus vans were parked.

He brought Rudy's body to the makeshift morgue at the clinic, covered it with a sheet, then called the number he'd been given to contact the field HQ in the Game and Fish trailers west of the Institute. Brianna answered, and when he told her Rudy was dead and someone needed to retrieve the body, his words were met with a very long silence. When she finally spoke, her voice was choked. "We'll be right over."

She came with two of her team, bringing a body bag, a stretcher, and "Mallory's" dusty blue Volvo, whose keys she handed to Cam. He stayed with them until they left, then went up to his fifth-floor office to revise the date on his resignation letter and print it out. Sealing it in an envelope, he took it with him to his apartment. There he shaved and showered and packed his things, all the while trying desperately not to think about Lacey, a feat that increased in difficulty the longer he went without hearing from her. Still, he clung to the delusion that Rudy had gotten her away, telling himself she'd been sent on to Phoenix after the rescue, and was just waiting for his call. He'd make it as soon as he got the number from Brianna.

On some level he knew he was being utterly irrational, but he wouldn't let himself think about that, either, because thinking in rational terms would lead him to a place he did not want to go.

He was standing over the duffle bag, going through its contents before he returned it to Brianna, and had just finished erasing the memories of both his BlackBerry and the tiny computer and keyboard when the BlackBerry rang. Shocked, he stared at it for a moment, wondering who would be calling him with Rudy dead; then he realized it must be Brianna and answered it.

"Cameron?" asked a familiar voice.

Suddenly his ears roared and his knees wouldn't hold him up. He sagged onto the bed. "Lacey?"

"You're alive! Oh, thank God," she cried, hysteria raising the pitch of her voice. "I thought for sure you were dead. When the tunnel collapsed—"

"Where are you?" he asked, his voice stronger now, his heart hammering against his breastbone.

"I didn't know where to go. I've got Zowan and Terra with me. Well, not exactly with me, but I don't know who to trust, so it's hard . . ."

"Lacey! Where *are* you?"

"I'm in the Madrona Lounge—"

"I'll be right there," he said, and cutting her off, he threw the phone and his resignation letter into the duffle bag, grabbed it and his suitcase and backpack, and took the service elevator down to the main floor. There he burst out of the car only to stop dead at the sight of her. She stood at the mouth of the elevator lobby, wearing her own jeans and top, turning toward him now at the rumble of the doors opening. Her face was white as a sheet, though her eyes and nose were red as if from weeping. He let his bags fall to the floor, crossed the space between them, and swept her into his arms.

Her emotional control shattered as she clung to him and wept. "I thought you were dead," she sobbed into his shoulder. "Mr. Mallory's team went down after you, and then Swain blew the tunnel. . . ." He held her close as she told him of the cave-ins and the massacre Swain had perpetrated on the Edenites, and how they'd been left for dead, but Zowan had led them out through the passages behind the Star Garden. It had taken them all afternoon to reach the campus proper, because they were terrified one of the security patrols would find them and finish the job Swain had started. She'd left the clones in a warehouse out by the Vault. "I didn't know what else to do."

"You did good," he told her, releasing her to take her by the shoulders and look into her eyes. "You couldn't have done better. Come on." He steered her toward the stairwell. "I've got a car again, so let's go get them."

As they drove around the outer service road, he told her some of his side of the story, including what Gen was doing to cover everything up. She was indignant at the notion of just letting her get away with it but saw the futility of any other route once he'd laid it out. "Our priority now is to get those kids out of here," he said. "My friends should be able to work up some official identities for them, social security numbers, birth certificates, that sort of thing. We don't have to say they're clones, either, just children of the cult members. Who's ever really going to know?"

She accepted his reasoning without comment and they fell into silence for a bit. Then she asked timidly, "And what about us?"

"I've got my resignation letter in the duffle back there and a bit of money saved up. I think I'll head up north to visit my parents and my brother for a while. After that, I don't know." He pulled in at the warehouse she'd indicated, switched off the engine, and looked over at her. "I'm pretty much waiting for the Lord to show me what He wants me to do next, and I have no idea what that will be." He gave her a half smile. "But you're welcome to come with me, if you want."

Her lovely eyes widened. "Come with you? You just said you don't know what you're going to do."

"That's true. But my parents would love to entertain us. They have a beautiful big house up in Cottonwood, lots of wooded land to walk through, a stream, horses to ride, trails to bicycle on. It would be a time to get away and take stock, figure out your next step."

"We barely know each other."

"Well, we could remedy that there, too."

She looked suddenly stricken, her eyes welling with tears. "I thought I would never see you again—that God had brought you into my life just long enough for me to fall in love with you, only to snatch you away forever. I swore after Erik I would never be impulsive again, but now here you are, asking me to go away with you. . . ." She fell silent, the tears glistening on her lashes.

He shifted around on the seat toward her, touched her cheek with the back of his fingers, then leaned forward and kissed her. It was a hundred times sweeter for having almost lost her. Her hand came up to press against the back of his neck, and he felt the same fire ignite in him as he had in the gardens.

Finally, reluctantly, he pulled his mouth from hers, then touched his forehead against hers. "Can I take that as a yes, then?"

She giggled. "I suppose so."

A flash of movement by the warehouse door caught his attention, and he glanced around. "Hmm. Looks like Zowan's getting impatient. I guess we better go over there and fetch them."

KAREN HANCOCK has won Christy Awards for each of her first four novels—*Arena* and the first three books in the LEGENDS OF THE GUARDIAN-KING series, *The Light of Eidon, The Shadow Within,* and *Shadow Over Kiriath.* She graduated from the University of Arizona with a bachelor's degree in biology and wildlife biology. Along with writing, she is a semi-professional watercolorist and has exhibited her work in a number of national juried shows. She and her family reside in Arizona.

For discussion and further information, Karen invites you to visit her Web site at *www.kmhancock.com.*

# Looking for More Good Books to Read?

You can find out what is new and exciting with
previews, descriptions, and reviews by signing up for
Bethany House newsletters at

## www.bethanynewsletters.com

We will send you updates for as many authors or
categories as you desire so you get only the
information you really want.

## *Sign up today!*